RELENTLESS PASSION

"What are you going to do?" Summer asked fearfully as Brent held her immobile against his lean, muscular frame.

"Ten years ago the earl took what was mine," he said, and the years of hate and anger cut through his flaring desire. "Now I'm going to take something of his."

"No," Summer moaned. "Please don't!"

Brent forced her to turn toward him. He cupped her face in his hands. "I haven't been able to get you out of my mind all day," he said in a voice husky with passion. "The thought of you has been driving me out of my senses."

He took her mouth in a hungry kiss, and the feel of his firm, warm lips on hers nearly paralyzed her. His hands roamed over her at will, going where no hands had ever gone, doing what she had never imagined hands were meant to do. She was stunned, but an answering chord sounded within her and she realized with a shudder of anticipation that she wouldn't stop him now even if she could....

The Captain's Caress

Leigh Greenwood

LOVE SPELL NEW YORK CITY

To my family, who has given
up so much so I may write.

LOVE SPELL®

July 2005

Published by

Dorchester Publishing Co., Inc.
200 Madison Avenue
New York, NY 10016

ISBN 0-505-52646-8

Printed in the United States of America.

Visit us on the web at www.dorchesterpub.com.

The Captain's Caress

Chapter 1

"Hurry up, or I'll come in and drag you out myself," Charles Ashton shouted through his daughter's bedroom door. "Your trunks are already loaded, and that damned prig is standing at the door looking as though one more breath inside these walls will choke him."

Abraham Brinklow, agent in the proxy marriage of Gowan McConnel, the earl of Heatherstone, to Summer Ashton, was so anxious to leave he would have fetched Summer himself if doing so would have reduced by as much as one minute the time he had to spend in her father's company. He hoped the girl took after her mother, for he shuddered to think of what would happen to the house of McConnel if any future earl should in the least resemble Ashton.

Summer descended the broad staircase with a quiet dignity that was at variance with the slovenly impatience of her sire; it cast into even greater relief the differences between them. A fixed gravity that made her look older than her nineteen years had replaced the tears and despondency of the past week.

1

"I'm ready," she said in a soft voice in which resignation was the only discernible emotion.

"You surely took your time, but I guess it doesn't really matter. I'm never *ever* going to have to stand around waiting for you again," Ashton said cruelly. "Good-bye, and good riddance."

"Aren't you coming with us?" she asked, surprised into raising her eyes.

"Hell no. I'm not going anywhere in this damned heat. She's yours now," Ashton barked at Brinklow, who couldn't disguise his relief that Ashton would not accompany them to the ship. "If you lose her, the earl can take his money out of *your* hide." Ashton gazed contentedly at the documents that put ten thousand pounds into his hands. "I've got all I want right here."

Summer turned and walked out to the waiting carriage without a parting word. Her father had heartlessly sold her into marriage, thereby stripping her of all feelings of love or belonging; his final brutal rejection had severed the last tendril of attachment. Nothing remained now but hurt and a profound feeling of betrayal.

Firmly resisting the temptation to take one last look at the only home she'd ever known, Summer stared before her with vacant eyes as the carriage rolled down the long drive. She felt cornered, caught between a vindictive father and the censorious representative of a husband she'd never seen, but whose shadow loomed ominously over her.

At times during the past week the whole scheme to marry her to the Earl of Heatherstone had seemed so fantastic she could almost believe she had dreamed it, but when she'd been dragged before a priest who'd solemnized the marriage despite her protests, she knew the nightmare was real. She had considered running away, but the marriages of all her friends had been arranged and no one thought her ill-treated.

"Why should I feel sorry for you?" her closest friend had

asked in a jealous pique. "I'd marry a leper if he were an earl and wealthy enough to take me off this island." Only Summer's mother could have understood why she looked upon her wedding day as an end rather than a beginning; but Constance Ashton was dead and Summer had no one to turn to.

As the hired carriage lurched over the ruts and stones of the unkept driveway, Brinklow studied his new mistress in silence. To him, anyone from the Caribbean was unworthy to become the Countess of Heatherstone, but even his unyielding Calvinistic soul had to acknowledge that Summer was a vision to gladden any man's heart. She sat upright in her seat, her long brown hair falling over slim shoulders bared by a deep neckline and sleeves pushed low on her arms to keep her cool. The simplicity of her gown outlined her slim figure, accentuated by the bright yellow ribbon at her waist. Soft brown eyes stared at him from under golden lashes, while the rich creamy color of her skin was heightened by the spots of color in her cheeks.

"Does the earl hope for an heir?" Summer asked uneasily, breaking Brinklow's rigid silence.

"It is natural that a lord as wealthy and influential as the earl should hope for a son to carry on his ancient line," intoned Brinklow, unbending slightly. The power, wealth, and grandeur of his employer was Brinklow's favorite subject, and he readily expanded on the bright prospects of the young man fortunate enough to be the earl's first-born son.

Summer didn't speak again until they neared the waiting ship. "Does the earl travel from home often?"

"The earl is frequently called upon to advise persons of importance," Brinklow announced, "and of course he undertakes a great amount of business in Edinburgh and London, but Glenstal is an excellently furnished castle and you may be assured that your comfort will be well attended to at all times."

Their arrival at the dock brought Summer to the final step

that would cut her off from her home and irrevocably thrust her into the arms of a complete stranger, her *husband*. Unwilling to leave the carriage until the last minute, she hung back while Brinklow conferred with the captain of the ship which was to carry her to Scotland, but once she placed her feet on the deck, once she realized there was no possibility of turning back, her courage began to assert itself, and she approached her fate with unsuspected courage.

"Welcome, miss. Your maid is waiting in your cabin. You'll find it down those steps at the end of the galley." Captain Bonner's greeting made it abundantly plain that he didn't relish having women on board his ship.

"I am the Countess of Heatherstone," Summer informed him quietly. "I have no doubt my husband is paying you handsomely for the use of this vessel, so please have someone inform my maid that I await her attendance. And I would be pleased if you would accompany me to my cabin and see that I am provided with all I need for this journey."

Brinklow gaped in dumb surprise. He had assumed the new countess to be only the stunned, helpless creature he had known the past week. But Summer had decided to fight and to survive. The ship was her first battleground.

"This is my vessel," Captain Bonner blustered.

"If the terms are not acceptable to you, inform Mr. Brinklow at once so that he may make other arrangements." Bonner paused to gauge Summer's determination, but she didn't give him enough time. "Please make up your mind. I'm tired and wish to lie down."

Captain Bonner barked out an order, and a few minutes later a short, stout woman of middle age and sympathetic mien bustled on deck.

"Lord 'a mercy, milady, to think I never knew you'd arrived. And me trying to make something out of that cabin, which I never will because anybody knows you can't make silk out of sack cloth." She glared at Bonner.

"I'm sure you've done quite well," Summer replied, checking an overwhelming desire to throw herself into the arms of this big-hearted woman. "The captain has offered to provide us with anything we need. Can you give him a list?"

"A list is no trouble, but finding a way to get the two of us settled in that little bitty hole is more than I can do." She turned to the irate captain. "You can begin by finding a lantern that gives off more light than smoke, a chair without the canes broken, a bowl and pitcher, a table, and a wardrobe."

"Do you think to take over the whole ship?" Bonner asked angrily.

"It's paid for, so we might as well have the run of it; your nasty sailors do. And don't go disappearing before I've had my say, or you'll not find as much money waiting for you at the other end as you supposed."

"I always heard the Scots were tight-fisted."

"Don't think to insult the earl by saying he's fool enough to pay for more than he gets. Now you come along with me, milady, and I'll settle you in for a nice rest before this hateful tub starts to rocking fit to make you queasy. If you think it's a penance now, that's nothing to what it's like at sea."

Summer was all too ready to put herself into the capable hands of this dauntless woman who, needing only the presence of her mistress to buttress her commands, proceeded to spare neither captain nor crew. Before they set sail, Captain Bonner was thinking that a cargo of Spanish bulls might have been preferable to these two women.

"My name's Bridgit Barlow," the spritely lady announced to Summer as she closed the cabin door in Bonner's scowling face. "I'm not rightly a lady's maid, I'm a housekeeper by training, but I'll see you're cared for until we get to Scotland and I can tend to you proper."

Able to restrain herself no longer, Summer sank down onto the bed with a sob. Instantly Bridgit was beside her, gathering her into her arms and rocking her gently.

"Now, now, there's no call to cry," she said soothingly, patting Summer's head all the while. "I know it's hard to leave those you love, but we all have to leave our parents when we marry." When Summer cried even harder, she told her, "Go ahead and get it out of your system if it'll make you feel better. But when you've dried your eyes you'll see what a wonderful future awaits you. It's not every girl that's able to marry a rich lord in a fret to have her with him. I can't wait to see his face when he sees how pretty you are. You'll soon have half the country at your feet. But don't worry, I'll be there to see that you aren't bothered too much. After all, even a husband will get underfoot if you let him."

Chapter 2

The man stood motionless and alone at the bow of the ship as she dipped and rose, cutting through the waves of the placid Atlantic with rhythmic ease. His tall, muscular frame was silhouetted against the morning sky, and cool breezes tossed his sun-bleached hair about and made his loosely tied shirt billow behind him like the sails of his ship. Trousers, short and threadbare, clung tightly to his powerful thighs, while his bare feet and legs glowed like burnished copper in the still-cool sun. There was about him a tautness, a sense of contained power that made him appear, even at rest, about to explode with vital energy. The powerful ship beneath him seemed but an extension of himself.

All around him Nature did her best to draw his thoughts from the dark memories that troubled him. The sky, arched over limitless horizons, was the azure blue immortalized by poets, its enormous expanse broken by billowing clouds that rose like gigantic mountains disdaining earthly foundations. Huge sea birds, not yet hungry enough to dive, hovered with

7

weightless ease on outstretched wings as they rode the powerful Atlantic drafts. A school of fish scattered before the ship as she knifed through the water, and the dolphin that had followed the large craft for days in search of food, darted playfully through the swells leaving all competition in their wake. The outstretched sails were filled by the brisk wind that bore the ship on her way. She was a pirate ship, speedy and efficiently designed.

There was no thought of attack that day, so the decks of the *Windswept* were quiet. She was heading for home after long months at sea, her hold bursting with prizes taken from less swift vessels. Bolts of priceless silks and velvets were piled high in the hold. Indeed, every available space was so tightly packed with rare woods, thick furs, ingots of copper ore, and casks of wine that the crew was forced to sleep in shifts. Now, as the early afternoon sun warmed the decks, some of the men were enjoying a siesta.

The lone sentry paused in his leisurely scanning of the horizon, his eyes focused on a tiny speck in the distance. He wondered whether to notify the captain immediately or to wait until he could identify the craft's flag, but the sounds of vigorous steps on the wooden deck caused him to look up in time to see his captain heading toward him with ground-devouring strides.

"You'd better keep a sharp eye out," Captain Brent Douglas said, stepping over a slumbering sailor. "We'll need lots of time to wake these sleeping beauties." A volley of guttural snores reverberated over the deck.

"They don't look very lively," Bates agreed, trying to smile despite the nervous excitement that filled him whenever the captain addressed him. "There's something on the starboard side, sir, but she's too far away to see more than the sails."

Brent's keen eyes peered into the bright sunshine. "She doesn't look like a large ship, but we should be able to tell something with the glass in half an hour." Brent turned away, then wheeled back to study the tiny dot once more, unable to shake the feeling that the distant craft was no ordinary vessel straying across his path. He tried to ignore the unwelcome sense of foreboding, but it wouldn't go away and that angered him. He had risen to his present position because of a cool head and careful judgment, not imagination and guesswork. "We don't have room for anything else unless we store it in my cabin," he said, showing his perturbation. "Keep your eye on her, but we'll let her pass to the north."

"Yes, sir." Bates was relieved to learn that they wouldn't be taking another ship. He was anxious to get to Havana and start spending his share of the profits.

"I'll send Smith to check on her later," Brent said. After leaving the quarter-deck, he stopped to talk with a seaman indulging in a leisurely stretch, but Bates noticed that he glanced out to sea several times before disappearing below.

"I wonder what's bothering the captain," Bates commented, as much to himself as to the mate who had wandered up to join him. "It's not like him not to know his own mind."

"Maybe he's trying to figure out how to pack more into the hold," suggested his friend. "The captain isn't greedy, but he doesn't make a habit of passing ships by."

"It's not that," Bates mused after a pause.

"Why don't you ask him if it worries you so much?"

"And get my head snapped off for my pains?" Bates demanded of his grinning companion. "I'm not such a fool. If you're so brave, Sam, why don't *you* ask him what he thinks about when he goes all glassy-eyed and starts staring out to sea, looking like he's about to commit murder."

"Likely it'd be me that was murdered if I was to do a tomfool thing like that," Sam replied with a shiver.

"Then see you don't go giving advice you don't follow yourself," admonished Bates.

Thirty minutes later the captain, coated, booted, and armed with sword and pistol, gazed wordlessly at the approaching ship through a powerful telescope. "What can you make out?" he asked, handing the spyglass to Bates.

Whatever is bothering the captain, Bates thought as he lifted the glass to his eye, is bothering him real bad. He examined the ship briefly. "She looks like a Scottish merchant vessel. Probably out of Edinburgh, and carrying a light load of tar and shingles." He handed the glass back to Brent who studied the ship carefully once again.

"It's probably just as you say, but we're going to take her nevertheless. Everyone needs tar and shingles." Once the decision was made, uncharacteristic languor fell from Captain Douglas like a discarded cloak. "Smith!" he bellowed at an extremely thin man of neat appearance who came at a run. "Get those lazy dogs on their feet. We'll never capture that ship if we wait for an invitation."

"We're wallowing about like a sea cow as it is, sir. Are you meaning to tow her into Havana behind us?" Only Smith was privileged to question the captain's orders.

"Are you hoping I'll let you sail her yourself so you can show me up?" Brent's eyes twinkled at Smith's energetic denial, and he then declared, "We'll only take the best of what they have. You may need to pack things a little tighter, but the men can double up."

"They've already doubled up," Smith reminded him as a few brave souls groaned aloud.

"Then let them double up again," Brent roared unsympathetically. "They'll have more than enough room when we reach Havana." He looked about him at his still-drowsy crew. "With all the sleep they get on deck, you wouldn't think they'd have any need of a bunk." Some of the younger hands fidgeted nervously, but the veterans merely grinned. "Make sure they're wide-awake, or we'll be the ones getting a dunking in the Atlantic. Take the usual precautions, but let's hope they decide not to put up much of a fight. Now turn to!" he shouted as he walked away.

At the sound of his booming voice, men appeared as if by magic. They went about their preparations with practiced efficiency, each sailor knowing exactly what was expected of him. Captain Douglas wouldn't sail with a man who had to be driven to his work; more than one reluctant seaman had found himself cast adrift or left to the mercies of a victimized ship's crew.

The captain remained on deck throughout the wait. From time to time he used the glass to study the approaching ship, more out of habit than from necessity. Her disorganized crew's futile attempts to prepare some kind of defense were almost comic, but Brent's mood was solemn. His attitude communicated itself to his crew and they went about their work without the noisy shouts of encouragement that usually accompanied their battle preparations. A warning shot fired across the bow of the other vessel was not returned, and the men of the *Windswept* prepared to board without opposition.

"They ought to show some kind of fight," Smith said in disgust.

"Stop moaning. There'll be enough fights the next time out to satisfy even your bloodthirsty soul."

"Is there going to be another voyage?" Smith asked with deceptive casualness. "Now that you've got that plantation, I wondered if you meant to settle down."

"A planter's life is too quiet for a man like me."

"You won't have any trouble finding a wife," Smith ventured tentatively, not meeting his friend's eye. "Once it gets about you're thinking of getting married, they'll come at you so thick you'll need me to sort them out."

"Not to marry a condemned murderer." Brent spoke with studied indifference, but his gaze turned steely.

"You never murdered anybody, sir."

"Unfortunately, not everyone has your faith in me," Brent responded. He gathered up his pistol and buckled on his sword. "I'll probably roam the seas forever like the Flying Dutchman."

"But his curse was lifted when he found a girl who'd be faithful to him."

"Well I'll be damned, Smith. I never knew you went in for reading old stuff like that."

"You know I'm more comfortable with my figures," Smith replied diffidently. "My old mother used to tell the little ones stories and the Dutchman was her favorite, probably because of my dad. He did all the roaming while she took care of us and waited for him to come home." He picked up his weapons. "We never did find out what became of him."

"It looks like neither of our mothers got much good from the sea. I don't suppose a wife of mine would like it any better. Let's go relieve this captain of his cargo," Brent said, dismissing the subject of his future. "Then he can finish his trip with an easy mind."

Smith wondered what Brent Douglas really *did* think. One never knew, but with his black moods becoming more frequent, he was fixing to do something, even if he didn't know it.

The *Sea Otter*'s crew was only vaguely aware of Captain Douglas's reputation, but the sight of his towering six-foot-four frame striding about on deck with an unmistakable air of command had driven any thought of resistance from their minds.

Smith broke off a rapid conversation with the *Sea Otter*'s first mate, a worried crease between his eyes. A quick conference with the *Sea Otter*'s captain did nothing to lighten his expression. He schooled his features to their accustomed passivity as he turned to Brent, but his eyes were wary.

"Williams has gone over the cargo lists with their people and it seems that about all they're carrying is a woman."

"Why would anybody be fool enough to waste a whole ship on one woman?" Brent demanded, angered to find his efforts wasted. "Who is this invaluable female?"

"The Countess of Heatherstone." Whatever response Smith may have been expecting, he was astonished to see his captain go deathly pale under his tan.

"Are you sure?" Brent demanded in a dry whisper. "You've *got* to be sure."

"I spoke to Captain Bonner myself," Smith assured him. He could not account for Brent's unexpected response, but he was certain the countess's name was not unknown to his captain.

Brent didn't hear Smith's reply; his mind was awash with memories he had spent ten years trying to forget. He heard, once again, his father's smiling promise to return with enough riches to pay their debts. He saw his mother, her eyes haunted, sitting by the parlor window, waiting for a letter from the husband she would never see again. He remembered every word of Ben Potter's explanation of how the earl had robbed Brent of his future. He closed his eyes tightly, but he couldn't block out the picture of Gowan lying in a pool of blood while a young boy stood over him, riding crop in hand.

"Do you want to speak to their captain?" Smith asked tentatively.

"Yes," Brent said, with a visible effort forcing himself back into the present. "It's time I met the leader of this faint-hearted crew."

Smith looked keenly at him, but for the first time in many years a curtain was drawn between them. With an uneasy mind, he led Brent to where Captain Bonner waited.

A middle-aged man of large stature, Captain Bonner carried surprisingly little weight on his tremendous frame, and the two men made an imposing picture as they faced each other. But Bonner's eyes didn't flash with Brent's keen intelligence, nor did he move with restless energy.

"I believe we are fellow countrymen," Brent began easily.

"You're English!" exclaimed the scowling man.

"No. I'm Scottish, but I doubt you'll find that an adequate excuse," Brent responded, smiling at the familiar reaction. "I'll spare you the trouble of telling me what a disgrace I am to my country. That *was* what you were going to say, wasn't it?"

"That and a great deal more," asserted the outraged man.

"Save it for our next meeting. Right now I'm in a hurry and I need the answers to a few questions."

"Your man already has our bills of lading. He probably knows more about our cargo than I do. *I* don't concern myself with freight," Bonner concluded with a haughty sneer.

"You should. It pays your wages." A snicker from the ranks of his own men cut off Bonner's intended reply and caused him to flush with impotent fury.

"My first mate tells me that your cargo consists of a woman. That's unusual. Is it also true?"

"Of course it's true," Bonner replied, infuriated. "Do you think I'd lie about anything as easily verifiable as that?"

"I should hope not," Brent said with an ironic smile.

"If you'll take the trouble to locate a Mr. Brinklow, he'll tell you that he's the agent who hired the *Sea Otter* to convey the countess to Edinburgh."

"Find me this Brinklow at once," barked Brent.

"Here he is, sir." Some of the hardness in Brent's eyes dissolved as Smith motioned one of the crew to bring the man in question forward.

"Am I correct in assuming that you have already sent someone to request the countess's presence on deck?" he asked, and Smith nodded. "There are times when I'm not entirely sure I trust you," Brent said with a wry grin. Smith relaxed a little; the captain seemed to be recovering from whatever had set him off so badly.

As Brent looked Brinklow up and down, the incensed agent bridled like a setting hen confronted by a fox. He was unsure of what this enormous man with the mocking eyes was about to do, but he knew it would be worth his life if he allowed anything to happen to the countess.

"Blackguards like you should be driven from the sea," he declared in a frightened, squeaky voice. "You ought to be hung, and your head placed on a spike. You're an abomination, and the Lord's wrath will be visited upon your seed for generations to come."

Smith struck the red-faced little man a sharp blow across the face. "No one talks to the captain like that," he said sharply.

"Don't stop him." Brent was laughing. "Can't you see he's suffering from mortal fear for his hide." Amusement danced in his eyes, but a hint of steel lay behind it. "It's a good thing I don't have any *seed* as you so quaintly put it. The little devils would be in for a nasty time of it, but I didn't ask you here to discuss my Judgment Day. Who is the woman you're calling the Countess of Heatherstone? I never heard that the earl was married, and I can't believe he'd be letting his wife run all over the world by herself if he had."

"It's not expected that a common criminal should be privy to the private concerns of an earl," Brinklow said, eying Brent with righteous indignation. "My mistress is indeed the Countess of Heatherstone, and if you so much as lay a hand on her the earl will destroy you. He's a great man with many powerful friends. There's nowhere you can hide that's beyond his reach." Brinklow allowed his arrogance full rein, secure in the belief that his employer's name was sufficient to instill mortal fear in the heart of this godless pirate.

Smith advanced upon him once more, fists ready, but Brent motioned him back. "I'm not frightened by your threats, but

I am tired of this meaningless bombast. Gowan is a hell-born devil and an unprincipled rogue. He'd steal food from an orphan if he could see any gain in it, but your warnings have inspired me with a determination to see this countess of his. It's rare that a mistress is able to inspire such loyalty in her servants. Has anyone found her yet?"

Chapter 3

Summer paced restlessly about the cabin, her eyes darting fearfully in the direction of each new sound. "I've got to know what's happening, Bridgit. Can't they tell you anything?"

"Not a word that makes any sense, milady. The captain's shaking so hard he'd rattle the bark right off himself if he was a tree. He doesn't know whether those cutthroats mean to board us or just come alongside. They fired over the bow so maybe they didn't mean to do us any harm."

"But don't you think that means they want something, and they intend to come take it?" Summer asked anxiously. "If they just wanted to talk, why couldn't they simply wave a flag or something?"

"They can't be pirates, milady. They wouldn't dare come this close to England."

"My father used to say that some of the bold ones would sail up the Thames itself. But what could pirates possibly want with us?"

"I don't know, but if we stay quiet maybe they won't bother us." A knock on the door dispelled that comfortable hope, and caused Summer to nearly jump out of her skin. "Who's there?" demanded Bridgit planting herself between the door and her mistress.

"The name's Williams, ma'am. I'm second mate on the *Windswept*."

"What do you want?"

"Captain Douglas extends his greetings to the countess. He's by way of being a countryman of hers and would like to convey his compliments to her on her recent marriage, in person." However surprised Summer might be to receive such a politely worded request, she had no intention of allowing anyone to enter her cabin. She shook her head vigorously.

"The countess is not feeling well enough to leave her cabin."

"I'm certain the captain would be happy to see her ladyship in private." Summer shook her head more frantically than ever.

"The countess doesn't want to see the captain at all," Bridgit replied tartly. "Take him our compliments and say the countess begs to be excused."

"I don't think I can do that," Williams answered, unperturbed as ever. "If you can't come out to us, we'll have to go in to you."

"I have no intention of letting you in, you rude man." Bridgit's courage was fortified by the locked door between them, but the scrape of a key turning dismantled that line of defense, and to her horror the door swung open to admit a well-muscled man of medium height and gaunt face.

"I relieved your captain of his keys," Williams said by way of explanation as Summer sat down with a plop.

"How dare you enter a lady's chamber unbidden," scolded Bridgit as soon as she had recovered the use of her tongue.

"The captain wants to meet the countess," Williams answered politely, "and he doesn't take kindly to giving orders a second time."

"And *we* are not accustomed to taking orders from nasty bandits, footpads, or whatever you call yourself," replied Bridgit indignantly.

"I don't suppose it matters what you call us, but I can't ever recall anyone disobeying the captain's orders."

"There's a first time for everyone, even your captain," Bridgit retorted. She was provoked by the easy confidence of the man. "You take yourself back through that door and tell him the Countess of Heatherstone doesn't appear on command for anyone."

"I don't rightly think I can do that, ma'am."

"Why not?"

"I don't have the courage," he said, grinning good-naturedly.

"You've got brass enough for anything," Bridgit responded, indignantly stamping her foot.

"Then you'll come with me?"

"Not one inch!"

"I suppose there's nothing for it but to carry the countess out to him."

"What!" Summer was shocked into speaking.

"If you can't walk by yourself, I'll have to fetch someone to carry you. But you're such a little bit of a thing," he said, looking at her slim figure, "even an old man like me could lift you real easy."

"Don't you even *think* of laying a hand on the countess." Bridgit declared. She was prepared to defend her mistress at her own peril.

"It's no use," Summer said, accepting the inevitable. "He's going to make me go."

Williams nodded. "When the captain wants something he means to have it, and he seems mighty set on seeing you."

"What can he possibly want with me?"

"I can't speak for the captain, your ladyship, but I can promise you you'll suffer no hurt. The captain is a great gentlemen."

"Well, I can't possibly go like this. I've got to dress."

"Your ladyship looks fine to me, if you'll pardon my saying so," Williams assured her, admiring the shapely body that could not be hidden by the thin material of the dress.

"Don't be absurd, you brazen man," said Bridgit. "No lady is fit to be seen without she's properly dressed, even if she *is* being pushed about by uppity rapscallions. You wait in the passage and I'll let you know when the countess is ready."

"I hope you don't mean to take long. The captain never understands it when he has to wait."

"We'll be as quick as may be," Bridgit promised, shoving him from the room. She locked the door and turned expectantly to Summer. "What do you plan to do, milady?"

"Change my dress and fix my hair," Summer said running to her trunk. "I can't possibly be seen in this old muslin."

"Milady! You can't mean you're actually going to see that dreadful man!"

"What choice do I have?" Her muffled voice came from deep inside the trunk.

"But you don't know what kind of disreputable rogue he might be. He could do *anything!*"

"He's less likely to do it on deck in front of people," Summer countered. She retrieved a dress from the bottom of the trunk. "And you heard that man say he'd carry me out if he had to. Well, if I must go, I'll go on my own two feet looking like a countess, not like some scared little girl." She held a gown up and considered her reflection in the mirror. "Now stop complaining about what can't be changed and help me dress. That man is not going to wait forever."

"A pox on all men!" Bridgit exclaimed as she moved to help her mistress.

* * *

Summer stepped boldly onto the deck of the *Sea Otter,* then paused to let her eyes adjust to the bright sunlight. She wondered what kind of man received such absolute obedience from hardened outlaws. The captain couldn't be anything like the planters she had known; they had neither the trust nor loyalty of their men. Curiosity and an odd desire for excitement overcame her trepidation, and she moved toward the waiting men.

Brinklow bustled up in an attempt to shield her from the curious stares of the gawking crewmen, but she swept imperiously past him in search of the man who was so determined to meet her. Her eyes swept over those nearest her; instinctively she knew that none of them had the power to hold the destiny of men and ships in his hands, and her gaze moved on, darting from one man to another until it came to a shuddering halt against the imposing form of Brent Douglas. Summer felt as though she had run full tilt into a stone wall, and the shock of the impact left her feeling bruised and breathless.

He was the most magnificent creature she'd ever seen. Sapphire blue eyes stared at her from under thick brows bleached as blond as his hair by sun and salt. Every detail of his proud profile had been chiseled with infinite care, but none more so than his broad, tapering nose or his parted, sensual lips. And not even his elaborate finery could disguise the powerful chest and bulging muscles that made his body a work of art.

A surge of energy coursed through Summer's body, and she moved toward him with a sinuous grace that made every man present aware of the months he had been without a woman.

A path opened before her. Even Brinklow, loudly blaming Bridgit for his mistress's shocking behavior, let her pass unhindered. Summer lowered her eyes, not sure whether she did so from fear or embarrassment. For a moment, only the muted fall of her footsteps broke the silence; then she became aware of the sound of ragged breathing. It reminded her so strongly of the utter exhaustion that follows the performance of a backbreaking task that she directed a questioning glance toward Brent. What she saw nearly rocked her off her feet.

Fury, incandescent in its intensity, burned in those hard blue eyes, a fury so hot she could feel it scorch her skin. She tried to draw back, but she couldn't. Riveted by his gaze, she was impelled to draw nearer to him. His look contained nothing of admiration or curiosity; his scrutiny mercilessly appraised her as if she were an object to be bought and haggled over. She felt his eyes strip her naked, and then burrow deep into her soul.

Chilling fear shook her, and she lost all desire to meet this frightening man. She wanted to run, to hide behind Bridgit or anyone who would deflect the searing gaze of those uncompromising eyes.

"I hope we haven't inconvenienced you, Countess." His harsh voice easily reached everyone on deck. "I was eager to meet the woman who would sell herself to Gowan for his money and title, but I never expected to find her a girl young enough to be his daughter." She shrank under the blast of his withering contempt, but he reached out and pulled her closer to him. "Don't be so quick to draw away. If you can endure Gowan's company day after day, you should be able to tolerate mine for a few minutes."

"Please let me go. You're hurting me." The lash of his scorn tore at her courage like a rasp at soft wood.

"Not until I have a good look at you."

"It is an outrage that this madman should be allowed to attack your passengers," Brinklow shouted at Bonner as he scrambled past open-mouthed crewmen to reach Summer's side. "If you don't put an end to this monstrous affront to a noble family's honor, I shall see that you lose your ship, and that *all* of you"—his waving arms encompassed the crews of both ships—"rot in the bowels of Newgate." He opened his mouth to say more, but surprised everyone by crumpling to the deck with a dull thud.

"His voice grates on my nerves," Smith explained, calmly wiping the butt of his pistol.

Summer looked from one man to another. Horror-stricken, she knew there was no hope of deliverance.

"Please let my mistress go," Bridgit begged, pushing in between Summer and Brent. "Your rough and angry ways are frightening her." But Brent's grip did not loosen.

"I'd have thought she had enough courage to face a dozen men like me," he sneered. "It must take nerves of iron to live with a man like Gowan."

"Sir, you're insulting," expostulated Bridgit.

"But then I have found that greed can assume many guises, even wide-eyed innocence." Brent let his gaze rest on the soft curves of Summer's body, the swell of her creamy breasts, and he felt a surge of desire flare through him. Unaccountably, that only infuriated him all the more.

Summer's own anger flamed rapidly now and it consumed her fear. Who was he, this arrogant young outlaw, to demand that she leave the safety of her cabin to be openly insulted like some nameless jade! She faced him with a proud tilt of her chin.

"Sir, I do not know what I have done to offend you so greatly, nor can I fathom why you should publicly abuse me in this cruel manner. Furthermore, I cannot accept such an unflattering reading of my husband's character from a man who is himself wholly lacking in honor or integrity."

Brent's face grew more threatening with her every word, and his crew fidgeted nervously. Summer, too, felt her surge of fury waver before his sulfurous gaze, but she pressed bravely on.

"Now that you have seen me, I desire to return to my cabin. I find your company distasteful."

"You act the role well," jeered Brent, "but a woman who sells her virtue, even in marriage, is no better than a harlot." Brent ignored the murmured protest from his crew. "Indeed, I have more respect for a prostitute who plies her trade honestly, than a woman who hides behind a coronet."

Summer went white under the lash of his scorn, but she refused to lend credence to his staggering accusations by running away. "You cur!" she cried, striking at him.

"So milady doesn't like to hear the truth?" Brent said, easily catching her wrists.

"How *dare* you speak to me of truth when you have made no attempt to discover it," she raged, struggling to hold back tears of anger and mortification. "I'd never sell myself to anybody, most particularly for money and a title." But the words rang false in her ears. Her father *had* sold her and she was sure this terrifying young man would admit no distinction between force and willing compliance.

"I'm not impressed by outraged virtue, nor will I let you hide behind the shield of your rank and sex. I've known your husband all my life, and no decent female would marry him."

"I don't believe you," Summer protested, her dismay at the picture he painted of the earl greater than her anger at his slander of herself. His harsh laughter only intensified her disquiet.

"Either you're a blind fool, or you're afraid to admit to yourself what Gowan is *really* like. He's a viper! There's nothing too low for him, not stealing from his best friend or murdering an old drunk and blaming it on an unsuspecting boy. He has wealth, but he stole it; he has power and influence, but he bought it."

"Stop!" Summer begged, but Brent drew her closer.

"How can you allow such a villain to enter your bed, take you in his arms, and make love to you?"

"Don't!" she sobbed.

"Only a wanton could swear to love, honor, and obey that devil's spawn."

Brent's concentration narrowed until he thought only of Summer and his hatred for Gowan. Long-simmering enmity and burgeoning desire fanned the coals of his rancor until it became a raging inferno that threatened to consume him. It erupted in an unreasoning tidal wave of abuse.

"Your precious husband is an outcast from society, a slave to greed, and a master of deceit."

Summer raised her hands to ward off the scalding torrent of words, but they kept coming, battering her until she could stand no more.

"His tenants curse his name, and his neighbors shun his company. He is a byword little boys shout at their enemies, a specter parents use to frighten naughty children."

At last Brent paused, nearly spent by the force of his own emotion, but Summer had already fainted.

"You horrid brute!" Bridgit shrieked as everyone stared in dumb silence, too numbed by the swift course of events to move. "See what you have done with your hate and your talk of evil. *You're* the one who's poisoned, not this poor child." She lifted Summer's head onto her lap and gently massaged her temples. "Someone bring me some water. You," she ordered, pointing at a slack-jawed youth standing near her, "keep the sun off her face."

"She just fainted," Brent rasped in a frayed voice. "She'll recover soon enough."

"You're a brutal, wicked man," Bridgit ranted, not ceasing to fan Summer with her open palm.

"Smith, we're taking her with us. It'll be easier if you move her, before she revives. Have someone fetch her trunks. You," he said addressing Bridgit, "see that her things are packed, but don't worry about your own."

"You can't mean to take this poor child without someone to see to her?"

"That's exactly what I mean to do."

"What can you want with her?" Smith asked. He was badly shaken to question Brent before the crew.

"We'll get loaded a lot quicker if you don't question my orders," Brent barked. "Throw a bucket of water over that agent and bring him here." Smith's steady gaze did not quail before Brent's angry glare. He was the only one who guessed how close Brent had come to losing all trace of humanity under the stress of the hatred which had simmered inside him for ten long years.

Within moments a soaked and barely conscious Brinklow was hauled before Brent. He shook the dazed man like a rag doll. "Listen carefully to every word I say, and carry it back to the earl exactly as I give it to you. Do you understand?" Brinklow nodded, too afraid of being shaken to bits to open his mouth.

"Tell Gowan his former ward has taken his lovely young wife to Biscay Island. If he wants her he'll have to come after her." Brent took painful hold of Brinklow's ear and pulled him closer. "And be sure to tell him he won't be dealing with such a green boy this time. Can you remember all that?" The poor man nodded again, barely able to think of anything but the throbbing pain in his pinioned ear.

"One more thing." Brent's voice sank to a whisper. "Be sure to tell Gowan that he doesn't have to worry that any harm will come to her. I'll treat her exactly as he would himself." Brent's laugh did not encourage others to join in. "Exactly as he would himself," he repeated. Brent released Brinklow's ear so suddenly the demoralized agent almost fell down; then he spun on his heel and thundered an order to his crew. "I want to be under sail in half an hour." He left them without another word.

"He didn't even so much as look to see if she was still breathing," Williams marveled, staring after Brent's retreating figure, "and he leaves you and me to carry her on board.

That's not like the captain and I've known him nigh on to six years. I told her the captain was a great gentleman, that he wouldn't harm her." He shook his head in shocked disbelief. "And she was such a pretty little thing, too. I can't figure out what got into him."

"It can't be the girl," said Smith, feeling extremely ill at ease. "It must be her husband."

"He's got no call to make off with a man's wife no matter what kind of scurvy rogue the man might be. I'd just as soon have nothing to do with holding countesses for ransom. You mark my words, the captain will come to rue this day's work."

"Maybe, but that's no concern for the likes of you and me," Smith responded, and then both men went about their tasks. It was never wise to keep the captain waiting; in his present mood it was positively foolhardy.

Chapter 4

Summer opened her eyes to a blur of light. She became confused and then alarmed as the figures around her gradually began to disentangle themselves and take shape. Absolutely nothing was familiar. She rushed to the porthole, but only the familiar limitless expanse of blue Atlantic met her gaze. The sun was an enormous orange ball riding on the tossing sea, and the ship seemed to be sailing right into its waning rays. But that's west, she thought. Why were they sailing *away* from Scotland? Why wasn't she in her own cabin? Where was Bridgit? Was that terrifying young man real, or was he just part of a horrible nightmare? Battling rising panic, she tried the door, but it wouldn't open. *She was locked in her cabin!*

Then all at once she knew; she was on the pirate ship. The pit of her stomach contracted painfully. What were they going to do with her? It would be months before the earl could arrive and ransom her. What would happen to her in the meantime? A sharp knock at the door nearly caused Summer to jump out of her skin.

"Are you awake?" demanded the unmistakable voice. Summer backed away, too frightened to reply. The knock sounded again, louder this time, but she still didn't answer.

"The mercenary little adventuress is still out cold," the captain said in disgust. "I can't imagine she has too many waking moments when Gowan's home." She heard a key being fitted into the lock and watched the handle turn as if by itself.

"Don't come in! I'm awake," she cried desperately. "Please send Bridgit to me."

"I'm already in," Brent announced as he closed the door behind him, "and I left Bridgit on the *Sea Otter*."

Summer was paralyzed by fear; she felt utterly defenseless before this terrifying man who had already bludgeoned her into unconsciousness with the fierceness of his hatred. Now she was alone with him, a prisoner on his ship, completely at his mercy; she couldn't bring herself to even think of what he might do to her. She tried to appear undaunted as she stood facing him, but it was impossible to ignore her trembling limbs.

"Where are you taking me?" she asked, afraid of the answer. "We're not heading toward Scotland."

"Who told you that?"

"Nobody."

"That's very clever of you," said Brent, impressed. "But I should have guessed you'd have to have some intelligence to trap Gowan into marriage."

Rising anger gave Summer's reply a sharp edge. "You don't have to be a genius to know we're not heading east if we're sailing directly into the setting sun. Why did you take me off the *Sea Otter*? What do you intend to do with me?"

"That's two questions at once," Brent said. Under other

circumstances his dawning smile might have allayed her fears; now it gave birth to a strange disquiet.

"We're headed for Havana to sell our cargo. Then I'm taking you to one of the islands to await Gowan's reply."

"Are you holding me for ransom?" she asked. Brent thought of his mother waiting patiently year after year for letters that never came, dying a little bit each day, and an implacable light glowed in his eyes.

"I wouldn't exactly use that term, but I guess it'll do as well as any," he said.

"What do you mean by that?" Summer asked, distrusting the hardness she detected in his features. "Why else would you keep me here?"

"There's a small matter of three ruined lives to be accounted for," he said bitterly. "You're small compensation for so much destruction, but I intend to extract a costly vengeance."

"What are you talking about?" she cried.

"Retribution!" he growled with explosive force.

"But why?" she asked, her voice dry in her throat.

"For what your husband did to my family and a poor old sailor who tried to help me. I've waited for ten long years, and I can't think of a better way to repay Gowan than through his own wife." The look of steel was back in his eyes.

"But why me?" she pleaded. "I've done nothing to you."

"You don't matter," he said roughly. "You're only a pawn, a means to plunge my knife into Gowan's belly." But even as he spoke the words, he knew they were untrue.

When Smith had told him the *Sea Otter* carried Gowan's wife, he had barely restrained a shout of joy. By holding Gowan's wife for ransom, he could wreak some small measure of vengeance. But when Summer had appeared instead of the middle-aged woman he'd expected, the thought that such a beautiful creature could agree to become Gowan's wife fanned his rage until he was unaware of the naked desire that swept over him.

As he looked at her now, her lovely face flushed, her eyes wide with apprehension, and her rapid breath thrusting her ripe, full breasts against the tight bodice of her gown, he became conscious of a longing inside him that had nothing to do with revenge—a deep animal need to satisfy his passion with this girl who excited it. The yearning was so strong it sapped the strength of his hate and turned it to hunger. His fingers itched to caress the soft skin of her cheek, to glide down the planes of her bare shoulders until they encountered the uplifted thrust of the heaving breasts that teased and taunted his senses.

Conflicting emotions battled within him, so fiercely that they left him feeling weak. With solemn determination, he averted his eyes from Summer's tantalizing image and pushed the distracting thoughts aside.

"I came to tell you we dine in an hour. We brought all your things on board." He pointed to the trunks and clothes scattered around the room. "But I'm afraid my men don't know much about packing women's clothes." The change of subject seemed to help and he felt some of the tension drain from his aching limbs.

"They've probably ruined everything," she snapped.

"You can buy more. No countess would be satisfied with so little clothing." His anger blossomed anew as he remembered she was Gowan's wife.

"Well this is all I have now, and not even you can expect me to appear in gowns that are crushed or torn."

"Nonsense," said Brent. He picked up a chemise that lay on top of one of the piles. "This isn't torn at all." The thought of her slim body clad only in the delicate fabric caused his blood to warm and eased his anger.

"I might wear it if I were the mercenary strumpet you take me to be," she said snatching the garment from him and blushing to the roots of her hair, "but I'd starve before I'd sit down to dinner in my underwear." A spontaneous smile raced across Brent's face and transformed him into a handsome young man with laughing eyes that nearly took her breath away.

"We'd probably starve as well," Brent said with a hot glance. "There's not a man on board who could spare a thought for food with such a sight at the table." Summer struggled to regain control of her weak limbs. The feelings that had swamped her when she'd first seen Brent threatened to overwhelm her again. His abundant animal magnetism made her feel like a swimmer being pulled under by hidden currents.

"That's not my idea of a compliment," she managed to reply after a struggle.

"I wasn't trying to compliment you," he said bluntly, "but I'm not blind. You have a beautiful body."

"I would never appear so improperly dressed," Summer said, flustered. She labored to regain some of her poise, but she was unnerved to discover that she was pleased by his straightforward admiration.

"Pity," said Brent, giving Summer a look so heated that she flushed and threw the petticoat from her.

Lowering her eyes, she tried very hard to fight the frightening attraction she had for this man. "You'll have to go now," she said more quietly. "I'll need every possible minute if I'm to clear away this mess and be dressed in time. It's going to take me longer without Bridgit."

"Things aren't as bad as you think," he said, the twinkle in his eyes becoming so pronounced that Summer felt her knees weaken. "I have to dress, too."

"So?"

"This is *my* cabin. My clothes are here."

"But that's impossible!" Summer gulped in consternation.

"I can help you clear away this mess and show you where

to put your clothes. I will even hook up your gown." He gave Summer such a hungry look that she felt her clothes had suddenly vanished, exposing her to his ravenous gaze. She backed away and sat down on the bed, jumped back up again when she realized where she was. Brent's twinkle of amusement threatened to expand into a laugh.

"You can't mean it," she stammered. "I've never done anything, I mean, I wouldn't do anything, I mean, oooooh, I don't know *what* I mean," she exploded in desperation, "but you can't stay here. I'd faint with mortification."

"Do you faint often?" Brent asked curiously. "I'm afraid you're going to be unconscious a lot during the next few weeks." He moved to a bureau and began to take out stacks of clothing. "I'll give you half of the drawers, but you'll have to make do with that. There's not a spare inch from bow to stern. We're riding so low now that a good storm would force me to throw a fortune into the sea just to stay afloat."

"I hope we run into a hurricane and you have to throw *everything* overboard," Summer said spitefully.

"You'd better hope we *don't*. The first thing to go would be your trunks."

"You wouldn't dare!"

"I most certainly would. This ship is a business. I can't make a profit throwing my goods into the sea. But your clothing is another matter. Besides, Gowan will buy you more." The sound of that hated name caused his wrath to arc again. He was having trouble remembering to be angry with this entrancing girl, and the fierce catapulting back and forth between opposite passions threatened to turn his mood completely black.

"Not even you could find new clothes in the middle of the Atlantic," she said crossly.

"Then you'd have to wear that dress until we reach Cuba."

"That could take months. It would be in shreds."

"You'll forgive me if I hope for a small storm at least," Brent said, grinning at her in a way that caused her heart to flutter uncomfortably in her chest. "That's a sight I'd give half my shares to see."

"I'd wrap myself in a sheet and not set foot outside this cabin, even if it took years for me to be rescued from this detestable ship," she said furiously.

"In that case, I suggest you pray for fair weather," snapped Brent. "Now, charming though it may be to talk with you, I have to dress. I'll help you with your gown, or you can wear what you have on. It makes no difference to me."

Summer glowered at him; she was trapped and had to accept his presence, but she didn't have to accept his help. "It'll take me half a day to put all these things away properly," she said in a sulky voice, turning to the piles of clothing scattered about the room. "Go have your dinner. I'll stay here."

"You'll dine with everyone else. I won't have you starving." Brent's tone admitted of no argument. "There, I've cleared this chest. It's not much space, but you can't expect me to throw all my clothes out. Not unless you're willing to do the same."

"You're the most ill-mannered man I've ever met," Summer retorted, although she was discomfited by her reaction to his nearness.

"Because I think you'd look lovely in a shift?" he asked, feeling hot desire surge through him again.

"That's not what you meant, and you know it," she said, stamping her small foot. "It's mortifying, and I can't wait until the earl gives you the beating you deserve." Brent drew near Summer, his expression so grim that she looked about for a place to hide.

"No one," he growled, "and most especially the earl, is going to beat me. I suggest you remember that you're under my protection now. I've treated you with great tolerance up to this point, but if you continue to behave like a spiteful shrew, I may change my mind."

"If you call abducting and abusing me tolerant behavior, you're insane," asserted Summer. "Now you're threatening to violate every concept of modesty and propriety as well. I suppose that's some more of your *tolerant* behavior?"

"Don't get worked up over nothing," he said sharply. "You're only changing your clothes."

"This isn't nothing," she said, seething. "You talk about me sitting down to dine half-dressed like it's a harmless joke instead of a painful humiliation. And if you think I'm going to stand here sorting my linens while you stare at me you're out of your mind," she added with a flourish.

"I don't give a damn when you sort them," Brent shot back at her. "I've seen too many females in underwear to be interested in yours. You can hang these items from the masts for all I care, though I don't advise it. After so many months at sea the men are easily distracted, and they might get the wrong idea."

"You're the most heartless, cruel, inhuman! . . ."

"Maybe, but I don't make a habit of standing around talking arrant nonsense. Now I'm going to change my clothes. You can waste your time calling me names if you like, but dinner is still at seven." With that ultimatum, he took off his coat and folded it up neatly. "I don't have a valet, so I will show you how to take care of yourself." He pulled off his tie and began to unbutton his shirt.

"Oh," she said in a faint voice, and buried her face in her hands.

"You must learn to make the most of limited space at sea, but you'll never do that if you keep your hands over your eyes." He wanted to stay angry, but her attraction was so great he found himself acting like a schoolboy trying to impress a girl.

"It's indecent," muttered Summer.

"I take that as a personal insult. You may not think me handsome, but you don't have to call me indecent."

"You know you're not . . . you know I didn't mean," she stammered. In her agitation, she uncovered her eyes and they fell on Brent's well-muscled chest, shoulders, and arms. His discarded shirt lay at his feet. "Oh my God," she whimpered, and sank down on the bed, too weak to put her hands back over her eyes.

"See, it's not as bad as you thought." Brent sat down to change his boots.

"It's horrible," Summer said in a tremulous voice, but she was unable to take her eyes off the overwhelming male body in front of her. He was so near she could reach out and touch him. Summer had seen bare-chested men before. The muscular workers in the sugar-cane fields rarely wore more than a loincloth, but somehow it had never mattered. This man began to pull off his boots, and she felt shattered, helpless before the powerful force of his presence. She tried not to look at him, but her eyes persisted in devouring every inch of him, from the short amber fur that covered the center of his chest to the deep tan on his shoulders and arms. Every detail seemed to fit perfectly into the mesmerizing force of the whole, resulting in an almost lethal dose of raw male power.

Brent's huge muscles flexed, strained, and rippled as he worked to pull off the tight-fitting boots; they played across his chest, down his powerful shoulders, and along his straining forearms, rippling his smooth, tanned skin and making him look like a huge sleek cat stretching its muscles for the sheer pleasure of it.

After a struggle, Brent got his boots off and rose to put them away. In spite of herself, Summer watched as he moved across the cabin in stockinged feet, his lithe grace as sensual as it was inviting. Fingers of charged excitement raced hither and thither through her body, churning up unnamed feelings and causing her to tense with excitement.

As he reached up to place the boots on a shelf above his head, his tall frame, tapered from broad shoulders to narrow waist, was displayed for easy viewing. His torso was smooth and glowed in the light, his stomach was flat and taut. Summer was fascinated and watched helplessly as he twisted and bent to put things away or to retrieve items he wanted.

A wicked grin danced on his lips when he turned to her and began to undo his breeches. That was too much for Summer. With a smothered moan, she threw herself upon the bed and buried her face in the pillows. Her long burnished locks were all that Brent could see.

A robust chuckle escaped him. "That's not a very flattering reaction, milady. Don't you find me attractive?" Beyond the power of speech, Summer could only shake her head. "My vanity has led me into error again," he said in mock distress. "Smith often tells me that preoccupation with one's appearance is an unhealthy obsession." He dropped his breeches to the floor, and their soft plop sent shock waves racing through Summer's every fiber.

"Maybe you'll be good enough to satisfy my vanity on one point. Am I more pleasing to the eye than your precious husband?" Summer didn't answer. "Don't be afraid to look at me. I'm not embarrassed," he assured her.

Summer shuddered convulsively, and pulled another pillow over her head.

"Come now, milady, it can't be that bad. After years of watching nearly naked men in the fields, you're surely not suffering from an excess of modesty."

Summer clapped the pillows tightly over her ears.

"No? Well, maybe I was mistaken, but I'm disappointed." He put on fresh britches and laced them up. "I was looking forward to hearing my praises on your lips. I guess we'll have to save that for some other time." He reached for a clean shirt and began to button it up. "You'd better be thinking about what you want to wear. There isn't much time left and you haven't laid out anything yet. Dinner waits for no one on the *Windswept*, not even the captain." Finished with buttoning his shirt, he sat down to put on his shoes. "Of course, you can wear that gown if you like, but I think I ought to point out that, what with throwing yourself about, it's a good deal crumpled. You do have lovely hair, but as you've got it under a pillow at the moment, I'm unable to say whether it stands in need of attention." Brent stood up and began to tie his tie. "I'll send someone to give your shoes a good brushing, but of course you'll have to decide which pair you're going to wear. That can't be too easy with your face buried in the sheets. On the other hand, maybe you already know what you mean to put on." He paused, raised his chin, and then let it settle slowly into the soft, snowy folds of his cravat. He studied himself in the mirror to see that his appearance satisfied him. Assured on this point, he began to brush his hair. Brent never wore a wig, and his glistening locks fell easily into place with a few practiced sweeps of the soft brush. After one last look in the mirror, he turned back to Summer.

"You can dig yourself out now," he said, repressed laughter in his voice. "Except for my waistcoat, which I will put on as soon as I find it, I offer nothing to offend your modesty. I make no guarantees as to your reaction to my face, but at least my propriety is beyond question."

Summer stirred, but she didn't lift her head from the bed.

"Oh, come now. This pretense of maidenly modesty has gone on long enough. If you don't begin changing soon, you'll be late for dinner, and no one will forgive you if you spoil one of Jacques' dinners."

"You promise you're dressed?" a muffled voice asked from under several pillows.

"For God's sake, woman, I said I was, didn't I?"

Summer took the pillows off her head and tentatively opened her eyes.

"I had to make sure," she said, sitting up. Brent was just making the final adjustments to his waistcoat when she saw him, and her eyes opened wide in wonder. He was a god, by far the most handsome man she'd ever seen. She had never had a clear image in her mind of the man she hoped she would meet someday, but she knew in an instant that she was looking at him now.

He wore black patent leather shoes, rounded at the toe and decorated with silver buckles. His powerful calves were enclosed in tight white hose, and the bulging muscles of his thighs strained against dark green skin-tight satin breeches that left no doubt of his masculinity. His waistcoat was of a rather plain design, but loosely cut so as not to confine his body too tightly. A snowy cravat billowed at his throat, and his hair was tied with a black ribbon at the back. His only jewelry was a pair of heavy gold rings set with precious stones—he wore one on each hand—and a gold chain that was attached to the watch which he kept in his right pocket. He was everything she'd hoped, dreamed, and prayed for, the perfect embodiment of a young girl's dream, and he stood right in front of her, still grinning at her in a way that made her mind go blank and her body become a limp, nerveless bundle.

With one last look in the mirror he turned to Summer. "I have a few things that need attending to, so I'll leave you alone since you don't seem to appreciate my presence." He reached into a narrow closet and pulled out the most gorgeous coat Summer had ever seen. Its coloring matched the green of his breeches, and it was decorated with silver braid and black buttons. "I think you ought to reconsider my offer," he said as he struggled into the tight-fitting coat. "You have no idea how helpful I can be in the bedroom."

Summer blushed all over again. "I don't want your help," she declared quickly. "I can take care of myself."

"You'll be glad to have it," he insisted, smoothing out the wrinkles on the sleeves. "I'll come back in half an hour. Be ready, or you'll sit down in what you have on."

"I'll be ready," she pledged, so glad to be spared his bedeviling presence that she would have promised anything. "It won't take me very long if I can find what I need," she said, surveying the disorder around her.

"If you can't find it, do without it. I doubt anyone would know the difference." He left her without waiting for a response.

For a few minutes Summer was too unnerved to move. That she was a prisoner on a pirate ship was almost too fantastic to believe. But that she was about to dress for a formal dinner prepared by a French chef was too incredible even for a dream. This day was assuming nightmarish proportions. Who was this man that could maintain such a table at sea, and what did he mean to do with her?

She broke out of her reverie with a jerk. She had to hurry, or she'd never be dressed before he returned. She doubted that he kept his temper when anyone displeased him, and she had not the least doubt that, if she were not already in her gown, he would *put* her in it. The thought lent speed to her movements. She didn't want to give him any excuse to touch her; she wasn't sure she could stand it.

Chapter 5

A sharp knock at the door startled Summer into fumbling with her buttons. "Are you ready yet?" called the now-familiar voice.

"Almost," she answered, as Brent's imposing frame filled the doorway. "It'll just take a minute more." She tried once again to do up the buttons at the back of her dress, but she still couldn't reach all of them.

"Let me do that," Brent said. "You'll give yourself a back-ache, and not be done before midnight."

"I can do it by myself," Summer insisted, twisting away from him. Brent took her firmly by the shoulders.

"Don't be a fool. You know you've been trying to button that dress for the last five minutes, and you'll still be at it an hour from now if I don't do it for you. I promise I won't rape you before dinner, so there's no need for all this running away."

Summer was speechless; Brent had put her barely realized

fears into words. "You should be ashamed to mention such a subject before a lady," she said after a stunned pause.

"I'm not that weak-minded," replied Brent, fastening the last button. "You should never be afraid of words."

"But words and thoughts are the precursors of action," she argued. "The more familiar you are with an idea, the less fearful you are of its taboos."

"Well you're certainly not stupid," he said with less mockery than she expected. "I was sure only a featherhead would marry Gowan."

"You don't need to go into that again," she answered coldly. "You have made it quite plain to me *and* to every man on the two ships how you feel on that subject." Brent raised his eyebrows as she stopped to gather up a shawl.

"Feisty little filly, aren't you? I'll wager you and the earl have some rare evenings in that draughty old castle of his."

"What passes between my husband and myself is no concern of yours," Summer said in her most haughty voice. "I don't discuss such matters with anyone."

Brent's eyebrows drew a little closer together and the lines around his mouth tightened. "I don't plan to *discuss* them either. I have something very different in mind," he said, his voice devoid of all warmth.

Summer wondered about the significance of his words and his abrupt changes of mood, but there was nothing in his impassive face to give her a clue as to what his thoughts might be or what he was going to do next. He was the most contradictory, unpredictable human she had ever encountered, and she fervently wished she had never set eyes on him.

Brent took her shawl out of her hands, draped it over her shoulders, and opened the door. "After you, milady," he said, standing back. The passageway was too narrow for them to walk abreast, and Summer had to step aside to allow Brent to throw open a door only a few steps away on the opposite side of the passage. She stepped into a medium-size room with a low, beamed ceiling, almost entirely taken up by a large table. A half-dozen men, anxious and ill at ease, rose to their feet when she entered the chamber; the one she knew to be Smith came forward to lead her to her chair.

"Good evening, milady," he said, looking a trifle uncomfortable in this unfamiliar role. "We're pleased you could join us."

"Sit down, Smith, and dispense with the pretty speeches," Brent growled. His rude words and the curious staring eyes all around her made Summer acutely uneasy, but Smith seemed unaffected. He escorted her to her place at the foot of the table with deliberate calm, and then seated himself on her right. Brent gave the signal for the first course to be brought in, and thus began the most memorable meal of Summer's young life.

The seven men at the table ranged in age from thirty-three, Smith being the oldest, down to about seventeen. Talk was not confined to one's neighbor, and, on occasion, it became rather boisterous. The men grinned sheepishly and dropped their voices to a polite level whenever the captain called them down, but minutes later they were noisily trying to make themselves heard over their tablemates once again.

Summer ate her dinner in near silence; she didn't feel comfortable among so many strangers and she didn't have much to contribute to the conversation. The men talked of the recent wars in the American colonies and of the continued friction at sea among England, France, and Spain. They took sides on various issues and cited facts to support their opinions. They were familiar with various methods of warfare, the most recent battles, and the individuals that figured prominently in them. And their references to politics showed that they had a grasp of the fundamental problems behind these international conflicts, and were able to discuss their effects on the participants.

Summer didn't have the slightest idea what they were talking about half the time. She answered any remarks addressed to her as quickly as she could and then relapsed into silence. After several polite efforts to include her in the conversation, the men left her to her own thoughts.

Summer felt deprived as she listened to one youth excitedly discuss the efforts of Pitt to establish English dominance at sea. She was not stupid and she had a great deal of common sense, but her life had been bounded by her home and the plantation; no one had ever talked of anything else. Her parents had rarely entertained, and they had received news from the outside infrequently. Neither of them was interested in the turbulent forces at work in the new world or in the continuing conflicts of the old. And certainly neither had thought of developing Summer's mind. Indeed; no one would believe that she *had* a mind after watching her stare at her plate all evening, ashamed to open her mouth.

"I'm afraid we don't know how to act when there's a lady on board," commented Smith.

"I don't understand much of what they're talking about," Summer said with a bleak smile, grateful for his thoughtfulness. "Maybe I'll learn something if I listen."

"It's still unkind to exclude you."

"But if they cater to me they won't be able to talk about the things that interest them most, and that will ruin their evening." She looked at Brent, who was patiently explaining a fine point to his eager listeners. "It's bad enough they have to share their table with me. There's no reason for them to adjust their conversation to include me."

"They've already adjusted their clothing," Smith observed dryly. "It won't hurt them to make a few more alterations."

"I was wondering if all pirates dressed like nobility when they came to dinner," Summer said. She was startled to see the smile vanish from Smith's face.

"If you would be willing to accept a word of advice, milady, I would suggest that you not refer to the men as pirates, or to the *Windswept* as a pirate ship."

"But it is, isn't it?" She faltered before his glacial stare. "I mean, you do stop ships and take their cargo."

"That is true as far as it goes," Smith said, without easing the severity of his tone. "We are commissioned by the Dutch government to harry the shipping of any country that attempts to establish dominance over the Atlantic. Our purpose is to keep the seas free."

"But isn't that what the English want, too?"

"Not in the eyes of the Dutch."

"I'm sorry," she apologized. "I don't know whether you're doing the right thing or not, but I perceive that you *think* you are." She looked so perplexed that Smith relaxed. He wondered what she could be thinking about so intently; a few seconds later he found out.

"There is something I *do* know about, however; and that's being taken prisoner against one's will. You can say what you like about Pitt and the Dutch, but you had no right to take me off the *Sea Otter*. I don't come under any commission, I don't belong to the English, I'm not cargo, and I'm not an instrument of war. You've taken me from my family and those hired to protect me. I have no idea what you mean to do with me, nor do I have a way to prevent it." The confidence and animation in Summer's voice was so marked that Brent broke off his conversation.

"What are you two talking about down there? Is Smith telling you off-color stories?" he asked.

Summer choked down a burst of anger.

"We were just discussing a point of international law and its application at sea," Smith answered calmly.

"We're not discussing anything so elevating," Brent said, directing a quizzical eye toward Summer's angry face. "Maybe we'd better save our conversation for later and listen to you." Smith felt a trifle put out by having caused attention to be focused on Summer, but she was not about to back down despite the shortcomings of her education.

"We've just finished, Captain," she replied coolly. "It would be too repetitive to go through our arguments again." The young officers stared at her, mouths open; no one spoke to the captain like that.

"If you don't mind, I would like to retire to my cabin." Everyone except Brent hastily scrambled to his feet as Summer stood up; he rose leisurely and deliberately walked to her side. "I can find my own way," she said, determined to be free of him. "Mr. Smith can escort me if you're afraid I'll get lost."

"I'm sure he would"—Brent smiled—"but I intend to escort you myself. He can bring the others up to date on *international law* while we're gone." He waited expectantly for her to return his verbal thrust, but instead she threw him an aggrieved look and started from the room. However, before she reached the door, she turned back to the men.

"Thank you for allowing me to join you this evening," she said to the still-standing officers. "It has been an unlooked-for pleasure." She then turned sharply on her heel, hoping to escape through the door before Brent could stop her, but he was standing behind her, his hand on the knob; it was impossible for her to go anywhere until he was ready.

"The pleasure has been ours," he replied with a broad grin she didn't think she liked. There had been a threatening undercurrent in his voice which Summer didn't understand, but then she understood little about this disturbingly handsome, oftentimes frightening, young man. She decided she didn't like him. She knew she didn't trust him.

Summer walked swiftly down the passageway. The cabin door was unlocked and she stepped inside, but not so quickly that she was able to close the door on Brent.

"That was unkind," he said with exaggerated chagrin. "I

might get the impression that you don't want me to come in."

"I don't," she responded promptly.

"And after all I've done for you."

"After all you've done for me!" she repeated, stupefied.

"I let you share my quarters. I even moved half my clothes to make room for yours."

"If you hadn't taken me off the *Sea Otter*, you wouldn't have had to move or share *anything*," she snapped.

"I admit I'm not an ideal substitute for your maid, but Smith and the boys have got to be better company than that twisted persimmon Brakeslow, or whatever you call him."

"Brink-low," she enunciated, trying to hide an appreciative grin.

"And without praising myself to the skies, I've got to be a cut above your cowardly Captain Bonner. As to whether I'm an improvement on your husband, well, we'll just have to wait and see about that, won't we?" Summer lost some of her color and all willingness to be amused.

"I wish you'd go away. I'm tired and I want to go to bed."

"It's early yet."

"Not for me. I'm used to an early bedtime and a light supper. It's not good for you to eat so much at the end of the day."

"I'll remember to tell Jacques," said Brent with a crack of laughter. "From now on we'll have fruit, with bread and cheese for those who feel the need of something a little more sustaining."

"You don't have to make fun of me," Summer said resentfully. "I know I act like a rustic; I am one. But I also know there's no way to get fruit and cheese in the middle of the ocean, and that men who work in the riggings all day need something more than a banana for the evening meal. But people like you should watch how much they eat."

"*People like me!*" Brent roared, his words so explosive

Summer reeled back. "Just what in hell do you mean by that extremely ill-chosen phrase?"

Summer went weak-kneed with fright before the lightning flashes of his blazing eyes. "I don't mean anything in particular," she said, hoping to soothe the pride she had so unexpectedly lacerated. "I just thought that since you didn't do as much work as the other men . . ."

"What makes you think that?" he demanded, his rage growing rather than subsiding.

"Well, you don't go into the riggings," she blurted out. "And you don't haul the ropes or row the boats," she added desperately. "So you can't be getting as much exercise as the men who do the heavy work."

Brent was shaking with such rage Summer thought he was going to strike her. He picked up a wooden chair and, with an incredibly quick wrenching motion, tore the back from the base. Then with one rapid move after another he snapped the inch-thick oak dowels that formed the back as if they were pieces of dried sugar cane.

"Before the week is out, I'll show you the kind of exercise I get on this ship," he said in an ominously quiet voice. "Then I'll let you decide whether I'm an armchair leader like your Captain Bonner. Until I do, make the most of your privacy. You're not going to have very much of it."

Brent slammed out of the room without looking back. Word quickly spread through the ship that the young countess had made the captain so angry that he'd stormed back into the dining room, picked up a knife, and thrown it at the wall. It had come to a quivering halt between the eyes of King William V of the Netherlands. Not even Smith had ever known Brent to do anything like that. Everyone was at pains to move quietly and speak only after giving thought to each word. The last person to make the captain that mad had been pitched overboard into a boiling sea.

"I knew that girl would mean trouble," said Smith after

they'd left Brent alone with his brandy. "She hasn't been on board half a day, and already the captain is mad enough to murder his mother."

"What could she have done?" wondered one of the younger men.

"You can never tell with a woman," Smith informed him. "I wouldn't have thought she was the kind to go about causing trouble."

"But she's a real beauty," pointed out another.

"That just makes it worse," Smith said morosely. "Did you ever see a man kick up a fuss or fall into a thundering rage over an ugly female? It's always the pretty ones that cause the trouble, and that one is pretty enough to cause a whole war."

"I never thought of it like that." This comment came from one of the younger men. He was digesting this novel idea.

"Ordinarily you wouldn't have to, you being at sea all the time," Smith said, "but now that we've got a female on board, we'll be lucky if we make it back to port without some kind of upset."

"Aw, come now," said a third, "one little bit of a lass can't do all that, even if she is a countess."

"Then you don't know anything about women," Smith said with biting emphasis. "One little lass can do a whole lot more than that, and without being a countess. You listen to me: never underestimate *any* female, especially if she's young and pretty. There's no such thing as a little lass when she looks like our countess yonder. She's Delilah, Jezebel, or anyone else you please all rolled into one, but whatever you call her, I call her trouble. You wait and see if I'm not right."

As they went off to their cramped quarters to get what sleep they could, they took Smith's words with them. He was not a talker and seldom gave unsolicited advice, but when he did speak, it paid to listen.

Chapter 6

The sound that woke Summer was slight, the whisper of stockinged feet moving across the floor, but her heart almost jumped into her throat.

"Who's there?" she called, hoping desperately no one would answer.

"I am." The reply was immediate. "Who did you expect?" It was Brent's voice.

"I didn't expect anybody," Summer responded, too relieved to be angry. "What are you doing here?"

"Where else should I be? It's my cabin."

"I don't care where you go just as long as you leave the minute you find what you're after."

"I know exactly where it is." His voice was unusually tense, and his hands shook slightly as he lighted a small bedside lamp.

The tiny flame illuminated his quarters with a soft shadowy light. Pieces of furniture stood in relief like ghostly bodies casting impenetrable black shadows behind them, and the rich brown and polished-copper tones of the cabin glowed with a luminous warmth that seemed to make them pulse with life. Summer had never seen anything so eerie. She huddled down under the covers.

Brent took off his coat, folded it carefully, and put it away. He did the same with his waistcoat. The ribbon that held his hair in place was rudely cast to the floor, as was the crumpled but still-snowy white cravat. Summer watched as if hypnotized as he unbuttoned his shirt, stripped it off, and cast it into the same pile. Then he sat down to take off his shoes, and she was once more lost in admiration of the play of muscles over his chest and across his shoulders. Even in the dim light, she could easily see the rippling rhythm of his massive sinews.

Her earlier sense of excitement began to steal over her again. She wiggled in the bed, unable to be still, yet incapable of taking her eyes off the man before her. Brent tossed his shoes into a corner and pulled off his long calf-clinging hose. He then flexed his toes, glad to be freed of the confines of shoes and hose. Summer had never really looked at a man's feet before, and she was surprised to find that such a humble member of the body could be so attractive. They were long feet, a little on the narrow side, but strong and supple.

No concrete images took shape in Summer's brain; her mind was too untutored to be able to give shape and form to her instincts, so she let her thoughts wander along uncharted paths, carried on by a sense of anticipation and pleasurable discovery. But her daydream came to an abrupt halt when Brent stood up and began to unlace his pants.

"What are you doing?" she cried, jerked out of her pleasant fantasy with a suddenness that was physically painful. "Stop! Don't you dare do that!"

He paid no attention, but undid the last button and

stepped out of his pants. Summer dived under the covers with a muffled shriek.

"Do you hide every time Gowan undresses?" Brent asked. "It must get awfully tiring."

Summer didn't answer. The tumultuous sensations coursing through her body so confused her brain that her thoughts made no sense.

"Where should I undress if not in my own quarters?" Brent asked as he shed his last piece of clothing.

"You should undress where you're going to sleep," Summer stammered.

"I am doing that."

Summer's whole world began to disintegrate; nothing related to anything as it should anymore, and she felt herself being drawn into an enormous maelstrom, against her will.

"But there's only one bed," she said, trying valiantly to keep a grasp on reality.

"That's all we need," Brent replied, and Summer could feel the heat in his voice.

"We?" Her voice was barely audible.

"You don't think I'm going to sleep by myself, do you?" He sat down on the edge of the bed.

"But you can't sleep in my bed."

"You've got that wrong. You're in *my* bed."

"I'll get out."

"But I don't want you to." His fingers traced her outline through the bedclothes. "You're too much of a temptation."

"I don't mind sleeping on the floor," she said desperately.

"But I mind very much."

Even with her head under the covers, Summer sensed his hot hunger. He lay down on the bed beside her and pulled the pillow off her head.

"Please don't," she begged, struggling to keep her hold on the only barrier between herself and this man who threatened to overwhelm her with his untamed animal desire. But he was much too strong, and easily pried the pillow from her grasp.

"I want to see your face," he said. "It's quite lovely, you know."

His breath was hot on her cheek. "This is no time to be talking about my face," she said, attempting to pull the sheet over her head.

"Then I'll talk about the rest of you. It's just as enchanting." Passion throbbed in his voice as his arms encircled her waist; her flesh felt as if it were being burned with hot irons. She tried to push his hands away, but she couldn't do that and still keep her hold on the sheets. She lost on both counts. His strong arms encircled her like metal bands, holding her immobile against him.

"What are you going to do?" she asked fearfully, still hoping that something would intervene to save her from what appeared to be her certain fate.

"Ten years ago the earl took what was mine," he said, years of hate and anger cutting through flaring desire. "Now I'm going to take something of his."

"No," Summer moaned, no longer able to doubt what he meant to do. "Please don't!"

"Why should you care? Once you sell yourself, one man's as good as another," Brent said brutally. His hands audaciously explored her body through the thin gown that covered her.

"You have no right," she protested, trying to protect herself from his ravaging hands, trying to deny that her body was responding eagerly to his nearness.

"I'm a lot younger than Gowan," he whispered seductively in her ear. "I can offer you a vigorous, virile body, and I promise I won't turn over and go to sleep immediately afterward." He started to tug her gown toward her head.

"Don't!" she cried out, but again he was too strong for her, and he steadily raised the gown until he slipped it over her head and dropped it to the floor. She lay still, too mortified to move, her hands over her breasts and her body twisted toward the wall.

Brent forced her to turn toward him. He cupped her face in his hands, but Summer kept her eyes tightly closed. "I haven't been able to get you out of my mind all day," he said, his voice husky with passion. "The thought of you has been driving me out of my senses."

He brushed her cheeks with his lips and then took her mouth with a hungry kiss. Summer had never been kissed, and the feel of his firm, hungry mouth on hers nearly paralyzed her. He cupped her firm breasts in his hands and gently massaged their rosy peaks; she tried to turn away, but he held her fast. Summer wanted to hate what Brent was doing when his straying lips began to tease and tantalize her breasts, but arcs of pleasure raced about her body like sparks from exploding fireworks. This unexpected response confused her so, she was hardly able to resist, and Brent pressed his attack with increased intensity.

His hands roamed over her at will, going where no hands had ever gone, doing what she had never imagined hands were meant to do. Her mind was stunned, but an answering chord sounded within her body, and the arcs of pleasure became more frequent, her resistance less determined.

She continued to struggle against him, but she felt the heat of him against her skin, burning into it with white-hot intensity and destroying her will to resist. She knew she should fight for her honor, she thought she wanted to, but it was becoming harder and harder.

"Let me go," she begged, but there was an urgency in her plea. Brent was too wrought up to pay any heed to her. His lips found hers as his arms enfolded her in a crushing embrace, and his tongue raked her mouth, bruising it and searching out every morsel of her sweetness. Their long limbs entwined, bringing Brent to a point of almost uncontrollable urgency. She felt his knee go between her legs, exposing the entrance to the very soul of her to his persuasion. Fear caused her to struggle harder, but her cries of protest were blocked by his lips; her strength was no match for his. Her thighs were forced apart and she felt him search for her, find her, and explore her.

Summer felt as if the whole cosmos were exploding about her. Her body was no longer obedient to her will; it seemed to take on a life of its own, ignoring every restraint she tried to put upon it. "Please don't!" she cried desperately as Brent's hot shaft of desire began to enter her, but tendrils of intense heat and pleasure spread through her loins, and her body accepted, even welcomed his entrance.

Brent had passed beyond the boundaries of restraint and he pressed deeper, moaning with barely contained passion. However, when he encountered an unexpected barrier, he drew in his breath in a gasp of surprise. Summer lay rigid and frightened beneath him, expecting some unnamed terror; she felt the taut, rigidly contained energy of his body and sensed that something explosive was about to happen. Instead he continued to torture her breasts with his lips, to tease her citadel with his hot shaft, until she was sure she would scream in agony. Waves of unnamed desire surged through her as she squirmed beneath him, pressing herself against him, instinctively inviting the release her mind didn't even suspect existed.

She felt Brent tense, gather himself, and then he thrust into her with brutal force. She uttered a long, shuddering moan of agony and her body sought to repel his next attack. She felt betrayed, lulled into a false sense of safety; if she must suffer such pain and disgrace, she'd rather be dead.

Brent paused to allow the pain to recede, but Summer's loveliness stoked his passion and it was impossible for him to think of anything but his urgent need to fulfill his desire. He held her in his arms and covered her face with passionate kisses before entering her slowly, fully, and then with greater force and deeper penetration.

Summer felt she would burst with the size of him. As the wall of pain and shock began to recede, she was aware of a deep-seated need to respond to him, to match his need with her own. Tentatively, and then with greater urgency, she responded to his measured strokes, finally rising to meet him and falling away when he withdrew. Her responses, limited and unskilled as they were, drove Brent beyond touch with anything but his own tumultuous senses, and his overheated blood raged through his veins, blurring his reason. He drove into Summer with increasing rapidity until his breath was coming in short, hot gasps. She struggled to keep up with his movements, caught between the shock of what was happening to her and the kaleidoscope of sensations blasting her body into nothingness.

Finally, with an incredible moan of exquisite pleasure, Brent flung himself at her and Summer felt the release of his heat deep within her. Her own half-born passion withered and died as he collapsed at her side, spent by the violence of his own release.

Brent lay without speaking until his breathing resumed a comfortable rhythm. Summer didn't attempt to cover herself or turn away from him. She was too shaken to cry.

"You're a virgin," he said unnecessarily.

"Not anymore."

"Why?"

"What do you mean *why?*" she asked, a splinter of anger in her voice.

"You're Gowan's wife. How did you escape being bedded by him?"

"I've never met the Earl of Heatherstone," she said in a flat, dull voice. "I was as close to Scotland as I've ever been when you took me off the *Sea Otter*."

"You can't expect me to believe you've never even seen

Gowan, or set foot in Scotland!" said Brent, sitting bolt upright in the bed.

"I was married by proxy. Brinklow was escorting me to Edinburgh."

"Why did you agree to marry a man twice your age, especially one you'd never seen?"

"My father forced me," Summer said, tears beginning to flow at last. "He had gambling debts and the earl was willing to pay a lot for me." She tried to wipe some of the tears away with the sheet.

"There's no end to the evil that man does," said Brent grinding his teeth.

"I begged Father not to make me marry him, but he wouldn't listen. He just kept on drinking until he couldn't hear anything I said."

"Then why in the name of hell and all the demons that toil there didn't you tell me?" demanded Brent in a long, whispered snarl. "Why did you let me go on thinking you'd sold yourself to that devil like some high-priced harlot?"

"I told you over and over again that I wasn't any of those things you thought," she reminded him.

"But you never said anything about not having been in Scotland."

"Would you have believed me?"

"Probably not, but I do now."

"Thank you, but it's already too late," she said miserably. "You can't give back what you've just taken, I can't say it was all a big mistake and then forget it. Oh, God," she wailed, "what am I going to do? What am I going to say to the earl?"

"You don't have to go to Scotland," Brent said, as uncertain of what he meant as he was certain he didn't want to hand her over to Gowan.

"I have nowhere else to go. My father won't take me back. Even the earl probably wouldn't want me if he knew."

"I can take you to Havana with me."

"What for? I will *not* become your mistress. Besides, I know the earl will come after me. You said he always gets what he wants; I'm his wife so I'll have to go with him. What will I tell him? How will I make him believe that it wasn't my fault?"

Brent tried to comfort her, but she fought him, pounding on his chest with her balled-up fists. "Beast!" she sobbed. "You've ruined me with your hate and your lust!" Her grief overwhelmed her and she collapsed into Brent's arms. She held tight to him, responding readily to the strength of his embrace. Holding her close as she poured out her sorrow, Brent kissed her gently, tenderly, wiping away her tears with his fingertips, tasting their salt with his lips.

Summer found herself responding to the warmth of his body, the strength of his arms, the security of his embrace. Against the fear of an unknown and threatening future, she clung to him, igniting once again the fires of his passion. Flames cooled momentarily by exhaustion leaped to white heat and engulfed them both, bearing them along on an ever-widening circle of surging energy. This time Summer responded immediately. Deep within her, she knew a compelling ache, an urgent need that demanded fulfillment; and she moved to meet Brent as he entered her again.

Her response electrified him and he moved more and more rapidly within her, teasing, tantalizing, coaxing her to his level of pulsating intensity. Suddenly Summer felt a burst of energy pick her up. She clung to Brent, greedily drawing on his energy, demanding that he give her even more. Then, with one final blinding surge, the world seemed to explode around them and a new sense of fulfillment and release claimed her.

Chapter 7

The sun had been up two hours when Summer woke. She almost purred as she stretched, enjoying the contact of her flesh and crisp, cool sheets, indulging in a luxurious yawn before she abandoned herself to the equally delicious feeling that something wonderful had happened. Then her eyes fell on the trunks piled against the wall and memory flooded back, bringing with it bitter shame.

Summer sat up with a jerk. She could barely accept the actuality of her deflowering, and she was incapable of facing Brent. She quickly scanned the room, but he had disappeared.

The soreness in her loins confirmed last night's events, and Summer dropped her face into her hands and then uttered a small groan as the full enormity of her humiliation sank in. There was no turning back now; her life would never be the same.

But hadn't it changed already? Was she any more adrift now than when her father had forced her to marry a stranger and go thousands of miles from her home? If the earl was as cruel as Brent had said, would she be any better off as his wife? Would he care what happened to her now?

It was useless to cry or smash her few belongings, yet Summer longed to hurt something as much as she had been hurt. A huge ache expanded like a bubble to fill her chest; it threatened to explode and take her last shred of self-control with it. She had been exploited by a father who should have loved and protected her, had been left to the mercy of pirates by a husband who should have treated her as his most precious possession, and she was now on her own. Her situation was much too desperate for tears; crying was only for people who could dry their eyes and find that everything was all right.

She stood up with a sigh of grim resignation. What was done was done; now she had to concentrate on what to do next. It was going to be impossible to avoid the consequences of the past night, but she promised herself that Brent would pay dearly for what he had done.

Yet a nagging voice inside her kept saying that she was almost as much to blame as he, that she had accepted him, that she had been a willing participant. Summer didn't want to listen to this voice, didn't want to acknowledge anything about last night except her pain and humiliation; but she knew she was going to have to admit her own responsibility for what had happened someday. Not now, however. Terrible things had happened to her in the last few weeks, and she needed to blame everything on Brent just to keep her sanity.

With dawdling steps Summer walked over to the washstand; there was still some water in the pitcher. When she had washed her face and carefully removed every trace of last night's tears, she turned her attention to her bloodstained thighs. Refusing to think of how the blood came to be there, she resolutely finished bathing herself, then turned a pair of expressionless eyes toward the mirror.

As her gaze focused on her naked body, she wondered at

its power to attract two such different men as the earl and the captain. Surely there should be something she could see, but Summer found nothing that hadn't been the same for weeks and months, even years. With a fatalistic shrug she picked up her discarded nightgown and folded it into a small square. "I didn't get much chance to use that," she said savagely as she tossed the garment into a drawer and slammed it shut.

She was in no hurry to dress; she had no place to go, nothing to do, and no one to see. Yet she unconsciously took extra care with details she had formerly given scant attention. A lock of hair wouldn't behave as it should, and she spent additional minutes coaxing it into place. She didn't like the line of her lashes, the color of her cheeks didn't seem quite right, and weren't her lips a little too pale? For the first time she wished she could add a little color to her skin. She gave her face a last critical look, then turned to the problem of choosing a dress.

Summer didn't own a single dress that she hadn't already worn so many times she was ashamed to put it on again, so she turned hopefully to the dazzling wardrobe that the earl had sent as a wedding gift, but the weather was much too hot for silks and satins, quilted brocades or fine wools. She picked up a soft chemise and held it next to her. It was certainly thin enough, but even the petticoats were made of layer upon layer of stiff material. She would have to be content with one of her old gowns. She barely had time to put on her dress and tie up her hair before a knock sounded at the door.

"May we come in, milady?" an unfamiliar voice called. "We have the captain's bath." Summer was startled out of her composure. Where were they going to put a bath? It was unthinkable that they would bring it into her cabin. But before she could protest, two young boys, straining under the weight of a large copper tub, staggered into the room and deposited their burden in the middle of the floor.

"I hope we didn't wake you, milady," said the youth with sandy hair and freckles.

"No, you didn't wake me," Summer replied numbly.

"The captain likes to get started powerful early," the boy said, staring at Summer with open admiration, "but it doesn't suit everybody to be up and about at such hours."

"Th-th-that's all right," she stammered, wondering how to escape before Brent came back. In her agitation she failed to hear approaching footsteps, and she nearly jumped out of her skin when Brent's voice roared from the open doorway.

"The captain particularly likes his crew to go about their business without useless chatter. That water won't jump into the copper by itself, so you'd better give it some help."

Brent's displeasure reduced the youths to quaking incoherence, and they hurried from the room. "I begin to wonder if either of those lads will ever amount to anything," he said, looking over his shoulder at the retreating boys. "Show them a pretty face and everything goes out of their heads." He waited expectantly for Summer to respond, but when she said nothing he moved impatiently about the cabin collecting what he needed for a bath. "They were supposed to have the tub filled by eight o'clock, but the fools were afraid to come in with you in here."

"Do you have a bath every morning?" Summer couldn't believe she had just asked such an improper question.

"Yes, but not always here. Sometimes I swim in the ocean, and at other times we rig up a shower on deck. But the sea is cold, even in summer, and I look forward to an occasional warm bath in front of a fire."

"How do you build a fire on a ship?" she asked, curiosity battling her shame.

"We use small oil burners with reflectors. They're not as good as a log fire, but they serve the purpose."

The boys returned, straining under their load of hot water.

"Don't slop it on the floor," Brent barked. "I don't want to slip and break my head because you don't know how to pour water out of a bucket."

The boys hurried away, to return again and again until the huge copper was filled with steaming water.

"That's enough for now," Brent said, finally. "Remember to have it ready on time tomorrow."

"Yes, Captain," was all they dared say before effacing themselves and escaping as quickly as they could.

"I'm forgetting my manners," Brent said, as he placed a chair and towel within reach of the tub. "Would you like a bath?" Summer shook her head vigorously. "Are you sure? It's no trouble to have more water brought in."

"Thank you, but I don't want a bath," she insisted.

"Suit yourself." He stripped quickly and stepped into the tub. Summer was no longer shocked that he would undress in front of her, but she still hid her eyes. This time, however, she used her hands instead of a pillow.

With an appreciative sigh, Brent settled down into the water until it was right under his chin. "Will you hand me the soap?"

"What?"

"The soap. I can't reach it."

"Where is it?" she asked, being careful to keep her eyes averted. The knowledge that he was naked beneath all that water made her feel weak.

"Next to the basin." The force of her attraction to him was pulling at her, but she was determined to overcome it.

"Here," she said, handing him the soap, her eyes directed at the ceiling.

"I forgot my sponge, too."

She dropped the sponge into the water.

"Thanks," he said, and she retreated to a chair in the far corner. She meant to keep her eyes in her lap, but they kept straying back to his head of luxuriant, short-cropped hair.

Brent washed his feet, raising one after another out of the water. She was so mesmerized by the power of those muscular limbs that she was caught off guard when he stood up unexpectedly. She blushed again and hid her face in her hands.

"Do you have a headache?" he asked turning around to look at her as he covered his whole body with thick lather.

"No." Her voice was no more than a faint whisper. "I feel fine."

"Good, then you can wash my back." He sat down and splashed water all over himself to rinse off the soap. "I can't reach it."

"No," she said softly.

"What did you say?" he asked, still splashing. "You'll have to speak up."

"I said I wouldn't wash your back," Summer answered, louder this time.

"Then I'll wash yours," Brent replied, smiling at her the way a cat smiled at a cornered mouse. "I'd enjoy that even more."

"You won't do any such thing," she said, a trifle shrilly, a look of frightened disbelief spreading over her face. "I don't want a bath."

"You have a choice," he said, still smiling. "One or the other. Which will it be?" He watched her steadily and his strong white teeth seemed to glisten in the light as she shivered with shame. "Make up your mind. The water's getting cold."

Summer dragged herself from the corner, not daring to raise her eyes. Every movement seemed to make her humiliation deeper.

"If you don't look where you're going, you'll end up in the tub after all." Brent laughed as she nearly stumbled over the chair. "I'd love to have you join me, but not head first."

Summer froze, embarrassed. She felt degraded.

Brent held out the sponge, but she made no effort to take it from him. "I'll guide your hand to my back," he teased, putting the sponge in her palm. "Then you won't have to look at me."

"No, thank you." Summer trembled from his touch. "I can do it myself."

Summer's scrubbing was so tentative that Brent could hardly feel it. "Put your back into it," he ordered.

Summer felt that she was going to die, but she scrubbed harder, covering first one shoulder and then the other. She rinsed them both and then scrubbed his lower back.

"Mmmm, that feels wonderful," Brent purred. "Are you sure you won't scrub the rest of me?"

Summer dropped the sponge as if it were a burning coal. "I've finished," she said, drying her hands.

"Hand me that towel before you go."

Before Summer could move, there was a great swishing of water and Brent stood up in the tub, dripping wet, but as proud and magnificent as a Michelangelo statue. With an audible gasp, Summer dropped the towel into the water and clamped her hands over her eyes, but not before she had a picture of his overwhelmingly masculine body etched into her brain.

"Now look what you've done," Brent protested. "You'll have to get me another towel from the cupboard."

"I can't," she groaned, keeping her hands over her eyes, unable to move from the spot.

"I'll drip water all over the floor if I go."

"I *can't!*" she said miserably. "I really can't."

"Oh, all right." He sounded only mildly put out. Summer heard water slosh about as he got out of the tub. Then his feet padded softly on the floor. A cupboard was roughly thrown open, and the barely audible sound of clothing being thrown about came to her ears. "You're lucky I have some extras, or you'd have to go ask Smith for more." Summer felt that her torment would never end. "You can open your eyes now," he said. "I'll stay covered long enough for you to run back to your corner." Fearful that if she delayed he might not cover himself at all, Summer dropped her hands and ran quickly to the chair at the foot of the bed. She sat, her eyes fastened on her lap, but she was prepared to shut them on a second's notice.

"You shouldn't be so squeamish," Brent said, as he dried himself off. "I'm not hard to look at, at least so I've been told." He tossed the wet towel to the floor, and Summer's eyes snapped shut. "You might as well get used to me. I'm going to be around until we reach Havana, and I don't plan to keep my clothes on all that time."

Summer shuddered.

Brent slipped into a luxurious ruby red robe that reached his ankles. He walked to the door and shouted down the hall. "More water!" He turned to Summer, leaving the door open. "Now it's your turn."

Summer's head jerked up at his words. Her heart beat wildly, and her eyes were so unfocused by terror that she could hardly see her tormentor though he stood less than ten feet from her. "I don't want a bath."

"The water's warm and relaxing," he said. "You'll feel much better afterward." Before she could recover the use of her tongue, the boys were trooping in with more cans of hot water. In a remarkably short time they had finished, and she was once more alone with Brent.

"Come on, there's nothing to be afraid of," he assured her. "I'll even help you undress.".

"No!" she nearly shrieked. "I can't take a bath in front of you."

"But I insist," he said, and she knew by the hard glint in his eyes that there would be no turning him from his purpose. He took her by the hand and pulled her to her feet, then almost dragged her toward the tub that stood so ominously in the middle of the room. "Let me help you with your ties."

"Don't touch me," she whimpered. Her hands flew to her waist and feverishly covered the knotted sash, but Brent firmly removed them and undid the sash with one quick movement.

"Stand still," he commanded. "I can't undo these buttons with you squirming like a captured pig."

Summer tried to remain rigid, but the feel of his fingers moving down and over her bosom as he meticulously undid each button nearly drove her into a frenzy. When he slipped the dress over her shoulders and dropped it to the floor at her feet, she thought she couldn't stand any more. He quickly undid her light petticoat, and she stood revealed in her shift. She was covered with embarrassment, and could only hope that she would die and never have to look anyone in the face again. But worse was yet to come.

Abruptly Brent was quiet. The mocking tone left his voice, the insouciant lightness vanished from his movements. His mind and body were heated by rising desire. His touch became heavy, his fingers clumsy; and he fumbled with the strings. As he slipped the straps of the shift over her shoulders, letting his hands linger on the satin-smoothness of her skin, the warm scent of her body gave him a heady feeling of intoxication. He tugged gently and the shift slid over the curves of her body to fall noiselessly into a circle at her feet.

Like a man in a trance, he drank in every breathtaking detail of her body, from the luxuriant fall of burnished-copper hair to toes wriggling in a sign of her inner torment. He wondered again how Gowan had had the luck to chance upon this supremely lovely creature. His hand reached out to touch her, but she shrank involuntarily from his touch.

"You'd better get into the tub before you catch cold," he

said. A constriction in his throat made it difficult for him to speak. "Let me give you a hand. You might fall."

"I can do it myself," she said, weak with shame. She drew her hand behind her, but he reached out and took it.

"Don't be a fool. It's not worth cracking your skull against the tub."

"I don't want your help. I don't want you to touch me at all," she said tersely.

"Try to accept my help graciously for once."

She did not answer him, but she did let him assist her into the tub. She immediately sank so low in the water Brent wondered if she meant to cover her head.

"You don't have to drown yourself just to get away from me," he said acidly. "I'll leave you alone if it's that painful." He stalked over to the chair in the corner and dropped onto it, muttering curses and swearing to blind himself rather than succumb to her allure.

But his eyes would no more leave her than his mind would refuse to think about her, and the heat of his anger quickly ebbed to the warmth of desire. His gaze feasted on the loveliness of her curving lips, her dainty nose, the alabaster creaminess of her complexion, and on tresses of molten copper that cascaded over the edge of the tub. He felt hypnotized.

Desire tormented him as she moved slowly and quietly in the water. She was turned slightly away from him, and the early morning sun cast her silhouette into well-honed relief, sharply outlining her every movement. With fluid motions she washed her limbs one at a time, and he felt mesmerized, incapable of breaking the spell that held him lightly yet so securely. With a tremendous effort of will he wrenched himself away from the siren call of her overwhelming femininity.

"I'll wash your back for you," he said, starting up from the chair like a stag erupting from the forest. He took the sponge, mindless of her protests, and roughly scrubbed her back, too caught up in her to know what he was doing.

"You've washed the same spot at least three times now," Summer told him with some umbrage. The sound of her voice broke the spell, and he gave her back the sponge. He felt as weak as a baby when he sat down again.

Brent closed his eyes. Slowly his sense of detachment began to fade and he felt a part of the world again. He got up, deliberately walked to the cupboard, and took out a towel. "I'll dry you," he said, and waited silently for Summer to step out of the tub.

She had no wish to leave the safety of the bath. Its warmth eased and comforted her, but she was weary of crossing wills with Brent, tired of the humiliation of being forced to obey his commands. He had almost destroyed the last remnants of her pride. She clenched her teeth and, eyes tightly closed, extended her hand for help out of the bath. She stepped onto the soft rug and felt the enveloping folds of the towel surround her. Then to her considerable surprise, he began to pat her dry.

Her protests were in vain. Nothing seemed capable of stopping those hands, those horrible patting hands that went everywhere with bold and insistent strength. She burned with humiliation, felt cheap and tawdry; but those hands wouldn't let her go, wouldn't heed her outcry of rage when they strayed.

Then, as suddenly as the patting had begun, it stopped. But Summer's relief evaporated when Brent let the towel fall to the floor. Now no barrier protected her from the burning intensity of his eyes. She could track his ravenous gaze by the trails of fire it left on her body. She wanted to scream, to yell heathenish curses, to scratch out his devouring eyes, but she couldn't move. She couldn't even cover her shame.

"Come," he said simply; he led her to the bed and placed her upon it with infinite gentleness. She watched with wondering eyes as he loosened the tie that held his robe closed.

She wanted to turn away, but she couldn't; her eyes remained wide and staring, drinking in the glories of the male body that stood before her. Any lingering shred of control she had was dealt a telling blow by his overpowering presence. His sensual grace seemed to permeate the whole atmosphere. She stared openly, greedily, committing every detail of his being to memory—powerful calves and thighs, muscular chest and shoulders.

Her eyes found his and locked, held by the intensity of azure pools filled with a wealth of desire. The heat and intensity of his need scorched her; she felt drained by it. She unconsciously moved over so he might lie beside her.

Brent gathered her into his arms, pressing her close to him, breathing in the warm fragrance of her freshly bathed body, enjoying the feel of her skin on his. His lips found hers in a gentle kiss. They almost pleaded with her to join him in the celebration of their union. Against her will, she responded, relaxing into his embrace and returning his kiss. Her response was warm and peaceful, but capable of becoming turbulent in the flash of an eye.

Brent continued to kiss her with gentle insistence—her face, mouth, and eyes. His legs intertwined with hers, and she could feel the heat of him on her abdomen, pulsating and insistent. Instincts buried deep within her body began to stir under the stimulus of his passion, to warm and respond to his nearness. His hands caressed her, and a low moan, primeval in origin, escaped her lips. It sent a shiver of excitement through Brent. His kisses intensified and his hands moved with ever-increasing urgency. Every part of her was alive as she twisted with rising anticipation, drawn to him, pressed against him, pleading for the union that would make them one.

Summer felt Brent's knee move between her thighs, and fear and anticipation battled for supremacy. Her mind and body pulled her in opposite directions until she lost all control. Her agitated confusion excited Brent, and he could no longer contain his growing passion. He moved above her, entered her, easily at first, then more roughly. Her fear of pain receded as wave after wave of pleasure surged through her, ridding her of all doubt and confusion. Her whole consciousness was concentrated on the oncoming swells that threatened to bear her helplessly away. All desire to resist or to stoically endure his advances evaporated. She clung to him as though he were her only means of crossing the swollen river of passion that threatened to overflow its banks and to drown them both in its swirling eddies and crashing falls. As Brent increased the tempo of his lovemaking, an abrupt thrust drove her to new heights at which she could share equally in their pleasure. She clung more tightly to him, her nails digging into his back as her mouth sought his, eagerly meeting his lips and trying frantically to say what their bodies were already saying for them. With each thrust, Summer felt herself being lifted a little higher until she felt she had lost contact with all solid objects except the pulsating body driving her own into a fiery spiral.

Brent's movements became uneven and labored, his body was almost rigid with intense pleasure. In one final agonizing effort he drove deep within Summer, then a deep shuddering sensation swept through him draining him of tension and leaving him weak and gasping for breath.

As Summer received the molten evidence of his heat, she felt that her insides were branded forever. She arched under him, thrusting herself against him, drawing every drop of pleasure from him, forcing him to drain himself dry in an effort to satisfy her. Then one final, explosive blast of pleasure surged through her, and with a moan torn from the very depths of her soul, she threw herself against him, to be locked in an embrace that would only be broken when the raging fires within them had cooled to glowing embers.

Chapter 8

"May I come in, milady?" It was one of Brent's young officers. Summer scrambled out of bed and reached for her clothes.

"You'll have to wait," she called out. "I'm not dressed." She pulled her shift over her head and looked for something to cover herself. Her glance falling upon Brent's red dressing gown, she threw it on without hesitation. "What do you want?" she asked, opening the door a couple of inches.

"Good morning, milady," the young man said politely. "Captain Douglas wants to know if you're ready to join him for the midday meal?"

"I'd prefer to eat in my cabin."

"I'll have to ask the captain," he said a trifle uncertainly.

Summer dressed quickly. She was very hungry and hoped her food would soon appear. But a few minutes later she was dismayed to hear heavy footsteps coming down the passage and a booming voice. The next moment the door was thrown open and the captain's huge form burst into the small cabin, his vital presence filling it to overflowing.

"What is this I hear about having lunch in my cabin?" he asked, looking like a man who has been dragged away from important business due to an inconsequential interruption.

Summer was determined that she was not to be intimidated by his size and bullying attitude, but she almost changed her mind when she saw the mood he was in.

"I would like to eat in private," she muttered.

"Why? What are you afraid of?"

"Nothing," she replied, finding it hard to face his forbidding glare. "I just don't feel quite up to talking with people."

"Nonsense," he said briskly. "It's not good for you to be cooped up all day. Besides, this ship's too small for you to start trying to hide."

"I'm not trying to hide. I just want to be alone."

"Well, you can't. This is not a luxury yacht, and Jacques doesn't have time to be making up trays. The crew has a full load of work; I can't have you adding to it."

"It's a pity you didn't think of that before you took me off the *Sea Otter*," she snapped.

"I'm not sorry about that." Brent grinned and cast a leering glance at her body.

"Well, I am. At least you could have let Bridgit stay with me."

"I'll see that you're cared for, but you can't expect to have your meals brought to you." Summer looked so small and vulnerable that some of the harshness left Brent's voice. "You don't have to worry that I'll forget you," he reassured her softly. "Now let's go before Jacques comes after us with a bowlful of French curses." He held the door for her, but Summer turned back.

"Hurry up," he called, not quite so softly.

"I'm looking for my shawl," she said. "I can't go to the table looking like this."

"What's wrong with the way you look?" he asked, gazing purposefully at the bodice of a low-cut gown that exposed half of her creamy bosom. "I think you look charming."

"Thank you," she said in a clipped tone, "but I'm not the strumpet you take me for. It's not my habit to advertise wares I don't intend to sell." She picked up her shawl.

"Where did you learn to talk like that?"

"My father had some pretty unsavory friends," Summer mumbled, blushing and turning away. "I suppose I shouldn't have spoken so boldly, but I can't forget all the things you said to me yesterday."

"I won't say them again."

Summer regarded him with skeptical eyes. It would be nice to have someone take care of her, but she didn't think this passionate man would be able to maintain a disinterested attitude for very long.

"In the meantime, we'd better hurry," Brent continued. "One of my rules is that anyone who's late to a meal doesn't get anything to eat."

"You can't mean that," Summer objected, moving quickly to the door. "I'm terribly hungry."

"One of the privileges of a captain is being able to change the rules," Brent said as he followed her from the cabin. Summer's laugh rang down the passageway, and there was a sudden jauntiness to Brent's step.

"But you can't do it very often," he added. "It would weaken morale."

"Maybe it would help if I smiled at everyone," she said with a saucy look.

"You'll do no such thing," Brent commanded, not amused. "Captives are only allowed to smile at the captain. It's a law of the sea."

"You haven't given me much reason to smile at you."

"I thought I had," Brent responded, a hot gleam in his eyes. "It looks like I'll have to try again."

"That would be nice," she said, trying to recapture a light note. "But make sure you tell me when you mean to start. I might not be able to tell otherwise."

"Vixen." Brent chuckled as he held open the door. "Say much more and I'll reverse my opinion of you."

"That would have to be an improvement on what you think of me now," Summer responded as she passed him.

A wave of relief swept over the men who were muttering anxiously among themselves about the captain's lateness when the pair walked in smiling and apparently in good spirits. After last night, they weren't looking forward to dining with Summer, for that might mean the captain would be in a dangerous mood for the rest of the day.

"I beg your pardon for my lateness," Summer apologized as they rose in unison, "but I'm not yet familiar with your schedule, and it takes me longer to dress without my maid." She gave Brent a pointed look. "I promise not to be late again."

Unprepared for such an apology, the men were uncertain of how to respond to it, but what struck them most was the manner in which she delivered it. Even though they couldn't point to any specific difference in her behavior, they sensed a slight change in her relationship with Brent. They glanced questioningly at their captain, but he gave no indication that he noticed.

When the meal began, Summer became silent, and the normal pattern of conversation soon sprang up. But the men weren't able to put Summer out of their minds as completely as they had on the first night.

"I should have thought of bringing a female on board long ago," Brent said, taking note of the men's unusually careful grooming. "These young scamps have been spending extra time in front of the mirror, though not with complete success.

Kent has finally managed to shave all of his face, but young Jones has wrapped his neck in a tie too ambitious for his skills." The two gentlemen named flushed self-consciously. "And our entire store of soap must be gone. I've never eaten with a sweeter-smelling bunch of men. Makes me think I'm in a harem."

"I'm flattered to think that so much importance is attached to my presence," Summer countered, taking pity on the embarrassment of her companions. "You are a handsome group of men, a sight to please the eye—and the nose," she added with a demure smile.

Brent's burst of laughter startled one poor lad into choking on his wine. "I'll have to remember not to give you an opening like that again, or you'll have them so bedeviled they won't be fit to do their work."

"I'm sure they have too much presence of mind to become rattled by a few compliments," Summer declared.

"Compliments from lips such as yours are potent," said Brent wryly. "A woman with a smooth tongue can always be dangerous."

"Not to a man of character," Summer insisted.

"You haven't studied your history, or you wouldn't say anything so stupid," Brent stated bluntly.

"I didn't mean it that way," Summer replied, hurt by his ill-mannered response.

Smith watched her silently, certain that Brent had underestimated the character and force of this girl. He couldn't say why just yet, but he feared Brent had gotten himself entangled and that his involvement would have disastrous consequences. If Smith had his way, he'd put the young woman in a boat with some food and water, and leave her for the next ship to find. Her fate wouldn't weigh on his conscience for long; he believed nothing should take precedence over the welfare of the ship or the success of their enterprise. And in

Smith's eyes, Brent was endangering both by keeping Summer on board.

Had he but known it, Summer agreed with him. As she undressed that night, certain of its end and of the ends of all the other nights she was aboard this ship, she felt uneasy. Already her attraction to Brent was growing. She had a tendency to let her glance linger on his features; she remembered the strength of his arms, the power of his body. He was a magnet pulling her in his direction. She wasn't at all sure she wanted to go that way.

Certainly it would be wonderful to be cared for by such a man. It wasn't every girl who could be loved, even for one night, by a man who so far transcended her dreams. But there was danger in it as well. What did she know about him? Only that he was a pirate who had captured and ravished her in the same day, no matter what Smith said about the Dutch government and freedom of the seas. But what more could she expect from a man who had never pretended that she was anything more to him than a means to cold-blooded revenge?

And that wasn't all. He had scorned and mocked her in front of his men, had called her every name a woman dreads to hear, had accused her of behavior that was cruel and despicable.

Against that could be placed only his slight softening toward her since he'd learned she had never seen Gowan. It was true that he expected his crew to treat her with respect, but privately he had changed little. He still bullied her and ordered her about.

No, there was a third side consideration, and it was the most important. What was her future going to be, and would Brent be a part of it? She was the legal wife of the earl, bound to him by the ties of church, state, and social custom; but she could never be Gowan's wife, not in the accepted sense. Still, she couldn't stay with Brent. She doubted he'd be willing to give up his ship, marry, and settle down; yet she'd never dream of staying with him otherwise.

Summer couldn't face the prospect of sailing the seas as Brent's mistress, cut off from the only kind of life she had ever known. Soon she would find herself with another man, and then another, until it wouldn't matter who she was with. After a while she wouldn't even remember their names. Rather than confront that possibility she would go back to the earl. Even his curses would be preferable to that kind of degradation.

But would the earl come after her? Would he acknowledge her if she reached Scotland on her own? After he learned who had ravished her, would he renounce her?

Brent woke early. Summer was nestled in the corner of the bed, her back to him, and the sight of her naked body brought back the memory of the past night and of the preceding nights. A smile of satisfaction touched his lips and his sleepy eyes softened. Now that she was no longer a part of his revenge, his anger toward her had disappeared. In its place was a strong desire to be near this lovely girl who challenged his control over his senses. Her long tresses lay tumbled over her brow. He reached over to pull them back from her face, but the shift in his weight caused Summer to stir. She squirmed into a tighter ball, but, unable to settle down again, she moved about seeking a more comfortable position. She finally ended up half on her back and half on her side, with one arm across her chest. Brent thought she looked miserably uncomfortable.

He studied her closely, marveling at the loveliness of her whole body. Her smooth soft skin was velvety to the touch, and he ran his hand along her side and over her abdomen, letting the tips of his fingers barely touch her. He took a lock of hair between his fingers; it was silky soft and its burnished-copper highlights showed red-gold in the weak morning light. When he touched her cheek and brushed her lips with his fingertips, she dashed a hand over her face as though to brush away an insect. Brent picked up the sheet from the floor and spread it over her. She might as well sleep as long as she liked.

What was he going to do with her? He couldn't send her back to her father, and he was not willing to turn her over to the earl.

He poured water from the pitcher into the basin and splashed it over his face. That refreshed him, but didn't answer his questions. He took out his shaving gear and quickly removed the latest growth of whiskers from his smooth, tanned face. As he patted his skin dry, he glanced at Summer once again. She lay facing him now, and the quiet innocence of her face tugged at his heart. It was impossible to look on anything that lovely and not desire it, not long to hold it close. Yet it was also impossible to regard her guileless face and not want to protect her.

He drew on a loose shirt and brief pants that covered little of his powerful body and concealed none of his bulging muscles. He would have to keep her with him until he could find some solution. Maybe he would think of something before they reached Havana. If not, she'd be safe enough on Biscay Island.

He took one more look at the sleeping girl before he left, but his mind was not at ease.

Chapter 9

Summer sat cross-legged on the bed, chin in her hands, the covers wrapped tightly around her. It was difficult to believe that only seven days had passed; so much had changed in that time it felt more like seven years. She was no longer a naïve girl uncomfortable in the presence of most men; she was now a woman learning that the pleasures to be found in the arms of a man were wonderful and exciting, quite unlike anything she had previously experienced.

Brent's image flashed into her mind, and she smiled as she remembered little things about him. It wasn't that she had become immune to his muscular body or his virile good looks. She still felt weak whenever he was close to her, but she had begun to see things that she hadn't had time to notice before: his hair was actually brown, but was bleached by the sun; he cocked his head to the right when he was amused; his eyes were not a pure blue, but took on a greenish hue when he became passionate.

She smiled languidly as she lay back down and snuggled

up to her pillow. Life on the *Windswept* was spoiling her. She had all morning to get ready for lunch, and all afternoon to get ready for dinner, which was what she should be doing instead of daydreaming. But the weather had turned cold enough to make the bed deliciously snug, and the temptation to stay where she was just a little longer was too great to resist. With a sound that could have been mistaken for a purr, she rolled over and pulled the sheets under her chin.

"It's cold enough to make your teeth chatter," Brent announced striding into the cabin, bursting with energy and infectious good cheer.

"I know," said Summer, snuggling deeper into the blankets.

"You'll have to wear something warm tonight."

"I don't have anything warm." She stifled a yawn. "It never got cold at home."

"There must be something in one of those trunks. No one can have that many thin dresses."

"I've got the clothes the earl sent, but I don't know how to wear them."

"Where are they?"

She pointed to a chest against the wall nearly twice the size of the others. "Bridgit was going to teach me, but she never got the chance."

"Never mind about your damned maid," he replied, tired of her carping about the missing servant. "I probably know more about women's clothes than she does."

"How could you?"

"I've taken a lot of them off," he said, grinning attractively at her.

Summer blushed rosily. "What an awful thing to admit, and you're not even ashamed."

"Why should I be? They were just as anxious to get out of their clothes as I was to take them off," he said nonchalantly, opening the trunk.

"I still think it's disgraceful," she insisted, trying to ignore a twinge of jealousy. But Brent wasn't listening to her; he was turning over gown after gown made of the finest materials.

"Gowan must really have been taken with that portrait," he said with a sharp whistle. "He'd cheat the parish priest if he could, but these clothes had to cost him a fortune." Brent admired one particularly lavish gown. "He must have wanted you a lot."

"He gave Father ten thousand pounds for me."

"What?" Brent thundered, whipping around to face her. "Are you sure it wasn't a thousand pounds, or even a hundred?" His voice was so unyielding, Summer remembered the day he'd captured the *Sea Otter*.

"Father told me his debts came to just under eight thousand pounds and that there would be some money left over." The strange look in Brent's eyes made Summer uneasy. He ground his teeth so hard his jaw muscles stood out.

"He must have wanted you very badly indeed," he said, almost to himself. "I wonder why?"

"Father said it was because of my youthful beauty, and my innocence," Summer stated modestly.

"I doubt that," Brent rasped. "Gowan never put any value on those qualities before. It's certain no one ever knew him to pay money for them."

"All Brinklow mentioned was some nonsense about my family and breeding. Even I didn't believe that." She was piqued by Brent's refusal to believe she was worth more than a hundred pounds.

"What exactly did he say?" Brent asked impatiently.

"I don't remember. I didn't like the man and I didn't listen very closely to what he said."

"Try to remember," Brent urged, persistent as a hound after a lost scent. "It might be important."

"I think he said the earl valued my bloodlines, that I came from an important family. He felt that with my beauty and breeding I would make an admirable countess." She looked annoyed. "He sounded more like he was talking about a race horse."

"There must be something in that," Brent mused after a pause, "but I can't see it. Gowan was never interested in marriage, not even when several well-dowered ladies did their best to catch him. And that was before he became rich by robbing me," he added with savage emphasis. He sat absentmindedly in front of the open trunk speculating on several possible answers, but none satisfied him. He looked so fiercely angry that Summer didn't dare make a sound.

"I can't find anything here but formal gowns," he said, coming out of his trance at last. "What else have you got?"

"There's a smaller trunk." Summer was relieved to see him looking more human, and she recalled that the second trunk contained many more gowns.

"Well, you'll just have to wear one of these," Brent declared, returning to the first trunk and selecting several items in rapid order. "You'll certainly be the best-dressed woman on the Atlantic." He dumped the armload of clothes on the bed. "I'll help if you want."

"But this is underwear," protested Summer looking at the flimsy garments.

"What did you expect to put on first?"

"But I can't put on underwear in front of you."

"Why not?" he asked, genuinely surprised. "I've seen you in less." He grinned so broadly she ached to slap his face.

"That's different," she said, refusing to be baited. "I really would feel like a strumpet if I put these things on with you watching."

"I can't see that it matters."

"Well, it does," she assured him.

"All right. I'll leave for a few minutes, but don't take too long. I'm anxious to get to the stockings."

"Go away," she said, blushing in spite of herself. As soon

as he closed the door behind him, Summer picked up the flimsy chemise and the drawers. I might as well be naked, she thought. Then she threw off the sheet, climbed out of bed and said out loud, "I don't know why I'm hesitating over underwear. It's the only thing I *do* know how to put on." She held the garments up for closer inspection, then donned them. It was cold in the cabin and she was already covered with goose bumps. She intended to put the stockings on herself, but she was barely seated when the door opened and Brent stuck his head in.

"I thought as much," he said accusingly. "Trying to cut me out of the fun." He took the stockings out of her hands and expertly ran them up on his fingers.

Summer stifled an urge to pull the sheet over her head again; she felt like a lewd and abandoned female.

"Now give me your foot," he ordered.

Reluctantly Summer raised her foot and Brent slipped the stocking over her toes. Then with deliberate slowness he drew it over her heel and ankle, up the calf, and over the knee, to where it was attached to the drawers. Summer held her breath as his hands moved along the inside of her thigh, then let out a long, pent-up sigh of relief when the first stocking was attached. She had barely recovered before Brent said, "Now the other foot." Once again the bold fingers slid the stocking over her toes and gently, steadily, irresistibly they traveled up her leg. Brent was breathing hard before the second one was attached, but Summer wasn't breathing at all.

"Now for the corset," he said, standing up abruptly. "You're not going to like this at all." His words released the tension. Summer felt weak and deflated, but Brent, recovering more quickly than she did, held up an evil-looking contraption made of heavy linen and strings. "Pull in your stomach," he said. Summer did, and before she had time to let it out again he wrapped the corset around her waist, encasing her middle in a merciless band of whalebone.

"I can't breathe," she wailed, knowing the terror a horse feels the first time a cinch is tightened around its girth.

"It's not nearly tight enough," Brent told her. "I've got to pull it in two more inches."

"I'll die," she moaned, but Brent pulled and tugged until she felt unable to breathe. No cry of pain, no plaintive entreaty stopped him until he had reduced her waist to eighteen inches and the rest of her body to agony.

"That's enough," he said at last.

"Uh," wheezed Summer. She was too miserable to talk.

"Stop complaining, or you'll go to dinner as you are," he threatened. "Now put your shoes on."

"I can't bend over," Summer groaned. She couldn't see her feet or the high-heeled, embroidered satin shoes with pointed toes and silver buckles.

"I'll put them on for you." Brent laughed. "But you have to pay a forfeit."

"What?" Summer asked suspiciously.

"I get to take your stockings off again."

"I've changed my mind."

"It's too late," Brent said. "Sit."

She managed to lower herself onto the bed. The touch of Brent's hands caused her whole body to tremble, but she controlled herself until he cruelly tickled the bottoms of her feet.

"You devil!" she shrieked, and managed to put her foot into his stomach even though she couldn't break his grip. "That's unfair and completely unworthy of a gentleman."

"True, but I couldn't resist," Brent confessed, his smile making Summer forgive him instantly. "Sit still and I promise I won't tickle you again." He slipped the shoes on, then helped Summer to her feet.

"I'm not used to high heels," Summer said, walking rather uncertainly across the floor.

"Then you'd better practice. I can't have you falling on your face in front of my officers."

"I'm not that bad," she protested, indignantly.

"Good. You'll need to be steady on your feet with the size of this petticoat." He pulled out a stiff white garment that seemed to grow larger as it escaped the confines of the trunk.

"Do I have to wear *all* of that?" she asked startled.

"Of course."

"Can't I just wear one of my old dresses?" Summer was rapidly becoming disenchanted with her new clothes.

"Stop complaining." Uncompromisingly, Brent placed the petticoat around her waist and tied it securely at the back.

"Don't women ever get tired of all this stuff?" she asked, unhappy with the weight of the petticoat and the discomfort of the corset. After years of wearing light, loose clothing, Summer was utterly miserable.

"They get used to it. Now turn around so I can put on the bodice." Summer meekly allowed him to spin her about, button up the bodice, and attach the sleeves. His hands did their work efficiently, but in her mind they lingered much too long over the buttons across her bosom.

"Don't squirm so," Brent commanded, but it was impossible for her to stand still under his touch. Her skin was alive, every nerve ending painfully sensitive. At last Brent released her, and she breathed as deeply as she could in that confining corset.

"Is that for me?" she asked in wonder when she saw the underskirt of white silk embroidered in a flower-like design copied from the French mode. She could hardly believe that anything so beautiful was meant for her.

"It takes forever to attach this thing," Brent said gruffly, "so don't move."

Summer was acutely aware of his hands on her waist and hips even though she tried to peek over her shoulder at her reflection.

"Not until you're completely dressed." Brent gave her a playful slap on the behind, and Summer obediently stood still until the overdress of cobalt blue satin with silver trim and a flounced hem was in place. "Now you can look at yourself." Brent stepped back and really saw her for the first time.

Summer almost raced to the mirror, but she came to an abrupt halt before the unfamiliar sight that met her eyes. She couldn't believe that the vision staring back at her could possibly be her own self.

"I'm pretty," she said, turning to Brent and bubbling with excitement. "Not even Mama would recognize me now." In her own eyes, the transformation was nothing short of a miracle, and she looked at herself again, almost afraid her likeness would disappear if she turned away for too long. "I *do* look pretty, don't I?" she asked excitedly.

"Much more than that," Brent said, unprepared himself for such loveliness. The tension in his voice belied his calm exterior, as did the burning intensity of his eyes. "You're really very beautiful."

"Am I?" Summer flushed with pleasure.

"I've never seen anyone more beautiful."

"Now, I *know* you're not telling me the truth," she said, afraid to let herself believe his extravagant praise.

"You don't have to rely on my word alone. At dinner, the men's eyes will tell you the same thing."

Summer realized with a sickening jolt that she wouldn't care if the rest of the world thought her a veritable witch as long as Brent thought she was pretty. That realization was so momentous she could only mumble a reply.

"I have to go," Brent said, striving to refocus his mind on his duties while his eyes traveled hungrily over Summer. "I've already stayed too long."

As soon as the door closed behind him, Summer sat down with a plop, the painful pinch of the corset all but unnoticed now. She tried to concentrate on the unfamiliar process of applying makeup to an already perfect complexion, but Brent's image kept intruding on her mind and she snapped the case shut in disgust. She could no longer ignore the fact that she was falling in love with him.

How could she do such a thing? How could she even *think* of falling in love with a man who had kidnapped her and then forced himself upon her in an act of revenge? Brent had no qualms about using her to satisfy his own physical needs without showing any regard for her wishes. But she loved him. . . .

She smiled to herself as she recalled the way his hair ruffled in the breeze, a stray lock always falling over his eyes. A little shudder of delight ran through her as she remembered the feel of his powerful arms around her and recalled every detail of his beloved face.

But the smile faded from her lips and the animation in her eyes dimmed. What possible chance did she have for happiness? He liked her well enough, but she wasn't sure his attraction went beyond the pleasure he took in her body. Even this might not be enough to hold his attention once they reached Havana. She had no illusions about her lack of sophistication or her inability to compete with seasoned beauties of practiced charm, and she doubted her youthful allure would be enough to keep him at her side for very long.

Her spirits sagged. Much as she ached for his presence, she knew that physical love would not be enough for her. He had to love *her*, the person inside the softly curved body, the girl behind that pretty face. He had to cherish the impish spirit that hid behind the twinkling eyes and demure smiles.

But who was she? She hardly knew herself. She had been so overshadowed by her mother that she'd never had a chance to think for herself. The freedom she had enjoyed stemmed from the isolation of their plantation, not from any desire to help her develop her own personality. Why hadn't she been taught to think? Why was it so important to know how to walk across a room, to speak to a man when she had nothing of importance to say?

There's no use sitting here and feeling sorry for yourself, she thought. You'd better try to get him out of your mind before it's too late. He probably won't even remember you once he reaches Havana. She walked over to the porthole and looked out. The sky was a misty gray and the wind whipped the waves into white-capped peaks, but that wouldn't last long. Yesterday's breezes had borne the softness and warmth of the Caribbean; their time at sea was drawing to a close. Once on shore there would be so much work he wouldn't have time for her.

And then there were all those women. Brent rarely mentioned them, but Summer knew they were there. It was impossible for her to believe that any woman could look at him and not feel as she did.

This thought made her so dejected that she felt like crying. You can't possibly weep at dinner, she told herself. Her mother had once said that men didn't know what to do with a crying female so they usually got angry. She doubted Brent would be any different.

She sniffed defiantly and dared even one tear to run down her cheeks. Only her glistening eyes hinted at the grief she resolutely held back. I will not become a sniveling miss, she thought, nor will I become a slave to a lot of muscles and a pair of blue-green eyes. I'll just have to put him out of my mind. If Mother could endure life without the man she loved, then I can.

"I am able to take care of myself," she said aloud. She knew it wasn't so, but that was something she refused to admit, even to herself. Things would become too desperate then.

She heard those familiar steps coming down the passage and her chin went up. Hers was an old and aristocratic name;

she would not disgrace her heritage. With eyes that glittered a little too brightly and a smile that was pinned too rigidly to her lips, she waited for Brent. She hoped he couldn't see that her heart was breaking; yet she hoped he would care enough to sense her unhappiness.

Chapter 10

The men did notice the difference. An awestricken silence fell over the room when Summer walked though the door, her petticoats rustling and her rich silks making their clothes appear ordinary by comparison. Even phlegmatic, disapproving Smith agreed that the countess was a stunning young woman. He's already lost, Smith said to himself, when he saw the smile curving Brent's lips.

"I told you their eyes would pop out," Brent said, his laugh not entirely hiding his jealousy. "Close your mouths, you gawking fools. You look like orphan boys in a pastry shop."

At his stern words his men recovered their wits, but throughout the evening their eyes turned toward the foot of the table to enjoy looking at Summer, to imagine that she was somehow their own, or perhaps to convince themselves that she wasn't an illusion conjured up out of the cold Atlantic mists to tease their senses. They included her in their conversation more often and listened politely to what she said; they were gradually beginning to accept her presence as a natural circumstance. But even Summer's overwhelming transformation couldn't keep their minds off the upcoming competitions.

Two years earlier Brent had inaugurated a series of contests to break the monotony of long sea voyages. In addition to being a much enjoyed break from the grinding routine of the ship, they provided a focus for the men's time and energy during lengthy periods of waiting and they helped them maintain the skills on which their lives depended. Practicing and bragging went on sporadically during every voyage, but the serious competing was saved for the trip home when the hold was full and they were in the mood for celebrating.

"Horton has been practicing for a week," Caspian said. "He's determined to throw farther than you this year, Captain."

"Trying to get a head start on me?" Brent chided.

"Not that, sir," Horton muttered, fully intending to break Caspian's neck when he got the chance. "Just trying to do my best."

"And hoping his best will beat yours," Caspian needled.

"Everybody is practicing this year. We're determined that someone is going to defeat you in at least one event."

"Are you going to enter all the events, sir?" asked a new crew member who was looking forward to participating in the games for the first time.

"I'm not a Hercules, no matter what Smith says." Brent laughed.

"Which events do you favor?" asked the young man.

"I'll have to decide who's getting too big for his britches first." They all laughed good-humoredly, each disclaiming that he was cocksure, but ready to point out a mate who could be taken down a notch.

"I think you ought to tell us," said Lane.

"So you'd know which events to avoid?" quizzed Caspian.

"I know I can't outrun the captain," Lane admitted, unabashed. "There's no disgrace in that. But I suspect he could lap me before he'd gone twice around the deck, and that *would* be a disgrace." His frank admission was received with loud guffaws."

"I appeal to you, ma'am." Lane caught Summer by surprise. "Is there any disgrace in declining to fight when you know your opponent is sure to win?"

"I don't think it is a disgrace," she said thoughtfully, "but it's no honor either."

"What did I tell you," crowed a delighted Caspian. "You can't back out now."

"Milady, look what you've done to me," Lane cried in mock despair. "Now I'll have to enter and *prove* the captain's superiority. I'll never be thought a man."

"But that's only part of it," Summer insisted earnestly, "and sometimes not the most important part."

"The captain's probably better at all the other competitions, too," sighed Lane, amid general hilarity.

"Maybe so," Summer continued. Her smile threatened to cause Lane's heart to leap into his throat. "But you can't finish second to anyone in honor and integrity."

"No one wants to be beaten out of sight," contended Lane. He was too young to value honor above recognition.

"If you strive to improve yourself every time, then you're just as much a winner as anyone else, even if you don't come in first," Summer asserted confidently.

"The countess has given you some excellent advice. You would do well to heed it," said Brent. He gazed at her, his glance compounded of surprise and respect. "It's unusual to find such wisdom in one so young."

"I'm sure they know these things already," she said self-consciously. The men attributed her nervousness to embarrassment, but she knew it was due to a strange new excitement that shook her like a tree in a hurricane. It had come over her when Brent had looked at her with admiration, maybe even pride. It made her bones turn soft and her tongue lie dead in her mouth.

Get a hold of yourself, you little fool, she told herself. You can't turn into a tongue-tied idiot every time the man looks at you. Everybody on the ship will know you're in love with him.

"I think it would be nice if the countess would agree to present the prizes this year," Smith suggested. "It would give the men something to look forward to." Everyone greeted the idea with enthusiasm. "Of course, with your approval, sir."

"Since I intend to compete, it would be better to have another presenter," Brent said thoughtfully. "Maybe the countess would consent to be a judge as well."

"I couldn't possibly," Summer objected. "I don't know a thing about your contests."

"We already have judges to make sure the rules are followed. All of you would have to do is declare the winner," explained Brent. "You can practice by watching the men as they train."

"I know I'd get much too nervous," Summer argued, protesting her unfitness for the position, but the men enthusiastically disputed with her, and finally overcame her resistance.

"Well, if you really think I can," she agreed at last, "but you must promise to teach me what to do so I won't make any mistakes." There were immediate offers of help from all around her.

"*I* will organize the countess's instruction," Brent informed them, quelling the hubbub with one glance. "Each of you will be assigned to help her with a specific event. That way it won't take too much time away from your duties."

Or allow anyone to spend too much time with the countess, Smith thought to himself.

"As soon as Smith has made up a list of contestants I'll name your chores."

"I'll get started right away, sir."

"Perhaps you should write everything down so the countess will know what to look for. We can go over it during dinner, or at some other time," Brent said, giving her a provocative glance.

"These are going to be the best games we've ever had," claimed an excited Caspian, "but we ought to have ribbons, and prizes, too."

"What for?" someone asked.

"For the winners."

"That's a splendid idea," agreed Summer, catching some of his excitement, "but what can we find in the middle of the ocean?"

"There're lots of things in the hold we could use," suggested Horton.

"If you young idiots think I'm going to hand over our hard-won treasure to a bunch of stumbling amateurs you're badly mistaken." Brent's tone was uncompromising, and Horton looked abashed.

"But surely there's something in that vast pile of pillage you can bear to part with," Summer said before she had time to think.

"My vast pile of *pillage*, as you so quaintly put it, is not to be used for trophies." Brent's voice had a biting edge to it. "I will not allow you to dig through it like children looking for sugarplums."

Now it was Summer's turn to look discomfited.

"I'm sure if we all look among our belongings we will find some things that might be of use," Smith said calmly, for he sensed the strained atmosphere. "And if you will permit it, sir, I will undertake to go through the hold for such items as have little or no trade value."

"I won't have you neglecting your duties," Brent said severely.

"I would naturally do it on my own time," replied the unflappable Smith. "I don't anticipate it to be an arduous task."

Brent yielded grudgingly. "The goods belong to the whole crew, so you'll need their permission as well. I can't have the men saying that their profits were taken from them without their consent."

"I'll see to it," the efficient Smith assured him, and everyone at the table breathed a little easier. No one could be comfortable when the captain was in a difficult mood. Even Smith, who had been with him longest and had the right to disagree with him, took pains to do so carefully. Brent was not one to act hastily or foolishly, but neither was he accustomed to weigh the consequences when he did act.

"Caspian, you can help the countess with the races and the swimming tomorrow. Since they're two of my strongest events, I take it you won't be entering them," Brent said derisively.

"I'll be happy to help the countess in any way I can." Caspian grinned, not the least abashed by Brent's sarcasm. "I can help her with the wrestling too, since that's also one of your strongest events. Besides, I'm not in your weight class."

"Lane will do the wrestling. You must also attend to your duties," Brent said snappishly. Caspian showed no sign of being disturbed by the captain's irritation, but the other men made their excuses and left Brent alone with his brandy. Even in the middle of the ocean, there were less dangerous ways to enjoy an evening.

The men practiced whenever they could take time out from their work; that meant anytime between daybreak and midnight. Rather than climb the stairs from her cabin a dozen times a day, Summer began to spend most of her time on deck. Some of those working out were self-conscious at first.

A few did try to get to know her better, but one look from the captain was enough to convince the most foolhardy to keep his distance. It was impossible for the crewmen not to stare at Summer, but they took care to keep their eyes on their work when Brent was about.

And that seemed to be just about all the time these days. He might *say* he needed to practice as well as anyone else, but it was obvious that his practice took second place to his interest in the beautiful countess.

The crew had no inkling of the deepening closeness between Brent and Summer. They'd rarely seen her, and his treatment of her on that first day remained strong in their minds. Smith was the first to notice the change, but he never shared confidences with anyone except Brent. And junior officers held their captain in such awe, thought him so godlike, that it was a jolt to find he was subject to the same emotions and desires that plagued them. They attempted to question Smith, and were expertly snubbed.

However, when Summer began to put in regular appearances on deck, the whole crew had an opportunity to observe Brent and Summer, and it wasn't long before everyone decided that the captain was smitten at last. He tolerated no familiarity with the countess, and barely restrained himself from treating an imagined insult to her with the same severity he usually reserved for insubordination. Only Brent remained unaware of the real extent of his feelings.

There had never been any room in his thoughts for marriage. For ten years he had devoted all of his time, energy, and concentration to two things: his career at sea and his hatred of Gowan. These existed side by side, each giving way to the other when necessary. There was no conflict, no sacrifice of one for the other, because Brent had realized that the only chance he had to bring Gowan to justice was to gain command of a ship and to have the power that came with that command.

He well knew that Summer was having an effect on him, but he was convinced that his attraction to her was only physical and that he could forget her just as easily as he had all of the others. Since there was no need to consider that unpleasant course of action at the moment, he put it out of his mind. He now accepted her presence at the table as a matter of course, and he firmly believed that his concern was only to protect her.

Brent was unaware that he glanced up at her a hundred times during an evening. And he didn't see the smile that touched his lips, the light that glowed in his eyes, or the relaxation of the muscles in his jaw when he gazed at her. He was unaware that the evidence of her presence in his cabin—slippers, a ribbon, a brush—gave him a deep sense of contentment, a feeling of pleasure that was new to him. He studied her, thirsting to know what she was like, trying to fathom her depths through the things she did and said.

But the most profound change in him, one he never suspected and would have vehemently denied, was that he would give up his desire for revenge rather than lose Summer. He had no inkling of this transformation, nor was he aware that, as she had become a part of him, his hatred for Gowan had become less intense. In just a few weeks, Summer had become just as much a part of his days as his duties on the ship he commanded. He no longer thought of himself singly, even in his own mind; she was always there. Even more than his boyhood home, she was necessary to his happiness and well-being, and each solution he came up with for her future was automatically rejected if it failed to keep her at his side.

Chapter 11

The first day of the games dawned bright and clear; the usual turbulence of the Atlantic had died down; and the bright sun, quickly absorbing the cool of the morning, insured it would be hot by noon. At the same time, feeding seabirds reminded Summer that Havana and their journey's end were near. Very soon now she would be on her own, and she couldn't afford the emotional luxury of being in love with Brent. She reminded herself of her vow to fight any temptation to think longingly of his comforting strength or to give in to the hypnotizing effect of his smile.

The men had been up before dawn—some testing muscles and reflexes or limbering up by running around the deck, others setting up the courses and insuring that the day's events would go quickly and smoothly. But the busiest person of all was Smith, for the success of the games rested squarely on his shoulders. It was his task to keep the lists of contestants, determine the order of the events, oversee them, and make sure that all preparations were completed. Summer did her best to help, but she was so nervous and excited she took up as much of his time as she saved.

Brent moved among the men, saying a few words to each and wishing them all good luck. His encouragement was warmly received even by those who knew they had little chance of besting him, and soon he had established an atmosphere of cheerful camaraderie.

"I don't think I'll ever be able to remember half of them," Summer said to Smith as she quickly reviewed the rules for a contest she had never even heard of until a few days ago.

"You'll do just fine," he assured her. "Just remember to watch very carefully as they cross the finish."

"But that's the trouble. I get so excited I'm afraid I'll be cheering instead of watching."

"Who are you cheering for?" asked Brent, as he came up from behind her. "I'm going to be mighty upset if you're pulling against me." He was cooling off from his morning exercise, and a fine film of perspiration caused his scantily clad, deeply tanned body to glisten in the sun, highlighting every muscle and sculpted curve. He looked like a god, a hero from some ancient legend. The pit of Summer's stomach knotted and her knees grew weak.

"I didn't say I was cheering *for* anyone," she mumbled, blushing and lowering her gaze. "I just said that I might be cheering." She raised her eyes again; she had to learn not to cower before him.

"We can't have a judge who cheers for her favorites, or one who gets so excited she forgets to watch the finish."

"I'll do my best to be impartial *and* to watch carefully," she said coldly, her resentment rising. "I realize how much these games mean to the men, and I wouldn't do anything to spoil them, but I did warn you that I am completely without experience." It was just like him to find fault with her even before she'd had a chance to prove herself.

"Everybody's anxious to win," Smith interposed diplomatically. "It's particularly important this year because of the prizes and the fact that you're going to present them."

"I hope the men appreciate those blasted prizes," Brent grumbled. "Your pack ransacked every inch of this ship, not to mention the time they spent away from their duties." He directed a baleful glare at his first mate, but Smith didn't flinch. "I think the men are ready to begin," he announced moodily.

"It'll just take me a few minutes more," Smith told him, not taking his eyes from his task.

"How do you feel?" Brent asked Summer, his tone more kind now.

"Nervous," she confided, steadfastly trying to ignore his inviting smile.

"The first events will be easy. They're foot races. There's only room for two or three runners at a time."

"I'm still nervous."

"You'll calm down once we begin."

"If you'll come with me, milady, we can get started," Smith said. "Captain, since you have to run in the third heat, you'd better go warm up."

"You give orders very well." Brent laughed. "You sound more like a captain than I do."

"He *looks* more like one, too," Summer commented. Brent's brief pants exposed almost his entire body to the glistening sun, and she had hardly taken her eyes off him since he'd joined them.

Brent drew himself up. Muscles tense and bulging, he met Summer's critical glance with an imperious look. "*Who* looks more like the captain?" he asked, daring her to compare his physique with that of the much less well-developed Smith.

Summer smoothly corrected herself. "I meant to say that Smith is *dressed* more like a captain."

"That is true," Brent replied, but he gave her a satisfied smile.

"You look more like a castaway." Summer repressed a fervent wish to be cast away with him. "I'll bet the earl would never recognize you if you returned to Scotland looking like that."

"The earl wouldn't have to worry about recognizing him," Smith observed dryly. "The captain would freeze to death in the first snow."

Brent eyed the two of them, a frown gathering on his forehead. "A little more of this, and I'll set you both adrift. I have a position to maintain in the eyes of the crew."

"If you didn't look like one of them, you wouldn't have to worry about it." Summer let her eyes wander over him with leisurely nonchalance, hoping that they didn't show how powerfully his presence affected her. "Of course there are some things that clothes can never do, but when it comes to conveying rank and station, they are an absolute necessity."

"I'll remember that when I feel the need to make a good impression," Brent responded coolly. "But right now we're wasting time." He walked away, and Summer had to tear her eyes from him. How could she get him out of her heart when she couldn't keep from staring at him?

"First set of runners," Smith called out, and three young men of nearly the same size and age lined up at the line drawn on the planks of the deck.

"You all know the rules," he said. "Start at the sound of the pistol and run four times around the deck. Remember to stay outside the red barrels. Anyone going inside is automatically disqualified. You can cross over in front of a runner as long as you're far enough ahead not to impede his race. The winner qualifies for the next race. That clear?" The three nodded. They were impatient to begin. "Are you ready?" called Smith, and they knelt at the line. "Get set. Go!"

The last word was punctuated by the loud report of a pistol, and the three men sprinted toward the bow of the ship. The outside runner, shorter and lower to the ground than the others, made a faster start and was able to cross over to the inside before they reached the first turn. It was a sharp bend that doubled back almost one hundred and eighty degrees in three or four strides. The runners slowed abruptly to keep from colliding with the rail, then accelerated quickly, the shortest man still in the lead. They rounded the broader turn at the stern at a faster pace and pounded past the starting line for the first time, about two yards apart.

The order remained unchanged during the second circuit, but during the third, the trailing runners began to close the gap. They fell back on the turn coming onto the last full circuit, but made a supreme effort to pass the leader before the short run to the bow. Once again the leader held his place. On the far side the second-place runner was passed by the last runner, who ran up to the leader's heels just as they made the final turn. He angled out from behind the leader two strides before they hit the stretch so that when they straightened out he was only a yard behind with a clear shot to win.

Not daring to even glance at the men coming toward her, Summer stood at the finish line, her eyes fixed on the spot where they would cross it. She didn't want to be involved in the contest, she just wanted to see which color passed the line first. She heard the thunder of their sturdy feet pounding toward her, and her heart beat faster and faster. "Oh please, don't let me get it wrong," she pleaded softly. Then a blur of color passed before her eyes, and she called, "Green!" loud and clear. Summer had just called her first race.

"You won't get a closer race than that, and you got it right on the button."

She hadn't noticed Brent come up behind her during the last lap.

"Thank you," she said, beaming with pride in spite of her effort to remain cool. When he looked at her like that, it was impossible to think of anything except the color of his eyes.

"Why don't you watch the beginning of the next race with me?"

"I'd better stay here," she decided. "I'll get too excited if I watch the whole race." She didn't add that his physical presence would destroy her concentration as it was doing at the moment. She pretended to close her eyes against the glare of the sun, but the image of mighty limbs and a tanned torso was burned into her memory. Just knowing he was within inches of her fingertips was enough to bring a flush to her cheeks.

The winner of the heat came up to receive congratulations from the captain. Summer smiled and offered him her hand. The poor man was exhausted, but his shining eyes bespoke his pleasure in the captain's words and his delight in being able to touch Summer's dainty hand.

"If you smile like that at every winner, they're all going to knock themselves out trying to win," Brent barked, heedless of listening ears. "I can't afford to have good men disabled." He sounded disgruntled.

"I'll do my best not to overexcite them," Summer snapped. "It's a shame it won't work on you," she added.

"Has just the opposite effect, doesn't it?"

Summer turned her back on him, not daring to meet his laughing eyes. "Not even a dunking in the Arctic Ocean could cool you down," she said, hoping the sting of her words would wipe the smirk off his face, but Brent grinned even more broadly.

"If I had you to keep me warm, I could melt the whole polar cap." He looked at the thrusting curves of her breasts, the outline of her hips and thighs as the wind molded her dress to her body. "With the sight you're affording us right now, we may overheat long before noon."

Summer tried to pull her thin dress away from her body, but it only whipped more tightly about her legs. Brent's crack of laughter did nothing to improve her temper, and all at once she found his presence less exciting. "I can't concentrate on the next race when you are intentionally making me angry. Please go away."

"Certainly, Countess." He only called her Countess when he was angry or trying to aggravate her. "I can save it all for tonight when you'll be able to concentrate on me *alone*."

He whispered the last word in her ear before going over to the runner kneeling for the start of the second race.

"That man is a beast," Summer said under her breath. "I don't know why I let him taunt me like that. I'd like to shoot him."

Bang! The pistol shot startled her. But three sets of feet pounding the planks of the deck reassured her that all was normal. All she had to do was keep track of the number of laps and then wait to see which color crossed the line first.

It was green again, but the race was easier because the winner came in a full yard before his closest opponent. The third race found Brent competing against the two tallest runners; he won easily after leading all the way.

"Where's my blinding smile?" he asked, in a voice calculated to provoke her. "You can't give me less than you give my crew."

"I wish I didn't have to give you any more than I give your crew," she said in a low hiss.

"Captains always receive special treatment," he retorted. Then he took her chin in his hand and forced her head up until her gold-flecked eyes met his azure blue ones. "And I intend to claim the winner's privilege."

She wrenched her face out of his grasp. "Don't be too sure. You haven't won yet." The fire in her eyes matched the heat that coursed through her body.

"But I shall, Countess, I shall." He chucked her under the

chin and walked away, leaving her shaking with rage. She felt that she had been humiliated in front of the whole crew, and she burned with a desire to punish him. But before she could indulge in any wishful thinking, the pistol sounded and another three runners were pounding toward her. Maybe he'll slip and crack his head, she thought savagely, but she didn't put much faith in that idea.

The morning wore on, and contest followed contest. Teams competed for the best time in setting a sail, in taking one down, and in climbing the rigging and descending. There was a tug of war, a contest of brute strength in which contestants struggled to haul up the ship's anchor, and there were many contests involving various weapons, some of which Summer had never seen. "Does anyone get hurt?" she asked Smith, as two men dueled with long swords whose curving blades flashed in the sun.

"Not often. The judging is based on skill in handling the weapon, not mere strength. If they inflict an injury they lose points or are disqualified. That shows a lack of control, both in the handling of the weapon and of the temper. And control is something the captain prizes."

"Is everything the crew does planned according to the captain's wishes?" she asked, revolted.

"Of course," Smith replied. He was surprised that Summer would even think it necessary to ask such a question. "The captain's word is law on any ship."

"The captain, the captain, the *captain!*" she repeated, loathing in her voice. "I've heard that word until I'm sick of it!" She thought of his earlier treatment of her. "I'd have thought you'd have too much pride to give in to everything he says. Does everyone quiver and quake each time he opens his mouth?" Summer fought to keep a hold on her emotions; she hoped Smith wouldn't see that a breaking heart was at the root of her angry tirade.

"I don't think you understand the nature of the relationship between a ship's crew and its captain," Smith answered, at a loss to explain the vehemence of her outburst.

"I understand that not one of you has the backbone to stand up to that grinning bully." The accumulated wrongs she'd experienced closed in on her, and she became so angry she started to shake. "You just say '*Yes, Captain*' and '*Of course, Captain*,' and then run off to do his bidding like good little boys."

"As I said, you don't understand how a captain and his crew work together." Smith decided not to try to explain the complex relationship to Summer. "I doubt anyone can who hasn't been to sea at least once."

"If this is the result, I don't want to understand it," she said pettishly. She swept her arm around to indicate the whole ship, and nearly hit Brent across the chest. "Oh!" she gasped, and jerked her arm back to her side.

"Is the countess preaching sedition and trying to foment rebellion?" Brent chuckled.

"I was just trying to explain how a captain and his crew work together," Smith explained.

"I'll wager she didn't understand," Brent said. He smiled at Summer in that superior way that made her long to hit him. "I'm sure she feels that you indulge me too far, and take my commands with too much complacency." Summer flushed deep red at the accuracy of his words. "She probably believes that a little well-timed opposition would do me a world of good, that it might even keep me from becoming too spoiled and set up in my own conceit."

Summer started to turn away, but Brent grasped her wrist and forced her to look at him in the eye.

"Am I right?" he said, giving her that galvanizing glance that never failed to set her pulses racing.

"The countess did feel that the men might express themselves a little more freely," Smith said smoothly. "But I pointed out that she would need to spend more time at sea before she could appreciate the relationship between a captain and his crew."

"And what did the countess have to say about that?"

"At that point you came up, sir."

"Too bad I didn't wait a little longer. Her answer might have been very revealing."

"As to that, sir, I wouldn't venture to say," remarked Smith.

"You're a wise man, Smith. I suppose that's why I put so much trust in you."

"Thank you, sir. I deeply appreciate your confidence."

"Be careful not to lay it on too thick," Brent chuckled humorlessly. "You'll have the countess fairly bursting with indignation. She might even accuse you of licking my hand like a whipped dog."

Summer was so blazingly angry that she nearly gave utterance to the first incautious thought that came to her, but she managed to check her tongue. "I would never refer to Mr. Smith in anything like those terms," she declared.

"What kind of words would you use to describe me?" Brent asked, his strong white teeth bared in a full smile and his enormous eyes twinkling with wicked pleasure.

"I wouldn't demean myself by using the words capable of describing you." Summer's suppressed anger made her voice quiver. "But I can assure you I don't share the crew's feeling."

"I'm glad of that," Brent retorted. "I wouldn't be able to turn my back if they felt like you. But then they're sound men, of good moral character and well brought up. They've been trained in the common civilities, and have been taught to obey those who know more than they do." He noted that Summer's eyes nearly jumped out of her head at the intentional brutality of his words. "They understand loyalty, as well as how to exercise a little common sense. That does give them the advantage over you, doesn't it, Countess?"

"Of all the loathsome, cruel things to say." Summer's entire body was shaking with fury. "You should be tied to a rack and pulled apart with hot tongs."

"I would love to continue this conversation, but Smith thinks we should get on with our business."

Smith studied his lists and didn't look up at the mention of his name.

"And I have to get ready for the next event because I'm in it."

"You despicable . . ."

"Don't waste it all," he said in an infuriating whisper, a knowing glint in his eye. "You can save the rest for tonight."

Summer thought she would either die right there or break out into blood-curdling screams. Only Smith's presence enabled her to keep from throwing herself at Brent and clawing his smirking face to ribbons.

The effort she made to control her wrath was so intense it was visible, but she turned to Smith and said in as normal a voice as possible, "We're late. We'd better get started before the men begin to wonder what's wrong."

Chapter 12

"You need to move to the rail, milady. The swimming trials are next. They'll finish between the ship and that boat off the bow. We'll start just as soon as the men get into the water."

Smith moved away, and Summer was glad to have a few moments alone; the day had not gone as she planned. You certainly haven't succeeded in getting Brent out of your mind, she lectured herself. If anything, you're worse off than before. You can't even look at him without going to pieces, and all he does is make fun of you. She thought of the way his eyes twinkled when he laughed, and a slow smile spread across her face dissolving her ill will.

She turned her face into the wind; the breeze cooled her brow and whipped her long tresses back from her face, causing their copper highlights to glisten in the sun like something alive.

Brent saw her from where he was preparing to dive into the water, and the sight of her profile destroyed his concentration. She looked like a Norse goddess carved into the prow of an ancient fighting vessel. She leaned forward from the waist, one hand raised, her thrusting bosom outlined against the horizon. The wind swept her hair behind her so that it looked like the flowing mane of a wild stallion, and her thin gown, plastered to her limbs, revealed the clean lines and delicate curves that made her allure almost too powerful for Brent to endure.

"Get her off the rail before she starts a riot," he shouted to Smith before diving into the sea to conceal his own inflamed condition. The cool, invigorating water slowly drained the heat from his loins, and he climbed back up the ladder with lithe, powerful movements, vowing all the while to get Summer out of his system.

Since he'd captured her, a conflict had been growing within him. He was only now beginning to recognize it; it threatened to outstrip his control. Every day he came closer and closer to surrendering to an overwhelming desire to put aside his responsibilities and capture this entrancing young woman, to give in to the powerful attraction he felt every time his eyes rested on her delicately chiseled face or her slim, rounded body. So far he had resisted this temptation, but each day his feeling of unrest grew, and he was finding it more and more difficult to appear uninvolved, to sustain the lighthearted banter that masked a molten volcano of passion. It was a good thing their journey was almost over. He climbed onto the deck, relaxed once more, and, as far as anyone could tell, was completely in control of himself.

The swimmers started about thirty yards off the starboard side of the ship, crossed in front of the bow and swam the length of the ship about thirty yards off the port side; they then crossed behind the stern and turned again. From there it was a straight shot to the finish. The men could choose to compete in the sprint, one lap around the course, or the distance swim of four laps. Brent had entered both.

Summer called the preliminaries easily. The lengths of the

races and the increasingly rough water resulted in the distances between contestants being greater than in the foot races. By the time Brent won his second race, Summer had cooled off enough to be able to call his name without feeling that she was choking on the words. She couldn't help but admire the clean strokes and powerful kicks that propelled his body through the water with an ease that belied his speed and power, and she found it impossible not to gaze longingly at the lean, powerful body that allowed him an easy margin of victory.

"You have no backbone, Summer Ashton," she muttered into the breeze that blew her words out to the secretive sea. "You're a foolish, giddy, shrewish-tempered, simple-minded fool who sighs and moans at the sight of his body. If you don't start using your head instead of your emotions, you're going to make a pathetic spectacle of yourself."

"Did you say something to me, milady?" Smith had come up behind her as the last set of swimmers had rounded the boat off the stern to head toward the finish of the race.

Summer yanked her mind back to her task. "I was talking to myself. I guess I got into that habit from being alone so much."

"Sailors do it too. It can get very lonely at sea, especially if you're the captain."

Smith looked at her with sympathetic understanding and her eyes suddenly filled with moisture. She dashed her hand across her face to brush away the teardrops shimmering on the ends of her long lashes.

"I'd better pay attention to my job before I do something terrible." Summer tried to smile.

"There's no surprise in this race, ma'am. Young Lane is at least twenty yards ahead. If he swims like this tomorrow, he'll give the captain some real competition, especially if he persists in entering both races."

"Don't the men resent Brent's beating them so often? He

must have won half a dozen times today." It was exactly seven, and she knew it.

"The crew takes pride in the captain's accomplishments. They're very proud to have been asked to serve under him."

"But he treats them like slaves, ordering them about, shouting at them if they don't get the job done exactly as he likes the first time." Her temper was rising again, and she tried to calm herself, knowing it was useless to become enraged over a situation she couldn't change. "I don't understand how they can listen to the sound of his voice without becoming angry."

Smith searched for the right words. He knew it was important that Summer understand the captain, not in his role on the ship, but as an ordinary person. It was senseless to deny the evidence of his own eyes. These two were deeply in love and were groping desperately, trying to come to terms with something neither of them had wanted or anticipated.

"If you could see the captain when we're in a hard fight, or when the ship's in danger, you might understand what the men feel and why they gladly accept his abuse with cheerful smiles."

"They're mad," she snapped.

"Not at all," said Smith, with a rare smile. "Though I guess you could be pardoned for thinking so. The captain's the first one on deck when there's any sign of trouble. He never holds back or spares himself because of his position. He's in there with the rest of us as long as there's any danger to the ship or the crew. You might think the men were talking about some imaginary hero if you could hear them bragging about him in port, but you'd be in no doubt over how they feel about him."

"I still think you're all mad," Summer said, refusing to be mollified. "*I* don't see any sign of the courage and consideration you're talking about." She ground her teeth at the memory of the last weeks. "All I see is an overbearing, egotistical bully set upon having his way and running roughshod over anyone who doesn't say yea to his every wish."

"I know he's really not like that," Smith said, abandoning any hope of making Summer understand. "But I imagine in your present circumstances you can't help feeling unhappy and resentful."

Summer's eyes flew to Smith's face, then quickly turned away. She had no doubt that everyone knew exactly how things stood between her and the captain, but to have it put into words, even in a vague allusion, was mortifying. "Isn't it time we ate?" she asked, changing the subject.

"Yes, but we still have a lot of work to do before this afternoon's events."

"Why can't we wait until tomorrow? Everyone's worn out."

"We can only give two days to the games. Tomorrow's events are so grueling the men would need several day's rest before they could compete again, and by that time we'd be in port."

"When do we start again?" she asked wearily.

"About six o'clock." He looked about the deck. "It seems we're going to be late," he said realizing that they were the only ones standing about. "Everybody else has already gone."

"Then let's hurry," she urged. "I don't want to give his holiness any excuses to get on his high horse." She hastened away without waiting for Smith to follow, her angry strides evidence of the embroiled state of her emotions.

I don't know what the captain did, Smith thought to himself, but he certainly went to work the wrong way this time. Unless I'm greatly mistaken, they're crazy about each other, but neither one of them will admit it. I wonder if they know it themselves.

The midday meal was a quiet affair. Except for some light banter about awkward spills and lost footing, the men concentrated on their food and excused themselves as quickly as possible. Everyone still had a day's work to squeeze in before the games resumed.

"I'm afraid we're rather dull company this afternoon, Countess," Brent said, eying her with an inquiring look. "You seem rather quiet too."

"I apologize for failing to bring mirth and sunshine to your table, but I don't seem to be quite myself today," she replied with a brittle smile. "Probably too much excitement."

At those words Brent's eyes narrowed and his concentration sharpened. "I wasn't aware that anyone had given you cause for immoderate excitement," he said, his glance less pleasant.

"If it comes to *cause*," she burst out, unable to contain herself now that they were alone, "your treatment of me has given me ample reason to feel more than immoderate excitement. I can't think of a single thing you've done that doesn't cause me to tremble with rage."

"Then let me give you a few examples," he said, laying down his knife and fork and fixing her with a glance that was merciless and unyielding. "You are a captive, an article of war, a piece of property if you will, that I, the stronger player in this game, have captured and may use to my advantage." Summer turned white with fury, but he swept relentlessly on. "By the rules of the game, I may use you as I like. The most common use for a female is to be thrown on her back to satisfy the crew."

"Since that's how you've used me, I fail to see the reason for my supposed gratitude."

"Then be still and I'll tell you." Summer had half risen in her chair, but at those words she sat down hard, unable to believe that he had actually spoken to her in that manner. "You have *not* been left to the mercy of the crew. On the contrary, you've been spared any regular contact with them. You are housed in the best cabin, and are allowed to move about unhindered. You dine at my table, enjoy my officers' company, and you are treated by them in a manner befitting your rank and station. In allowing you to judge their contests and confer the prizes, the crew has signaled you out for a special honor. You even have the right to make virtually any request it is within my power to grant."

"Except for release and freedom from your disgusting attentions."

"You aren't stupid, so don't talk as though you were. What would you do if I let you go? Swim to Havana? I had thought," he went on, the wicked smile she found so difficult to endure curling his lips, "that my *attentions* might partially compensate you for the inconvenience of your captivity."

"I can hardly believe my ears!" Summer gasped. "I never thought anyone could be so conceited, so *blind* to the way I feel. Do you think that your attentions could be anything but a purgatory I pray nightly will be quickly ended and fully revenged?" The gold in her eyes was gleaming as they changed to a tawny yellow, in them a molten, incandescent glow.

"It must be that in your inexperience you don't know how to appreciate what you have," he said, mocking her almost beyond reason. "My *attentions* have always been welcomed, and by ladies of higher stations than yours. It has been said, I've been told, that to lie in my arms is heaven on earth." He laughed at her fulminating rage. "I gather you don't agree."

"Agree with the wanton, abandoned women you find in back rooms and filthy alleys?" She almost choked on the words, and her body became rigid with fury.

"I don't have to look for my women in alleys or anywhere else," he said, interrupting her with a leering grin. "A lingering glance, a whispered promise, light kiss—and they can't wait to search me out." He stood up and took a step toward her. "They're all too willing to bring their bodies, and their honor, to my bed."

"You fiend!" she cried, recoiling in unfeigned revulsion.

"But I accept only the most beautiful," Brent crooned, stalking her like a large sleek cat. "They cry and moan, but they can't wait to come back for more."

"Well, I for one don't want any more. Keep away from me," she exploded, backing around the table.

"I must not have treated you very well. I'll have to make sure I do better tonight," he taunted her, the greenish tint of passion beginning to light his eyes. "Or should we start right now?"

"Don't touch me!" she shrieked, wrenching open the door. "I'd rather drown first."

"But I'm such an excellent swimmer I'd be sure to save you."

"Beast!" she stormed at him, and ran from the room, to hear the echo of his rich, mocking laughter in the passage.

Chapter 13

Summer was ready to resume her position by six o'clock. A long nap and an afternoon of solitude had done much to calm her temper and soothe her irritated nerves. Besides, she thought to herself, if I don't go up on my own, he'll send someone after me. Or even worse, he'll come drag me on deck himself.

That last thought reminded Summer of all the reasons she had to be angry with Brent, and she renewed her resolve to drive all warm feeling for him from her heart. But there was no evidence of his earlier pique when she reached the deck. He came toward her immediately, his face transformed by a devastating smile.

"Did you have a restful afternoon? The roses are back in your cheeks." He brushed her face with his fingertips, and her initial resolution to strike his hand away was recast into a longing to press his smiling, self-assured face to her heart.

"You were a little worn down at midday. You shouldn't have let us tire you so."

The unmistakable sincerity in his voice caused Summer's will to dissolve even further. Instead of telling him that the only things that tired her were his constant demands, she struggled to keep her determination from melting completely under the warmth of his gaze.

"I feel much better," she said, favoring him with a mechanical smile. "Solitude is a wonderful restorative."

"You're likely to have a lot more of it soon," he remarked offhand, as he led her to where the final foot race would begin. Why was he always throwing half-phrases and unexplained statements at her? They drove her crazy. She longed to ask what he meant, but there wasn't time, even if she could have trusted him to give her a truthful answer.

This race would decide whether the captain or a short, compact member of his crew was the fastest. I hope that little man runs him into the ground, Summer thought rancorously. It's time someone beat him.

"Watch Wells on the turns, Captain," a voice called out. "With those little legs he can turn faster than a cornered Jaguar."

"He looks like two crabs in a tangle," contended another. "He's fast enough, but the captain'll eat him up in the last lap."

The contestants ignored the good-natured banter, each concentrating on putting forth his utmost effort.

The shorter Wells, starting on the inside, bounded away from the starting line like a jackrabbit. Brent, larger and much stronger, started slower, but he gained quickly once he hit his stride. Before he could take advantage of his momentum, however, they reached the first turn. Wells barely seemed to slow down, but Brent had to come to a virtual stop and then accelerate all over again, giving Wells an advantage of several yards. Brent wasn't as badly handicapped by the broader stern turn and he gained ground, but before he could pass Wells the sharp bow turn restored Wells's advantage, enabling him to stay in the lead the second time around the deck.

The third circuit was the same, and it was obvious to all the spectators that Brent was furious at his inability to take advantage of his greater strength and speed. On the fourth and last circuit Brent was once more two yards behind, but he made up the whole distance down the backside. On the stern turn the spectators thought the captain was going to run up on Wells's heels, but he came off the turn with only a yard disadvantage. In the final straight both men dug in, but Brent produced a burst of acceleration that left the crew with mouths agape. He shot past Wells and hit the upper deck in full stride. Realizing that he was beaten, Wells slowed down before reaching the finish.

To the surprise of the new recruits and the raucous delight of the veterans, Brent didn't slow down in the least; with a tremendous leap, he dived over the rail, into the clear blue sea. A huge cheer sounded when he broke the surface and the crew rushed forward to pull up the rope ladder; everyone wanted to have a hand in helping their leader aboard.

At a distance from the press of cheering men, Summer clung to the rail for support, her heart pounding madly, her knees buckling under her. In spite of her vow, she had found herself cheering for Brent; when it had seemed his gallant effort would come to naught, she'd felt a stab of disappointment. And she had stood frozen with fear when he'd been running too fast to stop, horrified by the thought of his broken body being hurled back at them by the ironlike oak of the bow rail. A scream of pure terror escaped her when he vaulted into the sea.

Her cry was drowned amid the shouts and hoots of the crew who knew better what to expect of their captain. She rushed to the rail, hope that he was still alive in her breast. When he broke the surface of the water, wearing his usual arrogant grin and accepting the cheers of his men with the aplomb of a ruling monarch, Summer sagged against the rail, weak with relief but angry with him for causing her to undergo such fright. The two emotions warred within her, neither winning, and the conflict unnerved her so severely she began to shake.

"Are you all right, ma'am?" Smith inquired. Summer faltered badly, nearly losing her hold on the rail, and he reached out to support her. She tried to wave him way, but he persisted and she gave in, relieved to have someone to lean on, even if it was just for a moment.

"I'm fine," she insisted, but she did not sound fine. "It's just that I thought . . . when he fell over the edge . . . it was something of a shock."

Smith rebuked himself. "It's a pity I didn't think to warn you. The captain has a habit of doing that. Rocks the pins out from under you the first time you see it, but he never comes to any harm."

"He should," she said, regaining a bit of her spirit. "I mean, he will if he keeps doing crazy things like that," she corrected herself.

"The captain's a very lucky man," said Smith, guiding Summer to a seat on a pile of ropes so she would have an unobstructed view of Brent as he climbed aboard in triumph. "No matter what happens he comes through without a scratch. The men know he's lucky and they're sure it rubs off on them."

As Summer watched Brent receive the adulation of his crew, she felt a tug at her heart and a quickening of her pulses. He was the most devastatingly gorgeous man she'd ever seen, and looking at him now, a natural smile on his face and friendly words on his lips, she forgot all the unpleasantness that lay between them. Conscious only of a surging desire to be near him, to share in the warmth of his friendliness, to claim some part of him as her own, she was jealous of his men, of their freedom to be near him, to enjoy his confidence and easy friendship without constraint.

"They really like him, don't they?" she said more to herself than to Smith. "He seems so different with them." There was an unmistakable wistfulness in her voice, and Smith felt compelled to respond to its plea.

"The captain is a very approachable man. The men feel free to take their problems to him, and they swear by his judgment."

"Why don't I feel like that? What makes him so different with me?"

"The captain is a very handsome man," Smith spoke carefully. "Some women will do anything to attract his attention."

"I'm sure of that," she said, astringency back in her voice.

"They come too easily, so he doesn't always value them as he ought."

"If the way he has treated me is any example, they would *have* to come on their own. No woman could possibly interpret his manner as inviting." She stood up to shake out her skirts and her mood changed. "We'd better go. I have a presentation to make, and if I'm late he's bound to think it was on purpose."

They go at each other all the time when I swear they mean to do just the opposite, Smith said to himself. I told the captain no good would come of having a woman aboard, and so it has turned out.

The group around Brent divided to make way for Summer. "I have to congratulate you, Captain, on a most spectacular finish," she said stiffly. "I was certain you were going to be beaten this time."

"Are you sure the right word isn't *hoping*?" he asked. A slight tensing at one corner of his mouth belied the merry twinkle in his eyes.

"I always cheer for the captain," she said, looking at him through her lashes and giving him a coquettish smile. She prayed the tinge of color in her cheeks would go unnoticed. "What else can a captive do?"

"Tell the truth," laughed Brent, admitting that she had gotten the better of him. "Before you perjure yourself again, let's go see if Nolan can lift as much weight as he claims. We still have three events before dinner."

"I'll never understand those two as long as I live." Smith scratched his head as he watched them walk away together. "They argue over nothing and then make up when I'm expecting them to take up cudgels. It wouldn't be worth it to me."

Nolan lived up to his promise and they moved quickly through the toss to the final event, the short swim. Brent won easily, but not by the wide margin Summer expected. "He's saving his strength for tomorrow," Smith told Summer, who had become resigned to having Smith as her personal shadow.

"What for?"

"The distance swim and wrestling. He knows Lane is going to press him. Lane pretends to be lazy and uninterested in winning, but he's just the opposite and the captain knows he'll have to do his best if he wants to beat him. But what really has him worried is that he also has to wrestle twice during the morning. Nolan is favored to be his opponent."

"Do you mean the man who won the weight lifting?" Summer looked to where a very large and brawny man of about thirty was moving full kegs as though they were empty. "But he's even bigger than the captain. Brent will never be able to beat him."

"He did last year, but then he didn't have to swim against Lane, who was out with a sword wound."

"Do you think he'll win?" she asked, and her anxiety was apparent in her voice.

"I don't know, milady, but if anyone can do it, the captain

can. He doesn't know what it means to give up. He always thinks of something that catches us by surprise."

"Let's hope his powers of invention don't run out before tomorrow. In the meantime, all this excitement has made me ravenous. I think I could eat everything on the table."

"If the persecuted looks his helpers are wearing are any indication, Jacques is preparing to serve up a truly royal banquet."

Brent approached them. "As long as the food's good, he has my permission to scare every boy in the kitchen out of his wits. You'd better get a move on, my girl. Dinner's in less than an hour, and if you don't start getting dressed soon, I'll have to see that you do."

Summer bridled instantly.

"I'd better get started as well," Smith said, excusing himself. "I've got half an hour's work to do yet."

"I hope you pay him well," declared Summer as she watched Smith retreat.

"Why?"

"Because he gets more done than any three people on this ship. And he puts up with your high-handed orders and cutting remarks without losing his temper or appearing to want to aim something hard and sharp at your head."

"Unlike you?" Brent asked, helping her down the steep steps.

"Definitely not like me. If I were Smith, I'd walk off this ship so fast it'd make your head spin."

"But Smith has one very valuable trait that can't be bought," Brent said, eying her with a nettled glance. "Loyalty. He wouldn't leave for any other position on the sea."

"Not even for his own ship?" Summer inquired, subduing a flash of anger in favor of curiosity.

"Not even for that."

"But why?" she asked, passing into their cabin as Brent

held the door for her. "I thought having a ship of his own was the great desire of every seaman."

"It is, and Smith is no exemption, but he knows how much I value him."

"How do you manage to garner all this loyalty? I can't see what you do to earn it."

"I'm sure you can't, but in this case you have it backward. *I'm* the one who's loyal to Smith."

"You?" she exclaimed as though the thought were beyond comprehension.

"Yes, me. Don't you think I can have any of those finer feelings you perceive in everyone else?"

"I don't mean it like that," she said, truly sorry for her choice of words. "It's just that I can't imagine why you'd feel that way."

"There's a great deal about me you don't know," he said as he stripped off his pants. "Smith was quartermaster of the first ship I signed on when I ran away from home. I didn't know anything about being a sailor, and I probably wouldn't have survived that first year if he hadn't taken me under his wing and helped me avoid the mistakes so many boys make during their first time at sea.

"I was awfully stupid," Brent confessed, smiling at the memory of hard times made softer by the passage of the years. "I didn't know anything, was afraid of everything, and had been so petted and spoiled that I didn't know what it was to take hard knocks and stand on my own two feet." He hesitated over his choice of shirts.

"I don't know why he didn't despair of me, but he never did. I took up a lot of time he could ill spare, and brought him trouble from the sailors who considered it their privilege to tyrannize over new recruits. Smith is not a big man, and he has the appearance of a clerk, but of all the people I would hate to have as my enemy, Smith heads the list."

"Smith?" said Summer, looking up from her mirror. "But he's the nicest man on this ship."

"Not when someone's threatening him. Before the end of that voyage, there wasn't a man aboard, except the captain and the first mate, who didn't make it a point to stay out of his way."

"I guess it was hard for you, not knowing what to expect."

"I know you don't think a great deal of me now, but you'd have turned up your nose in scorn at the poor fool who'd signed on thinking he'd come back in a few short months and reclaim his home." Brent smiled, but the curve of his eyes didn't hide his bottled-up bitterness. "I was even less prepared to do that than you are to be Gowan's wife." It was a shock to Summer to realize how thoroughly she'd forgotten her husband.

"It might not be so terrible," she said, but in the pit of her stomach a painful knot formed.

"It would be much worse than you imagine, but you don't have to worry about that. You'll probably never meet him."

"Why not?" Summer slewed around to face Brent, eagerly looking into his eyes. "I thought you said he was going to ransom me. That's what you want, isn't it?"

"It was at first." Brent's countenance was expressionless, and hope died in Summer's breast.

"Do you think he will send someone, or come himself?" Her voice was flat, unemotional.

"I'd be able to answer that question if I knew why he wanted to marry you, but I can't think of any reason he'd be so anxious to get you back that he would travel three thousand miles. He'll most likely send Brinklow with an offer." Brent's eyes warmed with desire as they rested on Summer's bare shoulders. "If Brinklow tells him what you really look like, he won't believe he's getting anything but damaged goods."

Summer blushed scarlet and bit her lip.

"Since Gowan knows I'm the one who's holding you, he would guess how I mean to take revenge," he added.

"And you didn't disappoint him, did you?" It galled Summer to be called damaged goods. She rose to select a gown. "You've effectively ruined me for any husband."

"Except myself." Two words, but at last he had given her some indication that he might care for her. Summer's resistance collapsed, and she admitted that she was already helplessly in love with him.

"No one wants a debauched woman," she answered, trying to keep her voice calm. "Not even as a servant."

"But you're not a debauched woman to me."

"Why do you keep taunting me!" she flung at him, naked despair in her voice. "You know you can't wait to be rid of me. There're only two reasons you come near me: lust and revenge. You must be sorry I'm not a simple native wench you can put ashore at the next port and then forget."

"Who could stop me from doing that, treating you *just like a simple native wench?*" he said, his voice like iron. "And what would prevent me from forgetting that I ever set eyes on you?"

"Nothing," she said piteously, and the fight went out of her. "Nothing and no one." Her shoulders drooped as she was overcome by the futility of her situation.

"I don't intend to dump you anywhere," said Brent, as he ceased buttoning his shirt. "You are lovely and you have a most inviting body."

"How easy it must be not to think of anything except your lusts," she reflected rather sadly. "That way you have nothing to regret. Unfortunately, I have other matters to consider, and there are lots of things I regret."

"I can think of only one."

"What's that?" she asked, unable to still her tongue.

"That there is so much between us you find difficult to forget."

Summer's heart lurched painfully in her chest, hope once again tormenting her. Surely he wouldn't keep saying these things if he didn't mean them, but if he did, why did he continue to use her so cruelly?

"I'll *never* forget what lies between us no matter what happens," she announced passionately. "It may not be of much importance to you, but it is to me."

"Anything can be forgotten or forgiven," he said bracingly. "All you need to do is put it out of your mind. Then you can start over with a clean slate."

"There are some things a person never forgets," Summer proclaimed angrily. She snatched up her gown and drew it over her head.

"Nonsense. You only remember unpleasant things if you want to."

"Trust a man to come up with a stupid remark like that." Summer pulled irritably at her gown to settle it into place. "You act as though forgetting involves nothing more than turning your back."

"You can do it if you want to," he insisted, a note of entreaty in his voice. "Here, let me help you before you rip your gown."

"Just keep your hands on the buttons," she snapped impatiently, but she stood still as he deftly assisted her, though her thoughts were in utter chaos. She wanted desperately to believe him, yet she was afraid to. There was so much to hope for if she could trust him; there was so little to live for if she couldn't.

Chapter 14

Summer couldn't sleep. Brent's words kept ringing in her ears, needling her until her brain was seething with speculation. She distrusted his every utterance, but his assurances continued to spark tiny flames of hope in her heart. She told herself that she was an idiot to heed such tempting beacons of hope, but every time she lay back to sleep, unbidden dreams of blissful tomorrows made their way into her consciousness to fret and bedevil her.

It was hard not to think of Brent when only a black, hopeless future lay ahead. She couldn't go back home, and even if there was no possibility that Brent wanted her, she could never love the earl or anyone else.

Something told her there must be a way out, a path to happiness, if only she could find it. She couldn't give up hope just when she'd glimpsed the bliss to be found in the arms of a very special man. It would have been far better if she had gone straight to the earl without meeting Brent; she would have been miserable, but she would never have known this rapturous torment, this agony of being in love.

You're a simpleton to place any dependence on words spoken only to calm you, she told herself angrily. You'd better be giving some serious thought to your prospects before you find yourself forced to do anything just to stay alive. Mooning over a brute of a pirate is a sure way to end up with no future at all.

In spite of Summer's attempts to sustain her anger by enumerating Brent's iniquities, she was forced to admit that she was hopelessly in love with him. That awful realization made her feel like a wandering soul willed by unfeeling Fate to worship the agent of her own destruction. Her anger rekindled every time she thought of the humiliation she had known at his hands, but then she pictured him as he moved about the ship, looking like a young god, and everything else became meaningless. While envisioning his muscled torso or his handsome, sun-bronzed face, all she could remember was the comfort she found in his arms.

She would not give up just yet, not as long as they were at sea and there was still time for him to learn to love her. She forced herself to smile even though she felt like throwing herself on the bed and crying her heart out. She might *be* desperate, but her pride would not allow her to advertise that fact.

Moodily Summer stared out the window. Multicolored stars distributed by a prodigal hand littered the dark velvet sky, and a soft breeze gently caressed her cheeks, cooling some of the turbulence within her. She rested her chin on folded arms as she gazed absently at the moon. Riding low on the horizon, it cast a pale yellow trail across the rippling waves, its hypnotic presence lessening her tension and easing her fears. Soon the soothing waves of sleep began to lap at the edges of her mind, beckoning her into the blissful relief of unconsciousness.

You're acting like a hopeless romantic, she told herself as she sank lower and lower into a subliminal world. When he smiles at you, you forget every cruel, degrading thing he's ever done. And you let his occasional flashes of humanity deceive you, though he's proved over and over again that he's an unfeeling monster. Any man who would force his attentions on a helpless young woman night after night can't be trusted, not *ever*. He never balks at embarrassing you in front of the crew, he cruelly abuses you if you dare to disagree with him, he laughs at you when you make a mistake. He's a brute and a bully, he's obsessed with his bestial lusts, and he's only nice to you occasionally because you're pretty to look at. If you think for one minute that this experience can be turned into an enduring love, then you're witless enough to deserve the dreadful fate in store for you.

Feeling that she had effectively dealt with her tendency to depend upon such a mountain of conceit, Summer sighed and sank further into her stupor. As the last anchors of inhibiting consciousness were unleashed, the image of Brent's laughing face floated before her mind's eye. Then it haunted her dreams like a gadfly, always flitting beyond her grasp, laughing at her efforts to capture it or to escape its bothersome presence.

The door swung open without a sound. Brent stood framed in the opening, through which a shaft of light fell to illuminate Summer's shadowy figure.

"Not asleep yet? Dare I hope you were waiting up for me?" he asked, closing the door behind him. There was a hint of hopefulness behind the mockery in the softly spoken question.

Summer woke from her light slumber. "I knew you would come," she said sleepily.

"That doesn't sound like an invitation."

"You've never needed one."

"Nevertheless, I would enjoy feeling your arms about me in a real embrace. It's hard to make love to a limp fish or a snarling catamount." He loosened his tie.

"It's dangerous for a fish to get too close to a shark," she answered in a listless voice.

"Is that how you see me?" he asked, genuinely surprised.

"Sharks are predators; they devour whatever they choose and destroy their victims in the process."

"I plead not guilty to the last charge."

"I suppose you think the first one isn't important."

"Not if it doesn't hurt you."

"Did you ever consider what might hurt me?" she asked, somewhat embittered. "You never ask what I want."

"You wouldn't let me come near you if I did," he said, grinning in a way that caused her heart to flutter. "Think of all the pleasure you'd miss, and the agonies I'd suffer every time I set eyes on you." He pulled off his shirt and tossed it into the corner.

"Do you think I enjoy being mauled every night?"

"That's not exactly how I'd put it." Brent sat down to take off his shoes. "But I remember a definite improvement in last night's performance." He tossed aside one shoe. "I particularly liked the way you responded to my kiss with your tongue." He tossed aside the second shoe. "Of course I found it very encouraging when you cried *'More, oh please, more!'*"

"I don't remember last night." As she lied Summer saw the ground caving in under her. "But I do remember that I never invited you to share my bed."

Brent stood up and loosened the strings of his pants. "I keep telling you this is my bed, and may I remind you that you're still in it."

"I'll be happy to get out."

He dropped his pants to the floor. "But I don't want you to go," he said sweetly. He faced her in fully aroused splendor. "I'm anxious to take up where we left off."

Summer recoiled from the sight that frightened and fascinated her at the same time. "You're nothing but a low, rutting beast," she hissed, but her words lacked conviction.

"It's not my fault that the sight of your incredible loveliness excites these low desires in me. If you looked like a peasant wench, I wouldn't be so anxious to share your bed."

"If I were a peasant wench, I wouldn't be here," Summer retorted. He sat down on the bed, but she moved as far away from him as she could.

"Talking about things that don't exist is a waste of time. You look like Venus must have been meant to look, and I want you so much it hurts." His voice was rapidly losing its clarity, and he pulled her inexorably toward him. Slipping his left arm around her and dipping his right hand into her gown to cup a firm breast, he kissed its hard nipple, letting his tongue tease her as he gently forced her back down on the bed.

"But I don't want you to want me," she protested faintly, her breath rough and uneven. "I want to be left alone." She squirmed as he slipped the gown over her shoulders and exposed her other breast to his hot hunger.

"That can't be helped," he murmured as he peeled the gown from her. "You might enjoy our moments together if you didn't fight me so hard." His lips played across her belly causing her muscles to tense. And when his hand found the inside of her thigh and then boldly entered the soft warmth between her legs she nearly ceased breathing altogether. She gasped and her body rose off the bed as his hand and then his lips caused an explosion of intense pleasure to erupt through her loins and race to every part of her body. She was horrified that he would take such advantage of her helplessness, but she was beyond resistance.

White-hot throbbing pleasure sapped her strength, and all determination to resist wilted in the steaming atmosphere of his torrid desire. She gave in to his advances, floated on waves of the enslaving sensuality that engulfed them both. Each was absolutely necessary to the fulfillment of the other. Beyond considering anything except her need to be one with the man she loved, Summer abandoned all restraint and threw herself wholeheartedly into the hot embrace of her lover. She clung to him, driving him with her demands, scorching him with her heat, until they reached a consummation almost too exquisitely painful to endure.

Chapter 15

The cool morning breeze struck Summer with bracing force when she stepped out on deck, her limbs heavy with exhaustion, her brain still numbed by sleep. As usual she had been the last to wake, and she was very late; several events, including Brent's first wrestling match, had already taken place.

"Are you trying to show me how uninterested you are?" he asked, although giving her a bright smile of welcome.

"I can't seem to wake up," she said, repressing an urge to indulge in a delicious yawn. "I never slept this late at home. Maybe it's the sea air."

"Did you help with the running of the plantation?" Brent inquired companionably as he offered her a seat.

"I managed the house after my mother died," Summer replied. She was distracted by the nearness of his barely clad body as he settled down next to her, but she managed to keep talking. "My father wasn't very good about paying the bills, or seeing that things were done on time." Her eyes wandered to his powerful thighs, and as she remembered the feel of his Herculean limbs, her pulse began to race.

"It sounds like you ran everything by yourself."

Startled, Summer said, "I'm sorry, I didn't hear you."

"It seems I can't even hold your attention when I'm next to you," he remarked, obviously irked.

She couldn't possibly tell him it was his nearness that was distracting her. She remained silent.

"I said you must have practically run the plantation by yourself," Brent repeated.

"I did. Father could be a great help when he wanted to be, but he didn't really like being a planter." Summer attempted to adjust her chair.

"Did he grow up in England?" Brent rose to rearrange her chair, and thrust his torso so close to her shoulder she could smell his skin. A torrent of debilitating excitement washed over her, leaving her faint. She closed her eyes, hoping he would move before she started to lose focus.

"My parents came over from Scotland right after they were married," she explained, her eyes still closed. "I don't think either of them wanted to do it, but my mother had tried to elope with another man and there had been some sort of scandal." She opened her eyes, but Brent's body still blocked her view. She shut them again, trying to stop the tremor beginning to overtake her. "Mother managed things until she died of a fever. After that, Father never really tried."

"Are you feeling all right?" Brent asked, looking at her closely.

"I have a slight headache."

"Are you sure that's all?"

"Yes. But if you don't really need me, I think I'll sit here a little while longer."

"Stay as long as you like." His massive bulk filled her visual field and made her tremble even more. "Are you *sure* you're well?' he asked again. "Maybe I'd better have the doctor look at you."

"That's not necessary. I really do feel better."

He felt her forehead. "It's not hot."

If he doesn't leave, I'm going to scream, she thought, gripping her chair tightly. "I'm all right, really I am. If you don't go, you're going to miss your event."

"I don't think I ought to leave you alone."

"There's nothing wrong with me," she claimed, desperate now. "Send Smith or the ship's doctor if that will make you feel any better, but I am fine."

"I think I'll stay with you."

"You know you can't. Lane has been dreaming of racing you for two years. You mustn't disappoint him now."

"I don't swim yet. This is a wrestling match."

"That's just as important. You can't win unless you wrestle, can you?"

"No," he admitted, grinning at her dogged insistence. "If you're sure you're all right . . ."

Good God, would the man never go away! "Yes," she said, trying not to scream the words at him. "Now go before you're disqualified."

"I'll be back as soon as I can."

"Just go." Summer's desperation was so thinly veiled she feared she couldn't stand much more.

She didn't have to hear the squeak of his chair or the soft padding of his bare feet on the painted deck to know he had gone. The easing of the unbearable tension in her limbs told her as clearly as her eyes and ears could that he was no longer by her side. She let out a long-held sigh, and her body melted into the chair.

She had looked forward to watching all of his matches, but now she felt that if she didn't get some time to herself, if she wasn't free for a while of his dominating male presence, she would do something desperate. She was losing control over herself, and she knew it.

They had passed some kind of limit last night, breached some invisible barrier. She had been attracted to him from the first, but though he had consistently worked to get within her defenses, she had never completely succumbed to his seductive powers. She had kept some distance between them, even if she had done that by whipping up her anger over his thoughtlessness. But that had ended last night. She had been defenseless before his passionate lovemaking.

They had made love twice. She didn't see how he could have any strength left after their draining consummations. Yet here he was, bristling with energy, ready to compete in any event, whereas she felt as though she'd been doing hard labor. Her head didn't ache, but everything else did.

It was chastening to discover that his mere presence could make her tremble. If she didn't take some time to calm her senses, she'd make a fool of herself before they reached Havana. She had to stay in this chair until she could face him without feeling like she was going to pass out, even if it took the rest of the morning. They had held some games without her; they could do so again.

She leaned back, let the breeze ruffle her hair and swirl her dress gently about her ankles. Its soothing warmth eased the stiffness of her body, and the gentle rocking of the ship calmed her tortured mind. As her muscles relaxed, she allowed her shawl to slip from her shoulders, then sagged against the ropes of the chair, sinking more and more deeply into its welcoming depths. Gradually she slipped back into the welcoming arms of gentle sleep, her worries lulled by dreams that caused her lips to curve in a smile of pleasure.

"The captain insisted I check on her even though she's still asleep. She looks fine to me, but he's been running over here every five minutes for the last hour."

"She's probably just tired. A good night's rest should put

everything to rights," Smith declared. There was an uncomfortable pause as the ship's doctor digested the meaning of those words.

"I can't see any reason to wake her," Smith continued, "especially since she seems to be sleeping peacefully. Just keep an eye on her and call me if anything happens. I won't be far away."

"Make sure you aren't. If she really is sick, you're about the only one who can keep the captain from running his sword through my heart."

"I doubt anybody could stop him if you let anything happen to her."

"Things have gotten that bad, have they?"

"I think this one's going to last."

"But she's already married."

"I know that, but you tell that to the captain."

"Not me. The last time I tried to tell him anything, he locked me in my cabin with a blasted monkey. You can laugh because he'd never do anything like that to you, but it's pretty awful to sit in the dark for three days and have your food shoved under the door."

"There's no point in either of us saying anything. He knows the mess he's got himself into, and if he means to persist, there's nothing we can do to stop him."

"I don't understand. He's always been such a sensible man, one you could count on to use his brains."

"I would say this comes under the heading of the inevitable."

"It's madness if you ask me."

"Maybe not," Smith said, looking at Summer's sleeping form. "Maybe not."

Loud cheering brought Summer out of her dreams with a confused start. She looked around, wondering at the source of the noise. The crew, bunched at the rail and moving down the length of the ship in a loud, milling mass of jostling bodies, were shouting their enthusiastic encouragement to someone in the water. None of the occasional words she could catch made any sense. Then she heard someone call the captain's name and was instantly wide-awake; it was the distance swim, and if she didn't hurry she'd miss the whole race.

Ignoring her dizziness, she scrambled to her feet, rushed to the rail, and tried to push through the press of bodies; but no one offered to let her through. She tugged at the arm of a big burly man she didn't remember seeing before.

"What's happening?" she cried. "Who's winning?" A sudden increase in the cheering drowned out her efforts to gain his notice, and she moved from one person to the next until she came to one of the young officers dangling from the rigging. She pulled doggedly at his sleeve until she got his grudging attention.

"Mr. Caspian, please tell me what's going on," she pleaded. "Is the captain in this race?"

Young Caspian looked down into her soft, gold-flecked eyes and breathtakingly lovely face, and he almost lost his balance. All thought of the race left his mind. "I beg your pardon. I couldn't hear what you said." Her hand was on his arm, and she stared at him with such intensity he felt his tongue cleave to the roof of his mouth.

"What's happening?" she asked again. "Why is everyone yelling?"

"It's the race," he said, dazed.

"I know it's a race, but which one? Is the captain in it? Is he winning?"

"They've just finished the third lap," he mumbled, still in a trance.

"Who's ahead?" she asked with rising irritation. "I can't see through all these people. Can you see the race? Don't stand there like a dolt!" she ordered sharply. "Tell me what's happening before I push you overboard."

Caspian tore his eyes off her exquisite face. "They're just rounding the stern," he said finally. "The captain is on the inside. I think he's slightly ahead."

"He's winning!" Summer exclaimed, jumping with excitement.

"Not yet," said Caspian, dampening her enthusiasm. He strained to follow the distant swimmers as they churned through the water. "Lane's pulling up. He's even with the captain now."

"But the captain will pull away again, won't he?" Summer asked, wanting to be reassured.

"I don't know. He's got to be mighty tired. He wrestled three times today, and Lane is just doing this one event."

"But he's so much bigger and stronger than Lane. Surely he can swim faster."

"He's not doing it now. It looks like Lane has pulled ahead. No, they're still even, but the captain has got to be bone tired."

"He must win," Summer really spoke to herself. "Why didn't I stay awake?" She didn't stop to ask herself how her staying awake could have helped Brent, but she felt that it would have made a difference. "How much farther do they have to go?"

"This is the last lap. They'll finish at the bow in just a few minutes."

"I've got to see the finish," she declared, and ran to the front of the ship like a coursing hare. The swimmers were just coming into view and she could see them in the distance. She followed them with such intensity that she failed to notice Smith until she bumped into him. "Excuse me," she mumbled absently, not taking her eyes off the furious battle in the water below.

"I'm glad you woke up in time to see the finish," Smith said, calm as ever. "This is the most exciting race we've had all day."

"He's going to win, isn't he?"

"I don't know, milady. The captain has never lost before, but not even the captain is made of iron."

"But he *can't* lose! It's not fair."

"That was the captain's choice, milady. Anyone may enter as many or as few events as he likes." He watched the two swimmers, still neck and neck, their powerful strokes knifing through the water, their kicking feet creating boiling white wakes. "He's got a chance. I was sure Lane would leave him on this last stretch, but the captain is still even with him. No, Lane's pulling ahead now."

"No!" screamed Summer. She raced back along the rail heedless of the crew, dodging ropes and poles, screaming her encouragement to Brent. With less than fifty yards to go Brent was gradually falling behind. His strokes were still clean and powerful, but Lane was clearly in control of the race. Summer's voice rose until it cut through the masculine roar around her. She saw Brent glance up briefly at the ship, and a shiver of excitement ran through her. He had seen her. He knew she was cheering for him, that she had forgotten everything except her desire to see him win. Her eyes sparkled and her body radiated vitality as she urged him on to victory.

With a flurry of rapid strokes that set the crew to shouting, Brent began to cut into Lane's lead. He poured every ounce of his waning strength into those last yards.

She's completely wrapped up in the captain, Smith thought. He looked from Brent to Summer and back again. All she can think of is helping him win.

But before Summer could utter another cry of encouragement, a shout came from the lookout: "Sharks!" Her blood ran cold. Above the cheers of the crew and shuffling of feet on the wooden deck, the cry came again. "Sharks on the starboard side."

Instantly the crew scattered. One group ran to the two

long-boats which were ready to be lowered at a moment's notice. As two seamen manned the winches, the men in the boats locked their oars into place so they would be ready to row the instant the boat hit the water.

A second group swarmed down the sea ladders ready to help their exhausted mates out of the water. Most of the swimmers had abandoned the race, but the leaders continued to head toward the finish line, each concentrating on the other and on the last agonizing yards still to be covered. They swept by Summer paying no heed to the shouts from the ship or to the oars being splashed to divert the sharks' attention from the vulnerable swimmers.

"Why don't they stop?" Summer had found her voice at last. "Why doesn't someone do something?"

"They're going to finish the race," Smith said, and for once his voice was not calm.

"But they must stop," Summer declared. "Somebody's got to make them." Out of the corner of her eye she could see the other swimmers climbing up the sea ladders. "Please, stop them," she pleaded, unable to take her eyes off the battling pair.

"There they are!" a voice called out. She could see several fins cutting the water less than fifty yards from where the two swimmers, nearly exhausted, were struggling to make the last ten yards. Brent's tremendous effort had strained even his powerful frame, but he was slowly and painfully inching up on Lane, the tension in his face betraying the intensity of his determination and the terrible cost to his body.

Summer plodded blindly along the deck staying as close to Brent as she could. Her throat was so parched from fear that she couldn't utter a sound, and the usually gruff, unemotional crewmen behind her were strangely quiet. Only the noise made by the swimmers' kicks and the vigorous thrashing of oars broke the tense silence. A third boat was in the water now so that one was on each side of the swimmers and the last was positioned at the finish to haul in the exhausted combatants as soon as they completed the race.

"For the love of God," Summer groaned, "won't somebody pull them into the boats! Why do they wait?" She grabbed Smith's arm. "They're going to be killed."

"I think they're safe," he replied, showing some of his habitual calm. "The men have them surrounded. It's not likely a shark can get through to them now." But the words had hardly left Smith's mouth when Summer's grip on his arm tightened.

"Look at that one," she said in a deathlike whisper. With a quick movement, one shark had separated from the group, its speed and manner of swimming changing abruptly. It had scented prey and was closing in for the kill. As Summer watched that protruding fin rapidly near Brent, she froze.

Moving almost as quickly as the shark, one of the boats changed direction. In a quick wrenching motion, it cut across the trail of the swimmers, nearly running across the driving feet of the two men as it was deftly positioned between the charging shark and its intended victims.

When the shark found its path blocked, it quickly cut around the boat and headed straight for Brent's legs, its great mouth wide open. The voracious creature was so close that Summer could see its three rows of teeth; they could cut a man in half with one snap of those powerful jaws.

"Brent!" A single terrified shriek ripped from her throat. She was drained of color, unable to move, helpless to do anything except watch this nightmare unfold before her. Then just as she was sure she would witness a tragedy that would haunt her for the rest of her life, a young man stood up in the rocking boat. Raising an oar over his head, he brought it down with stunning force on the head of the onrushing shark. The enraged beast's mouth slammed shut with an audible snap, and it came to a dead stop. But not before it had struck the boat with enough force to pitch the young sailor into the boiling water on top of the infuriated monster.

"Oh, my God," ejaculated Smith.

Unable to endure any more, Summer fainted. She slid quietly to the deck, unnoticed and unaided.

Chapter 16

When Summer opened her eyes for the third time that morning, the first thing she saw was Brent's face. His eyes were filled with concern, but her relief at seeing him was so great she feared she might faint again.

"You're safe!" she exclaimed, remembering the shark.

"I'm not a bit worse for a little excitement."

"But the shark?" she questioned.

"He's not doing as well." Brent laughed, and his gleaming white teeth reminded her of the shark's lethal weapons.

"But I saw him. He was so *big*." Summer shuddered.

"He's not so big now," Brent responded, laughing even harder. "And he's got something else to do with those teeth than try to chew up my crew."

"What happened to the boy?" she asked, suddenly remembering the heroic youth.

"He's still a little weak from attempting to ride a shark bareback, but he's unharmed."

"But I saw him fall on top of that monster. How did he get away?"

"You've asked enough questions for the time being," Brent said solicitously. "Lie here and rest for a while. I'll tell you all about it later."

"Brent Douglas!" Summer sat up, a martial light in her eyes. "If you *dare* leave me here without telling me what happened, I'll . . . I'll . . ."

"Just what will you do?" he asked, his amused smile duplicated on the dozen faces around his.

"You're a beast and a bully," she said, taking refuge in the words, "and there's not a decent bone in your whole body." A volley of laughter ran through the gathered seamen, causing Summer to scowl angrily.

"I'm certain the countess will be able to recover her strength more quickly in private," Smith suggested, casting a significant glance at the men clustered about.

"Back to work, all of you," Brent ordered. "I want this ship under full sail in less than thirty minutes, and that won't happen if you stand about with your mouths open like fish waiting for a hook." As the men scattered to attend to their tasks, Brent said to Summer, "You can remain on deck if you like, but stay off your feet. Smith will see to you until I get back."

"Don't hurry," she retorted. "I need lots of rest. Who knows when a little excitement might send me off again. And, goodness knows, your presence is enough to give a healthy person a fit."

"You're making a quick recovery. I expect you to be in fighting trim by the midday meal."

"That man!" Summer declared, exasperated. "I wish the shark *had* bitten him. Smith." She turned to the first mate, determination shining in her eyes.

"Yes, milady." He smiled. "I'll tell you anything you want

147

to know. If I don't, you'll be in a high fever when the captain returns and he'll hold me responsible."

Summer blushed. "It's not that bad. The captain's not really worried about me."

"Begging your pardon, milady, but I don't agree. Now what do you want to know?"

Summer almost forgot about the shark in her desire to ask Smith what he had meant, but she forced her thoughts back to the race.

"What happened to that boy?"

"The captain and Lane were being pulled into the boat when Silas fell in. Before anyone could stop him the captain dove back in to rescue the lad."

Summer's eyes widened in disbelief. "But he was exhausted from the race. Besides, he didn't have any weapon. What did he think he could fight that shark with? His rapier wit?"

"We were wondering the same thing," Smith answered, doing his best to preserve an unrevealing countenance. "But the captain has fooled us many times before. We should have known he'd have something up his sleeve."

"Since he was practically naked, it couldn't have been much of a surprise to anyone, not even the shark," Summer snorted.

"Milady, don't you *like* the captain?" Smith was momentarily diverted by the sharpness of Summer's rejoinder.

"We're not discussing my opinions," she said firmly. "What did he do?"

"The shark was thrashing about looking for something to chew up," Smith explained, "so the captain shoved the oar Silas had dropped into its mouth. The beast was so crazed with anger it bit the oar in half, but the splintered wood stuck in its throat. When the shark opened its mouth to dislodge that, the captain jammed the other piece of oar in. That

148

caused the shark to thrash about so, it nearly dumped every-one into the water."

"The crew pulled Silas and the captain back into the boats and headed for the ship, and not a moment too soon. A piece of the oar punctured the shark's mouth and it started bleed-ing. Within seconds the other sharks had scented the blood and closed in. I don't think they even realized their prey was one of their own kind."

"Did they actually kill the shark?" Summer asked, her eyes wide with wonder.

"As far as we can tell. Before long the water will be filled with sharks from miles away, all ready to devour anything in their path."

"Can't we leave?"

"The captain is seeing to that now. There's no danger to us, but it's bad luck for a ship to be followed by sharks. If we don't shake them before they recover from their feed, we're bound to have at least one on our trail looking for garbage."

"Ugh!" said Summer. She quivered with disgust and fear. "It's absolutely revolting to think about that."

"It's not something you want to discuss over a meal."

"I don't think I can eat a thing," she declared. "Maybe I'll lie down in my cabin."

"Yes, milady, if you really think that's what you want to do."

"What do you mean?" Summer asked. She could tell from the tone of his voice that he had more to relate.

"Well, I rather think the captain is expecting you to join him at table."

"If that's all, he can do without me." She was disappointed. "I'm sure I'll feel well enough to join him by dinner."

"But it'll be too late then."

"Too late for what?"

"For the celebration."

"Will you stop talking in riddles?" Summer was exasperated. "What could he possibly be celebrating? Not even your beloved captain could be so crass as to gloat over a bunch of dead sharks."

"I don't think he has sharks in mind."

"I think you've been in the sun too long. Maybe *you'd* better lie down."

Smith's smile turned into an infectious grin in which Summer recognized the same reckless courage she saw in Brent.

"If you don't stop smirking at me like you know all the answers, I'm going to have Brent throw you to the sharks. Then we'll see how fast *you* can swim . . . *the race!*" she exclaimed, her eyes bright with excitement. "That's what you're trying to tell me, isn't it?"

Smith nodded.

"He won, didn't he?"

"Yes, milady, he certainly did." Without warning Summer jumped up and threw her arms around Smith's neck, laughing and hugging him at the same time. The poor man was unprepared for her assault and staggered backward, his own arms instinctively closing around her waist to keep her from falling.

"What the hell do you think you're doing?" a voice thundered.

If Summer hadn't been so beside herself with happiness, she would have seen the murderous look in Brent's eyes or she would have sensed Smith's trepidation. But she was too elated to be aware of either. In one quick movement, she released Smith and threw herself at Brent.

"You won!" she cried happily. "Smith just told me you won the race."

"Is that why you're throwing yourself all over my officer?" Brent asked, his face clearing somewhat. Smith began to think he might be allowed to live if she just didn't do anything else foolish.

"Yes." Summer laughed with uninhibited delight. "I was so afraid you were going to lose. It wasn't fair either, not after you had done so much more than anyone else."

"And it mattered that much to you?" Brent was used to winning, everyone expected it, but no one had ever been afraid that he might lose, or so rapturously happy that he had won. It was a new experience for him, and he didn't know how to react to it. He felt uncomfortable, as if he were somehow bound to this strange, elfin creature that had so completely captivated him.

"Of course it did," she replied. "Didn't you hear me cheering for you? I was sure you saw me when you looked up."

"I did," he said, gazing at her with an unfamiliar warmth in his eyes. Suddenly she didn't feel giddy or foolish anymore; she removed her arms from around his neck, but he wouldn't let her go.

"Release me," she begged, embarrassed now.

"I'd rather not. I like having you here."

"You can't stand here hugging me in front of the whole crew. What will they think?"

"It's not my behavior that is shocking them. Everybody saw you throw yourself at both of us. I merely caught you so you wouldn't fall."

"You're the most impossible man I've ever met," Summer said, but then she laughed. "I don't think you've ever been caught without a retort on the tip of your tongue."

"What makes you think that?" he said, setting her on her feet.

"You're never at a loss. You always seem to know what to do," she said, adjusting her dress and then smoothing it out.

"You flatter me," he said, and the laughter faded from his eyes. "Smith can tell you that I've gotten myself into one mighty tangle, and I still don't know how to find my way out."

"What's that?"

"Don't you know?" he asked, watching her closely.

"How could I? I've only known you for a few weeks. You've had years and years to get in and out of scrapes I wouldn't know anything about."

"I did rather well for myself then."

"I might have known you'd blame it on me."

"On the contrary, that's a compliment."

"I don't know what's wrong with everybody today," Summer complained. "First Smith talks in riddles, and now you aren't making any sense either. I've had too much excitement to be able to concentrate on any more obscure conversation. I'm ready to eat. Smith said that you insisted I join you for the celebration. Why?"

"Because, my sweet simpleton," Brent said after a pause so long she began to feel uncomfortable, "it was seeing your intense face at the rail that gave me the determination to win."

Summer turned pink with pleasure. "You really mean you won that race because of me?"

"Do you find that so hard to believe?"

"Nothing like that has ever happened to me before. It's wonderful," she said, clapping her hands together with delight.

"Let's not get too excited about it." Brent gazed at her, his expression compounded of doubt and hope. "I don't want you grinning at the crew, or encouraging them to indulge in foolish acts of heroism."

"I'd never do anything like that," Summer said, indignantly. "What kind of girl do you think I am?"

"I don't know," Brent said with unaccustomed gravity. "I begin to doubt that I ever had the least idea what you're like."

"Well, it's not very flattering for you to think I'd run about simpering at the crew."

"I humbly beg your forgiveness."

"I'll bet this is the first time you've ever done that," Summer marveled. "I'm surprised the words didn't stick in your throat."

"I'd get down on my knees if that would convince you of my sincerity," he responded, the twinkle in his eyes suddenly becoming more pronounced.

"Don't you dare," she said quickly. "You've already given these men enough reason to whisper about me. I won't let you give them more."

"If anyone dares say a single word—"

"Don't be stupid. Of course they won't open their mouths around you. Nobody wants a broken head. But if you thought I could be on this ship for more than ten minutes, let alone ten weeks, and not give rise to all kinds of speculation, then *you're* the one who's naïve."

The significance of her words struck Brent for the first time. Smith thought it odd that a quick-witted man like the captain should have overlooked such a little thing, especially when it was so obvious to every man on the crew.

"But there's no point in crying over what can't be helped," Summer said pholosophically. "Now let's go eat. I'm starving. I haven't had any food all day."

"In that case, milady, allow me to escort you to the banquet so that the celebration may begin."

Brent took Summer by the arm and led her off most correctly, but his step had lost some of its jauntiness, his voice some of its insouciant gaiety.

Chapter 17

Summer stood at the bow of the ship, staring at the busy, sultry harbor of Havana. It was late in the year and the weather was not very hot, but the air was so rich with moisture it hung like a thick mantle over every living thing, wringing out energy and making each breath an unrewarding effort. Heat rose from the town in unending waves, and was carried out to the bay by a languid breeze which then sloughed off its unwanted burden.

As Summer watched the slow-moving figures in the distance, she wished for the tenth time in the last five minutes that they were still out to sea where the air was clean and brisk. There, she had felt alive and invigorated even on warm days, but in the bay the air moved sluggishly. It came from land and bore the malodorous smell of filthy streets inhabited by clouds of the dreaded mosquitoes.

Brent had gone ashore as soon as they'd dropped anchor, and the crew were industriously working to ready the cargo for unloading. It was now late in the afternoon and he still hadn't returned, which made a discontented Summer even more unhappy that her unfettered days at sea had come to an end.

"We might be gone for quite a while," Brent had told her early that morning. "We have to find buyers and make arrangements for unloading the cargo. That's not always easy to do quickly."

"Will you be back before lunch?" she asked with a sleepy yawn, thinking of curling up again as soon as he left.

"Maybe, but most likely I won't return until late tonight."

"Tonight?" she exclaimed. She sat up quickly, all thought of sleep forgotten. "You can't leave me by myself all day."

"You won't be by yourself," he said, smiling indulgently. "Smith is the only one going with me."

"Can't he stay?" she asked, not in the least reassured by the presence of the other officers.

"He's the one person I can't do without," Brent replied, not understanding how she could feel alone in the midst of his crew. "There's nothing for you to worry about, and you'll have the entire day to spend as you like. The ship is at your disposal."

"That's not much of a temptation," Summer retorted. She couldn't steel herself to tell him there was nothing of interest to her on his blasted ship if he wasn't aboard, not with her hair in her eyes and her thin nightgown twisted around her thighs.

However, Brent didn't seem to find her dishabille at all unattractive. "You're a mighty big temptation," he said, letting his fingers travel up her arms and then brush her cheeks. His eyes wandered over her body, lingering on the long slender leg and thigh not covered by her gown, but not neglecting the full curves of hips and breasts the thin fabric barely obscured. He let his fingers travel up her leg, from ankle to hem, causing her blood to begin to boil. "If I stay here any longer, I might not leave at all," he whispered, his hot breath warming her ear.

Summer pulled his head down onto her breasts. "I would like that," she purred, but further words became caught in her throat as his hot lips touched the tender skin of her breasts and caused them to firm with excitement. Her body arched against him as the hand on her leg strayed between her thighs.

"Damn, now I'm going to have to get dressed all over again," he rasped, and quickly began to unbutton his shirt. But their swelling passion was interrupted by a sharp knock at the door.

"Blast and damn!" Brent cursed. "What the hell do you want?"

"The boat is ready, Captain." It was Smith's voice.

"Tell it to wait," Brent replied, breathing heavily. "I'm not ready yet."

"It's already in the water," Smith answered. "Should I tell them pull it up again?"

"I don't care what you tell them." Brent was torn between the mounting pressure of his physical desire and his duty to the ship.

"I can't understand you very well, sir," droned Smith's insistent voice.

"I'll be there in a minute, blast you," Brent bellowed. "I've just got to button my shirt." He wrenched himself away from Summer's arms. They were both panting hard and their senses were throbbing painfully from unfulfilled promise. "I've got to go," he said, beginning to rebutton his shirt. "You do understand, don't you?" Summer nodded imperceptibly. "I'll come back just as soon as I can." He eyed her sprawling, half-naked figure with undisguised desire. "I've got some unfinished business that needs my attention."

"Don't be gone all day, please," she begged, giving him a weak smile.

"I'll try," he promised, but Summer could tell that his passion was weakening with each button, her attraction fading before the pressure of his duties. "Now cover yourself up," he said, straightening his cravat and reaching for his coat. "I don't want Smith to see you lounging about so invitingly. At least one of us has to be able to keep business in mind." Summer righted her gown and pulled the covers up to her chin.

"Is this enough?" she asked a trifle pettishly.

"Not unless you cover your face as well." He leaned over to brush a lock of hair out of her face. "Even when you look like you've been riding in the back of a hay cart, you're the most adorable, captivating women I've ever known."

"Since I can't keep you here for a few minutes, that's not saying much for the other women you've met. Unless there were farm girls riding in those carts you were talking about."

"Silence, you abandoned hussy," he said, giving her clearly outlined backside a playful slap. "I never consorted with farm girls, with or without a cart."

"Then don't let me keep you from your highbred ladies any longer," she said, turning her back on him. "They must be biting their nails in impatience."

"I believe you're jealous, my sweet." An impish smile lighted his face when she angrily flipped over to face him.

"Me!" she sputtered. "Why should I be jealous of some olive-skinned seductress with bloodred lips and jet black hair?"

"When did you meet Consuelo?" Brent exclaimed, simulating surprise. "I thought you said you never left your father's plantation."

"You devil!" she spat at him. "How dare you imply that I keep company with the likes of your abandoned hussies."

"It surprised me, but you described Consuelo so exactly I thought you must have seen her. She moves in the very best circles."

"I have no desire to meet her or to know anything about the circles she inhabits, no matter how exalted."

"Surely you don't plan to stay in your hotel room the whole time we're in Havana?"

"Of course not. Why should I?"

"You'll have to, if you're set on avoiding all the women I've met. In fact," he added, a wicked glint in his eyes, "you'd better pull the sheet over your head when the maid comes in with your morning cocoa."

"You're a depraved, unnatural lecher," she charged, now goaded to fury. "Get out of my cabin this very minute. I don't want to set eyes on you again. You're a conceited, overbearing devil and the most black-hearted monster I've ever met."

"That's the second time today you've tried to throw me out of my cabin," he said, approaching the bed again. Summer rolled as far away from him as she could. "I'm going to have to teach you that it's not good manners to treat your host so rudely."

"You're a pirate, not my host," she flung at him. "And you're the last person on earth to have a right to criticize anyone's bad manners. You are the rudest and most insolent person I know."

Brent leaned over the bed to make a grab for her but Summer scrambled out of his reach. "You won't escape me that easily, you little hornet," he said grimly, and climbed onto the bed. Summer shrieked and tried to fight him off with balled-up fists and kicking feet, but Brent easily overpowered her. He held her down, wrists pinned on either side of her head. "Now my little spitfire, you listen to me."

"No." Summer rolled her head from side to side. "I won't listen to a single word. You'll probably lie anyway."

"I don't know anyone named Consuelo, and you won't meet the women I've made love to at every corner. Most definitely the maid who brings your cocoa is not one of them."

"I don't believe you. You're such a horny beast you couldn't leave any woman alone."

"I never said I was a monk," Brent said angrily, "but I'm selective about my women."

"I wouldn't have thought you could spare the time. Do you question them yourself, or does Smith interview them first?"

"You spiteful little jade. I've never seen anyone so ready to fly into a jealous fit over the slightest thing."

"If you call throwing armloads of mistresses at me after the way you've treated me these last few weeks a *slight thing*, then you're the vilest man in creation." Summer worked one of her legs free and gave him a painful jab in the ribs with her knee.

Brent was really angry now. "You intemperate bonehead. If you can't tell the difference between the way I've treated you and disinterested lust, then you're a featherbrained nitwit worth no more than a roll in the hay and a kiss good-bye."

Summer tried to kick him again, but Brent threw his whole body on hers and held her helpless beneath him.

"Get off me, you tyrant. You can go to all the almond-eyed whores you can find and stay as long as you like. I'm sure I don't mind. I probably won't even notice." She tried to bite him, but he moved out of reach.

"I don't know why I don't throw you overboard." He held her two hands in one of his, her chin with the other. "If you weren't such a cuddly little armful, I would consider it." He released her chin and let his fingers explore her breasts. "But it would be a shameful waste."

"You're diabolical," she hissed, "and I hate you."

"You're beautiful," he said roughly. The passion in him was stirring again, rushing to enslave his senses. His hot lips began to nibble one breast while his free hand caressed the other.

"Let me go!" she gasped, trying to push him away and at the same time trying to stave off the surge of desire flooding through her. "You're nothing but a low, rutting animal." She tried to twist away, but he held her fast and drove his knee between her legs, further immobilizing her and fanning the flames that licked at her resistance.

"Get your hands off me," she cried, but her words sounded more like an invitation than a dismissal, and Brent only redoubled his efforts. Summer made one final attempt to escape, but her heart wasn't in it, and she suddenly capitulated, throwing her legs around Brent and hungrily kissing the top of his head. He tore his lips away from her nipples to return her kiss, savaging her mouth with his, ransacking its far recesses with his tongue. When he released her hands, she threw her arms around his neck, pulling him to her with all her might. And his hands flew to his clothing, tearing off buttons and ripping seams in his haste to be free of any restriction.

"Captain Douglas." It was Smith's long-forgotten voice. "The men have been waiting in the boat for more than twenty minutes."

"You can take that goddamned boat and row it straight to hell!" Brent roared. "I'm not leaving until I'm good and ready." He turned back to Summer and the business at hand.

Chapter 18

"But I can't just walk in on your arm," Summer said for the sixth time. "I might as well announce that I'm your mistress."

Brent, the insensitive egotist, couldn't understand why she wasn't eager to march straight into the biggest hotel in Havana with him as though he were her brother. He stared at her as if she were crazy, then turned a deaf ear to her protests.

"Nobody's going to think any such thing," he said. "This is not London or Madrid."

"Have you ever taken a woman to a hotel?" she asked indignantly before she had time to realize what a stupid question that was.

"Lots of times."

"I don't mean some trollop," she snapped, trying to control her irritation. "I mean a respectable woman."

"All my women are respectable."

"Then I suppose you spent the night in separate suites?"

"What do you think I took them to the hotel for?"

"That's *exactly* what I mean. Respectable women don't stay in hotels unless they're properly chaperoned, not even in Havana."

"Well, you can't stay on the ship. It's not safe." Brent reached out and pulled her over to him. "I couldn't trust any man alone with you," he said huskily.

"Don't judge everyone by yourself." She removed his hands from her waist. "What's wrong with my staying here?"

"I have to meet with buyers in the city, and I'll be much too busy to row back every night to check on you."

"You don't have to come back. I'll be perfectly safe with Smith."

"Good Lord, girl! After six months at sea, would Smith, or anybody else in their right mind, want to stay on this ship with the whole city of Havana open to him?"

"Somebody has to stay here."

"Those aboard won't have time to take care of you," Brent stated in a manner that clearly ended the discussion.

"If you had brought Bridgit along, you could go anywhere you wanted without my being a stone around your neck."

"I've never felt that way about you, and you know it."

"No I don't," she said, hoping he would tell her exactly how he *did* feel. "What am I supposed to think when all you do is bark orders at me?"

He looked at her standing in the early morning sun, the rays shining on her still-bare shoulders, and he knew she would never understand why the mere sight of her made him more determined than ever to keep her by his side.

"The only way I can stay in that hotel with you and keep a decent reputation is as your wife."

"You'll have to think of something else. I can't have you married to two men at once."

"Would my being married make any difference to you as

long as my husband doesn't interfere?" she asked, greatly interested in his reply.

"It makes a great deal of difference, especially when your husband is Gowan." The thought of Summer in Gowan's arms caused the muscles across Brent's shoulders to become so rigid they strained the seams of his shirt. For a moment his hatred of the earl blocked out all awareness of Summer; he stared beyond her with a look of dogged determination that would have told any member of his crew the captain had made up his mind. And when that was so, there was no turning him from his course.

"He is my husband after all," Summer said. "I don't see what you can do to stop him if he decides he wants me back."

"He won't," Brent declared, abruptly returning from his thoughts. "Gowan never bothers with people who can't be of any use to him." Summer was irked to learn that Brent thought Gowan valued her so lightly he wouldn't make an attempt to find her. Yet the thought that Gowan might actually come after her frightened Summer so badly she would have swallowed any number of insults rather than face her lawful husband.

"If you don't get into that dress, I'm going to carry you ashore in your shift." Brent was impatient to be gone. He eyed her inviting curves and again felt desire stir in him. "It would certainly brighten the boatmen's morning, but I'd prefer your arrival to be less spectacular."

"I'll just take a minute more," Summer said. She was provoked but had given up on swaying him.

The ride to shore was hot and uncomfortable. The small boat pitched until Summer thought she was going to be ill.

"It's pretty rough," Brent sympathized, "but it won't last long."

"It's lasted too long already," she replied, trying to keep her mind off the stench of the harbor. Her head, covered by the wide-brimmed hat Brent had insisted she wear, hung list-lessly to one side. He had not missed the glances of the animal-like men who worked the docks. It was the presence of such men that had led him to decide it was unsafe for her to stay on the ship.

"Watch your step, or we'll both end up in the water," Brent cautioned as he helped her out of the boat.

Summer looked at the brackish water dotted with floating debris and her stomach heaved. "I've never seen such filth," she declared, remembering the times she had dangled her feet in the clean, clear water at the dock of her parents' planta-tion.

"If you could break Havana of leaving its garbage in the streets to be washed into the bay with the next rain, you would be doing everyone a service," he responded, though he did not seem to mind the filthy water that much.

"How does anyone stand to live here?" Summer asked.

But she didn't feel that way once they'd left the harbor be-hind. The streets were hot and stifling; however, the houses were beautiful. They had tile roofs, iron rails, and cool courtyards enclosed by high walls. Everywhere she saw the trees, shrubs, and flowers she had known since childhood, but instead of the random gardening of Mother Nature, these plants were arranged in endlessly varying designs, great num-bers of them being massed together to create awe-inspiring blocks of vibrant color. "I've never seen so many beautiful flowers," Summer commented.

"Wait until you see the gardens of some of the large es-tates. This is nothing compared to them."

Summer lapsed into a daydream, but she came wide-awake when she found herself stepping out of the carriage into the most enormous building she had ever seen. The *Casa Grande* was the largest and most luxurious hotel in all of Cuba. In only five years its fame had spread throughout the Caribbe-an, and people came to Havana just to see it.

Summer followed in Brent's wake, wishing she could become invisible, or at least go unnoticed in the furor caused by his arrival. She could practically *feel* accusing fingers pointed at her, could almost *hear* the scandalized whispers that damned her as a scarlet woman. Why had she let Brent talk her into leaving the safety of the ship? When would she ever learn to stand up to him?

Summer would have been even more upset if she had known that her compelling beauty had brought her greater attention than being seen in Brent's company ever could. Ignorant of the desire she kindled in the men she passed, she stared straight ahead and silently prayed that she would reach her room before her courage failed.

The lobby, reached by a short flight of steps, made Summer gasp. Twelve marble columns were arranged around it, topped by Ionic capitals supporting statues in dull gold. The extravagant plaster ceiling and the stucco wall panels were heavily decorated with gilt in contrast to the geometrically simple floor of yellow and blue tiles.

"How do you like it?" Brent asked as he watched Summer gaze about her in disbelief.

"It's a little overpowering." She faltered, hesitant to criticize. "But I've never seen anything like it."

"Alonzo will be pleased to hear that. He's always glad to hear guests praise his hotel." A short, stocky individual with fat cheeks, penetrating eyes, and boundless energy suddenly appeared before them.

"Señor Douglas," he gushed, as he directed young men to unload their trunks and fetch the baggage from the carriage, "I am delighted that you have favored my humble hotel with your presence."

"I wouldn't think of staying anywhere else," Brent said with an easy smile. "And I've brought you a very special guest this time."

"Your servant, *señorita*." Alonzo got his first good look at

Summer when she removed her hat. "We are honored that our roof is to shelter such a beautiful dove," he said smoothly.

Brent's eyes suddenly narrowed and glinted dangerously. "Before you jump to conclusions that may cause you considerable distress," he said in a voice that startled Alonzo into dropping his suave demeanor, "let me introduce the Lady Summer McConnel, countess of Heatherstone." Alonzo bowed deeply while Summer stared at the floor and hoped her complexion didn't betray her mortification. "Her husband is the richest man in Scotland, and I want you to take particularly good care of her."

"I am a complete fool, and should have my tongue cut out," apologized Alonzo. "It is a great honor to have you stay with us. If there is anything we can do to make your stay more comfortable, just name it. It will be done at once."

"As long as you're so anxious to please, you can find the countess a maid. Hers became too ill to continue the journey."

"Of course," Alonzo assured them with an ingratiating smile. "That will be no problem."

"And send a message to Clothilde. I want her to be here before noon with every dress she has in the place. The countess needs some new gowns. Hers are all too hot for Havana."

"Of course." Alonzo swallowed convulsively. "Which suite would the countess prefer?"

"Your best," Brent informed him, surprised at the question.

"It will be prepared at once," Alonzo replied. "And you?" he asked, without daring to look into Brent's hard eyes.

"Any suite you have as long as it's close enough for me to keep an eye on the countess." Brent fixed Alonzo with a brittle stare. "My first mate will share it with me. Mind you, I want that maid engaged by this evening. The countess must not be unattended."

Summer was too unnerved to protest in front of Alonzo,

but when he bounced away to correct some trifling fault in the service of another guest, she pounced on Brent. "Why did you have to demand the biggest suite?" she asked. "Why couldn't I occupy some modest room?"

"No one will believe your story if you hide in the attic. Either you play the part all the way, or we might as well go back to the ship." Summer longed to tell him that she *wanted* to do that, but Alonzo returned to escort them to their rooms. She followed the two men up the grand staircase that led to the first floor on which the largest suites were located. Surely even kings didn't live in places like this, she thought as she stared at the magnificence all around her. She had visited the homes of some very wealthy planters, but nothing she had seen could be compared to this hotel. A still greater surprise awaited her when she was ushered into her suite.

The huge room was decorated in the French style. The walls were covered with dark green and gold paneling on which Chinese and Turkish figures were carved, and enormous gilt mirrors hung above the companion fireplaces of pink marble. The floor was covered by a deep carpet, and the furniture was upholstered in fabric that depicted rustic scenes.

"This is the salon, *señora*," said Alonzo. "There is a dining room on the left, a small private parlor to the right. Off the bedroom you'll find a dressing room and quarters for your maid, and there are also rooms for your husband and his valet."

"You needn't bother with them," said Brent briskly. "Just see that the rest of the suite is prepared."

"But of course," Alonzo assured him. He could barely hide his relief that Brent was not going to share the countess's suite openly.

"Where are my rooms?" Brent demanded.

"Just down the hall," said Alonzo. "Come, I will show you."

With a sinking feeling, Summer watched the ornate double doors close behind the two men. She had to lean on the back of a chair to prevent herself from giving in to a mad desire to run after Brent. Though he was only a few steps away, she had never felt more alone in her life.

Until now everything had seemed real, at times painfully so, but real all the same; yet alone in this enormous suite she felt she was living a dream. Maybe it was the opulence of the hotel, but she clung to the memory of Brent's arms about her.

"I've got to stop acting like a scared rabbit," she said aloud, hoping the sound of her own voice would give her courage. "I'll never be able to take care of myself if I go to pieces over every little thing." She got up and looked about her. The overpowering grandeur of the room and the luxury of its appointments momentarily distracted her. She let her fingers wander over plush fabric and dark polished wood. She felt intimidated, threatened by the sheer extravagance of it all, and she longed for the comfortable plainness of her own home in which she was more important than the objects around her. Even the servants in a hotel such as this were bound to look down their noses at her.

She walked around a couch with a sculpted mahogany frame, then dropped onto its thick cushions, and stared ahead unseeingly. A soft knock at the door made her start up from the sofa like some forest creature looking for a place to hide. The knock came again, more insistently this time.

"Come in," she managed to say, one hand clutching her throat and the other grasping the arm of the sofa.

Chapter 19

The door opened and a bright, pixie-faced girl tripped into the room, words tumbling from her mouth in a torrent. She both surprised and reassured Summer.

"*Señora*, I'm your new maid! Isn't it wonderful that I don't have to make beds and clean up after messy people. Oh!" she stared at Summer, open-mouthed and unabashed. "The *señora* is so very beautiful. You are like a princess."

"I'm not a princess." Summer felt more like a frightened charwoman than royalty. "I'm really no one at all." Heartened by the girl's extreme youth, she managed a weak smile.

"You must not say that. Señor Alonzo told me that you were a real countess. He said I must be very careful not to make any mistakes." She suddenly looked suspiciously at Summer. "You *are* a countess, aren't you?"

"Yes, but—"

"Wait until I tell María," the girl squealed, clapping her hands with glee. "She will be eaten up with jealousy, the black-eyed slut!" She clapped a hand over her mouth and stared apprehensively at Summer. "*Madre* de Dios, *señora*, I beg your pardon. My horrible tongue."

"It's all right." Summer laughed, relieved to find her maid a guileless child and not the censorious woman she had feared. "I've often wanted to say something like that myself."

The girl broke into a giggle totally devoid of contrition. "I know I shouldn't say such things, and I confess to Padre Miguel every week, but I can't stop. María says I'll get into trouble someday, but I don't care for anything *she* says. She's a mean-hearted girl, and green with jealousy. You should have heard her scream when Alonzo said I was to be your maid and that she had to clean the rooms."

"I'm sure she is everything you say," Summer said. She decided to try to stem the flow of unwanted confidences. "But we can forget about her for the time being."

"It's impossible to forget María," the young maid declared emphatically.

"I'd prefer to talk about you," Summer stated. "I'd really like to know your name. I can't go around pointing at you every time I want something."

"*Perdôneme señora,*" she said, a delighted laugh rippling from her. "My name is Chichi."

"Chichi?" repeated Summer, curiously. "That's such an unusual name."

"I was christened Dolores Isabella Carlotta Beatrix," Chichi announced proudly.

"My goodness. What a lot of names for such a little girl."

"Nobody ever used them. My father said I chattered like a monkey. That's why he called me Chichi. Even my mother stopped calling me Dolores before I was six."

"I think Chichi is a charming name, and I'm glad you're my maid," Summer declared. "I was afraid they would send me some stiff Spanish lady who would disapprove of everything I did."

"Margarita would never agree to be maid to an English lady," Chichi told her earnestly. "She thinks all the English are sinners and seducers." The girl giggled. "She says that their souls will be the devil's food."

"Who is Margarita?" Summer felt overwhelmed by the introduction of yet another person.

"She's the housekeeper," said Chichi. She mimicked the walk and the stance of a stout, scowling, ungraceful woman. "She's always crossing herself and saying that the devil will devour our souls every time we laugh. *Estúpida!*"

"How horrid. I had no idea that Spanish devils were so hungry."

Chichi's tinkling laugh erupted spontaneously. "We think the devil tried to eat her soul, but it was so tough it gave him a stomach ache." She was overcome by laughter once again, but it stopped abruptly at a knock and the appearance of Alonzo.

"The countess's trunks have arrived," he announced sternly. As proof of his words, two young men struggled in under the weight of Summer's largest chest. "See that the *señora*'s clothes are unpacked right away." He glowered at the unrepentant Chichi until she took refuge behind Summer. When he turned to direct the men bearing Summer's second trunk, the spritely little maid made a face at him and then dashed for the safety of the bedchamber.

"If the *señora* is not satisfied with her maid, I will be happy to send another," Alonzo offered.

"No, I'm quite happy with Chichi." Summer schooled her features to impassivity.

Alonzo's rigid face relaxed into a smile. "She's a good girl, really, but she will talk the hind leg off a donkey. You have to be very firm with her."

"I don't mind. She amuses me."

"If you are quite certain," he said. He wondered if Captain Douglas would feel the same.

"Have you found a maid for the countess yet?" Brent demanded as he came into the room, his very presence charging it with energy.

"She's already unpacking the countess's trunks."

"Good. When will Clothilde be here?"

"I'm not certain," stammered Alonzo, avoiding those penetrating eyes. "I have not yet received an answer to my message."

"Good God, man, we can't sit about all day. The Governor's reception is tonight, and the countess has nothing to wear."

"I don't think Madame Clothilde will be able to provide a gown on such short notice."

"What you think doesn't matter. You did tell her I wanted her at once, didn't you?" Brent demanded brusquely, fixing Alonzo with the glare that never failed to reduce his crew to quaking incoherence.

"She must not have had time to respond to your wishes," Alonzo finally replied.

"Why not? Send someone over there and tell her to drop whatever she's doing."

"I'll have your message delivered right away," Alonzo said, quickly, glad to have an excuse to escape Brent's mounting temper.

"Perhaps we could go to Madame Clothilde's shop," Summer suggested.

"She can come here," Brent grumbled. He was completely out of patience. "She charges enough to take the trouble."

"But she doesn't know my size, my coloring, or what I look like. She can't possibly have any idea of what to bring for me to look at."

Alonzo paused in the doorway.

"I've already asked her to come here," Brent stated determinedly.

"I'm sure she'll be more willing to try to find a dress for

me if we make it easier on her. Her regular customers have probably ordered gowns for tonight as well."

"To hell with her regular customers," Brent stormed.

"You can't expect her to see this from your point of view. She won't want to endanger her regular income for someone who will be here only a short time," Summer pointed out rationally.

"All right," Brent finally said.

Summer turned to Alonzo. "Tell her we'll come to her shop as soon as she can be ready to receive us."

"Right now," Brent growled.

"Ask the messenger to hurry," Summer suggested, unwilling to test Brent's temper too far.

"I'll send María to her shop at once," said Alonzo. "Is there anything else before I go?"

"We'd like something to eat."

"Certainly," said Alonzo, bowing himself out.

"How that great fool manages to run this hotel I'll never know," Brent observed.

"With men like you making absurd demands at every turn, his job is not an easy one," remarked Summer.

"Now listen to me, *señora*," Brent sarcastically mimicked Alonzo.

"No, you listen to *me*. I won't go to this reception if you intend to make a scene everytime something happens. I won't even step outside this room if the whole town is going to be buzzing with stories about my unreasonable demands and your temper."

Brent surprised Summer by looking disappointed instead of angry. "Don't you like staying at this hotel?"

"It makes me feel positively wonderful," Summer said quickly, "when it's not scaring me to death. Why did I ever let you talk me into leaving the ship?" she groaned. "Maybe that wretched Clothilde won't have anything for me to wear and I won't have to go after all. Chichi can stay with me."

"Clothilde will find something if she has to spend the rest of the day sewing it herself. And who is this Chichi? She doesn't sound like a suitable companion for you."

"She's not a companion." Summer laughed. "She's my maid."

"If that fool Alonzo has palmed off one of his sluts on you, I'll wrap this crucifix around his Spanish neck." Brent picked up a large bronze cross from a side table.

"She's not a slut," Summer said indignantly. "She has a long list of proper Spanish names, but her father calls her Chichi because she chatters like a monkey."

"I'm going to see just what kind of joke Alonzo thinks he's playing." Brent stalked toward the bedroom door. "You," he shouted, "come out here at once."

Chichi catapulted through the door, nearly running into Brent. She gasped in fright at seeing his great size and the murderous look on his face. *"Nombre de Dios!"* she exclaimed, backing up a few steps. "Surely this is Margarita's devil." Summer was seized by a fit of giggles as the two took a moment to size each other up. When Brent saw that Chichi was indeed a charming young girl with a turned-up nose and a slim figure, his frown changed to an appreciative smile.

Chichi, too, had had a chance to appreciate Brent and to become aware of his magnetism. Her eyes began to twinkle, and she responded to his frank gaze with a pouting little smile and lowered lashes. "So, *Señora*, is this your earl?" she said moving closer to Brent and looking him over quite brazenly. "I would never have the courage to go behind the bedroom door with him. Surely he would swallow me in one gulp." Brent let out a crack of laughter, but Summer's mirth suddenly vanished.

"No, he's not my earl, you impertinent child. He's the captain of my ship."

"*Your* ship?" Brent asked.

"*My* ship," Summer repeated emphatically.

"The earl has entrusted me with the protection of his good lady," Brent explained more soberly, "and I'm taking her back to Scotland."

"This earl," said Chichi, a gleam in her eye, "either he is a god or a great fool."

Summer turned to her. "What do you mean?"

"Look at him," Chichi said, talking to Summer as if she were instructing a particularly dull child. "Is he not beautiful? Who but a *loco* would trust his young wife to cross an ocean with a devil like this? It is madness. It is tempting the Fates."

Summer prayed for an earthquake to swallow her.

"You're stretching my tolerance too far," Brent said. "You're pert and insolent, and your extremely foolish remarks have distressed the countess."

Chichi looked conscience-stricken. She ran around the sofa and knelt in front of Summer. "Please forgive my stupid tongue, *señora*. I would cut it out before I would make you cry."

"You should have thought of that before you opened your mouth," Brent said scornfully.

"Please don't send me away. I'll die if you do," Chichi said, taking Summer's hand and pressing it to her cheek.

Summer was recovering. "No, I won't do that. Alonzo might send me Margarita, and I wouldn't like her."

Chichi revived instantly.

"But if you ever do anything like that again, *I'll* throw you out," Brent said, his tone leaving no doubt in Chichi's mind that he would be as good as his word. "But I'll give you a good beating first," he added. "Have you finished the unpacking?"

"Not yet."

"Then you'd better get it done if you don't want to be mopping halls before noon." Chichi rose to her feet and walked quickly toward the bedroom door, but she turned around before going through it. She regarded Brent with a speculative eye. "This earl of yours, milady, what does he look like?"

"I beg your pardon?" Summer was taken off balance by this unexpectedly forthright question.

"Why do you want to know?" Brent demanded, a note of warning in his voice.

"Me, I could not do it," Chichi said and disappeared through the door. A muscle twitched at the corner of Summer's mouth. She looked up at Brent, who was staring after Chichi, his glaring look a mixture of anger and reluctant admiration, and the improbability of the whole situation struck her. She suddenly began to shake with ill-contained amusement.

"That impertinent wench will be strangled to death someday," Brent said with conviction.

"Not by you, I hope," Summer responded. "She thinks you're *so* beautiful," she said imitating Chichi, and then she fell into a chair, laughing.

For a moment Brent looked undecided, then he, too, broke into a grin. "Are you sure you want to keep her?"

"How could I give her up? She's certain to give me the latest gossip on half of Havana before breakfast."

"You shouldn't encourage her."

"I don't think I'll be able to stop her, but at least I won't feel like such a stranger."

"By tomorrow morning you'll be the best known stranger in town. You'll probably be showered with enough invitations to last a month."

The look of a hunted animal came to Summer's eyes.

"You don't have to look like the hangman's at the door," Brent said. "I'll be there to make sure Havana's young gallants don't begin to harbor unsuitable ideas."

"No you won't," Summer declared emphatically. "I may be frightened of meeting so many strangers, but I don't want you standing over me like a jealous lover. That's just the kind of thing that will confirm people's suspicions."

"I didn't say I was going to stand over you."

"But you will. I know you. The men on the ship hardly dared to speak to me for fear you'd murder them, and I can just imagine what you would do if some young and presentable nobleman began to pay me particular attention."

"You can spend your time talking with the other married women."

"Now you're being stupid. You insisted that I play this game by the rules. Well, you're going to have to do the same. Being admired and receiving flattering attention is part of the game. If I go to a ball, I have to dance. If people talk to me, I have to talk back."

"That doesn't mean you have to encourage them."

"I won't, but remember, you promised you'd do nothing to compromise me while we're here."

"I remember," Brent said hastily.

"Then you must treat me just like an ordinary passenger. See that I get where I'm going and *leave me alone*."

"Does that mean you're not going to let me into your bedroom after your maid has gone?"

"It means you're not even to knock on my door after I go to bed. Do you think your comings and goings would remain a secret for one day in a place like this? Do you think that Chichi, or any other maid you find for me, would keep such a juicy bit of gossip to herself?"

"Then what am I supposed to do?"

"Go to sleep like everybody else. What else were you expecting to do? Don't tell me," she said quickly when Brent broke into a leering grin, "I've heard more than enough about your women."

"Then why are you trying to drive me right into their arms?"

"I'm not, but I don't think there's any power this side of

heaven that can keep you *out* of some abandoned female's bed," Summer said furiously.

"If I can't have you . . ."

"I don't suppose it would be of any use to suggest that you go to bed alone. I will."

"But you *want* to go to bed alone. I don't."

"As long as she doesn't bite, you can't keep your hands off any female."

"That sounds like it might be fun. A little bit of danger adds spice," Brent teased.

"Not for me, or any other respectable person."

"What *do* you want?"

"What every woman wants: to have a husband and be respectable. No woman really wants to be a mistress. No matter how notable your lover, you're always on the outside. Since you forced me to come here against my will, it's only fair that you do everything you can to see that I'm not branded a harlot."

"I would wait until everyone was asleep. No one would ever know."

"No!" Summer insisted, stamping her foot. "You agreed to stay away from me as long as we were in Havana."

"I didn't," Brent barked irritably. "I just couldn't face the idea of your fainting dead away when some malicious fool asked you what it was like to be a pirate's mistress. Besides, judging by the commotion you caused on my ship, I'd be spending all my time fighting off Sir Galahads striving to save you from imagined dangers."

"If they were protecting me from you, there wouldn't be anything imaginary about it. You're the most dangerous creature I've met, and that includes that shark," Summer declared sharply. "Your lust and your need for revenge put me in this impossible situation in the first place."

She immediately regretted her words. The tension between them had been lessening, but it worsened again. What was done was done, and no good would be served by bringing it up all over again.

"I'd better go help Chichi if we are to get to Madame Clothilde's on time." Summer wanted to escape his abrassiveness. "Do you have to go back to the ship right away?"

"No. Smith will attend to it for me. I'm going with you to see that you get a decent dress for tonight. That's the least I can do for my good friend Gowan." He emphasized the earl's name.

"Please don't mention him," Summer said. "I never wanted to marry him, but at least it was an honorable bondage."

"And you're blaming me?" Brent's temper was rising.

"Who else can I blame?"

"Why not your father, or Gowan, or both?"

"They were thoughtless and selfish, but neither of them made it impossible for me to hold my head up in decent society. They abused me, but neither stole my honor and left me defenseless."

A knock at the door interrupted them, and Alonzo entered followed by a procession of waiters bearing trays and dishes. The antagonists were forced to bottle up their anger, but neither of them had wanted it to boil over into a full-blown argument anyway. The new understanding they had enjoyed these last few days had led them to a new appreciation of each other. But they knew there were still many unresolved questions, many raw hurts that were far from healed. And their stay in Havana was not likely to help them answer these questions or heal their wounds.

Chapter 20

Madame Clothilde's shop was a tiny, cramped building set between two large structures that seemed intent upon squeezing their neighbor into oblivion. Nothing about the shop, inside or out, showed it to be the most expensive dressmaker's shop outside Europe. It was badly overcrowded, jammed with piles of fabric, boxes, and every kind of accessory that could be bought. Though the furniture was of the latest style and quite expensive, it was likely to be covered by a bolt of cloth or a half-finished dress. Madame Clothilde's great mirror was the envy of all her customers, but as often as not it was blocked from view by a table, a chair, or Madame Clothilde herself.

"Bah! This heat," exclaimed the energetic lady as she bustled out to meet her special customers. "It's not so bad inside. You may have a glass of lemonade, Countess."

"I hope you plan to offer me something less likely to choke me," said Brent.

"I haven't forgotten what you favor, Captain Douglas."

180

Madame Clothilde favored him with a tiny bob of her head and a very broad smile. Summer looked suspiciously at Clothilde's angular middle-aged form, and Brent, following her train of thought, laughed heartily.

"Not this time," he whispered in her ear, as she settled into a chair Madame Clothilde had hastily cleared just before they'd arrived. "Too tough, though not without character."

Summer pretended not to hear him. Then Clothilde engaged her in some leisurely small talk while the refreshments were being served. But once the trays had been taken away, the dressmaker's smile became fixed and she prepared to do business with all the acuity of a successful shopkeeper.

"You are so lovely, Countess, it will be a pleasure to dress you. Will you be staying in Havana for a long time?" she asked hopefully.

"The countess is on her way back to Scotland and doesn't yet know how long she'll be staying in Havana," Brent said. He was anxious to get down to business. "What she needs now is a suitable gown for the governor's reception this evening."

"But that's out of the question." Clothilde was astonished. "No one can provide a gown on such short notice."

"I'm very sorry to have taken up your time. . . ." Summer began to rise, but Brent put a hand on her shoulder and forced her back into the chair.

"The countess needs a gown for tonight," he said in the voice he used to address his crew when they needed to be put in their place, "and it must be spectacular."

"Surely you see that what you ask is preposterous. Even with all my girls working on it, it would take a whole day to make a simple gown; for an extravagant gown, three or four days are needed, perhaps a week."

"Then put them all to work. I'll pay well if I'm pleased."

"But I have just told you it's impossible," Clothilde repeated, exasperated. "Even if I wanted to do it, I could not. I have other customers wanting dresses like that," she said, snapping her fingers in the air like a conjurer. "Everyone is suddenly unable to wait for five minutes."

"Your other customers are your business," Brent stated undiplomatically. "I'm concerned only with the countess."

"Your demand is without reason," Clothilde said angrily. "Cannot the countess postpone her appearance at least a day or two?"

"The countess will be gone before the governor holds his next reception," Brent explained. "You know how displeased he would be if we were to attend Don Ignacio's party or General Arista's ball without first attending his reception."

"And I suppose you expect me to provide at least two more dresses for tomorrow?" Clothilde asked in disbelief. Brent nodded and she threw up her hands in exasperation. "You are mad. I do not conjure dresses out of the air."

"Let's go," Summer begged. "It really isn't important."

"Clothilde could find a dress if she'd stop arguing and use her head," Brent insisted. A hissing noise from the affronted woman prompted Summer to rush on.

"It doesn't really matter what I wear," she said, trying to defuse the tension. "No one will pay any attention to a stranger."

"Look at that face and tell me she's going to be ignored in any room," Brent challenged, turning to Clothilde.

"The countess is very lovely." Clothilde was thinking it would be beneficial to her if Summer first appeared in one of her gowns. With the proper wig and jewels, the young countess would be a sensation. And unless Clothilde was mistaken, everyone would be coming to her shop in the hope that she could again accomplish what she had done for Summer. Two ideas burst into her head simultaneously, and she turned them around carefully while Summer and Brent argued in half-whispers.

"I think I may have found a way out of your dilemma,"

Madame Clothilde finally declared, interrupting a conversation she'd never heard. She hurried away and came back minutes later carrying a huge box. "I'd almost forgotten about this gown. It was ordered some time ago by a lady who couldn't pay for it, and no one else has had the right figure for it." When she opened the box, Summer drew in her breath.

"The young lady was about your size, Countess. If it's close enough, maybe I can have the alterations finished by this evening."

Summer wasn't listening. She was spellbound for before her was the most beautiful gown she had ever seen. It was made of silk of the deepest gold, and on its soft white underdress lilies were embroidered in gold thread.

"If you'll come with me, milady, we can see how it fits," the dressmaker said.

Twenty minutes later the door the two women had gone through opened and out stepped a vision that nearly took Brent's breath away. The gown was even more beautiful than he had imagined, but Clothilde had deftly touched up Summer's face and provided her with an enormous jewel-covered wig.

"There is almost nothing to do but take in the waist, make a tuck or two, and it might have been made for her. What do you think?" Clothilde asked Brent, but the question was superfluous. His reaction was written on his face.

Summer looked expectantly at him. She knew she had never looked lovelier, but she also knew it wouldn't mean a thing unless he thought so. She needed to hear it from his own lips.

Brent's eyes narrowed, and Summer could see his jaw begin to work. She waited nervously, not knowing him well enough to realize he was attempting to disguise his surging passion from Clothilde's prying eyes. Even after all these weeks, Summer's extraordinary beauty jolted him, but it wasn't that which held him immobile. Through the tangle of powerful and confusing emotions warring within him came the recurrent refrain: I must make her my own. No matter how, she *must* be mine.

"I think it'll do just fine," he said absently, "but she can't wear that wig."

"Of course," Clothilde agreed. "I have many more for her to choose from. This one is just for the effect."

"She doesn't need any effects."

Clothilde studied Summer carefully. "Nothing can compete with her complexion and her marvelous figure." She turned to Summer, "You will meet many women tonight whose jealousy will make them cruel, and I can understand them. It is unfair that you should have so much beauty and the rest of us so little."

Summer had never thought of herself as a beauty, but it gave her a twinge of pleasure to hear such flattery directed at her. She was even more delighted by Brent's admiration. She would willingly face a roomful of scowling grandees if he would always look at her with that ravenous expression in his eyes.

"I'll send the gown to the hotel the moment it is finished," Clothilde recalled Brent to his surroundings.

"You'd better send one of your girls along, too," he said. "The countess didn't bring her maid, and the girl the hotel provided seems inexperienced and undependable."

"I have just the girl for you, milady." Clothilde smiled. "Jeanne is quite mannerly, and expert in preparing a lady for a ball."

"What about the other gowns?" Brent asked.

"I've been thinking about them." Clothilde resumed her businesslike manner. "And I think I have found the answer."

"I knew you would as soon as you stopped going on about how impossible everything was," Brent said complacently. "You're a resourceful old bird." Clothilde couldn't decide whether she was more pleased by the compliment to her intelligence or more irritated by his insufferable manner. She thought of the profit she was about to make and decided that it didn't matter.

"I just happen to have a large number of gowns on hand because I'm preparing a trousseau. It will not be required for some time yet, so I will have a chance to replace any gowns the countess is able to use."

"But I don't look at all Spanish," Summer protested.

"The young lady in question was educated in Europe and has demanded all of the most fashionable gowns. She will look like a chicken dressed in the feathers of a bird of paradise. Quite sad, really." Clothilde shuddered. "It will be a relief to know that the countess will wear my creations. They are very lovely, really some of my best work."

"Can they be ready by tomorrow?" Brent asked.

"Not everything, of course, but if you will let me have a list of your engagements, I will see that alterations are made on gowns as they are required."

"Maybe Jeanne can serve as a go-between," Summer suggested. Knowing that Brent thought her ravishing had changed her whole outlook on their stay in Havana. Meeting and being admired by complete strangers no longer frightened her. She even looked forward to it.

Clothilde agreed. "That's an excellent idea. She will also know of anything that needs attention, or if madame has need of anything to complete her toilette."

"Box up whatever she needs and send it to the hotel," said Brent. "I want no effort spared in making sure the countess is the most beautiful woman there tonight."

Clothilde looked at Summer, resplendent in the sumptuous gown and glowing with youthful innocence and beauty. "I don't think there will be any difficulty with that," she said. "Now if milady will come with me, I must see to the changes that have to be made."

"If you're going to be forever trying on dresses, I'm going back to the ship," Brent declared. "I'll send young Lane to escort you to the hotel."

"I can have one of my girls accompany the countess if you like," Clothilde offered.

"No, I'd rather have one of my own men bring her. I'll be back in time to dine."

The warm excitement that had blossomed in Summer upon Brent's admiration began to fade at his departure. Now the dress didn't seem quite so lovely, and the room was hot and stuffy. She didn't want to spend the whole afternoon having pins stuck in her and being pushed, pulled, and tugged at by dozens of hands. She'd much rather be back on the ship in her thin muslins, the cool breezes on her face and her long hair tossing in the wind. She turned to Madame Clothilde, a definite pout on her ruby lips.

Clothilde had dealt with too many women for Summer's swift change of mood to pose a mystery, but a possible affair between Brent and the countess was none of her business. It did make her wonder whether she should reconsider her plans, however. She knew of at least three women who considered Brent their own and who would not readily accept another candidate for his favors. Such rivalries could be bitter ones, and Clothilde had every intention of turning them to her advantage. If Summer was going to be at the center of the storm, then the clothes she wore would receive particular notice. Clothilde made up her mind that they would be the finest she had ever designed. Everybody else could wait. At this moment nothing was as important as turning Summer out in gown after gown guaranteed to make her clothes second only to her beauty as a topic of conversation.

Chapter 21

"Madame is a real pleasure to work for," Jeanne told Summer, remembering the impatient and ungrateful young women that had driven her to give up being a personal maid and to work for Madame Clothilde. Summer had sat through having her hair dressed and her face delicately tinted without voicing a single protest. "It will only take a minute more," Jeanne promised as she pinned the last of the flowers in Summer's hair.

"The *señora* looks so beautiful," Chichi sighed, repeating her litany of the last hour. "Every man in Havana will be driven wild at the sight of you. They will all want to make love to you."

"You know that's a very improper way to speak to the countess, Chichi," Jeanne sternly reprimanded her. "Hand me those pins, and try to remember that you're only a maid." Chichi hated being scolded. She flounced away to find the required pins, then slapped them down within Jeanne's reach. But her ill humor only lasted a few minutes; she could hardly have been more excited if she had been going to the reception herself.

"Are you sure I look presentable?" Summer asked nervously, seeking reassurance as she thought of the many strangers she must face. "I must seem attractive."

"Attractive!" exclaimed Chichi incredulously. "The *señora* is *beautiful*, even more beautiful than the captain."

"That is high praise indeed." Summer relaxed a bit. "But don't let the captain hear you. He might become jealous."

"The captain frightens me a little," Chichi said, indulging in a pleasurable shiver. "The *señora* must have great courage. Maybe if he likes you tonight, he will keep you for himself." Summer stiffened.

"How many times do you have to be told to watch your tongue?" Jeanne admonished.

"A thousand pardons, *señora*, but the Captain looks at me as though he would like to make me disappear."

"He doesn't think you're a proper maid," Summer explained.

"But I am a wonderful maid," Chichi declared indignantly.

"You are not," Jeanne stated uncompromisingly. "You are flighty, and you talk when you should be working. If you don't learn to control your tongue, you'll be cleaning rooms for the rest of your life."

Chichi puffed up, ready to defend herself, but Summer intervened. "Do try to watch what you say, Chichi. If you aren't more careful, Captain Douglas is going to make Alonzo give me someone else. You really do come out with the most shocking things."

The vivacious girl crumpled into a demoralized little flower. "I'm sorry, *señora*," she whimpered dolefully.

"And don't start to cry." Summer spoke quickly. "I might cry too, and that would ruin Jeanne's work. The captain would be in a awful temper if he had to wait while Jeanne did it over again."

"The captain is not patient with you?" Chichi asked, wiping her eyes.

"Not in the least," said Summer, underscoring her words with a grimace.

Chichi's sadness evaporated, and her big black eyes began to sparkle with curiosity. Her romantic soul sensed that something lay behind Summer's words, and she regarded her mistress very much as a cat would regard a mouse hole.

"Don't you like the captain, *señora?*" she asked.

"The captain is a friend of my husband," Summer said with deliberate calm. It was essential that *no one*, especially a chatterbox like Chichi, suspect her real feeling for Brent. "He takes very good care of me, but he is used to commanding men and is unaccustomed to the ways of women."

"But that's impossible," protested Chichi breathlessly. "All of Havana speaks of his success with the ladies."

"If you don't watch what you say," snapped Summer, turning on the maid with a tigerlike pounce, "*I'm* going to have Alonzo send María to me *tonight!*" As Chichi quailed before her sudden fury, Summer rose to her feet.

"Am I finished? Am I ready to receive the captain?"

"Madame is ready to meet anyone," Jeanne assured her. "There won't be a more beautiful woman present tonight. You will break hearts."

Summer was greatly heartened by that thought. "I wouldn't want to do that, but it's nice to know that I will be presentable. I want to thank you both," she said to Jeanne and Chichi. "If I'm a success, I will owe it to you and Madame Clothilde."

"Oh, *Dios!*" Chichi exclaimed, unable to remain quiet any longer. "Are you blind? You would stop carriages in the street if you wore rags."

"She's right, *señora*, even though she shouldn't have said it," Jeanne said.

"Don't say another word," Summer commanded, "or I'll

burst into tears. Convey my thanks to Madame Clothilde for sparing you. And, Chichi, please wait up for me. I can't possibly undress myself."

"*Muy bien*, señora!" Chichi laughed. "I couldn't sleep a wink without knowing all about the party."

"You're an impossible girl," Summer chided, "but I'm glad I have you. Now open the door. I can't wait to see the captain's face when he sees my wig."

Summer sat without moving, her back ramrod straight, her eyes staring directly ahead. She had waited for two hours and still Brent had not come to her. She knew he wasn't going to; she had known it for some time, but she still couldn't admit it to herself. It was easier to search for excuses for his lateness than to admit that he cared so little that he had forgotten her.

She tried not to let herself think of the implications of his absence, but doubts and worries assailed her. She feared that she was unimportant to him now that he was back on his old hunting ground. Why should he restrict himself to the penniless daughter of a small plantation owner when he could attract the heavily dowered daughters of powerful, aristocratic Spanish families? What could she offer him to shift the balance in her favor? She had already given him her innocence and her love, but apparently that wasn't enough.

Chichi's words kept coming back to taunt her. How could she, an inexperienced novice, hope to hold a man whose prowess in the bedroom was on the tongues of everyone in Havana? Hadn't he repeatedly teased her about his women? Even Smith had tried to warn her. Why hadn't she listened to them instead of being so satisfied with her new gown and her flower-bedecked wig that she had completely forgotten about everything else?

Well, she was paying for it now. For the last hour jealousy had been eating away at her like hot acid. She struggled to curb her demon of resentment, to banish all thought of the partners who might be filling his arms. She tried to look at things less emotionally, but it was a futile task. She kept telling herself that he was only staying away from her because she had made him promise to do so. She tried to make herself believe that, but a headache was all she got for her pains.

"It's ridiculous to be sitting around dressed like this," she finally said aloud. Rising to her feet, she rang for Chichi. "I'm sure he'll be here first thing tomorrow with a ready explanation tripping off his tongue, but staying up won't bring the morning any quicker. I'm going to bed."

"We're not talking about your duties on the ship," Summer said furiously to Brent. "I realize they must come before me or a reception. We're talking about your abandoning me to go roistering about with your women. Don't expect me to believe that you were tied up with your business deals all night. Your carriage was seen leaving the hotel a little after midnight."

Summer shuddered when she recalled the embarrassment of explaining to Chichi why she had not attended the governor's reception after taking over an hour to get dressed. She had barely slept at all, she still had a throbbing headache, and her mood had not been improved by Chichi's chatty report over her morning cocoa that the captain had been seen in the company of a particularly beautiful and notorious marquise.

Brent was not accustomed to being raked over the coals by anyone, but particularly not by a female. *Any* female! "You can't expect me to give up all my pleasures," he exploded. "I have to have something to do with my time if I'm to stay out of your bed. Besides, nothing can protect your reputation better than to have it publicly known that I'm occupying myself in another quarter."

Summer couldn't tell him, for she hadn't even admitted to

herself, that she didn't want to give up having him in her bed. When she had demanded that he protect her reputation by keeping away from her, she'd never dreamed that she would have to watch him pursue another female, or that his interest in someone else would cause her such great agony. She'd told herself for so long that she didn't want his attentions that she had come to believe it. It was quite a shock to discover the opposite was true.

"Can't you ever think of anything else?" she demanded hopelessly.

"I think about you all the time, but I'll go crazy if I don't have something to do besides sit around torturing myself in thinking about your loveliness and the nights we spent making love. Why should I neglect all those lovely ladies just waiting to throw themselves into my arms?"

"You'll stop at nothing to satisfy your bestial cravings, will you?" Summer's tone was scornful, but she was torn between happiness at knowing that Brent still wanted her and agony that he would put someone else in her place.

"Oh, I stop at quite a few. I like my women soft and yielding," Brent crooned in her ear.

"That never stopped you from plaguing me constantly," Summer pointed out, aware that she was exposing her jealousy, but unable to stop doing so.

"You were the only woman at hand, so I made do with what I had."

"You worthless brute." Summer's raw nerves were further irritated by his needless cruelty.

"Not worthless," Brent needled. "I'm very useful in certain ways."

"A person only has value as he is desired," retorted Summer from between clenched teeth.

Brent laughed so heartily that Summer grew even more angry. "I suppose you think that has put me in my place, but I warn you it has put me on my mettle instead. Before the month is out, my lovely countess, you're going to want me."

"Never!"

"And I'm going to make you admit it," he declared with sudden intensity.

"Impossible!"

"I'm going to make you beg me never to let you go, to make love to you until we grow exhausted from trying."

"I'd die first," Summer swore.

"You'll finally learn what love really is, and realize that your life would be much poorer without it."

"I long to be taught that lesson," she flung at him, almost in tears, "but I'll never learn it from you. That is one thing you can't force me to do."

"Don't bet anything you value against it."

"I have nothing of value left," Summer said, utterly dejected. "You and my father have seen to that."

Chapter 22

"Madame will have to hold still, or I may have to do it all over again," cautioned Jeanne as she applied the faintest touch of rouge to Summer's cheeks.

"I don't want to look like a courtesan," Summer said pettishly. She had seen Brent just twice in the last four days and her mood was very brittle.

"*Señora*, you could never look like anything but a lady," Chichi assured her with unbounded enthusiasm.

"That's blind favoritism speaking," Summer said with a bleak smile. She had wrung from Brent a promise to accompany her to this affair and she was determined to look her best.

"Don't frown," Jeanne warned. Summer schooled her face to impassivity, but her thoughts remained in disarray.

Brent was almost never at the hotel during the day or the evening, but his carriage was seen to leave it late every night. Several times Summer was so desperate to know where he went, she had almost sent Chichi to find out, but each time she had held back, afraid of what she might learn. She had done her best to think of something else, *anything* other than Brent. However, she had little to do except dress and eat and await this evening of socialization. Now she was ready so there was nothing to do but wait.

"I'm finished, madame." Jeanne put away her pots and brushes.

Summer stared closely at her image, and for the moment Brent was forgotten. She still found it difficult to believe that the sophisticated, modish woman who stared back at her could be herself. Jeanne had done such a superb job it was almost impossible to tell she wore rouge, but her luminous eyes and luscious lips were highlighted to give her face a whole new character. She still looked like Summer Ashton, but she appeared to have a completely different personality. Her off-the-shoulder gown bared much of her breast, for it was designed to make the most of her physical allure without compromising her position.

"I look like the marquise," Summer said aloud, stunned to find that she looked as worldly as the dazzling Spanish beauty whose name was being coupled with Brent's more and more frequently.

"You are more beautiful than the marquise," Jeanne said firmly.

"Don't be absurd. I hear someone in the salon," Summer announced, suddenly forgetting everything else. "It must be the captain."

"You can ask *him*," suggested Chichi.

"I'd rather die!" Summer exclaimed. "And if you dare to open your mouth, you outrageous child, I'll choke you."

But when Summer entered the salon she found Lane, rather than Brent, waiting for her. Her first thought was that something had happened to Brent, but when Lane stood gaping at her rather than hurrying into an explanation she knew Brent wasn't coming. He had spurned her company once again. He hadn't completely forgotten her because he had sent Lane to take his place, but Summer would have preferred that he had sent no one at all. For a brief moment she was so heartsick she thought she would break down right in front of Lane and Chichi. What could this be but a clear message that the intimacy they had shared on the ship was over!

Summer had feared that this day would come, and she'd wondered how she would be able to endure it. Now she knew: she felt as though she had just died. Suddenly she was a hollow shell, completely empty inside. She could feel the loss, but not the pain. Unable to move, to speak, even to faint, she stood helplessly waiting for the shock wave to hit, knowing that it would almost be a relief when it came.

Lane hadn't seen Summer since she'd left the ship, and he was so stunned by her beauty that he didn't notice she looked like a statue.

"Milady, is that *really* you?" he asked, unable to believe the evidence of his own eyes.

"Of course it is the *señora*," answered Chichi, dancing about delightedly. "How do you like the countess?" she asked, bubbling with excitement. "Aha!" she exclaimed happily when she received no answer. "See *señora*, you have made him speechless."

"You're like a vision," Lane declared.

"I told you so, *señora*, I told you how it would be," Chichi said, gleefully jumping up and down like foam on a windy sea.

"Has anything happened to the captain?" Summer finally asked. It felt odd to hear herself speak. Her voice didn't seem to come from her own lips.

"The captain is fine," Lane answered, still too astounded to notice her shocked state. "You look so different I wasn't sure it was you."

"But where is he? He promised he wouldn't be late." Summer's words were spoken in a hollow, uninflected voice, and, upon hearing them, Lane noted her stupefied expression.

"The captain sends his apologies," he said, reciting the message he'd memorized, "but the press of business makes it impossible for him to accompany you this evening. I am to go in his place."

Summer felt completely deflated, utterly without value; she didn't really want to attend this or any other party. How could she smile and pretend to be gay when her hopes were in ruins? Even though she had told herself for weeks that this day would come and that she had no one to blame but herself, it was cruel to expect her to parade before the curious and cynical eyes of Havana's aristocracy on the heels of such a rejection. Summer was about to refuse to accompany Lane, but she changed her mind almost at once, anger and pride coming to her rescue.

Brent had used her, had shown a callous disregard for her feelings; there was nothing she could do about that. She had been his captive, physically incapable of holding him off; but she would *not* give him the satisfaction of knowing that she was suffering greater agony than she ever thought possible. She was a countess, and, if he wanted her to play that role, then she would do so. And she hoped Gowan *did* come after her. If she was lucky some fatal fever would carry her off before she reached Scotland; then Brent Douglas wouldn't have the satisfaction of knowing that she loved him and longed to feel his strong arms around her.

Summer told herself she didn't care if he did go to the affair—it wouldn't matter one wit if that predatory marquise was on his arm—she would show him *and* everyone else that the Countess of Heatherstone languished because of no one, especially not a pirate captain.

But after Summer had been socializing for two hours she wished she hadn't left the hotel. She was heartily tired of feeding fish, exploring grottos, and admiring exotic plants;

her new shoes pinched and her patience and good humor were at an end. Trying to remember names got on her nerves, but she continued to smile, all the while cursing Brent under her breath.

Finally, unable to stand it another minute, she sent her youthful escort to find her something to drink and wandered off to a quiet corner. She hoped he would not find her for several minutes; it was rude, but she didn't care. She needed to calm her nerves so she might stop looking for Brent at every turn, listening for his voice. He's with the marquise, she told herself, and you might as well get used to that fact. Saying he was protecting your reputation was just an excuse to be with some black-eyed witch. That way he didn't have to tell you he was weary of you; you could figure it out for yourself.

"You don't seem to be enjoying yourself." The voice came from behind the stone bench where she was seated; Summer started and turned sharply. She found herself looking into the face of a dark young man. It had a Spanish cast, and his black eyes twinkled merrily. He was tall and his smile was quite contagious. "Have you lost your way? You can't have been abandoned."

"I haven't been so fortunate. I'm just resting while my escort goes for something to drink."

"And I thought you were trying to escape a procession of young men too tongue-tied to put together a single intelligent sentence." He laughed.

"Well, yes," Summer confessed. "You've been spying on me and that's not nice."

"Not spying exactly, but I have been watching you."

"Then you know I've seen every part of the garden at least twice. It's really quite lovely, but it's impossible to admire it for a third time in the same day."

"I should think so." He nodded. "I'm surprised you didn't try to escape altogether. May I join you, or have you foresworn all human companionship?"

"I don't think you should," Summer replied. "I don't know you, and it's quite improper for me to be sitting with a perfect stranger in a retired part of the garden."

"That's easy to remedy," he said, promptly executing a formal bow. "*Señora*, I would like to introduce Gonsalvo de Aguilar, beloved only son of Vincente and Doña Isabella de Aguilar," he said in a perfect imitation of her host's voice and manner. "He is a handsome youth of upstanding habits, exemplary character, and the heir to a great fortune." Summer was shocked, but she burst into a ripple of laughter.

"And he is extremely modest."

"But I would never say such things about myself," Gonsalvo said, using his own voice now. "It would be much too impolite."

"But it's all right if someone else says them for you?"

"Of course. Who can argue with the Baron de la Rocha? Besides, he is a great admirer of my family and believes I shall become as fine a man as my father."

"Will you?" she asked, wondering what he would say next.

"His life has been but a prelude to the wonders I shall accomplish," her companion replied, seating himself next to her with a smile that was almost too broad to be genuine. "I shall perform such amazing feats that all of Spain will stand dumbfounded. The King himself will seek to reward me."

"And of course you will tell him of your deeds, just in case he happens to miss one or two?"

"Naturally. It is the duty of all loyal subjects to see that the King is well informed."

"But could such a hero as yourself remain the subject of a mere King?"

As Gonsalvo paused and wrinkled his brow in deep thought, Summer struggled to suppress a giggle.

"I cannot say," he finally replied gravely. "It would be extremely difficult to bend my knee to one so inferior, but as I do not have the royal blood in me, I cannot but see that I should have to accept him in the end."

"It would be a sacrifice," Summer stated in an unsteady voice.

"Yes," he responded, "but I should be quite ennobled by it." He stared straight before him as though concentrating on a beatific vision. Summer's laughter bubbled up.

"Do you always talk such perfect nonsense to strangers?" she asked as she moved a little away from him.

"Not unless they have a crease between their eyes, and are frowning as though they have lost their last friend."

"How unhandsome of you to describe me in such unflattering terms," Summer protested.

"But it was a beautiful crease and an entrancing frown," he added hastily.

"There is no such thing as a beautiful wrinkle," declared Summer. "A freckle is hardly a worse tragedy."

"As you have neither, you may continue to entrance me with the loveliness of your smile and the delicious sound of your laughter."

"You do know how to say pretty things." Summer favored him with a rueful smile. "I suppose you have half the girls in Havana hanging on your every word."

"All of them," he stated confidently. "Could you expect less?"

"Perhaps not." Summer admitted to herself that he was quite handsome and very charming. "But if you carry on like this I'm surprised that any mother would let her daughter come near you."

"But my father is very, very rich," he added.

"Ah," she said, a twinkle in her eyes. "I'm sure that accounts for it."

"Cruel!" he protested in mock despair as he slid to his knees before her with practiced ease. "Can you look upon these features I modestly claim as my own and dare to deny their hypnotizing effect on all beholders?"

"Quite easily," she answered promptly.

"Pitiless maiden," he groaned. "You have a heart of ice. I shall make it my task to melt it."

"Do get up and stop acting like a buffoon," begged Summer. She was beginning to feel uncomfortable. "I'm not a maiden, and if any of these hateful, disapproving women were to see us they would start the most alarming rumors."

"You're far too beautiful for the women to like you." Gonsalvo seated himself beside her. "You will have to resign yourself to being an outcast among your own sex, like the marquise."

"Don't you dare speak my name in the same breath with that *siren's!*" Summer commanded, trembling with suppressed anger. Her lighthearted mood was totally vanquished.

"When one thinks of the marquise, one also thinks of you, one beautiful thought giving birth to another," Gonsalvo explained with a smile. "She is famed for her thoughtless cruelty while you have earned a reputation for gracious modesty. Already the young caballeros are divided as to who is more beautiful. Many hold with the marquise because of her lush sensuality, but her adherents are steadily being whittled down by your spectacular figure and haunting loveliness."

"It is most improper for you to talk to me like this." It frightened Summer to learn that she could be the focus of any kind of controversy.

"Don't you want to know what people are saying?" Gonsalvo was undeterred by her criticism.

"No!" she replied vehemently.

"Not even if it's in your favor?"

"Not even then," Summer insisted, but not so firmly.

"You're right," Gonsalvo said, hanging his head in pretended chagrin. "I don't know what could have caused me to behave with such a lack of taste."

"You should be ashamed of yourself," scolded Summer eyeing him skeptically.

"I am," Gonsalvo professed with supposed sincerity.

"No you're not," Summer said calmly. "You're laughing at me, and don't mean a word you've said. You're just about the most brazen man I've ever met."

"I wish that were true." Gonsalvo smiled at her with a genuinely open look that melted her ire. "But since Captain Douglas's reputation for audacity is known throughout the Caribbean, I really doubt that it can be." Summer's heart lurched, and she quickly looked away to hide the grimace of pain she could not suppress.

"It is true that the captain is a bold man," she said, choosing her words carefully, "but I don't imagine that you're any different in your own way."

"I'm quite flattered to be held the captain's equal, Countess, but I know him well, and I'm compelled to admit that I have yet to discover his like." Gonsalvo's mocking eyes watched Summer closely, but she did not look up. Her heart ached so agonizingly, she wondered if she would be able to go on with the conversation.

"The captain is not without faults for all his renown." Her voice threatened to break.

"You tell me the captain's faults," Gonsalvo instantly was transformed into a conspiratorial child, "and I'll tell you everything I know about the marquise."

"I would never do anything so ill-mannered," she said, choking on the words. She could never tell anyone what Brent had done to her; it was locked inside her forever.

"But it would be so much fun. And it's not as though I'm a stranger. I've known the captain for quite some time; I've even done business with him. He asked me to keep an eye on you tonight." When Summer looked at him sharply, Gonsalvo added, "Oh, just to see that you didn't come to any harm."

"If you know the captain that well, you don't need any information from me."

"Not even one little bit of gossip?" he begged.

"No."

"Then I guess I'll have to bribe you."

"You can't." Summer was indignant.

"Are you sure?" he asked, for all the world as though he were offering her a second serving of dessert.

"Absolutely."

"That's too bad. I was sure you would like to meet my sister and spend the day on our plantation. You could go horseback riding, take a boat trip along the river, or spend the afternoon in idleness under the mahogany trees, enjoying the cool breezes and a delicious drink."

"That's a cruel temptation," said Summer.

"I never would have told you if I'd thought you could be tempted," he replied with feigned innocence.

"You told me because you knew I wouldn't be able to resist. Do you really have a sister?"

"I do, and my parents would be delighted to welcome you to Casa Carvalho. I will go find her right now, and then you can come visit us tomorrow."

"That's too soon," said Summer, flustered by the unexpectedly swift turn of the conversation. "I'm not sure what my immediate plans are."

"How long will you stay in Havana?"

"I don't really know," she muttered uncomfortably. "I suppose that depends on how long it takes Captain Douglas to dispose of his cargo. A few weeks maybe?" she said questioningly, expecting him to know more about the sale of cargo than she did.

"My sister and parents will be leaving in ten days and will be gone for quite some time."

"I'm sure I will have returned to Scotland before they come back." Summer's disappointment was evident.

"Are your days all taken up?"

"No"

"Could we arrange an afternoon visit?"

"I suppose so. In fact, there's nothing to keep me from it." If Brent was deputizing his friend to watch her, then why shouldn't she visit him? she asked herself angrily. After all, doing so would make it easier for Gonsalvo to keep an eye on her.

"Splendid. How about the end of the week?"

"Fine."

"I'll bring my sister to see you as soon as I can find her," Gonsalvo said. "My parents have already met you, and will look forward to seeing you again."

"Are you sure they will welcome me?" she asked, suddenly serious. "You aren't just saying that to get me to visit, are you?"

"Yes to both of your questions," he replied with a disarming smile. "My parents have already commented on your graciousness and dignity, and I know Anita would love you. She has already asked me to introduce her." Summer remembered the coldly formal couple she had met several nights before and doubted that Gonsalvo was sticking too closely to the truth, but she decided not to concern herself with that. The chance to get out of Havana, away from Brent and the marquise for even a few hours, was too inviting to resist. As long as she had been invited, she would go.

"It will also give me a chance to talk to you without being interrupted by youthful swains bearing drinks." Gonsalvo pointed to a young man who was looking for her amid the shrubbery.

"You are totally without conscience." Summer laughed. "And I probably shouldn't accept your invitation at all."

"But I haven't invited you. My parents will invite you, and you will be visiting my sister."

"I'm not quite sure I trust you, but I think I will come anyway—only if your sister will be present."

"She'll be there. And as a sign of my good intentions I'm going to disappear before your young man comes back." The hot and baffled swain had finally caught sight of Summer and was hastening to her side.

"Thereby investing a chance meeting with all the trappings of an illicit assignation," Summer informed him.

"There's no satisfying you," he complained. "Whatever I do, you want something else."

"Isn't that the way of all accredited beauties?" she asked ingenuously. "I was just trying to follow Roussillon's example."

"Spare me," he said without humor. "We have the original. A copy is totally unnecessary."

"Unkind." Summer was secretly pleased to find that at least one of her rivals was not so universally admired as she had supposed. "But I promise to behave as I ought. Now my sober escort draws near so you must go away. Your irreverent tongue is liable to cause me to say something that will disgrace me with the whole city."

"Nothing could do that."

"Well, I have no desire to tempt Fate too far. You must disappear at once."

"Your servant, Countess," he declared, and disappeared into the shrubbery.

Chapter 23

"Did the *señora* enjoy the evening?" Chichi asked as she helped Summer out of her light cloak.

"Not very much," Summer replied, wilting onto the sofa. She was getting used to accepting invitations on her own, but she had never given up hope that one evening Brent would suddenly appear and would go with her.

"How could you not enjoy wearing such beautiful clothes and meeting such grand people?" Chichi could not believe that possible.

"Can't you think of anything except social affairs, clothing, and men?" Why should Chichi be any different from herself? She could never think of anybody except Brent.

"What else is there to think about?" Chichi asked in wide-eyed wonder.

"Lots of things." Summer sighed. "But I can see it would be a waste of breath to point them out."

"Did the *señora* have lots of suitors?"

"Yes, you abominable girl. I had every man in the place at

my feet begging for a dance and swearing he would cut his throat if I didn't give him the flowers from my hair."

"Oh, *señora*," Chichi was ecstatic, "I knew you would slay them with your beauty."

"Hush, you absurd child. Nothing like that really happened." Summer went to the dressing table. "I'm only making fun of you."

"Men didn't ask you for dances?" Chichi asked, shocked.

"Well, yes, they did."

"And they didn't admire you?"

"Yes. At least, they said they did."

"And didn't you meet lots of rich and important people?" the girl asked, almost dancing around the room.

"Of course."

"Then you *did* have a good time." Chichi was delighted at having proven that Summer had enjoyed herself.

"You'd better hurry and help me get undressed, or I'll never get to bed," Summer chided. "Then I'll look like such a hag everyone will say that the countess is a witch and the sooner Captain Douglas takes her back to Scotland, the better." There were times when Summer almost hoped that Brent would take her to Scotland. At least they would be alone at sea, and maybe they could rekindle what they had felt for each other before reaching Havana.

"No one would dare to say such a cruel and stupid thing," Chichi stated categorically as she helped Summer out of her gown. "I know you were the most beautiful woman there tonight."

"But I wasn't. There were many beautiful women present."

"And who was as beautiful as the *señora*?" Chichi asked skeptically.

"Several ladies."

"Name just one," the little maid challenged.

"Roussillon de Cabrera," said Summer.

"Bah!" said Chichi scornfully. "She is lovely, but more mean-spirited than María."

"How do you know?"

"I have seen her."

"Where?"

"Here, at the hotel. Señorita de Cabrera does not wish to behave like a nice Spanish girl. She sometimes goes where another would not dare."

"She's old enough to know how to conduct herself."

"She's too old," sniffed Chichi with all the bravado of a sixteen-year-old. "She couldn't find anyone to suit her until she met the captain, but even with all her money, she is a shrew."

"How do you know this?" Summer demanded. "I will not have you telling me idle gossip."

"Oh no, *señora,* I would not tell you lies. The *señorita* cannot keep a maid. Havana is full of girls who tell of her selfishness."

"She seemed to be doing a lot of thinking about someone else this evening," Summer said savagely.

Chichi's tinkling laughter erupted and all seriousness faded from her face. "She thinks about the captain all the time."

"I'm tired of talking about her," Summer said petulantly. She twisted away from Chichi. "Besides there was a marquise there who was much more beautiful than Señorita de Cabrera."

"Señora Tragetto was there?" asked Chichi awestruck. "Did you talk with her?"

"Just a few words," Summer was at a loss to account for Chichi's look of stupefaction.

"What is she like? Is her skin as white as milk? Do the flames in her eyes really enslave all men? Is she really a witch?" Chichi asked breathlessly.

"I'm sure she's not a witch." Summer stood up to rid herself of her corset and petticoat. "But it is true that men flock around her." She wouldn't care if the whole world threw it-self at the marquise's feet just as long as Brent did not.

"Does she make men helpless? Do they fight just to hold her fan?" Chichi begged, enthralled.

"Where did you ever hear such utter nonsense?" Summer was poised between amusement at Chichi's gullibility and irri-tation at how close the girl's description approached the truth.

"They say that when she places a man under her spell, he can't break away."

"She is certainly very beautiful."

"It is said that she consumes men and they kill themselves when she casts them aside."

"The marquise is a very lovely woman and men are strongly attracted to her, but if you must know, I had more crowding around me than the marquise and Roussillon to-gether." Summer was exasperated, but Chichi skipped about the room in childish delight and the absurdity of the girl's re-action caused Summer's brief spurt of temper to die. Her boast now seemed cheap and tawdry.

"I shouldn't have said anything. You will oblige me by for-getting every word I said."

"Of course, *señora*, I have forgotten it already," Chichi said, her eyes twinkling.

"You're lying." Summer slipped her arms into her robe and then sat down so Chichi could comb out her hair. "You'll remember every foolish thing I've said and tell María just as soon as I've gone to bed."

"No, *señora*," insisted Chichi, abashed to have her plans so exactly anticipated.

"Don't bother to deny it," said Summer severely. "If you're going to be my maid, you've got to learn loyalty and discre-tion. That means you aren't at liberty to run about the hotel repeating every unwise word I utter."

"Of course, *señora*," the girl said meekly.

"And don't you 'of course, *señora*' me. Repeat one word

and I'll tell the captain. He will see that Alonzo dismisses you from the hotel."

Chichi was completely cowed by this threat. It wasn't easy to find good jobs in Havana. "I won't say a word, I swear. I love you, *señora*. I wouldn't do anything you didn't like." Her face puckered up.

"Now don't start crying. You haven't known me long enough to love me, but I do like you rather well and I would hate to have to get used to María."

"I'd die before I'd give up my place to María," Chichi declared dramatically.

Summer smiled conspiratorially at Chichi. "If you're going to help me outshine the local beauties, you can't be giving away all my secrets, can you?" Chichi's head bounced up and little imps began to dance in her smiling eyes.

"*Señora*, Jeanne and I will slave until you're the most beautiful woman in all the world."

"There's no point in trying for the impossible," Summer said dryly. "I'll settle for the general's ball."

"But that is a certainty," Chichi said elated. "With Madame Clothilde's gowns and Jeanne and me to dress you, no one can match you."

"Don't I get some of the credit?"

"Of course, and so does the captain."

"The captain? How can you give him credit for what I look like?" Why did everyone insist upon talking about Brent when the mere sound of his name caused her whole body to tremble.

"Just to be seen in the captain's company is a great distinction," said Chichi. "Everyone knows he sees only the most beautiful women."

"Let me assure you that he is not *seeing* me," rasped Summer, "and I intend to see that no one even thinks he is."

"I didn't mean anything improper," Chichi assured her, "though I'm sure no one would blame you if you did."

"Chichi!" Summer exclaimed.

"He's such a beautiful man," Chichi rhapsodized, "and his eyes shine with such a wicked gleam."

"I suppose it is his *wicked gleam* that attracts so many women to his side." Summer's tone was scathing. "It is wonderful that in this hot, steaming climate, his torrid energy can refresh and invigorate so many languishing females."

"The *señora* is angry with Captain Douglas?"

"I'm almost always angry with the captain," Summer replied. "He is the most difficult man I've met."

"And the most handsome," Chichi added.

"*And* the most handsome," Summer agreed. "But he is *not* the greatest gentleman."

"But he is so handsome it doesn't matter." Chichi became so enraptured she pulled Summer's hair quite sharply. "Oh I'm so sorry, *señora,*" she said contritely when Summer called her to order.

"Never mind." Summer's anger quickly subsided. "It's just one more thing I can blame on the captain."

"The *señora* forgives me?"

"Only if you promise not to say another word about the captain. Now hurry and go to bed. I don't want you nodding over your work tomorrow. We have a lot to do."

"I never would!" Chichi was indignant.

"You won't be able to avoid it if you don't get some sleep. This dratted affair is being held in the afternoon, and I won't be able to hide a single wrinkle."

"You don't have any wrinkles."

"I'll have crow's feet if I stay up any longer. I'm so tired I could fall down right where I stand. I'd wager I'm more exhausted than the captain and he's been working all day."

"Not all of it. He left here not an hour ago."

Summer stopped in her tracks. "What do you mean?" Brent *had* to have been working. The marquise had been at the party.

211

Chichi wasn't watching Summer and her reply was off-handed. "He came in a great hurry after you were gone and ordered his carriage to wait for him. He's probably gone to see his mistress." Summer felt blood begin to pound in her temples.

"Whatever the captain does is no concern of mine," she said angrily. "It wouldn't matter to me if he had a hundred mistresses." She immediately regretted this untruthful boast.

"Not even Captain Douglas could please that many." Chichi giggled as she picked up the countess's clothes and scampered off to the dressing room.

"The rutting beast." Summer stomped over to her bed, ripped off her dressing gown, and threw herself onto a cool sheet. "I don't care if he never comes back," she said out loud. "He's nothing but a brute, and I never want to see him again." She dabbed angrily at her streaming eyes with the corner of the pillow, but that didn't stop her tears. Fatigue and jealousy were too much for her, and she cried her frustrations and loneliness into her pillow.

"You're a great fool," she told herself after she had finally dried her eyes. "You're going to have to make up your mind what you want. You can't drive the man away and then expect him to remain at your side. You'll just have to put him out of your mind." She forced herself to think of all the new people she had met, but Brent's face kept intruding on her thoughts and before long she gave up.

"If you will be such a great bobby," she said in disgust, "then go ahead and tease yourself with him, but don't expect any sympathy from me."

Chapter 24

Summer saw very little of Brent during the days that followed. He attended to business and at night he went elsewhere. Bit by bit she got used to being alone.

She was positive that Brent went to see the marquise, or some other wanton, as soon as he left the hotel, and every night she wrestled with visions of what must be happening in some unknown bedchamber. Her stomach churned when she thought of Brent holding another woman in his arms, of jet black hair falling over his shoulders and crimson lips fastened hungrily to his. Sometimes it was nearly dawn before she fell into a fitful sleep.

Even during her waking hours, Brent's mistresses were rarely out of Summer's thoughts. Every time she was introduced to another attractive woman, a persistent question bedeviled her: "Is she his lover too?" This constant suspicion kept Summer's nerves on edge. As a result her temper was in shreds, and her pleasure in Havana was nonexistent.

Meanwhile, her acquaintance with Gonsalvo's family had progressed. His parents' acceptance of her was genuine, and she had liked his sister instantly. Anita was pretty in a modest way, but she didn't feel threatened by Summer's transcendent loveliness. Summer looked forward to the time she spent with Anita. To have a friend of almost her own age who was neither competitive nor jealous was a pleasure.

She wasn't as happy in Gonsalvo's company. True, he was a charming rogue, but she was not in the mood for rogues. However, every time she started to shy away from him, he would remind her that he was watching over her for Brent and her temper would flare. Then she asked herself, if Brent wanted her watched so closely, why did she hesitate to allow Gonsalvo to do it?

On the day of her visit to Casa Carvalho she was able to free her mind of the jealousy that ate away at her. Now Summer relaxed against the deep cushions of the coach and listened to Anita's gentle voice. There was a crispness to the air that was rare for the Caribbean, and she felt more alive than she had since she'd left the ship.

"I told Mama she was making too many plans," Anita was saying, "but she was afraid that you might become bored. She finds the country tedious and is sure that everyone else does too."

"Oh no," Summer assured her. "I never have anything to do in the hotel. Everything will be a special treat."

"You must promise to tell me if anything fails to please you or if you become too tired," Anita entreated her. "This day has been planned especially for you, and you'll hurt my feelings if you say nothing."

"I'm certainly enjoying being out of the city."

"Don't you like Havana?"

"I suppose I do," Summer admitted reluctantly, "but I grew up on a small island. At times I long to be back home, free to wander barefoot through the fields and the forests in a plain dress."

"It must have been very lovely."

"Not really," Summer replied honestly. "Certainly not when compared to the houses I've seen in Havana, but I loved it just the same. It was my home, and I was happy there." She was conscious of an unfamiliar sense of sadness. "I will probably never see it again."

"Do you ride?" Anita asked, hoping to find a subject that didn't depress their guest.

"Yes, but I didn't bring a habit."

"You can use one of mine."

"The countess couldn't possibly wear anything that would fit such a little dab as you." Gonsalvo was coming out of his trance. "Any habit of yours would hardly reach her knees."

"I won't be stopped that easily," vowed Anita. "If you want to ride, I will find *something* for you to wear."

The two girls laughed contentedly, and then wiled away the time until they turned into the avenue leading to the house.

Unlike most owners of Caribbean plantations who were content to carve a path through the trees, providing a route that was muddy half the year and rock hard the rest, Señor de Aguilar had laid down a drive and had planted trees on either side. Summer was impressed by the carefully manicured naturalness that prevented the avenue from looking too formal. The gradually increasing variety and liberality of the plantings aroused a sense of expectation in her, and she almost held her breath when they rounded the final bend and a full view of the lawn running down to the gardens lay before her.

"It's so beautiful," she whispered, realizing how woefully inadequate her mother's garden was. "How can you ever bear to leave it for the city?"

"It is lovely," agreed Anita, as the carriage passed beneath

215

the branches of giant oaks hung with moss. "Every time I return I ask myself the same question. It's so cool and peaceful after the noise and heat of the city that I can't imagine why I ever wanted to go to Havana in the first place."

"It's too quiet," said Gonsalvo. "If you stayed here too long it would put you to sleep forever. It's my home and I love it deeply, but I could not stay here all the time. I would miss the companionship, the gaiety, the life of Havana."

"How can you say that when it's only a short ride to town?" asked Summer. "You can have the best of both worlds."

"I suppose we are more fortunate than we deserve." Gonsalvo's eyes danced. "We have the dashing countess from the city in the solitude of the country."

"I'm not the least bit dashing," said Summer. "I'm really a country girl, and I intend to enjoy myself completely."

"How little we know of you," said Anita, half to herself.

Summer could have bitten her tongue. She was going to expose herself one day if she didn't learn to be more circumspect. Fortunately the carriage came to a stop and Señora de Aguilar, trailing yards of silk, hurried out of the hacienda to meet them.

"You must be uncomfortably warm from your journey," she insisted as she ushered Summer into a cool parlor and handed her a refreshing drink. "The heat always exhausts me so I have to rest frequently. To do even the smallest thing drains me of all energy." She sank into a deep chair in one of the dim corners of the room and gradually lost all animation.

"Mama, you can't greet our guest and then promptly close your eyes," said Gonsalvo good-humoredly. "My mother really can't stand the least exertion," he added.

"This is regrettably true," concurred the señora, not the least bit disturbed by her son's remarks. "I can no longer manage to work as I did when I was a young bride. Then there was no labor too exhausting for me to perform for my

children or my husband. Isn't that true, Vincente?" she asked
of her husband who had just entered the room and was greeting Summer.

"The heat this year has been very bad," Vincente de
Aguilar said quietly as he bowed over Summer's hand. He
was a tall man, and everything about him bespoke well-bred
ease, but Summer felt a barely perceptible sense of inflexible
purpose in him. "Refreshments are laid out in the salon, and
a picnic lunch will be served at the river house," he added.

"It sounds wonderful," said Summer. "I would love to see
the gardens."

"The gardens are my father's particular pride," Anita informed Summer.

"After the sugar mills, his horses, and his library," Gonsalvo explained.

"Don't let Gonsalvo mislead you," said his father. "It was
his idea to have a summer house built on the river, and he can
tell you as much about the grounds as anyone."

"I can hardly wait to see it all," Summer declared eagerly.

"You can't possibly mean to start now," exclaimed Señora
de Aguilar, aghast that anyone would even consider a walk
without taking a long rest beforehand.

"I'm not the least bit tired," Summer assured her. "I had
plenty of time to rest during the drive."

"No one can rest in a carriage," the *señora* stated with
feeling.

"Allow me a few minutes to change my shoes, and I will
join you," Anita said.

The house was a white, two-story wood-and-stone structure, typical of the Spanish-style houses generally found in
tropical climates. The windows were small, but porches ran
around the inner courtyard both upstairs and down. Two
enormous hundred-year-old oaks flanked the front entrance,
their huge branches rising above the roof to shade the front
half of the house during all but the hour at midday. While tall

shrubs and the flowering vines that grew up trellises protected the porches from the merciless glare of the tropical sun. Even though the house was very large, it nestled, like a small jewel, in the vast, meticulously manicured grounds that surrounded it.

The expanse between the house and the river was enormous. A small area was open to the full force of the sun, but in the remainder of the seemingly endless gardens dappled shade was cast by a bewildering variety of trees and flowering vines. In areas receiving the most light, beds of bright blooms presented a riot of color; shady spots were filled with ferns, vines, and plants with spidery foliage and variegated leaves. A series of paths, arbors, and alcoves provided access to the garden, and offered places of rest as well as focal points about which to arrange each part of the grounds. This magnificent display was tended by numerous gardeners who saw that everything was in perfect condition.

"It must have taken a lifetime to achieve all this," Summer remarked as the three young people wound their way down one of the many paths. "Everything is planned so carefully."

"It was begun by my father's grandfather," Gonsalvo told her, "and each son has carried on his work."

"There are so many trees and flowers that are strange to me. How do you remember them all?" Summer was dazed by the thought of having to learn the names of so many plants.

"We keep carefully detailed plans of the entire grounds in the library," said Gonsalvo, "and each time a new plant is set out, or dies, it is noted with great care. We can tell you every tree, shrub, vine, and flower that has grown here over the last seventy-five years."

"Seeing all this makes me wish I had taken more interest in our gardens." Summer walked around a stone bench that was nestled in the curve of a vine-covered arcade. "Mother didn't have much time to spare, and father disliked the tropics and anything that reminded him of them."

"I don't suppose it is reasonable to expect people who grew up in Scotland to have the same appreciation for the Caribbean we do," Anita said politely, but it was clear that she and her brother did not relish Summer's father's limited appreciation of a world they found so nearly perfect.

"Where is this river house I've heard so much about?" Summer asked, wanting to change the subject. "After all I've been told, I'm going to be very hard to impress."

Gonsalvo responded to her buoyant spirits. "It's just around that bank of hibiscuses. Remember I was not the one who praised the house, so don't be angry with me if it fails to meet your expectations."

"Are you running shy?" Summer asked saucily.

"Not exactly," he answered evasively.

"Covering your tracks then?" She gave him no quarter.

"Trying to cover all possibilities," Gonsalvo countered.

"He's trying to flatter you, no matter what he says," teased his irrepressible sister.

"Lead me on, gallant knight," Summer requested jauntily. "I shall be satisfied with nothing less than a slice of paradise."

And that was what she found.

On the other side of the hibiscuses the lawn sloped gently down to a still river that was no more than fifty feet wide at its greatest width. Its banks were lined with thick growths of water hyacinths and overhanging branches shaded the river's edge. Great clumps of moss trailed airy tentacles in the delicate breeze, while birds fluttered through the branches filling the air with their songs.

An island built of stone and covered with white sand dredged from the river bottom rose from the water about fifteen feet from the bank. It was reached by way of a moss-covered stone walkway capped by a green ribbon of grass. In the center of the island stood a newly whitewashed bower partly covered with wisteria vines whose pale purple blooms scented the air. Several chairs and lounges, generously provided with cushions, were placed in the shade, and a small boat was tied at the foot of a tiny dock. In the coolness of the bower stood a large table covered with enough food to feed ten guests twice as hungry as Summer.

"Do you like it?" asked Gonsalvo, the pride of possession in his voice.

"Oh, yes," Summer sighed, somewhat in awe of such consummate luxury. "It's the most beautiful place I've ever seen."

"You have made Gonsalvo your slave for life," chortled Anita, moving ahead of them. "He's secretly very proud of this island and loves to have it admired."

"Attend to your duties as hostess and stop trying to embarrass me," scolded her brother.

Summer couldn't remember when she had enjoyed food so much. Everything was deliciously prepared and beautifully served. She was loathe to destroy what had taken so much artistry to create, but her hosts showed no such reluctance and before long not a dish remained untouched.

But it was the enchantment of her surroundings that captured Summer's imagination. She leaned back on thick cushions and watched the play of light and shadow in the leaves high above her head. Gazing down then, she found the gently undulating beds of hyacinths hypnotic, and she succumbed willingly to a deep feeling of contentment. Water lapped against the cool stone base of the island lulling her, and Summer finally felt utterly at peace.

Chapter 25

"Would you like to go for a ride on the river?" asked Gonsalvo as he rose from the table. "The current is almost nonexistent at this time of the year. We can float idly along."

"That sounds like a lovely idea," Summer replied languidly, "but I've eaten so much I'm not sure I can move."

"I can carry you."

"How many times do I have to tell you to behave, Gonsalvo?" admonished Anita. "If you are going to upset the countess with your foolishness, I will not be able to leave you alone with her."

"Where are you going?" asked Summer, trying to clear her mind of the heaviness that seemed to weigh her down.

"I hate to admit it, but I don't care for boating on the river," Anita confessed, "particularly after I've eaten."

"I'll come with you," Summer offered.

Anita staunchly refused. "Absolutely not. Stay here and enjoy your afternoon."

"Are you trying to run away from me?" Gonsalvo quipped.

"Not at all," Summer languorously replied. "I just didn't want Anita to think I was deserting her."

"I'll have some refreshments waiting when you return," she offered. Summer made a face at the thought of more food, but Anita only laughed. "The river makes you hungry," she said.

Summer's and Gonsalvo's eyes followed her as she traversed the walkway to the riverbank. It took very little time for her to reach the bend in the path, turn, and wave to them before disappearing behind the hibiscuses.

"Would you like anything else?" Gonsalvo asked.

"I couldn't eat another bite. I'm so stuffed I just might stay here and go to sleep."

"If you must doze, it's much nicer on the river. The current is so sluggish you will hardly know you're moving."

"Where does it go?"

"It twists and turns through the estate for the next mile or two, and then comes out on the other side of the house a short distance from where we entered the avenue. It's a long ride to nowhere."

"That suits my mood."

Gonsalvo helped Summer out of her chair.

"Will the sun be hot?" Summer asked, remembering she had not brought a sun shade.

"The boat is fitted with a large parasol."

"You think of everything, don't you?"

"It's always wise to plan ahead."

"Now you sound like Captain Douglas," Summer complained. "It's too warm and I'm too full of your delicious food to listen to anything that sounds like good advice. I want to waste my time, be frivolous, and do absolutely nothing worthwhile."

"Admirable." He laughed. "Spoken like a true Spaniard."

"You Spanish can't be allowed to have all the fun," Summer decreed as she permitted herself to be led down stone steps to where the boat was tied. "If I'm going to spend the rest of my life freezing in Scotland, I'll be practical when I must."

"Does your husband know how much you dislike Scotland?"

"I don't actually dislike it." Summer chided herself for letting her tongue get away from her again. "It's just that after spending my whole life here, it will be very hard to get used to blizzards and frozen rivers."

"I should think it would be impossible." Gonsalvo had spent one winter in Madrid. "How do you keep warm?"

"With lots of roaring fires." Summer wondered how there could be a tree left standing in Scotland. "But I don't want to talk about the cold and snow. I want to enjoy this marvelous day. Oh, you have cushions, too," she said, and sighed contentedly.

"They are much more comfortable than wooden seats."

"I may stay here forever."

Summer settled herself while Gonsalvo opened the huge parasol and fitted it into the grooved slot at the side of the boat. Then she leaned back and closed her eyes.

"Don't wake me until tomorrow," she said.

"Don't you dare go to sleep on me," Gonsalvo ordered sternly as he cast off and steered the boat toward the middle of the river. "Some of the finest scenery is along the river."

"Describe it to me," Summer murmured. "I have a very good imagination."

"I think you ought to know a snake is about to drop on you from that limb overhead."

When Summer instantly opened her eyes and sat up, Gonsalvo burst into laughter.

"You beast," she said, trying not to smile. "I have a good mind to join Anita and let you have the river and its snakes all to yourself."

"I won't play any more tricks," he promised.

"You'd better not. I didn't come out here to be frightened to death."

Summer settled back to listen as Gonsalvo talked about the birds and the other creatures that lived in the gardens and the surrounding forests. But she didn't listen very closely. Instead, she watched the magnificent canopy overhead as their boat moved lazily in and out of the shadows. Her eyelids sank lower and lower, and Gonsalvo's voice grew softer and softer until it became no more than an indistinct murmur from somewhere far away.

Brent's boots pounded a drummer's cadence as he strode along the corridors. Smith had sent him back to the hotel after he'd started an argument for the fourth time that day, each time with a prospective buyer. He wasn't in a very good mood.

"I can deal with everybody much better when you aren't swearing and scaring people into having nothing to do with us," Smith had told Brent after the merchant had hurried away without agreeing to purchase anything.

"It's my ship and I don't have to sell to any of these timorous clerks you've rounded up."

"If you don't stop shouting at every person who sets foot on your ship, your cargo will rot or be eaten by rats before you sell it," Smith countered, not the least intimidated by Brent's intemperate rage. "Then it won't matter if your agents are courageous daredevils or cowardly fools."

None of the officers could explain the irrational furies that had plagued Brent since they'd reached Havana, but they took pains to stay out of his way. His rage was no less dangerous for being unexplained. Smith had born the brunt of

Brent's ill humor, but he remained unshaken, and treated Brent with an unfailing patience which caused him to grow angrier still.

"Why don't you tell me to go to hell or knock me down or put a bullet through me?" Brent stormed after Smith had stoically endured another of his vituperative tirades.

"You could break every bone in my body. And in your present mood, you probably would."

"You know I wouldn't," Brent began, but he didn't go on.

"No, not if you were in your right mind," Smith said gravely, "but in your present state I wouldn't care to risk it. One of us has to be in condition to tend to the ship's business." The truth of Smith's words made Brent so rousingly angry that he then worked off the worst of his spleen by quarreling with a crew of stevedores. He left them shaken, confused, and unable to account for the argument or its abrupt conclusion.

Smith knew what was troubling his captain, but he meant to let him discover it for himself. Brent wasn't going to be happy when he figured it out, but he'd be less likely to face up to the truth if it came from someone else. He had never been one to accept news he didn't like; he preferred to bend Fate to his will. At last, Smith suspected Brent would be the one who would do the bending.

Smith picked up his pen, then paused before turning to his ledger. He hoped Summer was at the hotel. Someone had to deal with Brent, and since she had destroyed his peace of mind, she should be the one to restore it.

Brent knocked sharply at the door of Summer's suite. When it remained closed, he struck the door so hard it rattled, but he still received no answer. Too angry to wait for anyone to bring a key, he smashed the lock and stormed in; there was no one there. Annoyed and perplexed, he strode to the bell rope and set about ringing it wildly. Someone had to know what was going on, and he was damned well going to find out. By the time he had paced the room for nearly ten minutes, he was in a black rage and was itching to tear someone to pieces. It was Alonzo who finally hurried into the room.

"Where in the hell is Summer?" Brent roared, too angry to remember to use her title.

"The countess has gone out," Alonzo gasped, out of breath.

"Where?" Brent demanded.

"Unfortunately she did not inform me of her plans."

"Then get me her maid."

"The countess gave her maid the afternoon off. I didn't even know that Chichi was absent until you began ringing the bell so frantically. I've already sent someone to fetch her."

"That scatter-brained wench was never worth a farthing," Brent gnashed his teeth, "but I thought she would at least stay where she belonged."

"I believe the countess gave her permission to visit her mother."

"I'm not paying her to visit her mother," Brent said with biting sarcasm. "I'm paying her, and you too, for that matter, to take care of the countess."

"I have every reason to suppose the countess is being well cared for," Alonzo disclosed, stung by Brent's unfair accusations.

"And exactly what do you mean by that, you miserable worm?" Brent advanced on the hotelkeeper with grim resolve.

"The countess spends most of her afternoons in the company of Gonsalvo de Aguilar."

"Do you mean to tell me you allowed her to leave the hotel with that rake?"

"I do not know for certain she is in his company," Alonzo countered, wishing he had remained silent. "It is just that he and his sister are constant visitors. I have seen no one else."

"His sister? Do you mean that tiny, squat creature?"

"He has only one sister." Alonzo was unruffled.

"That slithering reptile would be certain to keep his serpent's eyes hooded until he has his prey in his grasp," Brent shouted.

"But I thought he was a friend of yours, a business partner?"

"He's a lecher," Brent said brutally, "and he uses his charm and good looks to conceal an unwavering determination to seduce every female that interests him, no matter how briefly." Just then Chichi rushed in, breathless from running all the way back from her mother's cottage.

"Where have you been, you stupid girl?" Brent demanded, rounding on her with boiling rage. "And what do you mean by letting your mistress leave the hotel with a deceiver like Gonsalvo de Aguilar?"

"They are going to spend the day at Casa Carvalho," stammered Chichi, intimidated by Brent's rage.

"And you were such a blockhead that you let her go?" Brent roared so violently that Chichi retreated behind a large sofa. Alonzo turned pale, but stood his ground.

"How could I stop her?"

"You could have told her not to go." Brent felt that he was talking to two-year-olds.

"The de Aguilars are a very respectable family," protested Chichi, "and he said he was your friend."

"He is *not* my friend and he is *not* respectable. All you had to do was ask."

"But you weren't here. You're never here when the countess wants you," Chichi said with a hint of her old spirit.

"I never thought you were very intelligent, but I didn't expect you to be witless."

"You are the one who is always telling her never to listen to anything I say, that I am a great fool," Chichi shot back at Brent.

"And so you've proved to be." Brent gathered up his coat. "Alonzo!" he thundered, so ferociously the little man wondered if his time had come. "I want a carriage at the door in five minutes, and it had better be harnessed to the four best horses in your stable." Alonzo's eyes nearly started from his head. He opened his mouth to protest such an impossible order, but he closed it when he encountered the bloodthirsty look in Brent's eyes.

"Don't waste your breath telling me why it can't be done. If that carriage isn't waiting for me when I step out of this hotel, you've drawn your last breath."

Alonzo escaped Brent's presence determined to have a carriage ready in the required time if he had to stop one in the street and pull its rightful occupants from it.

"As for you," Brent roared, whipping around and causing Chichi to gasp in fright, "have everything the countess owns packed and be out of here when I return. I don't want to set eyes on you again, or I'll not be responsible for my actions."

"Please, Captain Douglas . . ." Chichi began, but her words were cut off by a blast worthy of a medieval dragon.

"Goddammit girl, do as I tell you," Brent said, then he opened Summer's bedroom door and watched coldly as the sobbing maid ran in. "Remember, you're to be gone before I get back," he commanded before striding out of the suite. He closed the door with such violence that one of the hinges was torn from the frame.

More than five minutes had elapsed before Brent appeared in the hotel courtyard, but a carriage was waiting and four fretting horses were ready to be off. Alonzo had instilled abject fear of Captain Douglas in the grooms, and had thus enabled them to harness a team in a time previously thought impossible. They, in turn, had communicated their fear to the horses, making them restless.

"There'd better not be a slug among them," Brent warned Alonzo as he climbed into the carriage and took up the reins. "Out of my way before I run over you," he shouted to the groom holding the lead horses.

Alonzo watched him disappear in a thick cloud of dust, greatly relieved that he was not the object of the captain's rage. He hoped that Gonsalvo had had the good sense to leave the countess in the company of his mother and his sister. Nothing less would be likely to convince Captain Douglas of the man's honorable intentions.

As the sun moved across the sky, a few iridescent rays slipped below the fringe of the parasol. Their heat made Summer uncomfortably warm and she opened her eyes. Gonsalvo was sitting beside her using his hat as a shield against the sun.

"A thousand pardons," he said, smiling in a way Summer found particularly attractive, "but I'm afraid I let the sun get in your face."

"Have you been shading me with your hat the whole time?" she asked, sitting up.

"You were dozing so peacefully I didn't have the heart to wake you."

"It was rude of me to fall asleep, but I've never been on a river before, and I feel wonderfully refreshed." She smiled, wishing he wouldn't sit so close.

Gonsalvo covered her hand with his, and gazed at her with a smile she didn't feel appropriate for casual friends. "I treasure any time I can spend with you."

"That's very sweet of you." Summer removed her hand from his. "But you shouldn't say it. And you shouldn't sit so close to me either."

"But I can't resist," he said, looking at her in a manner that increased her uneasiness. "Your presence is a drug that inflames my sense."

"I'd just as soon you didn't feel that way. I *am* a married woman."

"You can't imagine how happy that makes me."

"Why should that make any difference?" Summer asked. She was becoming agitated.

"An unmarried girl such as Anita would never be allowed so much license, but you may go where you please."

"It would please me to go back to the house. You must have a very strange idea of Scotland if you think it's all right for wives to wander all over with just anyone."

"There's no need to go anywhere," Gonsalvo said, moving even closer. "It's barely the middle of the afternoon, and there's still a lot of river you haven't seen."

"We can save that for some other time."

"But we can't leave now." Gonsalvo leaned so close that Summer could feel his breath on her neck.

"Why?" she asked distrustfully.

"The carriage is not here yet. It won't meet us for another hour."

"Then we can walk back."

"We can't reach the gardens from this part of the river. We have to wait until we come out near the avenue."

"Can't we go any faster?" Summer asked, flustered.

"That sounds like the request of someone who is not enjoying herself." Gonsalvo's voice was perilously close to a purr.

"I've had a wonderful time, but I'm rather tired of being in this boat."

"I'm afraid the boat is not provided with oars. It's only intended to float along with the current."

"You mean there is no way to get off this thing for a whole hour?"

"Not unless you're prepared to swim ashore."

"I'd drown in all these clothes!" Summer declared.

"Never fear, I'd save you."

"Thank you just the same, but I'd prefer not to be saved."

"You mean you'd rather drown than be with me?" Gonsalvo teased, but Summer was not in a mood to be amused. "I'm beginning to think you are angry with me."

"I'm not angry with you yet," she said, trying to remove her hand from his grasp, "but if you don't let go of me, I will be very angry indeed."

"But you have such an elegant hand," Gonsalvo declared, raising her fingers to his lips and dropping clusters of kisses on each knuckle.

"That's no reason for you to be slobbering over me," Summer said, exerting unladylike strength in an attempt to remove her hand from his. However, Gonsalvo was too involved to bridle at her words.

"Two such lovely hands," he crooned, possessing himself of the other as well.

"Did you expect me to have only one? Or were you hoping for a third so you could indulge yourself without restraint?"

"I need nothing more than the invitation of your lips," he said, and he gathered her in his arms despite her spirited resistance.

"My lips are not inviting you," Summer said impatiently.

"Your neck, your shoulders, your ears, even your elbows . . ." Gonsalvo continued his litany.

"You sound like a butcher inspecting a carcass he's about to cut up," Summer scoffed as she battled vainly to break his hold on her. "If I'd had any notion you were such a rude man, I would never have come with you."

"It's all your fault, fair charmer," he murmured as his hot lips began to plant little kisses on her neck and her cheek. "The narcotic of your nearness has destroyed all power to struggle against my longing."

Summer was able to twist her mouth away from his long enough to utter an impassioned shriek, but Gonsalvo was much stronger than she was and she remained in his arms.

"I have dreamed of this moment for days," he said. "Every time I have been near you, it has been an agony not to touch you, to caress your cheek, to tell you how much I love you."

"You can't love me," Summer declared in disgust. "You hardly even know me."

"I've loved you from the first moment I saw you," he insisted. "Since then you've haunted my dreams and filled my thoughts every waking moment."

"How dare you maul me like this!"

"I can't help myself."

"Get off me." Summer tried to push him away. "I'll never be able to explain why my clothes came to be in such a mess."

"You won't have to. Anita and my parents have gone to visit a neighbor. They won't return for another hour or more." Summer realized with a jolt that there was no one to help her. She was on her own with this man who seemed to have a dozen hands.

"I want to make love to you."

"In a boat in the middle of the river?" she exclaimed unromantically, unable to believe that he could be serious.

"I could make love to you any place on earth," he rhapsodized. "But here, amid the sublime beauty of Nature, it is a most appropriate place for our love to come to fruition."

"But I don't love you," Summer barked, and she raked her nails across his face leaving several ugly streaks that began to ooze blood.

"Bitch!" Gonsalvo yelped, no trace of the lover in him now. "I ought to slap you senseless."

"Now you show your real feelings." Summer sneered.

"But I do love you." Gonsalvo strove to recapture his first enchantment with the most beautiful face he had ever seen, but his words lacked conviction.

"Prove it by letting me go."

"I can't do that. I must have you."

"Not while I have breath in my body." Summer clenched her teeth and drove her knee into his stomach as hard as she could. "You're nothing but an overheated child," she fumed, her voice dripping with scorn, "and I was a fool to believe a single word you said." She stared at him, eyes flashing.

"By God, you're a beauty," Gonsalvo said suddenly, forgetting the pain in his stomach. "Captain Douglas may not want you any longer, but I do."

"Captain Douglas was hired to carry me back to Scotland, not to be my duenna. I doubt anyone foresaw that defending me against Havana's marauding caballeros should be part of the agreement."

"He was a great fool to have let you out of his sight, in Havana or in any other place." Gonsalvo's eyes were now glazed with libidinous desire. "Captain Douglas is a very careless guardian."

"The captain agrees with you, and intends to repair that oversight at once."

Summer and Gonsalvo froze as an unexpected voice promised destruction and deliverance.

Chapter 26

Brent had plenty of time during the drive from town to decide where to begin his search. He knew Summer was not likely to be in danger as long as she was near the house, but he visualized so many possibilities for Gonsalvo getting her off by herself that he pushed his horses to even greater speed. Soon, however, reason reasserted itself; there were only a few legitimate choices for daylight seduction. Gonsalvo could take Summer for a ride on the river, he could take her to one of the secluded spots for which his plantation was famous, or he could take her to another place altogether. Brent discounted the last possibility because such a move was bound to make Summer suspicious. Of the two remaining choices he was inclined to think that the river was the place to look. Gonsalvo's love of it and his use of it for romantic rendezvous were well known. Even in daylight, the river was a much better choice than two horses or a carriage that had to hidden from view. Having decided on which course to pursue, Brent was impatient to reach the de Aguilar estate.

An old woman was working a small garden plot along the road at the estate entrance. "Have you seen any carriages pass by here in the last few hours?" Brent called out.

The old crone looked at him suspiciously. "One," she finally answered without halting her work. "Señor de Aguilar's carriage, but it was closed." Brent cursed the Spanish habit of riding in closed carriages even in the hottest weather.

"Which way did it go?" The old woman pointed in the direction from which Brent had just come.

"What's that way?"

"Old Daquin's place. He's a cousin of the señora," she explained, becoming more talkative as she noticed Brent's good looks.

"Does the river run near here?" he asked.

She pointed to a rise in the ground yet some distance away. "On the other side of that ridge."

Brent instinctively knew that Gonsalvo had chosen the river. He whipped up his horses and headed straight for the spot the old woman had indicated.

"You're never going to be able to drive that through those trees!" she called after him, but he was already out of hearing distance. *"Loco,"* she muttered to herself.

The horses were unused to such terrain, and it took all of Brent's skill to maneuver the carriage through the tangle of trees and the tropical undergrowth. He was rarely able to get close to the river, but he never let the ribbon of water out of his sight, not even when he had to drive the rebellious team through a marsh or a rush thicket. After half an hour of struggling, the team was exhausted and Brent was wondering if he hadn't made the wrong decision. Just then a scream broke the silence. It was impossible to identify the source, but Brent had no doubt it was Summer.

Driving his team out of the bog to the more open forest nearer the road, Brent cursed Gonsalvo for being a lecher,

Summer for being a trusting fool, the horses for being iron-mouthed slugs, and himself for not watching her more closely. Smith had warned him that she'd get into trouble, but he had blithely assumed she would stay quietly in the hotel until he came for her.

As his lumbering team burst through a small thicket of ferns, Brent caught sight of a boat on the river. It was easy to see that Summer and Gonsalvo were locked in a bitter struggle. Brent cracked the whip above the horses's heads. The thick layer of leaves on the forest floor deadened the sound of the carriage, and his approach went unnoticed.

The river had eroded the bank under one of the large water oaks that grew along its edge, and the boat was floating toward the toppled tree that lay over the river, its trunk barely six feet above the shimmering surface. Brent jumped from the chaise and ran along the trunk with catlike agility until he was over the path of the approaching boat. But the currents swirling around the submerged limbs caused the boat to change course and Brent was forced to drop into the water. The river barely reached his chest, and he was able to wade out from among the branches just as the boat brushed past their still-green foliage. The shock to Summer and Gonsalvo couldn't have been greater if they had suddenly come face to face with a sea monster.

"*Sangre de Dios!*" cried Gonsalvo, unable to believe his own eyes. "Where did you come from?"

"That's not much of a greeting for an *old* friend." Brent grasped the boat and whipped it around until Summer was next to him. "Or maybe you wanted the countess all to yourself?"

Summer was so stunned she hadn't even taken advantage of Gonsalvo's slackened grip to wiggle free.

"Everyone knows she's your mistress, so you can stop with the countess bit." Gonsalvo fought to keep his balance in the spinning boat. "It's a little selfish of you to try to keep every beautiful woman in Havana for yourself. Not even you can satisfy that many."

Brent jerked the boat around so sharply that Gonsalvo, caught in the act of rising, tumbled into the river. Brent dragged him to his feet. "If you weren't such a putrid little piece of Spanish droppings I would beat you into the oblivion you deserve."

Gonsalvo didn't have Brent's strength or his height, but he slapped him across the face. "Do you English always fight with words?" he jeered. Brent raised Gonsalvo half out of the water with one hand.

"I'm from Scotland and we use our fists!" he roared. Then he dealt Gonsalvo a bone-cracking blow that lifted him completely out of the water and sent him flying through the air.

"Don't! You'll kill him!" Summer cried, finally finding her voice.

"Killing would be too good for this contemptible miscreant," Brent snarled. "His kind prey on innocent women and then cast them aside when they've ruined them. Did he hurt you?"

"No." She clasped her torn bodice in one hand.

"If he dared to lay one hand on you . . ." Brent grabbed the boat so it wouldn't slip away on the current.

Summer was careful to keep her hand on her bosom. "He just tried to kiss me," she said.

Brent was so relieved his released tension found expression in harsh words. "How could you have been so stupid as to go anywhere with that lecher? Even a fool like Chichi would have had more sense."

"I could have been carried off by green dragons and you wouldn't have noticed," Summer fired back. She then struggled to get to her feet in the unsteady boat. "I don't need you and I don't want you." Losing her balance, she grabbed at the parasol pole to keep from falling. When she did so, she lost her grip on her dress and exposed the rent in her bodice.

"That rotter! I'll have his blood for this!" Brent shouted. Gonsalvo barely had time to see Brent bearing down on him before he felt a pair of iron hands clamp around his throat. Brent lifted him from the water and whipped him about until Summer feared he would break Gonsalvo's neck.

"Stop, you're choking him!" she cried as Gonsalvo's face turned blue. But Brent was too angry to release his prey even though the man's eyes threatened to pop from his head.

"Let him go!" Summer shrieked. She stood up in the bobbing boat. "You'll kill him." In her excitement, she lost her balance and fell headlong into the water with a loud splash; that small mishap saved Gonsalvo's life. Brent immediately dropped him and dove after Summer.

"You would have drowned," he said as he scooped her up in his arms and held her close. The warmth in his voice nearly brought tears of joy to Summer's eyes.

"No I wouldn't," she said, unable to understand why she was suddenly laughing. "I'm an excellent swimmer, but you'd better get him out of the river."

"Let the fish have him." Brent was still holding her close.

"That won't do," Summer persisted, even though she wanted to forget Gonsalvo and stay right where she was. "It would cause a great deal of trouble if anything happened to him."

"I'll put him in the boat, but I'm going to leave him there, even if he floats out to sea."

"Just find him before it's too late," Summer urged, and Brent reluctantly deposited her in the boat, then hauled up the barely conscious Gonsalvo.

"Get him in the boat," Summer cried in alarm when she saw Gonsalvo's purple face. Brent draped his limp form over the cushioned seat. Gonsalvo's breathing was weak and unsteady, but he was alive.

"He'll be all right now," Brent said. "I'll leave him for his servants to find. If we're lucky a jaguar will get him first."

"Are you sure he's all right?" Summer questioned. "He looks awful to me."

"I've seen a lot of half-drowned men in my time. It was a pretty close call, but he'll make it."

Brent picked Summer up and headed toward the shore. Even dripping wet, the feel of her body ignited the flame that always flared in him and his pulse quickened. He looked at her face, nestled against his shoulder, and thought of the empty nights he'd passed in Havana, the painful evenings when he closed his eyes and imagined the smell of her perfume, the feel of her skin, the warmth of her breath. He relived the agony it had been to keep away from her, to pretend indifference, to hide his aching need from prying eyes.

Now, alone with her under the cathedral-like canopy of the forest, restraint fell from him. He was obsessed by her nearness, blinded by her beauty, oblivious to everything except his need of her. He rose from the white, churning water, an all-powerful Neptune, and set her on the moss-covered forest floor as carefully as if she were a delicate, priceless work of art. Then he knelt beside her, shivering from the intensity of his need.

The water molded Brent's clothing to his powerful form, so Summer was acutely aware of his growing desire. From deep inside her came an answering surge that swept her into the same storm of emotion that battered him so fiercely. She looked into his eyes, unquenchable hunger in hers. At this moment it didn't matter that he had deserted her for days or had spent his nights with other women. They were together, alone, and he wanted her as much as she wanted him. She opened her arms in a welcoming embrace and he fell into them with an anguished groan.

His lips met hers in a crushing, greedy kiss that seared her senses, as he surrendered to the desire that swept over him in pulsating waves. Her soggy clothes were stripped from her in quick, rough movements; he shed his own with equal haste.

And the sight of her unclothed body lying at his feet, perfect, tempting, welcoming provoked in him a craving that made his muscles ache. He threw himself upon her, entering roughly, thinking only of his need.

Summer joyously met Brent's ardor, but she was unwilling to be the mere object of his release. She encircled his body with hers and forced him to slow the headlong rush of his longing. Pulling his face down to hers, she kissed him so intimately that she drew from him a response never before plumbed. It grew in intensity until it consumed them both. Gradually Brent was drawn into the rhythm of Summer's body. They began to move in concert, each striving to meet the other's expectations. And as the tempo of their lovemaking increased, they were engulfed by the magnitude of their desire, overwhelmed by the force of their suppressed longing for each other. They were unable to think of themselves as existing outside those moments as their ecstasy grew and at last they achieved a union more perfect than any they'd enjoyed on the ship. They now knew that they belonged together, that their fusion went beyond the physical to the spiritual, to where creation ended and eternity began.

Chapter 27

"I don't know how I can face his sister after what happened today." Summer groaned as she snuggled down under the robe in the carriage.

"You won't have to face any of his family," Brent replied absently, carefully guiding his weary team through the last of the forest.

"But you know I'll see them," Summer insisted. "They go everywhere."

"You won't be here. We're leaving Havana tomorrow."

"Where are you taking me?" She sat up quickly. "You promised you wouldn't hand me over to the earl."

"I'm carrying you to my plantation, which is what I should have done in the first place. If I'd had any idea Gonsalvo and his ilk would take you for my discarded mistress, I wouldn't have brought you to Havana at all."

"There wouldn't have been any need for your *interference*, today or any other day, if you'd left me where you found

241

me," Summer retorted wrathfully, but she stopped suddenly, ashamed of her vixenish behavior, especially after the way she had welcomed his embraces on the riverbank. She reflected bitterly on the unfairness of having to be thankful to a handsome brute who deserved to be flogged.

"I haven't thanked you for coming to my rescue," she said stiffly. "It was most fortunate that you took the time and trouble to come all this way on the chance that I might need your assistance."

"If that is the way you talk when you're being thankful, I prefer your anger," Brent said scathingly. "At least then you don't sound like a mutton-headed fool."

"I was trying to thank you properly." Summer's anger flared. "Since the words nearly choked me, the least you could have done was to listen without making rude remarks."

"I hate mealy-mouthed females."

"You can be sure that I won't be *mealy-mouthed* again." Summer had a steely glint in her eyes. "I'll let you know exactly what kind of a cur I think you are."

"That's better." Brent laughed. "For a minute I was afraid you were catching a chill and would come down with a fever before midnight."

"If I ever have the good fortune to come upon you bound and defenseless," sputtered Summer, "I'm going to cut a hole in your belly and fill it with salt."

"That's dandy." Brent was enjoying her anger. "Don't give me an inch. Now you lie back and get some rest. I don't want you worn out when we reach the island. There is too much I want to show you, and there are hundreds of things I want to do."

"Where is this plantation?" Summer asked, unable to curb her curiosity despite her anger. "What's it like? Is it really a plantation, or is it just a house?"

"I don't think I'll tell you," Brent teased. "At least not

everything." She looked at him reproachfully. "It'll be easier to let you judge for yourself, but it is a real plantation. In fact I've gone to a lot of expense to see that it's in good working order. I'm anxious to see how the changes I've ordered are working out."

"Can I go with you, out on the plantation, I mean? I did a lot of work for Father and I could be helpful."

"You can go anywhere you please. I own the whole island."

"A whole island!" Summer was astonished. "It must be a huge plantation."

"No, but it is rather large," he said, his eyes twinkling. "Quite large enough to support me when I decide to retire from the sea."

"But what about your home in Scotland?" she asked before she stopped to think.

"I have no home in Scotland," Brent replied, and the light of happiness went out of his eyes.

"Who did all this?" Summer asked in open-mouthed surprise when she arrived at the hotel to find everything packed.

"That fool of a maid."

"But where is she?"

"I threw her out. She had no business letting you go off with Gonsalvo."

"There was nothing she could do to stop me," Summer protested. "You can't blame her for my mistake."

"I can blame her for not telling me," said Brent.

"Not after I lectured her on loyalty," Summer told him as she pulled the bell rope. "The poor child couldn't obey both of us."

"You're determined to spike my guns, aren't you?" Brent thundered.

"How am I suppose to change for dinner? I can't even get ready for bed by myself."

"I can help you," Brent said quickly, his sudden smile transforming his harsh expression and giving him a boyish charm.

"You will not!" Summer felt light-headed. She always did when he smiled at her in that way. "My reputation isn't so bad that I can afford to have you making free in my bedroom."

"Blast your reputation!"

"You nearly have, but there are a few shreds of it left, and I'm determined to hold on to them."

"Did you want me, *señora?*" inquired Chichi timorously, peeping from behind the bedroom door with wide, frightened eyes.

"Yes. I need to change my clothes."

"*Madre de Dios!* What happened to you?" Chichi exclaimed, forgetting Brent when she saw her mistress. Summer's hair hung in ugly strings about her shoulders and her dress, which, though it had dried somewhat, clung to her body with indecent clarity.

"You'll catch your death of cold," Chichi declared, pushing Summer toward the bedroom door. "You must have a hot bath and something warm in your stomach."

"If you don't take better care of the countess this time," Brent growled, "I will personally peel the hide off your body."

Chichi's burst of enthusiasm faded.

"Pay no attention to him," Summer instructed her through chattering teeth. "As long as you please me, you don't have to worry about anyone else."

It was obvious from the fearful glances Chichi cast in Brent's direction that she didn't put a great deal of faith in Summer's ability to protect her from his wrath.

"We leave at first light," Brent said, "so be sure the countess's trunks are ready to be carried to the docks by midnight."

"Aren't you going to take me with you, *señora?*" Chichi was visibly upset.

"I don't keep incompetent servants," Brent said firmly.

"Go take care of your business and leave us alone," Summer ordered, her vexation evident. "You're upsetting her."

"Fine thing. You're more concerned about a worthless maid than me."

"You can take care of yourself. She can't."

"That's the first compliment you've ever paid me, yet you managed to make it sound like a fault," he said as he left.

"There's no need for you to cry anymore." Summer guided Chichi toward the bedroom. "The captain's gone now."

"It's not that." Chichi hiccupped. "The captain scares me a little, but he would not make me cry."

"Then what are you crying about?"

"You are leaving."

"I'm sorry Chichi, but you knew from the first that I was only going to be here a short time."

"I know, but you had such a great success I thought you might want to stay."

"You know I must return to my husband," Summer said carefully. "I can't stay away from him forever."

"Does he love you?"

"What do you mean?" Summer was unnerved by the impertinent question.

"He hasn't given you a baby."

"How can you know that?"

"Everyone knows that you don't have such a perfect figure after you've had babies."

"But what has that got to do with my husband?"

"Captain Douglas is a very handsome man. You have said so."

"What are you trying to say?" Summer was no longer feeling sympathetic.

"Maybe he would give you a baby."

"One more word out of you, and I'll slap you." Summer advanced on the hapless maid with flashing eyes. "That's a rude and stupid thing to say, and if the captain ever hears of it, he will surely beat you. If that's what you think of me, I'm glad you're not coming."

Chichi tried over and over again to convince her mistress of her devotion, but Summer was too infuriated to listen to her arguments. She might *want* to tumble into Brent's arms, but she had far too much pride to do so.

Summer thrust her face squarely into the cool sea breeze. It was heaven to be out of the heat and the fetid closeness of Havana. Now there was no need to spend hours dressing or to wear clothes she didn't like. On the small craft were only Brent and the two crewmen necessary to help sail it. Smith had been left behind to see to the disposal of the cargo, and the crew had been dispersed until such time as Brent was ready to go to sea again.

"Smith can do just as well without me," Brent had confessed sheepishly when she'd asked why he wasn't staying. "My temper has scared off so many buyers he practically ordered me to stay away until I was human again."

Brent had also told her that he was taking her away for her own protection. "Whatever you find to do on Biscay, it won't include the likes of Gonsalvo de Aguilar," he had declared, a martial light in his eyes. "If that man ever dares to set foot on my land, I'll put an end to him once and for all."

"I don't think he'll be anxious to see either one of us again." Summer had been unable to suppress a smile of satisfaction. "No man can pretend to be a lover after his servants have fished him out of the river. They did find him, didn't they?"

"They must have. News travels fast in Havana, especially news that promises to turn into a scandal."

"I still think you were too rough on him."

"I wasn't as rough as I wanted to be. That scalawag ought to be wiped out."

A sharp retort had hovered on the tip of Summer's tongue, but she'd bitten back the words. However much she might revel in being able to throw his sins in his face, she was deeply grateful to him for saving her from Gonsalvo; and there was also no use denying that her feeling for him had undergone a complete change. She felt almost none of her earlier anger. Maybe it was because his abuse of her was beyond recall. Maybe it was because he had left her alone and for a fortnight her self-respect had not been bruised by the selfish demands he made on her body. Or maybe jealousy was a stronger emotion than all the rest, and now that she had him by her side again, she wasn't willing to give him up. She wasn't sure that it actually mattered. But she was more charitable to him than she had ever been; she even felt a companionable closeness that was new to her. They were more friendly than in the days before they'd reached Havana. Looking at his tanned profile, she realized that she was looking forward to the coming days.

"I thought you said it wasn't a large island?"

"It's not."

"We've been following the coast for the last hour and we haven't gotten halfway around it. You must have thousands of acres here."

"I don't know the size of the island, but I do know we have about two thousand acres in sugar cane."

Summer gasped. "But that's enormous. You must be terribly wealthy. I never knew pirates made so much money."

"I couldn't buy this island. Not even pirates are that rich."

"Then how did you get it?"

"You might say I won it on a wager."

Summer gave vent to a snort of disgust. "And Smith told me you never gambled. I should have known he was just trying to protect your reputation."

"This gamble had nothing to do with cards. The island was held by the previous captain of the *Windswept*, a man who was widely known for his cruelty. The actual owner wanted his island back and I wanted the ship, so we joined forces. Unfortunately Don Agustín was injured in the assault. It didn't seem serious at first, but he suddenly got worse and died. Now the island belongs to me."

"Didn't he have any heirs?"

"Only a sister, and she didn't want it. Doña Inés has never forgotten that I helped her brother, and unless I can think of some way to prevent it, she's going to leave me her fortune as well. Then I won't be able to set foot in Havana without expecting to be stabbed in the back by some Spaniard fearful that I mean to annex the rest of the Caribbean."

Summer interrupted him excitedly. "I see a break in the trees, and there's the dock. Are we finally coming to the house?"

"Yes. There are terraces down to the water, but the view is cut off by that grove of cyprus. You'll be able to see it in just a few minutes." Summer waited expectantly. Her excitement mounted as more and more of the beautifully planned grounds came into view. One terrace after another climbed up the hillside, each with a particular design and its own special plantings.

"How many terraces are there?" she asked, amazed. "I can count three already."

"Six including the one in front of the house."

"It must be huge," she said in wonder.

"It keeps a dozen men busy, but I can't claim any credit for them. They are the work of Don Augustín's family."

"Like Señor de Aguilar's garden?"

"Very much," he said, scowling at the unpleasant memory of Gonsalvo. "The two families used to be friends, and they began their gardens in friendly rivalry. There are none finer in all of the new world." The yacht approached the dock and at last Summer had an unobstructed view of the sweep of lawn that rose from the sea to the house high on the hill.

"It's breathtaking," she said, hardly able to believe her eyes. "How can you bear to leave it?"

"I've grown rather fond of it, but you can't sail a ship like the *Windswept* and have much time left to run a plantation."

Summer sensed his enthusiasm was not wholehearted. She supposed he was remembering his home in Scotland. To her, nothing in Scotland could compare to a beautiful home such as this, but she accepted the fact that Brent had loyalties she couldn't dismiss.

"It's the most beautiful place I've ever seen," Summer said dreamily. "I feel I've just awakened from a bad dream to find that I'm an enchanted princess who lives in a palace."

"Maybe you've come home," Brent said in an odd voice. Summer waited hopefully, but all he added was, "You don't have to leave if you don't want to."

"Good," she said, trying not to show her disappointment at his refusal to commit himself. At the moment it was enough for her to know that she was safely away from Havana and the people that had driven a wedge between them. For a while he would be completely hers.

"I can't wait until we dock. I want to see everything."

"You can't see much today. It's almost dark. You'll have lots of time to look into every corner tomorrow while I'm out checking into what has been going on since I was here last."

"I want to go with you, at least some of the time."

"What for?"

"I probably know more about running a plantation than you do," she said, proudly tilting her chin. "You forget that I was reared on one and that I helped run it for a year."

"True," he admitted. "All right, you can come with me, but you will have to prove your worth or I'll leave you at the house to deal with the kitchen maids."

Summer laughed. "You are a miserable wretch, Brent

Douglas. What are you going to do when I answer your every question and solve all your problems?"

"Thank you."

She was thrown off stride by his unexpected answer. "That's not much of a reward for expert advice," she said, recovering her balance.

"I haven't gotten the advice yet, but I'm certain it won't be without cost."

"You are unquestionably the most maddening, infuriating man I've ever met," Summer said without heat, "and I don't know why I continue to put up with you."

"Probably because I won't go away."

"You needn't remind me of that. I've been trying to get rid of you for months."

"You counted it a major sin when I disappeared in Havana," Brent retorted.

"That was desertion," said Summer, collecting her dignity and her skirts as she prepared to climb onto the dock. "No woman wants to be abandoned in a strange city."

"It seems like the same thing to me."

"You're a man."

"I'm glad you noticed."

"And," Summer ignored his interruption, "that's exactly the kind of remark I would expect from a self-centered, insensitive male."

"If men are such terrible things, I wonder why you females want to be around us so much."

"I've wondered about that too," Summer replied, pretending to consider the point seriously. "I admit that men are quite useful when it comes to chopping wood and frightening off wild animals, but the civilized world would be so much more *civilized* without them." Brent pulled Summer back from a particularly inviting path.

"So you would like to dispense with us altogether?"

"Not quite altogether," she temporized. "I do like you a

little, but it would be nice if you were tame enough to be brought into the drawing room without fear that you would overturn the coffee cups."

"You lying wench." Brent threw back his head and laughed. "You talk out of both sides of your mouth, and so fast you don't know what you're saying out of either side.

"As long as you don't know, I'm safe," she answered, elated by his lighthearted mood.

"But I do know," he said, grasping her arm more firmly as they began to mount a long series of steps. "You won't be happy until you've made me your slave."

"The idea of your unquestioning obedience to my commands *is* very appealing."

"Yet as soon as you have me under your control, you won't want me any longer. You'll start to complain about me and you'll long for some strong, ruthless brute to sweep you into his arms and carry you off."

"I won't!" Summer said emphatically. "That's exactly what *did* happen to me, and I can tell you that it's very uncomfortable. I think I would greatly admire a compliant husband who would pamper me and give me everything I wished for, one who would spend all his time trying to think of things to do to please me."

"I'll give you everything you want and I'll spend the rest of my life trying to make you happy,"—Summer's bones began to melt—"but I'll be damned if I'll lie down for you to walk on." Summer's bones stopped melting. "That doesn't sound like something I'd enjoy very much."

"Neither is being captured, seduced, mauled by Spanish wolves, and then hauled off to a remote island," Summer shot back, but her barbs fell wide of the mark.

"It beats sitting home sewing samplers and going to bed early," Brent scoffed.

"I never did any such thing," Summer professed, horrified by such a fate.

"But you went to bed alone."

"I most certainly did."

"That couldn't have been much fun," he said, putting an arm around her waist.

"Speak for yourself," she said trying to remove his arm because it was brazenly taking advantage of its position close to her breast. "You never asked me how I felt."

"Because you kept saying one thing and doing another," Brent taunted. "I liked your actions much better than your words." Summer was glad that he could not see her blush in the fading light.

"I'd prefer to talk of something else," she declared.

"I don't want to talk at all," Brent whispered. He buried his face in her flowing hair. "We could go wandering among the terraces and inspect the plants quite carefully."

"You wouldn't let me just a moment ago," Summer pointed out, caught between a frown and a laugh. "Besides, it's so dark I couldn't see my hand in front of my face."

"We won't need to see."

"I'm getting hungry," she said, trying a different tack. "I won't be able to stand up if I don't get something to eat."

"I can order a picnic basket," Brent offered hopefully.

"You are completely without scruples." Summer smiled in spite of her determination to be stern. "I'm convinced you would disgrace me right in the middle of this path if I would let you."

"I'll send for blankets and a pillow."

"You'll do no such thing," she said, unable to keep her voice steady. "I may not have much influence over your actions, but I will not be abused in public while the servants watch."

"They might learn something."

"Not from me. Now stop this nonsense and take me up to the house. I'm dying to see it."

"Maybe I should show you around." Brent's eyes were

alight with mischief. "It might help to get your mind off my body. You can't begin to know how tiresome it is to be continually fighting off your advances."

Summer stooped to pick up a large rock; Brent grabbed her hands when he realized she had every intention of hitting him with it. But Summer was laughing so hard it was doubtful that she could have done more than drop it on her own toes.

"I'm going to have to be on my guard," he said. "My reputation would never recover if I were knocked senseless by a mere girl."

"It would give me infinite pleasure to be able to knock you senseless."

"And you accuse me of abusing my power."

"You do. I only wish I had some power to abuse."

"You've got plenty. Every time you smile, thunder rolls and the earth quakes. You can do more damage with those eyes than I can with my sword."

"That's nice of you to say, even if it isn't true," Summer replied meekly. "It's flattering to be noticed."

"Noticed!" Brent shook her by the shoulders. "Men fall all over themselves just to dance with you, and you say it's flattering to have people notice you. I suppose you are aware that Gonsalvo *noticed* you?"

"I don't consider that a compliment."

"You might not have wanted his attention, but Gonsalvo is famous for his high standards."

"Like you?"

"Not at all like me. Everybody knows I like women, period!"

"I want to forget about Gonsalvo. Tell me about the house." They had reached the final terrace and Summer now had a full view of the large dwelling.

"And they say men are changeable," Brent grumbled.

Chapter 28

"Here come Juanita and Pedro," said Brent as two middle-aged servants hurried out of the house to meet them. "Since I'm alone in the world, they've made it their task to take care of me. Juanita likes to spoil me," he confided with a wink.

Along with every other woman who sets eyes on you, Summer thought.

"Señor Douglas, you've come at last." Pedro hailed them, his Spanish accent evident. "We had just about given you up."

"Given you up? How did you know I was coming?"

"No one told us you would be bringing a guest." Juanita was an incredibly fat woman with swaying flesh and limitless goodwill.

"This is Summer McConnel." Summer noticed that Brent hesitated over her name; it was the first sign of discomfiture she had ever noticed in him.

"It will be nice to have someone to pet and spoil," Juanita

declared as she gazed admiringly at the beautiful young woman she had just met.

"Don't go wasting any of your special treatment on her," Brent commanded. "There must be at least a dozen ways you haven't found to spoil me."

Juanita reprimanded him. "Now you behave yourself and stop giving the *señorita* a bad impression of me. I won't have you making free with my reputation."

"Pedro would cut me up and throw the pieces away." Brent chuckled.

"I'm not saying he wouldn't want to." Juanita regarded her husband fondly. "But facts are facts, and nobody would have a chance against such a bull as you."

"You know you shouldn't be so free with your tongue," Pedro chided. "It's not respectful."

"The captain doesn't mind," Juanita countered. "Besides, I don't think he's entirely respectable himself."

"You deserve her," Summer said, nearly choking. "I've finally found someone who's not afraid to give back what you dish out."

"Afraid of the captain?" a bewildered Juanita inquired. "Why's he's the kindest man in all of New Spain."

"Then he's got a double," Summer stated coolly.

"Summer is not afraid of me either," Brent said. "She also thinks that my manners could use some correcting."

"I'm sure we all could use some improvement, but I never knew much good to come from picking out other people's faults," Juanita replied, clearly taking exception to Summer's criticism of Brent.

"If we don't hurry, your dinner will be ruined." Pedro wanted to change the subject.

"How could you possibly have anything ready?"

"We started the ovens as soon as the yacht was sighted. I have meat on the spits and girls in the gardens picking vegetables. Dinner will be served by the time you finish dressing."

"Your trunks should be in your room by now, *señorita*," said Juanita. "I'll send my oldest daughter to help. She's a sensible girl. You just tell her what you want, and she'll see to everything."

"I guess I will have to wait until tomorrow to see the house." Summer stepped into the wide, cool hall.

"You'll have the whole morning to yourself," Brent responded. "I have to meet with my overseer, or he will never forgive me."

"He's been counting the days since you left," Pedro assured him.

"I see we shall be ruled by our servants. I have only one request to make," said Brent, stemming Juanita's retort. "I want to eat on the terrace. Summer has never had dinner under a tropical moon."

"All will be ready when you come down," Pedro assured them. "Now if there is nothing else . . ."

"Come, before they chase us upstairs," Brent said to Summer. "I'll show you to your room. I have no doubt the faithful Ana is already pacing the floor. And unless a kind providence has at last taken mercy on me and gathered him to his reward, which I hope is swift and terrible, the awful Miguel is awaiting me just as impatiently."

"You know you wouldn't have anyone else," said Pedro.

"Offer me anything this side of a monkey and see if I don't take it," Brent complained as he mounted the stairs. Summer was caught between amazement and a bubble of laughter. She had never seen Brent like this, but she liked the effect the plantation had on him; she hoped they would never leave.

Summer's trunks had been unpacked, fresh undergarments were laid out, and Ana was standing ready to iron the wrinkles from the dress Summer would choose to wear for the evening. A huge copper bath held hot water, a maid waited to help her out of her clothes, and a second maid stood by to bathe her. Summer wasn't used to so many servants, but she gave herself entirely into their hands. It was an unheard of luxury, and she loved every single minute.

She was undressed and led to a scented bath that gave off an intoxicating tropical bouquet. It was so relaxing she was tempted to go to sleep, but busy hands would not leave her alone and she was soon drawn from the water, engulfed in huge towels, and patted dry. Then one of the maids wrapped her in a luxurious robe, and she chose a gown sewn with tiny pearls for the evening. While it was being readied, the maids helped her into a light petticoat and seated her at the dressing table. Summer wanted only the slightest touch of makeup, but dressing her hair took time. She wore it in a knot on top of her head, ringlets cascading down at the back, and by the time this was done, she had decided against powdering it. Her dress, a rose-red silk with a deep bodice and tiny puff sleeves worn off the shoulder, was now ready. The sleeves and hem were ruched and an undertrimming of white lace decorated the hem, sleeves, and neckline. From among the remnants of her mother's jewels, those that had escaped her father's depredations, Summer chose a strand of pearls and small ruby earrings.

"The *señorita* is so beautiful," Ana said, using the very words Summer hoped to hear from Brent's lips. "It is a shame you do not wish to powder your hair."

Summer much preferred her own rich, russet brown coloring. "There isn't time now," she stated firmly.

"No. Everything would be spoiled," Ana agreed, prodded into activity by the thought of the dinner her mother was at this very moment bringing to a peak of perfection. "I will take you to the rose salon," she added.

"Good heavens, and I nearly chose the jonquil muslin." Summer laughed. "Thank goodness I decided on the silk."

"I would have told you."

"I certainly hope so. I would have stuck out like a goose among chickens."

Ana laughed when the lovely *señorita* compared herself to a goose.

The salon was empty when she threw open the double doors, and Summer felt a pang of disappointment. She knew it was vanity to long for Brent's admiration, and she scolded herself for being so vain as to pride herself on her looks and lineage. Well not lineage, she thought grimly.

Then she pushed that unpleasant thought from her mind. Tonight was going to be wonderful, it had to be. She and Brent would be even more alone than they had been on the ship. She tingled with excitement, and began to pace the room, unaware that her anxiety was giving her stride a very unladylike swing.

So much rested on this night. She knew Brent loved her, but did *he* know it? He was so stubborn he couldn't even see what was right before him; surely during the coming days and nights he must realize that he loved her, and that she had to become his wife.

Summer sagged against a table, and released an audible groan. What was she thinking about? She was already someone else's wife. That brutal fact she would have given anything in the world to be able to forget. It was so unfair, so cruel of life to show her Brent with one hand and deny him with the other. But it would do her no good to dwell on that. Something must be done, a way must be found out of her difficulties; but let that wait for tomorrow and sensible daylight. Tonight was hers, and she was determined that nothing would spoil it for her.

"I thought I heard someone in here," Brent said, entering through the open French doors, but he suddenly came to a stop and a low whistle escaped him. "You certainly made good use of your time." He recovered enough to offer her the glass of wine he held in his hand. "You take this. I need something stronger." He poured himself a brandy.

"Brent Douglas! If you dare tell me you can't sit down to dinner with me without getting drunk first I'll, I'll . . ."

"You're putting the wrong words into my mouth again," he said, taking a large swallow of his brandy.

"A truly chivalrous man would be paying me extravagant compliments instead of swallowing his brandy like water and looking at me as if I were some serving wench he was about to roll in the hay."

"Maybe that's because I can't think of anything except taking you straight to bed." Brent took another sip of brandy.

"Probably," Summer agreed. "You never seem to have anything on your mind except your ship or taking off my clothes as quickly as possible."

"Now there's a subject I would like to discuss."

"Your ship?" she asked archly.

"No, she-devil, talking off your clothes."

"After I spent an hour putting them on, the least you could do is admire me."

"I admire you without your clothes, too."

Summer sat down on one of the sofas.

"I'm going to pretend that I've just come down. I'm about to have a delicious dinner under a tropical moon. The softest of breezes is blowing, and I'm with a handsome man, even if he is a monster of selfishness who knows how to make himself very pleasing to a woman. I would like to enjoy the evening, to pretend that I am young and beautiful and that life is filled with happiness and excitement."

"That ought to be easy."

"I want to be told that I'm beautiful," Summer continued, ignoring him, "that my skin is like velvet, my eyes are like stars, and that men would die just for the chance to sit where you are now."

"They would."

"Will you stop interrupting and listen," she said, exasperated. "I want to walk in the moonlight, dance under the stars. I want to forget that there is anything or anybody in the world other than the two of us. I want you to tell me any man would be lucky to have me for his wife and that I'm going to meet some wonderfully handsome man, be gloriously happy, and have rooms full of children."

"I don't think I should let you have any more wine." Brent removed the glass from her hand. "A little more and you'll be discussing bridal gowns and the kind of wedding you want." That unfortunate remark burst Summer's bubble of happiness.

"You don't have to be so cruel," she said, losing her animation and heaving a tremulous sigh. "I know it's a futile dream, but I never had a chance to speculate on my future before I found myself in this impossible tangle. My problems are so insurmountable I can't bear to think of them. Instead, I make up fantasies about how I wish things had been. I know it's silly and childish, but they give me a few moments of happiness."

"I know how you feel." The sympathy in Brent's voice surprised her. "Things never work out the way we want, not even when they come out right in the end."

"Why?"

"Maybe that makes us appreciate our happiness more when we do get it, maybe that makes us stronger people. I really don't know, but there's no use being sorry for yourself or letting self-pity get in the way of doing something about your situation. Nothing is ever so bad it can't improve if you work at it."

"That sounds like a page from a Scottish book of proverbs." Summer sniffed in disgust.

"I promise I won't preach anymore tonight." He brought Summer to her feet.

"And I promise not to become maudlin again." She

walked toward the terrace. "It seems I'm always starting conversations I don't want to finish."

"That's because you let your worries get the best of you."

"And you let your lusts get the best of you."

"It's the best of you my lusts want," Brent countered.

"Devil!" she retorted, but her good humor was restored. "Let's eat before I give up on you completely and join a convent."

"That would be an awful waste of one of Nature's most perfect creations."

"You know, that's the nicest thing you've ever said to me, even if I do owe the compliment to your lust," Summer said as she stepped out onto the terrace.

"I can't see you or be near you without desiring you. And don't tell me I should love you for your mind. No mind or personality can make up for a body like a stick or a face like a shrunken skull."

"I shouldn't think it could." Summer giggled in spite of herself.

"If you were the most brilliant woman in the world, that wouldn't provoke the surge of desire I get just from touching your hand or kissing your lips. The smell of your perfume in my nostrils makes my senses ache."

"I doubt Juanita will think that sufficient excuse for letting her food get cold," Summer remarked, marveling at the number of dishes set out before her.

"Now who's the devil? You know you wouldn't like me nearly so much if I were as cold as that man Brinklow."

"But I *don't* like you." Summer gave Brent a provocative smile. "I don't deny that you are pleasant enough to look at, but I would much prefer to be sitting down to dinner with Smith, or even Caspian. At least then I would be sure that Juanita's food, and not I, would be the main course." She slipped around Pedro to escape Brent. "Careful," she warned, "or you'll overturn the table."

"Someday you'll be strangled and your body hidden under a bush."

"I cry peace," she said merrily, and allowed Brent to help her with her chair.

"Eat, you vexing female. For the present I'll do my best to behave like Smith."

"Oh, please don't try," Summer protested. "I'm persuaded the effort would derange you." The presence of the dour Pedro and the entrance of two girls who were bringing in the first course prevented Brent from sweeping Summer up from her chair and inflicting his own particular brand of torture on her. But she smiled at him in such a devastating fashion that his legs grew weak, and he sat down quickly. There would be time to exact punishment later, when he had gotten his quivering limbs under control.

Chapter 29

It was a perfect dinner. Pedro served them from trays brought from the house to insure their privacy, and Summer felt that nothing could ruin this night. The terrace was bathed in the light of a full moon, its pale gold rays augmented by lanterns placed on walls or hung from trees. These glowed like lesser moons against the dark shadows of the house and the gardens. On the table, candles glimmered within globes, wrapping them in an aura of warm, lustrous light.

A medley of sounds and smells filtered to her. The murmur of rustling leaves, the chirping of frogs soothed her senses. Odors of decaying leaves, freshly turned earth, and salt sea air became lost in the heavy perfume of the flowers that filled the terrace and surrounding lawns, some growing on plants in huge pots, other on thick borders, tall shrubs, or rambling vines. The extravagance of Nature's bounty made Summer feel almost drunk.

Filled with the soft, life-giving moisture of the sea, the

night air fell on Summer's shoulders like a velvet cloak, enveloping her in its soft warmth. It promised peace and plenty, and it eased the tension from her body, allowing her to luxuriate in this paradise that must have been intended for the gods.

Dinner began in a bantering mood, but during the course of the evening, the atmosphere changed, slowly at first, and then quite dramatically. When they finally rose from the table, their easy informality had vanished. In its place was pent-up excitement, intense concentration on each other. Their conversation slowed, became halting, and then virtually stopped. The few words they spoke were separated by long pauses.

At first Summer tried to sustain the faltering conversation. "We haven't been very talkative tonight."

"No." It was an unencouraging reply.

"I didn't expect to be entertained every minute, but neither did I anticipate having to talk to myself."

"I was thinking," Brent said unhelpfully.

"Are your thoughts private, or am I included?"

"You're very much included, but I'm not sure I want to share them yet."

"Sounds mysterious."

"No, just damnable!" he said with explosive fury.

Summer pushed her chair back. "In that case I'm glad you won't tell me. Maybe a change of scene will help you think of something more pleasant," she said provocatively. Brent rose quickly to help her with her chair as she gathered up a thin gauze wrap. "The moon is so bright I can walk about as if it were day. You may come along if you like, in case I stumble or lose my way."

"I'll trip you at the first step."

"I should never give you permission to lay a hand on me," she said, striving for a light tone. "You never neglect any opportunity."

"I never could stand the temptation of being near you without touching you."

"Did you every try?"

"In Havana, but I couldn't get you off my mind," Brent said. "Those were the worst weeks of my life." Summer halted and turned to face him, angry now.

"How can you say that when you pursued dozens of females right under the noses of half of Havana?"

"You know I wasn't interested in any of those women."

"Do you think I believe that?" she asked.

"It ought to be obvious."

"Well it's not. Explain it to me."

"You really don't understand, do you?"

"It's about as clear as the ravings of a madman."

"I *am* a madman. I have been for the last several months."

"I must have had too much wine. I don't understand a word you've said."

"You haven't had enough, or your feelings would tell you that I made my interest in the marquise and others obvious to keep anyone from guessing that the person I was really interested in was you."

Summer merely stared at him.

"I was sure you knew."

"No," she said, helplessly. "I never guessed." A soaring joy threatened to dismantle every bit of control she had.

"It was a mistake to bring you to Havana. With my reputation, the only way I could think to protect you was to let everyone see that I was interested in others."

"Are you trying to make me believe that your interest in the marquise was assumed?" There was a dangerous tone to her voice.

"Not entirely," Brent admitted. "I had known her before. Dallying with her is not without its rewards."

"So you lost sight of why you were playing at cat and mouse and proceeded to collect your reward every night."

Summer stepped angrily away from him. "Maybe you decided it was more fun to capture the cat than to protect the mouse."

"I didn't collect anything from Constanza, unless you consider the privilege of talking to her husband a just reward for fidelity."

"You can't really expect me to believe the two of you sat around her boudoir discussing the sea while the marquise slept demurely in the background."

"I was never in Constanza's bedroom, and her husband doesn't know any more about ships than you do, although he's an admiral of the Spanish Navy. God, he's an ass! No wonder Spain is losing her empire."

"Where did you go then?" she asked, confused. "Everyone knows you didn't stay at the hotel."

"I went back to the ship," he said, as though the answer were being pulled from him. "Didn't you guess?"

"How could I when I never saw you?" Summer was afraid to believe him, but she couldn't bear the thought that he might be lying to her.

"I couldn't have fooled anybody if I'd blabbed to everyone."

"I don't think I qualify as just anyone."

"That chattering fool Chichi would have spread the news all over town in less than a day."

Summer was forced to admit that was true. "But why did you do it?"

"You still don't know?"

"No," she replied, in a hushed voice.

He drew her so near she could feel his hot breath on her cool skin. "It was the only way I could keep my promise not to touch you."

"At least you could have told me you weren't spending every night with the marquise."

"I wasn't sure you were interested."

"When I didn't see you, I thought you didn't care anymore."

"I was *trying* to attend to the ship's business." He laughed humorlessly. "Smith practically ordered me to stop chasing all over the city and spend more time looking after you."

"Why?"

"Because you're mine."

"But you don't particularly like me, remember?" Summer studied his cravat. "I'm just a body with a pretty face."

"I never said anything that foolish."

"You certainly did, and a lot more I won't mention."

"You know it's not true."

"No I don't," she whispered, more softly than before. "You never told me."

"I've told you now."

"You've only said a lot of meaningless words. You haven't said anything to make me believe you've changed your mind."

"I brought you here, didn't I?"

"You could have brought hundreds of women here for all I know."

"I went to the trouble of hiring the most lavish suite in the largest hotel in town, bought you trunkloads of clothes. Everything I did was for you."

"You haven't done *anything* for me," she said, wondering what she could say to make him understand. "Everything you did was for you, for your pride in possessing me, your pleasure in admiring me, even your revenge against Gowan."

"I don't understand you," he said aggrieved. "You're beginning to sound like Smith. Have you two been putting your heads together to plague me, because if you have I'll tan your hides."

"There you go again, forcing people to your will without even questioning whether they might not know more than you do."

"I don't bend people to my will," Brent protested.

"But you do, even Smith. What can anybody else expect when you treat the person who's most important to you like that?"

"He's not the most important person to me," Brent said impatiently. "You are."

"I didn't know that." Summer made a noise that sounded like a sob. "How could I when you've never bothered to tell me?"

"But you had to know it."

"No I didn't. Remember, I'm the one who thought you were spending your nights in half the bedrooms of Havana. I'm not in on your little secrets."

"It's not a secret."

"*What's* not a secret?"

"That I love you."

"You don't!" Summer tried to keep her turbulent emotions under control. "You've let the wine and the moonlight go to your head."

"I know what I feel," Brent said, his voice rising. "If I say I love you, I love you."

"Is that an order?" Summer asked. A choked sound escaped her as Brent suddenly swept her up into his arms and crushed her to him.

"No, you hard-headed spitfire. It's a declaration. I love you, do you hear me? I love you like a man loves a woman he wants to keep by his side forever. I love you because you're beautiful, because you have the most inviting body I've ever seen. But I also love you because you're a termagant and I can't get you and your craggy temper out of my mind. I dream about you, and I spend every waking minute wondering where you are, what you're doing, and what lucky fool is close enough to reach out and touch you, to hear you laugh, to see the way your eyes sparkle when you're happy, to watch a smile curve across your lips, or enjoy the way your eyes crinkle when you're about to say something clever. I'm a man with a raging fever and there's no cure. The more I'm around you, the worse it gets. But when I'm not with you it's worse still. I can't sleep and I can't eat. My crew had begun to wonder if they shouldn't start looking about for a new captain. I paced the deck, I lost my temper without reason, I shouted and gave contradictory orders, and worst of all I haven't been with another female since I set eyes on you."

"You really *do* love me." Summer strove to keep from giving way to hysterical happiness.

"That's what I've been trying to tell you for the last half-hour, you adorable little idiot," Brent said roughly. "I love you so much I ache all over just thinking about it." Summer threw herself into his arms and covered his face with kisses, laughing and crying at the same time.

"And I love you, too, you big dumb ox. I've loved you almost from the beginning."

"Now who's telling lies?" he said, holding her even closer.

"Truly, I'm not. I tried to hate you for quite a long time, but I couldn't. It was your loyalty to Smith that utterly destroyed my resistance. After that I was so hopelessly in love with you that I was jealous of every woman you looked at in Havana."

"How could you think I would really look at anyone when I had you?"

"How was I to know you could live like a monk for weeks on end?"

"I've been going to sea for ten years, my poisoned-tongued Aphrodite. We're away from port for months at a time."

"Tell me again that you love me," Summer begged.

"I love you," Brent declared.

"Say it as though you mean it," she demanded.

"I love you, by God," Brent shouted, and sweeping her into his arms, he turned and mounted the terrace steps. "But I prefer to show you." He recrossed the terrace in a few strides, carelessly brushing the table with Summer's trailing gown and causing the wine glasses Pedro had set out to fall to the flagstones and break into tiny fragments.

"I can't wait any longer. Having you in my arms is more than a man can bear. I will do something wild if I don't make love to you. Tomorrow I may restrain myself, but tonight I'm going to make love to you until dawn."

"If you pull the curtains, we won't know when it's morning," she said teasingly.

"I may not stop when the sun comes into the room." Brent welcomed the look of invitation in her eyes.

"Don't ever stop," she pleaded. "I dreamed that someday you'd say you loved me. Now that you have I can't hear it often enough."

"I'll tell you at least once every day."

"Every hour," she said, floating on clouds of buoyant bliss. "I want to hear it when I wake up and when I go to sleep. I want to hear it in the wind, feel it in the air around me. I don't ever again want to have to ask myself if you love me."

"You won't have any doubts," he said, placing her on the bed and beginning to unbutton her dress. "I will devote all my time to proving to you that no one in the world means as much to me as you do."

Summer helped Brent slide the dress down over her body, and within seconds she lay before him as Nature intended her to be seen. Brent stared at her in awe, unable to believe that anyone could be so beautiful. She grasped his hand and pressed it to her warm flesh.

"Are you going to join me," she asked shyly, "or are you going to stand there gawking all night? I thought you were a man of action."

"I never refuse a lady." Brent shed his clothing without regard for strained seams and popping buttons. As he climbed into the bed, Summer enfolded him in her arms.

He kissed her deeply, and she responded with such burning intensity their bodies were driven to become one. Their limbs entwined, and the heat coursing through their bodies increased tenfold as it flowed from one to the other.

Brent's tongue raked her mouth and kindled in her a chord of response deeper than anything she had experienced. She flung herself at him, determined to become so much a part of him that he would never be free of her. Her fierceness had its birth in an unspoken fear that their love, removed from the hard realities of the world and declared in the isolation of the island, was too fragile to last. But something deep within her urged her to plunge into the vortex of this maelstrom, and her stormy passion was all the more compelling because of her desperation.

Brent met the challenge boldly and recklessly, marveling at the depth of love she was revealing. He loved her more than life, even more than his revenge. He knew he wanted to be with her forever, that he would never feel complete again without her. He was an adventurer who had taken her against all odds; he would hold her the same way.

They made love with an animalistic frenzy, each attacking the other, driven to insensitivity by the force of their own fevered passion, and their consummation was a brutal release of pent-up desire. Exhaustion only made their need more unbearable, but they were freed of their dammed-up energies.

They had destroyed the last barrier that kept them apart, and as their overheated senses cooled and the desperate rush to dash themselves on the rock of their passion subsided, they achieved a truer perception of the feeling that had come to exist between them. No more would they thrash aimlessly about, trying to search out the seat of their emotional needs in a game of sensual blindman's bluff. Their urge for physical fulfillment had been tested in the much larger crucible of their love, and had become just a part of a relationship no less powerful because it was complex.

"I always dreamed of what it would be like to lie with the

man I loved," Summer said softly. "Here, far away from the outside world, with your arms around me, I feel totally at peace."

Brent touched her cheek. "I had no idea that two people could feel this way. I don't think I wanted to, not after seeing how much my mother suffered."

"You should have left me on the *Sea Otter* and sailed away as fast as you could."

"I could no more have left you than I could have given up my own ship. I was hypnotized by that first vision of you stepping out on deck so proudly."

"I would never have known it from the way you treated me."

"Knowing that you were destined to belong to Gowan was a blow I couldn't endure. I was determined that you would be mine." Summer snuggled closer to him.

"Are you always so determined in your pursuit?"

"I never bothered before. If things didn't go my way, there was always someone else."

"There was never anyone else for me," she declared. "I had almost resigned myself to spending the rest of my life running the plantation for Father." She held more tightly to Brent. "I never dreamed that I would be dragged willy-nilly from that ship by a wild-eyed pirate, and held captive in his cabin for weeks. That kind of adventure only happens in story books."

"I remember numerous complaints about beasts, bullies, and people who bend the rules to suit themselves." Brent chuckled.

"You were heartless, but I never could stay mad at you for very long, even when you were behaving like a medieval warlord."

"Every time I looked at you I wanted to take you in my arms and hold you forever. My mind dwelt on the sight of your bare shoulder, the feel of your skin, even your crooked grin when you were up to mischief."

They reached out to each other, two souls crossing the abyss and leaving behind all desire to exist separately. They knew a gentleness they had not known before, a certainty that they were no longer entities, no longer alone. They could share without the need for words, achieve satisfaction through each other, give in the certainty that they would receive in return.

They now knew the meaning of oneness. They had acquired a deeper understanding of their love, and of each other. No matter what they must endure, they would not be torn asunder.

Chapter 30

Summer woke to sunlight streaming through the windows. She was strongly tempted to stay in the large fourposter, but as she stretched with feline grace, she was drawn to the life-giving warmth of the sun. Her room, at the front of the house, provided her with an uninterrupted view of the terraces that descended to the sea. It was a breathtaking sight, and she sank down onto a bamboo chair, hardly able to believe she could be so happy.

After weeks of doubt, worry, and fear, the island was a sanctuary, a quiet cove where she was protected from the whims of Fate by the one person she loved above all else. It was still hard for her to believe that Brent loved her as passionately as she loved him, but a thrill of exhilaration raced through her, swift as lightning, every time she thought of his strong arms or his hot, demanding lips.

All at once she had a tremendous desire to be up and about. She rang the bell, then ran to her trunks to look for something to wear. Her head was deep in the largest one when Ana entered with a towel and a basin of water.

"I wondered when you would wake," Ana said with a smile. "The captain gave orders that you not be disturbed."

"Where did he go?" Summer's voice was muffled by the trunk.

"He's out with the overseer. Carlos heard last night that the captain had returned, and he was here before Mama got the fires going this morning."

"How long will they be gone?"

Ana's eyes twinkled merrily as Summer raised her head from the trunk. "Carlos didn't look happy when the captain told Mama he'd be home by midday. The captain said he had better things to do than ride his rump raw, stare at a lot of sugar cane, and worry over problems he was paying Carlos to take care of."

"That sounds exactly like something Brent, I mean the captain, would say," Summer confided, a glimmer of a smile touching her lips. "He's rather impatient."

"Can I help the *señorita* with something?" asked Ana, belatedly becoming aware of her new duties.

"I'm looking for a yellow poplin dress covered with knots of blue flowers, but I can't find it anywhere." Perplexed, Summer opened the second trunk. "I wanted to wear it today."

"That's one of the dresses I ironed and put away." Ana went to the small dressing room. "I didn't know what you would choose to wear, and since I couldn't do everything last night, I just ironed a few dresses. Do you really wear these clothes when you're in Scotland?" she asked, lifting from the trunk a silk gown trimmed with lace and heavily embroidered.

"Yes, and with enough petticoats to slow a horse. Put it away. It makes me hot just to look at it. It's such a beautiful day I can't stay in this room a minute longer. I want to see the house, the lawns, the terraces, the stables, and just about every foot of land on the island." She suddenly felt a trifle embarrassed by her own enthusiasm, but Ana seemed to find nothing unusual in her attitude.

"Mama will be happy to show you anything you like. She and Papa were both born on the island and there's not much here they don't know about."

"Maybe you can begin by telling me why this room is so oddly furnished," Summer said. "It looks as though people have been stealing pieces of furniture from it."

"They have." Ana became aware of the unusual appearance of the room. "This was the old *señora's* room. After she died the old master could never bear to let anyone else use it, so it was left untouched. Whenever something broke in another part of the house, we would come here to find what we needed. You only have to tell me what you want and Papa will see to it. If the captain had told us he was bringing you, we would have prepared the room."

"A dressing table would do for now," Summer said. "I don't want to go moving things about without talking to the captain first. You never know what unaccountable notions men will take into their heads."

"Yes, *señorita*." Ana held up the dress so she could slip it over Summer's head. "Mama is always saying that men are the most contrary of creatures. No matter what you do they could have done it better and in half the time."

"That's the captain all over." Summer adjusted her gown with great care. She hoped Brent's eyes would always glow like aquamarines when they lighted on her. It gave her pleasure to know that she had the power to send his senses racing.

"You are very beautiful, *señorita*," Ana said simply. "The captain is a very lucky man."

"Let's hope he agrees with you." Summer blushed faintly. She felt that she was accepting affection and good wishes under false pretenses, but there was nothing to be gained by telling the truth. "I think I'll take a tour of the house first," she said, banishing that unwelcome thought.

"Should I tell Mama?"

"No. I just want to wander about."

"If you change your mind, the large bell in the hall summons outside servants, and the bellpull right next to it calls someone from the kitchen."

"You can start trying to make sense of all these trunks while I'm gone," Summer instructed. "I want the heavy clothes packed in one trunk and the other things gotten ready for me to wear."

"Yes, *señora*. Is there anything else?"

"No, just make sure someone calls me the minute the captain returns."

Summer's home had been constructed to bring cooling breezes into the house. There were porches on all sides, and halls bisected it to catch every available breath of air. But this house was built of stone and brick, much like the Scottish houses her parents had talked about, and Summer had never seen one like it. It had no inner court as was the Spanish custom, and no porches or halls that opened to the outside. The thick walls were broken by few windows, and the bare beams that supported the upper floor projected from the outer walls. Summer moved slowly down the wide stairs, conscious of the gloomy interior. There were no bright colors to lighten the atmosphere, no open doors and arches to give a feeling of light and space. It was cool and dark, but Summer didn't mind the heat as much as she minded the feeling of being closed in. Better ways to arrange the furniture flitted through her mind as she wandered through the rooms on the first floor, but she soon abandoned such thoughts to daydream about spending her life in this large, quiet house with Brent. She wanted to turn it into a cheerful, happy home. As she wandered from room to room, she pictured the house filled with people, children playing among the shadows and guests wandering contentedly over the terraces.

Summer went onto the terrace where they had dined the preceding night, and memories of Brent's lovemaking sent a thrill of excitement through her, bringing her to tingling awareness.

It was not a hot morning, but the blaze kindled within her combined with the heat of the sun to make her uncomfortably warm. She strolled from the terrace to seek the shade of the trees in the garden below. There, she found a bench along a winding path and sank down upon it. From this position, she had a partial view of the house and she could see the terraces descend to the sea. It was a lovely sight, and it encouraged Summer to feel that the house was not quite hopeless. She would have to speak to Brent. If it was not possible to alter the structure of the house, she would have larger windows cut out and convert others into doors that could be thrown open to the outside. She was deep in her plans when Brent's voice startled her out of her reverie.

"You can't go to sleep on me the first day you're here," he chastised playfully.

"I was just daydreaming." A rush of giddy excitement came over her at his unexpected nearness. He was smiling at her in that intense way he had when his eyes began to turn green with desire, and her pulse raced, preventing her distracted mind from focusing on anything in particular.

"I hope I was included in your dreams," he said, settling down next to her.

"I was just thinking of ways to open up the house. It looks more like a fortress than a home." She averted her gaze to allow her hot cheeks to cool and her whirling wits to slow down. She had to force her thoughts through the tumult of her emotions.

"That's what it was," he said, brushing a heavy fall of hair back from her upturned face. "It was built to withstand an attack from the sea." His fingertips lost themselves in the luxuriant locks that fell down the back of her neck.

"Is there any danger of that still?" Summer's voice trailed off into a whisper.

"No one dares when they know they'll have the *Windswept* swooping down on them before they reach the windward passages." He took her quivering fingers in both his hands and raised them to his lips.

"Ana said your agent was waiting for you when you came down this morning." She spoke in halting phrases, her heated mind barely able to piece together the words.

"The man is a workhorse." Brent placed kisses on her open palm. "If he had his way we'd have packed provisions and been gone the better part of a week." His lips moved to her wrists. "I told him I could see his sugar mill some other time; I was coming back to have lunch with you."

Summer's arms lay exposed to the touch of his foraging lips.

"Can I go with you?" she mumbled, all power to make conversation beginning to leave her.

"If you like, but I doubt Carlos will approve." His lips reached her shoulder and her head listed to one side, providing open access to the fluted column of her throat.

"Why?" she asked faintly.

"He doesn't think seafaring people know much about planting." Brent's voice became unsteady as the fire of desire spread through his loins.

"I know quite a lot about managing an estate." Summer struggled to retain her clarity, but his arms tightened about her, pressing her softness into his iron-ribbed chest, and she could resist the delicious languor lapping at her self-restraint no longer. She subsided gratefully into his ardent embrace.

"The midday meal will be served in the breakfast parlor," Pedro announced, stern disapproval in his voice.

"Damn the man," Brent muttered as Summer wriggled from his embrace and tried to repair the damage to her toilette. Her mood was fading rapidly and suddenly she laughed out loud.

"What's so funny?" Brent demanded, unamused.

"It's a good thing Pedro came along when he did, or you would have tumbled me right here on the path."

Brent responded with an inarticulate growl.

"You can tell me what you plan to do with the plantation while we eat," she invited, putting his arm around her and resting her head on his shoulder. "We can take up where we left off later."

But the meal didn't go quite as she had expected. Brent began to talk about the plantation and all he had seen that morning, and soon he was deep into the changes and improvements he wanted to make. Summer listened attentively, making few comments other than to ask a question now and then. She knew that much of what Brent had in mind was difficult or impractical, but she was surprised at the interest he was taking in his land and the grasp he already showed of its management.

"You sound like you've been a farmer all your life," she said as Brent helped her into the trap. He had insisted that he show her some of his fields immediately after they'd eaten, and the trap had been at the door before they had risen from the table. "I never imagined a sea captain would take more than a slight interest in a plantation."

"Neither did I," Brent confessed. He climbed up beside her and signaled the groom to stand away from the horses' heads. He backed his pair effectively, but after long years at sea, he lacked the style of one who had been raised as a gentleman. "I guess I learned about more in Scotland than guns and horses. I no sooner found myself the owner of this than I thought of all manner of changes I wanted to make. I intend to do even more now."

"Will you go to sea again?" The answer to that question was very important to Summer.

"I'm not sure. The Dutch aren't nearly so worried about the English anymore, and I don't want to go to sea as a pirate."

"You could become a legitimate trader."

"What's the excitement in that? Not even Smith would want such a tame ending to ten years of adventure."

"If you had a home to return to, maybe you wouldn't miss the sea so much," Summer said hopefully.

"Maybe I wouldn't, but even if I do give up privateering, I'll have to defend myself from other scoundrels just as the *Sea Otter* tried to defend itself against me."

"I never thought of it that way."

"I have. It would be better to settle here and make something of this place than to dwindle into a fat steward tending cargo."

"In that case, there is a question I would like to ask." Summer looked at him tentatively.

"What is it?" Brent's smile was so warm the thought almost left her mind.

"What's going to happen to me?"

Chapter 31

"You're going to stay here with me. I'm going to marry you."

Summer's heart leapt into her throat. He'd said it so simply as if he were telling her some ordinary piece of news. It was nearly impossible for her to speak, but she had to. She must know what he meant before she was swept away by the euphoria building within her.

"But I'm already married," she said with difficulty. "Legally I'm the earl's wife."

"You're not going back to Gowan," Brent barked. "I'll never let that man touch you."

"But how can you marry me when I'm already married? Will they let you?"

"Who is they?" Brent asked.

"I don't know exactly. Everybody I guess."

"They can't stop us."

"They can make it impossible for us to be happy together."

"You're the only one who has the power to do that," he

said, letting his hand slide suggestively along her side and up under her breast.

"Will you stop thinking about my body for once and listen to me?" she said, knocking his hand away.

"I can do both," he answered, considerably startled by the vehemence of her outburst.

"No you can't. In a minute I'll see your eyes begin to turn green, and I'll know you're out of reach." She moved away from him. "Please listen. This is very important.

"What I'm trying to say is that according to everyone else what we're doing is totally wrong. As far as they're concerned, I'm Gowan's wife. It really doesn't matter that I was forced to marry him. If I suffer in silence they'll pity me, when they remember to think of me, but if I pretend to be your wife they'll destroy us. They won't care how bad Gowan is. They'll only think I've committed a crime that cannot go unpunished."

"No one can destroy us if we don't let them," Brent declared.

"Try to understand," she begged. "They won't care if I'm your *mistress*, but I won't be allowed to be your *wife*. They'll refuse to recognize me, and I'll be ostracized if I attempt to force my way into their midst."

"I'll see that you're invited anywhere you want to go." Brent now had a martial light in his eyes.

Summer smiled lovingly at him, but shook her head. "This is one time you can't change the rules. You can't force people to accept those who trample on their social customs. That threatens everything they believe in, and they'll fight back. It wouldn't be easy for you either."

"I've been an outcast for years, but I've succeeded quite well in spite of it."

"It's not only you I'm concerned about. There are children to consider."

"We don't have any children to worry about."

"We will, and I don't want them to be brought into this world as bastards. And they would be because I'm not your wife, no matter how much I ought to be," she added quickly to forestall his protest. "It was wrong of my father to sell me to my husband, but that doesn't make the marriage illegal. Our children would never be accepted by the only strata of society they could really be a part of. Do you think the marquise would allow one of her sons to marry our daughter, even though she herself has seduced half the men in Havana?"

"No," he admitted thoughtfully, "she wouldn't."

"Neither would anyone else, and you couldn't expect our children to understand that." Summer paused briefly, and then continued as by an act of will. "I know what it's like to be unable to claim your rightful father, and I could never do that to a child of mine."

"What do you mean? Your parents were married."

Summer hung her head. "I never told you before, but Ashton is not my father. I didn't know it myself until a few months ago. He probably never would have told me, but when he ordered me to marry the earl, I vowed I'd run away or do anything else I could to keep from marrying a man I'd never seen. That's when he threatened to disown me, to throw me out of the house and tell everyone I wasn't his daughter. He swore he'd cut me off without a penny so no one would marry me and I'd starve or be reduced to doing anything to stay alive."

"The rotten bastard ought to have his neck wrung," Brent said savagely.

"He was drunk, and scared. He had enormous gambling debts, and was afraid of what would happen to him if he couldn't pay them off."

"Then who is your father?"

"My mother created a terrible scandal by eloping with Frederick Boyleston. Somehow he died a few days later, and she was forced to marry Ashton and come out here. I'm Frederick Boyleston's daughter."

"Thank God for that." Brent was unmoved. "Ashton is a commoner, but Boyleston comes from a good family."

"But I'm a *bastard*," she nearly shouted. "Don't you understand? You've been eaten up by hate for years because you can't reclaim your own land. I can't claim *anything*. My mother was the only person who would acknowledge me, and she's dead. Do you think the Boylestons would claim a penniless bastard? Mother's father disowned me before I was born, and Ashton is liable to do the same the next time he gets drunk. I'd be ready to swear an oath that the earl would rather have me drowned at sea than admit his wife is illegitimate."

Brent tried to calm her, but Summer was too worked up. The horrible secret had been festering inside her for months and she had to get it all out.

"I can never claim to be part of the Boyleston family, and our children wouldn't be accepted as members of yours. I can't bear to think of leaving you, but I can't face a life of ostracism. It would ultimately destroy us, if not because of what it did to us, because of what it did to our children."

"You don't have to worry about any of that," he said, taking her into his arms and holding her close. "I promise that before long we will be man and wife in the eyes of all the world, not just ours."

"Don't you understand? Don't you care? *I'm a bastard!* There's no way you can get around that."

Brent spoke sharply. "I'd rather have you illegitimate than think that Charles Ashton's blood runs in the veins of every child I sire." He put his fingers to Summer's lips to silence her protest. "I don't care who your father was. I fell in love with you as Ashton's daughter, and I'll go on loving you as Boyleston's. It doesn't make any difference to me." He stifled another protest. "Nobody knows anything about Boyleston and no one ever will. Your mother died without breaking her silence and Ashton has no reason to break his. But I can offer him plenty of reasons *not* to change his story. So, as far as the world is concerned, none of this ever happened. You have two legal and respectable parents, and before long you're going to be my legal and respectable wife."

"How?" she asked, hardly daring to hope he could find a way to dispel the troubles that dogged her heels.

"Smith and the lawyers will unravel the tangle."

"Isn't it impossible unless Gowan dies?"

"Maybe not. Since you've never met your husband and were married against your will, the best solution would be to have the marriage annulled. However, we may have to settle for something less satisfactory."

"What?" she said, almost afraid to ask.

"I've told Smith that if things begin to look impossible, he's to steal the records and destroy them."

"You wouldn't dare!" she gasped, horrified.

"I'd sack every church in New Spain if it would free you from that marriage. I'm not going to let anyone or anything stand in the way of your happiness."

"Can it really be done without causing a scandal or doing something terrible that people will never forget?"

"I'm a rich man, and I can't think of a better way to use my money than to buy your freedom."

"Can you promise something like that?"

"Do you doubt me?"

"No, but . . ."

"No *buts*. Either you do or you don't. Do you believe in me?"

"You know I do."

"Do you believe that I will do what I say I'll do?"

"Yes, as far as you are able."

"There you go, qualifying your trust again. Have you ever known me to fail?" he challenged. "Come on, have you?"

"No, I haven't," she confessed with a trace of a smile, "not even when I thought there was no way you could succeed. But then you never took on the whole western world."

"Then forget all your fears. We've wasted too much time on them already."

"That sounds agreeable to me." Summer repressed an urge to ignore any possible obstacles to her happiness. "I would like nothing better than to settle down here and raise a family of strong sons and beautiful daughters, but there is one more question that has to be faced." She hesitated, but knew she had to go ahead. "What about your home in Scotland?"

"I've told you before that I no longer have a home in Scotland." His voice was harsh, a look of dulled hatred filled his eyes, and his hands instinctively tightened on the reins. The horses reacted sharply to the sudden pressure on their tender mouths, and Summer allowed Brent time to get himself and the horses under control before she spoke again.

"What about your estates? Are they still yours?"

"As long as I pay the taxes Gowan can't take them from me unless I die without an heir, but as long as I'm outlawed they might as well be his personal property." He ground his teeth. "But I have better land here even if there's not so much of it. Why should I saddle myself with a run-down estate that's covered by snow half the year?"

"Will you be content here?"

"Yes!" That one strangled syllable convinced Summer that no matter what Brent did with the rest of his life, he would never forget his home or the manner in which he had been forced to leave it.

"You don't believe me, do you?" he asked after a prolonged silence.

"No," Summer answered quietly. "You could forget if you had left on your own, but not when you were driven out against your will."

"You're as bad as Smith. There's no reason to go back.

The estate has been going to ruin for years. My father went to sea to find the money to restore it, but it would now take a fortune to put Windswept back on its feet. It would be years before it could begin to pay back the investment."

"Have you forgotten your father's money?"

"That's beyond reach. My father trusted Gowan so completely that there's no way to prove the money ever existed, much less that it was mine. If any proof does exist, it's in Gowan's hands."

"Can't the courts help you?"

"The courts are Gowan's trump card. He doesn't have to lift a finger against me. He can even pretend to see to my part as my guardian and trustee while the courts do his dirty work for him. He's required to uphold any verdict they reach, and since there's only one verdict they *can* reach, he has me neatly boxed in."

"But someone must know something."

"After what happened to Ben, no one is going to come forward to speak against him."

"There's got to be some way."

"I've spent years trying to think of one, but I can't even get near Scotland as long as I'm accused of murder. That was Gowan's master stroke. There's no way I can be cleared, not with his men waiting to swear that Ben was last seen alive with me screaming at him."

"Were you?"

"Yes. I went mad with rage when he told me what Gowan had done, and I went straight to the castle and confronted Gowan with everything. Fool! Somehow I expected he would confess and everything would right itself. That was stupid, but I was too young and angry to think; I couldn't see that the most likely result would be that Gowan would find a way to get rid of me."

"People would have suspected him first if anything had happened to you."

"Not when no one knew about the money. All anyone knows is that I'm supposed to have killed that old man."

"What did happen to him?"

"I don't know. Someone must have overheard enough to tell Gowan that I knew the truth. Ben and I left the tap room still arguing, and we separated at the edge of the village. They found him in a ditch not far from his sister's cottage. He had been hit over the head and strangled. My riding crop was found nearby. I sealed my own fate by running away."

"There must be a way to prove your innocence."

"No way and no reason. I have everything I want right here."

"But Smith says you'll never be happy until you go back."

"Smith is a romantic fool for all his efficiency," declared Brent. "He listened to me too often those first years. All I could think about then was how much I hated Gowan. I counted the days until I would be able to wreak my vengeance. But when I saw you things began to change. I didn't care about revenge anymore. It took me a while to find that out, but now Scotland seems far away, too remote to be an important part of my life ever again."

"I can't believe that I can be a substitute for a lost estate." Summer was not sure quite what to think.

"I'd forgo the whole of Scotland before I'd hand you over to Gowan for even one hour."

Overcome by this tribute, Summer abandoned her effort to make Brent realize how important his past still was to him. She feared he would never be content as long as his family's name was sullied, but she decided she would talk of this some other time. She had never experienced the electrifying feeling of having the man of her dreams tell her she was more valuable than an estate, and she intended to bask in his love and enjoy his adulation to the fullest. She tightened her hold on Brent and leaned her head against his shoulder.

"Do you love me enough to let me change the house?" she

asked, looking up into his eyes and giving him her most tempting smile.

"Keep smiling at me like that, and I will let you tear it down block by block."

"I don't mean to do anything so drastic," she assured him, satisfied that he had given her permission to proceed. "I only want to open it up to the sunshine. It's so dark I feel I'm in a cave when I'm in that main hall."

"I've spent my whole life in the open, so you have my permission to do whatever you like."

Summer sat up, eyes alight, words about to cascade from her lips.

"Provided I approve of it first," he added hastily.

Her pent-up energy escaped in a chuckle. "I knew you were going to say something like that. You probably won't even allow me to use the estate carpenters."

"They'll be working on the mill, or the barns, or building kegs for the rum. You and I will have to build it with our own hands."

"In that case I'd better forget it. You'd probably do quite well at knocking out walls, but I have no faith in your staying around long enough to rebuild them."

"You dare to doubt my ability?"

"Your ability, no, but I do doubt your willingness to toil when you have others to do it for you."

"Wise woman. I knew there must be a reason why I loved you."

"You'd better not forget, you treacherous dog," she said, pinching him in the side and causing him to jump away from her sharp fingernails. The horses didn't understand the confusing signals coming through the lines, and one tried to stop while the other attempted to turn. "Pay attention to your horses. You've been at sea so long, you don't know how to guide anything without a rudder."

"You shall pay dearly for that bit of sarcasm, madame." Brent settled the horses, then taunted her. "I shall gamble away your dowry and leave you without a dress to your name."

Summer's gaiety vanished. "I have no dowry," she said as though she realized it for the first time. "It was gambled away before I was sold into marriage."

"You don't need a dowry." Brent put an arm around her.

"You ought to get your lawyers to look into my mother's will," she said angrily. "Half of the land was left to me, along with the house and the money. The money's gone, but the house and land are still there if Ashton hasn't sold them yet."

"I'll make you a bargain," Brent offered, realizing that the question of her dowry was likely to loom larger and larger in her mind. "If you can forget about your dowry, I'll forget about Scotland. Our lives can begin from this moment. We have only the future and each other. Can you do that?"

"I'll try," she said, looking at him with tears and love in her eyes. "I will try very hard."

"Good. I'm taking you to see the new sugar mills," he said kicking the horses into a trot despite the roughness of the track. "Tomorrow you can look at the maps of the island and you'll be able to understand how the plantation is laid out. This field is given over to grain for the cattle. It seems they ravage the crops unless they're kept fat and lazy. I told Carlos to run them loose in the swamp, but I don't think he wants to change the way they've done things here for ages."

Brent continued to talk of his estates, and Summer settled back to listen with the part of her mind that was interested in cows and sugar cane. Another part of her gave itself over to choosing materials to cover chairs and deciding on what new furniture the carpenters should build. There was some beautiful wood on the island. In time she could give the house a completely new look. She would have to see to the domestic arrangements as well. Juanita and Pedro did their work beautifully, but it was impossible for such a large house to be run by just two people. Brent's home had to reflect his wealth and power. It must be perfect.

Maybe she wouldn't need to become involved in the running of the estate after all. Brent seemed interested, and the overseer quite capable. Why not leave it to them? She could supervise the gardens. She might even design the public rooms as an extension of the gardens, with the terrace as a common meeting ground. Of course, that would have to wait until they had decided upon the changes in the house, but it was an idea that would bear some thought.

Brent continued to talk contentedly about the fields they passed. Summer nodded now and then, but became more and more lost in her own daydreams. She did not want to think of the past. Everything she wanted was in the future, and her future was right here.

"Hmmm?" she said, when Brent repeated his question.

"I've asked you twice if you didn't think that was the best looking bull you'd ever seen."

"He's beautiful, an absolutely perfect specimen," Summer agreed, not knowing whether she was talking about cows or alligators. Brent looked at her out of the corner of his eye. Her eyelids were closed, her head was tilted to one side, and an almost inane smile was spread across her face.

"You haven't heard a word I've said. You have no idea what I'm talking about."

"I do," she said dreamily, keeping her eyes closed. "You were talking about bulls, beautiful, perfect bulls."

"You've been in the sun too long." Brent stopped the trap and began to turn it around beside fields of ripening corn. "I'm taking you back to the house right now. I want you to lie down for a while. Don't even get up for a glass of water." He started the team homeward.

"I heard what you said," Summer murmured. "You were talking of bulls lying down until dinner time. See, I told you I was listening to every word."

Brent whipped the horses into a gallop.

Chapter 32

"Get those lazy girls moving," Pedro said to Juanita as he returned to the kitchen. "If we don't serve dinner soon, those two are going to eat each other right up. They're just about past human hunger now."

"You let them be." Juanita brushed butter on a fat squab. "There's nothing wrong with being in love. You tend to your business and get the first course served before it gets cold."

"Nothing wrong, she says," Pedro grumbled, loading the trays with steaming dishes of food. "The captain brings another man's wife here and you say there's nothing wrong."

"The captain can tend to his own business without help from you," Juanita scolded before pushing him out of the kitchen. "You just see you don't slop those peas over the hall floor, or you'll be the one who's not all right."

"If you ask me, he's stepped into a mite of trouble he can't handle," Pedro declared. "You mark my words, this is going to bring trouble, bad trouble."

"Pedro Martinez, you've never been right about anything in your entire life," his wife said fondly. "Why should anyone listen to you now?"

"Because it's not right, that's why, and I know it," he grumbled. "You just wait and see."

"I don't think Pedro's happy with us," Summer said to Brent as he sipped his after-dinner brandy. "I'm afraid you've gone against the poor man's principles." Summer had declined to leave Brent to enjoy his brandy alone, so they sat together on the terrace.

"Damn his principles." Brent snorted. "Pedro will do as he's told and keep his morals to himself."

"Do you think the rest of the servants know?"

"I don't care. None of it will matter in a few days. Now come here and take my mind off all these problems. There's a particularly lovely terrace halfway down to the sea. I want to show it to you."

"I'm not sure I trust you in the dark."

"Where do you trust me?"

"Nowhere, so now you'll ask me why the dark should make any difference," she chortled. "I know what you'll do if you get half a chance."

"No, you don't. You don't know much about me at all. If you think I'm going to make love to you on the goddamned grass when I've got a perfectly good bed upstairs you know even less than I thought."

"I most humbly beg your forgiveness," she said with exaggerated humility. "I will never question you again. Lead on, master."

"A little more of your lip and I'll tumble you in the grass after all. You deserve it."

"Aha! You admitted it, you confessed that you lied and that you are the treacherous lout I thought you to be all the time." Brent made a playful lunge for her, but she dashed behind the table. "I'll scream if you come one step closer."

"The first person to show his face will get his neck wrung for his pains."

"How unfair of you. How else am I supposed to hold off your improper advances?"

"You're not." Brent vaulted over the table and captured Summer before she could take a step. "Now, my little dewdrop, I'm going to lap you up and make an end of you." Summer happily subsided into his embrace, and they walked contentedly down the path that led to one of the sculptured terraces bathed in iridescent moonlight.

With misty eyes, Juanita watched from the house as they walked arm and arm. "Isn't it beautiful?" she said to Ana who was folding the last of the freshly ironed linen. "I never saw two people more in love."

"It shouldn't be hard to love her. She's so beautiful, and so nice too."

"The captain's not a hard mouthful to swallow either." Juanita chuckled. "If I weren't tied up to Pedro, I'd be making eyes at him myself. What a man!" She sighed.

"The captain's not going to be looking at a fat old woman like you." The outraged Pedro was bringing in the last of the polished glasses to store them in the cupboards. "It'd be enough to sour him on women altogether."

"Leave me be," Juanita replied with good humor. "I don't know why I put up with a dried-up piece of rind like you anyway. Never could understand what got into me to want to marry you."

"Couldn't have been much to choose from if he was the best of the lot," said Ana.

"He wasn't so bad once upon a time," Juanita quickly responded. She never allowed anyone but herself to disparage Pedro. "But he's gone off right sharply since then." Pedro reappeared from the cupboard, and with an expert flick of the wrist, he twirled a table cloth into the air above the two women. It settled over them, making them look like two humps on a camel's back. He then wrapped the two ends around the giggling women and drew them toward him.

"Any more of this and I'll hang you up in the smokehouse with the rest of the fat meat." Their giggles turned to laughter. "I'd get enough lard for a year's supply of soap." As the laughter turned to helpless shouts of merriment, a pitcher of water caught Pedro's baleful eye.

"Maybe this will calm you down a little." He dumped the water over the tablecloth. Most of it ran onto the floor, which would have to be mopped before they went to bed, but enough soaked through the cloth to get the women thoroughly wet. They emerged ready to do battle, but Pedro had already made good his escape.

It was fortunate for Brent that Summer was unaware of the interest they had inspired among the servants. He would have been inclined to punish them, then forget the incident; but Summer's evening would have been ruined. To her, it was pure bliss to be able to go about freely with Brent and not to have to hide her feelings. She luxuriated in this freedom, drinking it in as a dry desert absorbs an all too brief shower.

As she lay in Brent's arms and felt his warm body against hers, she could hear his soft rhythmic breathing in her ear. She snuggled closer, letting her hands rove over his hard, muscular body. Brent moved in his sleep, but when he did not wake, Summer continued her explorations. She was becoming less shy, but she still couldn't match his complete acceptance of their physical hunger. She enjoyed his explorations of her body, responded thrillingly to every new and exciting expression of their love, but she couldn't think of doing the same to him without turning pink, at least not while he was awake. She let her hands sink lower, timidly seeking the instrument of her pleasure. Gingerly she touched him there, amazed that anything so small, soft, and pliable could become so large and rigid. Then it began to change and within seconds it was full-blown and ramrod-stiff. She snatched her hand away.

"I didn't know you wanted me to wake up," Brent whispered, biting her ear. "All you had to do was ask."

Summer didn't have time to be embarrassed. Brent's passion exploded like volcanic lava, wrapping them both in torrid heat, wiping out all embarrassment or hesitation. Joyfully she met him in a union that seemed to release her from the limitations of her physical body. They were independent of weight and space, two spirits who needed only each other to be complete.

The weeks flew by, each one more wonderful than the last, until Summer found it easy to forget that she had ever heard of the Earl of Heatherstone or that Brent had once been a feared pirate. She settled into a daily routine that was at once satisfying and extremely pleasant. There was always a lot to be done, but the tropical abundance kept the job of providing for each day from becoming a burdensome task. If they didn't grow it or couldn't make it on the plantation, Summer had only to express a wish and Brent would send a boat to Havana to buy or order whatever she wanted.

"If you don't stop, I'm going to be afraid to open my mouth," she said one evening after a half-dozen men had spent hours hauling a huge mirror up from the docks.

"There's no reason why you can't have everything you want." Brent's smile was a besotted one. "I have enough money to last forever."

"No man has that much money." Summer laughed. "You've got to stop buying everything I so much as mention."

"Why?"

"A woman talks about a lot of things, it's fun to daydream, but I have to make choices or the house will end up looking like a furniture shop."

"Then I'll build you another house to put things in."

"We can't live in more than one at a time," Summer chided.

"Then we'll save that one for the children."

"They won't want it. Children never do."

"In that case we shall have to give it to Pedro and Juanita."

Summer laughed and then turned the conversation to other channels. She loved being spoiled, but she was also worried. Brent had been like this since they'd come to the island. At first she thought it was the result of the absence of outside pressures, but gradually she began to think that there were other reasons for his perpetual gaiety.

He worked very hard and was becoming increasingly involved with the plantation; he had even talked to Smith about the possibility of setting up a trading company. She had no cause to doubt his love or to question his unfailing attention to her, but she gradually became convinced that Brent was trying to run away from something. One day she figured out what it was: he had gone on being a pirate long after he'd needed to because he was running away from what had happened in Scotland and from the loss of his inheritance. Now he was using his love for her to do the same thing. With the passing of each day, she became more convinced that he would never be able to settle down and be contented, anywhere or with *anybody*, until he had laid the demon of Gowan to rest.

But he refused to talk about that.

"Why should I want to exchange this paradise for thousands of snow-covered acres?" he'd once asked when she had pressed him. She wasn't sure that he did want to return to Scotland, but she was certain that he would never rest easy until he could make the choice for himself.

But she didn't know what to do. She had talked to Smith when he'd spent a week with them before going back to Havana to settle the issue of Summer's marriage, but he hadn't been able to get to Brent or to figure out a way to get around the legal net that Gowan had set up. Summer had no desire to make her home in a land that was foreign to her, but she did want Brent to be happy. And she was certain that Windswept was as important to his happiness as she was.

"I'm going to have to start doing more of the work around here instead of letting you do it for me," Summer said to Ana as she handed her one of her favorite dresses. "I'm getting so fat I can't fit into half my clothes."

"The *señora* is not fat," Ana stated. She had long envied Summer's slim figure.

"And your mother is going to have to stop tempting me with dishes she knows I can't resist. Captain Douglas has already warned me that he'll give me away if I become as fat as Juanita."

"Nobody is as fat as Mama." Ana laughed as she handed her a rose silk dress. "Not even Papa, and he eats more than she does."

"But what could it be?" Summer asked, exasperated to find the rose silk just as tight. "At this rate I won't be able to get out of bed in a month."

"There *are* other reasons for a lady to become a little stout," Ana suggested.

For a moment Summer looked blank, then her eyes grew wide. "You don't think . . ."

"I couldn't say, but there are signs."

"I never thought . . ." Summer paused. "Oh my goodness," she suddenly exclaimed before running to the enormous mirror which had been installed in her room. She began to poke and prod her belly, then turned sideways to the mirror and studied herself intently.

"What do you think? I just realized that I haven't had my flow in months. I didn't even notice it."

"The *señora* has been very busy lately."

"But not busy enough to miss something like this." Summer was aghast. "Brent will think me a fool. My God," she exclaimed, suddenly realizing the full import of her discovery, "what will he think?" She slumped down on a chair, too perturbed to remember to put her clothes back on.

"Señor Douglas will be overjoyed," Ana assured her. "He will make a wonderful papa."

Summer smiled absently at the compliment. "I don't know. There is so much that is unsettled."

"What could be wrong?"

Summer didn't feel that she could explain the tangled web of her life to Ana, so she hurriedly dressed. She would have to tell Brent, but first she wanted to think. She wanted to have a baby, but she wished she hadn't become pregnant at this particular time. She didn't feel she needed any more complications in her life.

For weeks she had been making plans for the future, plans that covered almost every contingency. Oddly enough, she had forgotten the most obvious one.

Summer brought Brent his brandy and settled into the crook of his arm. "Tired?" he asked when she remained quiet longer than usual.

"No. Just thinking."

"Want to share it?"

She chuckled. "I suppose I will have to. It's half yours."

"I never trust you when you laugh like that."

"*You* don't trust *me*?" Summer exclaimed, sitting up and turning to face him.

"Is that so surprising?"

"I should say so. After the way you've used me and the absolutely terrible things you've done."

"It all turned out for the best, didn't it?"

"I don't say I'm not content to be where I am, but I can think of at least half a dozen ways I'd rather have gotten here."

"You have to admit they wouldn't have been half as exciting."

"Excitement's not everything. I'm right fond of a whole skin."

Brent ran his fingers along Summer's shoulder, making her whole body ache for him. "I don't see anything wrong with your skin as it is."

"You know what I mean, you infuriating man. Suppose you had a daughter and some pirate seized her and ran off to play house under the palms. What would you do?"

"This is not the same."

"It is. You're just trying to get out of answering my question. What would you do if such a thing happened to your daughter?"

"I don't know," Brent answered rather quietly. "I never thought of it that way."

"Well it's time you did, because you just might have one someday." Lord, what a way to tell him. When would she learn to lead up to things carefully.

"What are you talking about?"

"Even sailors know that women have babies and some of those babies are little girls who grow up into daughters that marry. How are you going to feel when you're a father?"

"I won't let any daughter of mine go to sea without me."

"Okay, what are you going to do if your son brings home a wife he took captive when he plundered a ship?"

Brent laughed, and took a swallow of his brandy. "No son of mine will steal his wife off a ship."

"Why not?" Summer said. "*I* was stolen off a ship."

"That's different."

"Only because it was you who did the plundering."

"What's gotten into you tonight? What's all this about?"

"I don't think I'm going to tell you." She pouted. "You're insensitive and unfit to be a father."

"I don't want to be a father yet."

"You should have thought about that before you pounced on me at every opportunity." She was making things worse with every word she uttered.

"Wait a minute. You're not teasing me, you're trying to tell me something," Brent decided, putting his brandy down and turning Summer to him.

"I told you that in the beginning."

"But you got off on this business about children playing pirates."

"You made me angry."

"I frequently do that, but it usually doesn't make you talk gibberish. What are you getting at?"

"Maybe it's better if I wait until tomorrow to tell you."

"No, tonight."

"You might not like it."

"I'm getting used to that, too."

"Beast," she cried, trying to push him away. He just held her tighter.

"Okay, I take it back. Just tell me what this is all about."

"I was just thinking that it would be nice to start having children. I'm not getting any younger, you know, and neither are you."

"You're twenty and I'm only four years older." Brent laughed. "I hardly think anyone's going to be calling you old anytime soon."

"But it's never wise to put off having children. Parents must be young and energetic to raise them."

"I don't intend to raise them. When the time comes I plan to hire a nurse and then turn them over to a governess or a tutor. But we won't have to worry about that for another three or four years."

"I'm afraid you're going to have to start worrying about it

a little sooner than that. Say, in about four or five months."
Brent's expression froze and his body became alarmingly
stiff.

"I'm almost certain that I'm pregnant." Summer watched
Brent expectantly, apprehensively, but he didn't move so
much as an eyelash.

"Say something," she entreated. "Don't just sit there.
You're scaring me to death."

"Y-you're going to have a baby?" Brent stuttered for the
first time in his life. "Are you sure?"

"Yes," Summer answered, not yet sure of how he was taking it.

With a shout that would soon bring everyone in the house
running to see what was wrong, Brent leapt to his feet. He
drew Summer into a crushing embrace, and then swung her
about until she was so dizzy she couldn't stand.

"I thought you didn't want a child for at least three years,"
she managed to say breathlessly.

"We can turn the empty bedroom into a nursery." He was
not paying any attention to her. "We'll have to hire a real
nurse, though, not one of the women here on the island, the
best one in Havana. I'll start Smith looking for one right
away."

"Slow down." Summer was feeling weak from relief. "We
don't even have a name for the child yet."

"He'll be named after my father."

"And if it's a girl?"

"After my mother."

"This is my child, too, you know. Don't you think I should
make some contribution to the name?"

"Well you can't really name him after Boyleston and you
don't want to name him after Ashton."

"If *he* is a girl, I insist that she be named Constance."

"It will be a boy."

"Just in case."

"It will be a boy."

"That is what we'll name our first girl then, when you're finally tired of nothing but sons."

"I suppose Constance Elizabeth sounds all right."

"With a name like that, she'd better not be a tomboy."

"With half a dozen older brothers, she won't be anything else."

Chapter 33

Summer stared at the heavy sofa with the high, elaborately carved back, and tapped her foot with dissatisfaction. It probably would be exactly the right thing for the entrance hall, but she didn't like it in the parlor; however, until she could find something else she would leave it where it was. They had to have something to sit on. The room did look better, but it ought to. They had spent weeks washing, scrubbing, sewing curtains, and polishing and rearranging furniture. Nothing short of complete redecoration would alter the heavy Spanish feeling of the house, but Brent had already signified his approval of the changes in their bedroom and in the dining room. Now that the parlor was in reasonable order, she need only think about the salon and the breakfast room. The rest of the house could wait until she could purchase more material and buy some new furniture. It wasn't likely that they would be entertaining guests soon, at least not until after the baby was born.

She smiled to herself at the thought. She was looking forward to the birth of the baby, but she was unsure of when to expect it. She couldn't remember having her flow since she'd left home; that would mean that the baby was due in about four months. But she was hardly showing, and it was Juanita's loudly stated opinion that Summer was not going to have a baby when she looked flat as a board.

"You can't be carrying anything bigger than a piglet, and you know Captain Douglas will never accept a runt for a son."

Summer always laughed when Juanita started up. Neither she nor Brent was in a hurry to have the baby. It could come when it was ready. But she was proud of Brent and of her new home, and she thought it would be fun to have a houseful of people. Nonetheless, regardless of when the baby arrived, she didn't intend to entertain until the legalities that prohibited their marriage were straightened out. Then she would put her plan into operation.

Summer had reached the conclusion that since Brent was giving up the sea, he had to have a new outlet for his energies and abilities. She knew he would never be content to live out the rest of his life on a plantation, no matter how large, no matter how many new inventions and projects he and the overseer could think up. Sooner or later he was going to begin to look farther afield for something to engage his curiosity, energy, and drive. She would be prepared. She wasn't going to leave their future to chance.

Summer had decided that Brent should become Governor of Havana. If he had an important job to do, maybe he would lose his unvoiced desire to return to Scotland. She didn't want him to be caught in Gowan's traps, enmeshed in the ponderous wheels of Scottish justice.

She crossed the hallway and entered the salon. When they did entertain guests, this would be the most important room, so she might as well begin to grapple with it now.

Summer was so deep in thought that she didn't hear the

door open behind her. The first suspicion that she was not alone came as a sixth-sense warning of danger. Telling herself not to be foolish, she turned around to find herself face-to-face with a perfect stranger.

She was so startled by his presence that she had no time to take in more than handsome aristocratic features and cold eyes before her gaze became riveted on the disfiguring scar that ran from his cheek to his temple, just missing the eye. The wound was an old one for there was no sign of redness, and the ridge of the healed cut had almost sunk to the level of the surrounding skin. But time had only thrown into relief the gathered skin, creating the impression that his features were being pulled to one side of his face.

"You scared me half to death," she said, trying to tear her eyes from the scar. "I didn't hear you enter."

"I apologize for the intrusion," he said smoothly in a deep, resonant voice, "but I found no one at the door, so I let myself in." The scar made its half of his face immobile.

"I didn't hear the knocker."

"I didn't knock."

"That would explain it," Summer replied, feeling unaccountably nervous. "I apologize for being rude," she said, pulling herself together, "but I don't know who you are. Are you looking for Captain Douglas?" If she was ever going to be a good hostess, she had to learn to handle strangers better than this.

"No. I was really looking for you."

"What could you possibly want with me?"

"That depends on whether you are who I think you are." The scar's immobility fascinated Summer, and she had to struggle not to let her eyes be drawn to it. "Are you the former Summer Ashton, daughter of Constance and Charles Ashton of Highland Glade?"

"Yes, I am. Is anything wrong? Has something happened to Ashton?"

"Not that I know of, but then I've never had the pleasure of meeting your father."

"Who are you?" Summer demanded, fear gripping her as she backed away from him. "What are you doing here?"

"I'm the Earl of Heatherstone, my dear, your legal husband, and I've come to take you home." Summer felt that her heart stopped beating; she fought for breath. Before blackness engulfed her she saw the earl advance toward her, saw that his thin smile made the scar curve and move like a living thing. With a despairing gesture, she whispered in a cracked voice, "*Brent!*," then she fainted into the earl's arms.

Summer woke to find herself lying on the sofa. She was allowed to wonder what had happened for only a brief moment.

"I'm delighted to see that you have rejoined us." The smooth voice of the earl recalled her to the horrible realization of his presence. To her dismay she saw that Pedro, Juanita, and Ana were seated across from her, their arms and feet bound and gags in their mouths. Several armed men stood between them and the door. The earl had come prepared to take what he wanted, with force if necessary.

"The gags may seem a bit unnecessary, but I cannot abide female screams," Gowan said in dulcet tones.

"Why are they tied?" Summer asked, perplexed.

"I thought that would be obvious," he replied. When she looked vacantly at him, he added: "I really can't have them running away to warn the good captain, or should I say your future husband? They have informed me that you are about to be married."

Summer did not respond.

"You have nothing to say? I should have thought words would come gushing forth. Any young woman who can garner two husbands in such a short time must have quite a lot to say for herself."

"I do not consider that I have a husband," Summer said defiantly.

"I take it the captain has not yet confirmed your union by the blessings of the church?"

"We have no union," Summer said flatly. She did not look up, so she missed the look of mingled relief and doubt that showed briefly on Gowan's face.

"You don't know how relieved I am to hear you say that, but I must inform you that I really can not allow you to marry the captain."

"You can't force me to go back with you."

"I would naturally hesitate to use force," he purred, "but I do feel that since you are my wife, it would be more fitting if you were to live under my protection than in a very dubious association of Captain Douglas."

"And do you think Captain Douglas would do anything worse to me than you will?"

"I'm not one to underrate the captain's charms. I realize my disadvantage," he made a faint gesture toward his scar, "but I at least have the advantage of legality."

"How can it be legal to purchase a wife as you would a slave?"

"I prefer to avoid such harsh words." Gowan grimaced. "Think of the exchange as value given for value received."

"You don't know whether I have any value or not."

"You do yourself an injustice," Gowan said with some sincerity. "I knew from your portrait you were lovely, but it didn't prepare me for the full measure of your beauty. My dear, you are truly a treasure and any man would be all too ready to pay a fortune to call you his own."

"I'd be more likely to believe this flattery if you would release my servants. I can't see their bonds as evidence of your supposed esteem."

"When a man finds himself in the fortunate position of possessing something of great value, to him and to other men," said the earl with suave control, "it is of the utmost importance that he protect his possession with all his resources. What would happen to my treasure if it were not properly cared for? Would its luster remain untarnished? If it were left within reach of the greedy and treacherous men that abound in this world, do you think it would long remain in the possession of its rightful owner?"

"I wish you would stop talking like I'm some great stone to be kept under lock and key," Summer protested. "I don't belong to any man."

"You are my wife," Gowan stated peremptorily, and Summer did not miss the flinty quality to his eyes. "As your husband I feel it is time that you came home. I have come to escort you."

"But Brent . . ." she began.

"I agree that it is rude to leave the good captain without a word of farewell, but I fear he might try to interfere with my plans and I would not like that. Your servants tell me his ship is expected any day now. It would be most unfortunate, and unnecessary, if my crew were to meet the captain's loyal men. I cannot help but feel that it would be better for everyone if we just left quietly."

"He won't let you take me."

"You mean without receiving his ransom? Without a crew to back him up, he really has no choice in the matter."

"He'll come after me," Summer declared desperately.

"I don't think so. Your man here, Pedro I believe his name is, can be relied upon to tell him what has transpired. You must not think that I don't appreciate his intervention, clearly Brinklow and Captain Bonner were not the men to see to your safety, but now that you are in my protection I feel I'm the one best suited to see to your well-being."

"I won't go with you," Summer said defiantly.

"I hope that force will not be necessary," the earl said with maddening calm that was tearing Summer's control to shreds, "but I am prepared to carry you to the ship if you are unable, or unwilling, to go to it under your own power." He reached out to take her hand, but she hid it behind her back.

"I don't have anything packed. I can't wear this dress all the way to Scotland."

"Your clothes have already been conveyed to the ship." Gowan's smile made Summer want to scratch his face. "Your maid was most helpful."

"Ana would not help you," Summer said, and she looked quickly at the sagging form of her maid.

"It is true that she did not want to at first, but once my intentions were made clear, she was most cooperative." Looking more closely, Summer saw bruises on Ana's dark skin.

"If you've hurt her, I'll never forgive you," Summer cried, leaping up from her chair.

"She's not hurt. She just needed to be persuaded." Gowan was beginning to lose his patience. "Now, time is running out, so I must insist that we make our departure. If there is anything you need, tell me so that we can be on our way."

"If Brent were only here . . ." Summer said despondently.

"It would be useless," Gowan stated flatly. "What could one unarmed man do against so many?"

The words had hardly left his mouth when the French doors literally exploded into the room. Its occupants, shielding themselves as best they could from a shower of glass and splintering wood, did not notice the body that hurtled into the room until it rolled against the legs of the men standing behind the sofa, throwing them to the floor. Then before stunned onlookers, Brent sprang to his feet, threw Gowan into the path of the men at the door, and before any one of his men had recovered their senses, he scooped Summer up and vanished through the shattered doors.

The earl's retainers stood gaping, unable to believe what their eyes had seen. "On your feet, fools!" Gowan shouted before he had yet found his own. "Alert the others. If we lose them in these jungles, we could search for weeks without finding a trace of them. Have your pistols ready. You come with me," he ordered one man as he raced through the doorway after Brent.

Summer had been too surprised to react when Brent had burst into the room, but as he carried her toward waiting horses she cried out, "Let me down. We can move faster if we both run."

"It's only a few paces. We must reach the jungle, and the only way to do that is to cross the open lawn. Ride as hard as you can and don't look back. The bullets will be meant for me." He put his fingers to Summer's lips to still her refusal. "I'll take a different route so I won't be such an easy target. I'll meet you at the pool," he said, throwing her into the saddle. He cut her horse across the rump with his crop, and screaming in pain, the animal sprang away, nearly unseating Summer. Brent threw himself on the back of his mount and galloped after her, his eyes busily searching the path they had just traveled. He had not gone twenty-five yards when Gowan and his men rounded the corner of the house.

"Too soon," he groaned, and whipped his horse to the right. Several pistols were discharged in his direction, but the shots went wide. He looked back and saw Gowan take careful aim. With an oath he drew his horse to the left and leaned out of the saddle to the side. A ball whizzed through the air where Brent had been just a fraction of a second before. "Just one more," he prayed softly as he righted himself and drove the frenzied horse forward.

Gowan threw his smoking pistol to the ground. "Give me yours. Stand still," he shouted as he steadied the pistol on the shoulder of the henchman and took careful aim at the fleeing Brent. He squeezed the trigger, and the figure in his sights flinched and lurched to the side.

"I've got him!" Gowan shouted triumphantly. "After ten years, I finally got him."

Summer looked back at the first sound of gunfire. She saw Brent cut across the lawn away from the bridle path and she drove her own mount on with renewed energy. But when the shots suddenly stopped she could not master her fear that something had happened to Brent. She turned in time to see him career in the saddle and fall lifelessly to the ground.

"Brent!" Wild sobs escaped her, and nearly blinded by tears, she turned her galloping steed around and raced toward his crumpled form. Tumbled from the saddle, she threw herself on his body. "Answer me," she begged between wracking sobs. "Oh God, please let him answer me." She cradled his head in her lap, but her desperate pleas evoked no answer. He was deathly pale and Summer couldn't tell if he was breathing. "Don't be dead," she sobbed hysterically. "Please don't be dead." She was too distraught to hear Gowan and his men approach.

"You're wasting your time." It was Gowan's loathsome, black velvet voice. "He will never speak to you again."

As he pulled her roughly to her feet, Brent's head rolled onto the grass where it lay motionless. Gowan slipped the toe of his boot under Brent, then flipped him over onto his stomach with a ruthless kick. Only then did Summer see the bloodstain spreading on his back. With a throbbing cry, she tried to break away from Gowan, but finding his hold too strong, she hurled curses at him through her sobs.

"Foul murderer," she cried, hitting and kicking him with all her strength. "I'll make you pay if it costs me my life." An extremely accurate kick to the groin made Gowan turn ashen with pain, and he knocked Summer to the ground, leaving her almost senseless from the force of his blow.

"I regret that I do not have time to trade insults with you," he said savagely, any trace of calm or velvet smoothness gone. "We had best be going. The shots are bound to attract attention, and the workers are not likely to investigate unarmed."

"I hope they kill you," Summer hissed.

"That is an extremely uncharitable view." Gowan's scar seemed to coil as his anger rose. "I would not like you to repeat it."

"Your likes are of no interest to me," Summer spat out.

"I see you have several extremely unladylike habits that I will need to break when I have you safely at home."

"There is no more you can do to me." Summer struggled to her feet.

"We shall see. Now let's go." He took Summer by the arm and started to lead her toward his waiting ship.

"You can't leave him lying on the ground like that. It's inhuman."

"Why bother with carrion?" Gowan's glance was pitiless. "Let the vultures dispose of him." Summer fell to her knees, too weak from shock and disbelief to be able to stand alone.

"In God's name, don't leave him like that," she begged. "At least let me cover him."

"Console yourself that is I, not you, who is leaving him to the vermin. On the whole, my sympathy is with the vermin." He dragged the sobbing Summer away to the ship, free of any apprehension of the vengeance to come.

The *Windswept* reached Biscay Island a week later. Smith stood watching as they prepared to drop anchor. He was not a man given to praising himself or to expecting praise from others, but today he was bursting with impatience for he knew the effect his news would have on Summer and his captain. The ship's bell had already rung, and at any minute he expected to see people coming from the great house to greet him.

The longboat was lowered and he reached the shore quickly, but still the wide expanse of lawn was as empty as the great sea he had just left. It's just my luck to arrive when everybody's away, he thought. I hope someone's around to tell me where to find them. But the house seemed shrouded in an unnatural quiet and a premonition of disaster began to nip at Smith as he started the long climb up to the house.

When he found the front door locked and his summons went unanswered, he could no longer deny his anxiety. He entered through the demolished doors, quickly passed through the salon, missing no detail of its disarray, and entered the hall.

"Hello!" he shouted, his call carrying to the back of the house.

"Mr. Smith, is that you?" a teary Juanita responded from the balcony above.

"What happened here?" Smith took the stairs two at a time. "Where is everybody?"

"We didn't know what to do," Juanita sobbed uncontrollably, "being left here by ourselves and no one to tell us how to care for the poor man."

"Will you stop blubbering and tell me what is wrong?" said Smith roughly. "Where is the captain? Where's his wife?"

"The mistress is gone," the heavy woman wailed, "and the captain is in his bed, dying."

Smith, so stunned he hardly knew what to think, lurched toward the bedroom without waiting for Juanita, but he stopped dead in his tracks when he stepped through the doorway. Brent lay as still as death in the middle of the huge bed, naked except for a pair of drawers. His entire chest was covered by a huge bandage stained with blood. Pedro sat by him, mechanically bathing his forehead, while another man, a stranger to Smith, checked his pulse.

"How is he?" Smith asked softly as he drew near the bed.

"I doubt he will live out the day." The stranger replaced Brent's hand on the bed. "I can't understand how he has lived this long."

"Who did this? Why?"

"No one is sure. Ask that man," he said, pointing to Pedro. "Maybe you can get more from him than I could."

"What happened Pedro?" Smith said evenly. "Where's the mistress?"

"The *señora* is gone." Pedro's voice had the quality peculiar to the mentally incompetent who are beyond the reach of their keepers. "Some man showed up with a lot of soldiers and took her away."

"What was his name?"

Pedro shrugged.

"I don't rightly know, but he kept saying that he was the *señora's* husband. He said she had to go with him."

"What happened to the captain?"

"You would not credit it unless you had seen it with your own eyes." Pedro was beginning to emerge from his stupor.

"Don't gab, man. Tell me what happened."

"The stranger had us tied up, and soldiers were all around. The captain crashed the doors like a cannon-ball and rolled right over everybody. Before anyone could get to his feet, he had scooped up the *señora* and run out the door." He stopped.

"Go on," Smith said impatiently.

"I don't know what happened next. We heard some shots, but it was a long time before anyone found us. They had already brought the captain up here. There was no sign of the *señora*. Carlos said he saw a ship sail away from the island not long before."

"She's alive then." Smith stood deep in thought for a moment. "So be it."

"What are you talking about?" The doctor thought he was surrounded by lunatics.

"Nothing that need concern you." Smith was coolly efficient once more. "All you have to do is see that the captain gets well."

"He's so weak now I can hardly find his pulse."

"You've got to bring him through," Smith ordered fiercely. "I'll see that you have anything you need, but you aren't to leave his side until he's out of danger."

"You must face the fact that it's highly unlikely he will survive," the doctor reiterated.

"You don't know the captain," said Smith. "He'll survive. He *has* to. The earl is not the countess's husband. The captain is, and neither of them knows it."

"I think this shock has unsettled your reason," the doctor stated. "Why don't you have a brandy?"

"My reason is quite sound," Smith declared vehemently. "Apply yourself to seeing that the captain doesn't slip his anchor; or you'll have cause to regret it. Now give me a list of everything you need. I can't be tending to things twice over, so make sure you don't leave anything out."

"You're wasting your time," the doctor repeated when he'd finished listing all he would need for the next few days. "You'd be better advised to have the carpenters start making a pine box."

"If I order any pine boxes, I'll order two of them."

Chapter 34

The cabin lay in near total darkness, only a thin stream of moonlight entering through the small porthole. Summer's restless movement could be heard above the sound of the waves slapping against the side of the ship, and as the minutes passed and her movements became more frantic, the enveloping gloom was punctured by mournful cries.

Suddenly, a piercing scream shattered the night and Summer sat up with a convulsive start. "Oh, my God, he's dead!" she cried, her hands pulling at her hair, her face twisted in terrible anguish.

Bridgit, dragged from a deep sleep, drew on her heavy robe and fumbled with the oil lamp. "It's all right, milady," she said as she set the flickering light beside the bed. "It's only a nightmare."

"But it was so real." Summer clutched the older woman. "There was blood everywhere."

"There isn't any blood. It was just a bad dream," Bridgit repeated. "It's all over now. You can go back to sleep."

"It will come again," Summer whimpered. "It comes every time I sleep, only it keeps getting worse. He looked so pale. I tried to touch him, but every time I reached out he moved farther away."

"It's all over now," Bridgit crooned. "Try to put it out of your mind. You've got to get some sleep or you'll never get well."

Hurried steps in the passageway diverted Summer's attention. She put her fingertips to Bridgit's lips and listened. Before either of them realized that the steps were heading in their direction, the door burst open and the earl rushed into the cabin.

Gowan had taken the time to put on his dressing gown, but his stocking cap had fallen from his head and his thick gray hair stood out like the spikes of a helmet. He was a forbidding man, and Bridgit couldn't blame Summer for becoming rigid with fear when he appeared without warning, tousled and intense, but that couldn't account for the hysterical screams she uttered one after the other.

"She sounds like she's being torn apart," complained Gowan, slamming the door behind him. "Make her stop before she wakes the whole damned ship."

"That's enough of this foolish noise, milady," Bridgit decreed sternly, putting her hand over Summer's mouth to muffle the screams. "It's only your husband."

But Summer's wails became more piercing, and without hesitation, Gowan crossed the room and slapped her hard across the face, stopping her in the middle of a scream. Her eyes fixed on him and she shook convulsively.

"Your lordship!" exclaimed a horrified Bridgit.

"Does she do this all the time?" Gowan demanded, cutting off Bridgit's protest.

"It's nightmares," explained Bridgit as she continued to coddle and pet Summer. "She can't seem to stop having them."

"Can't you do something?"

"It's been so bad lately not even the laudanum can stop them. I'm worried, your lordship. I fear her mind may be starting to weaken." Summer tapped nervously on Bridgit's shoulder and whispered in her ear, but her wide staring eyes never left Gowan.

"What is it, milady?" Bridgit asked, half-distracted.

"It's him."

"Now what could you be meaning by that?"

"It's him," Summer repeated, her eyes staring before her in wild-eyed fright. "The man in my dreams."

"Nonsense. You're just imagining things. That's the earl, though he doesn't look much like himself at the moment."

Gowan's eyes flashed angrily. "What's the foolish female talking about now?"

"Nothing, your lordship. She's just confusing you with one of her nightmares."

"It seems to me it's about time she was taken in hand," Gowan threatened menacingly. "Your molly-coddling hasn't done any good."

"If you want a wife who's stone dead, or mad as bedlam, you go right ahead," Bridgit declared wrathfully, "but you'll get no help from me. I'll have no hand in driving this poor creature to her grave."

"I wonder if she's the poor creature you think." Gowan peered intently at his cowering wife. "Maybe she's fooling you."

"Not with me sitting by her side every blessed minute for the last month," Bridgit stated indignantly.

"We shall see." Gowan was unconvinced. "But I won't put up with this once we reach Glenstal. I didn't travel six thousand miles to bring home a deranged female who will spend her life tied to the bed."

"The countess will get well real quick when she's kept warm and when her food will stay down." Bridgit looked fondly at Summer. "I remember how the roses bloomed in her cheeks when I first saw her. My, but she was a lovely thing then, all peaches and cream, and she had a proud straight bearing."

"If I hadn't seen her on that island I wouldn't believe you," said Gowan acidly. "All I've been privileged to regard since is a sickly, whining female with hair in her face and not an ounce of flesh on her bones."

"She'll do you proud once she's well again," Bridgit predicted. "You'll be the envy of every man in Scotland."

"Promises are easy to make," the earl said, his expression lightening somewhat, "but sometimes unaccountably hard to deliver."

"This is one your lordship won't have to worry about. Now you'd better get dressed before *you* catch a cold and I have the both of you on my hands."

"I've never been sick in my life," Gowan said regally.

"I'm sure your lordship's an example to us all." Bridgit hoped he would go before Summer said something else to set him off.

"I'll be back," Gowan said. He scowled at the shivering Summer before turning to go. "See if you can get some rest. You look terrible," he added as he departed.

Bridgit took a bottle from one of the dresser drawers. "I'm going to give you some more of your medicine, milady," she said, pouring the dark liquid into a glass. "It'll make you sleep better."

"I don't want it," Summer protested fretfully. "It tastes bad."

"I mixed it with some wine this time," Bridgit said, coaxing her to take the glass.

"I wouldn't mind the taste so much if it didn't make me feel sick."

"I'm sorry, milady, but if you don't get some rest you'll die before you reach the end of this blessed journey. And you know you can't sleep a wink without your laudanum."

"Most of me is dead already," Summer moaned. "My *husband* saw to that."

"Hush now. You know it's not Christian to talk about the earl like that."

"If you tell me one more time that I have to honor this infamous union because it's blessed by God and his priests, I'll throw this glass at you," Summer said, her ferocity belying her weakened condition. "I was forced to marry that murderer. Why can't one of these endless storms wash him overboard?"

Bridgit reproved her sternly. "You ought to get down on your knees and give thanks that you have a husband ready to risk his life just to rescue you from those nasty pirates. And him rich and powerful into the bargain. Mind you, he's a mite old for a young thing such as you, but he's still a handsome man, or would be if it weren't for that terrible scar. Turns my stomach at times, it does."

"He's horrible," Summer argued. She took a swallow of medicine and shuddered convulsively. "Why must it taste so bitter?"

"All medicine tastes nasty. It wouldn't work if it didn't. Now stop complaining about what can't be helped."

"You're heartless," Summer said, gulping down the last mouthful, "but I don't know what I would have done without you."

"To be sure things have been mortal bad," Bridgit said gruffly, "but you would have pulled through without me. You're a very strong young woman for all you've been feeling right poor lately. And though I know you don't want me to speak of him, the earl would have seen to you himself if I hadn't been here."

"That would have been worse than being alone."

"For the life of me, I can't understand why you have taken such a dislike to the man."

"Don't you know what he did?" Summer nearly shouted. She fell back on the pillows, trying to fight back the tears that began to fall. "Don't you know what he *did*?" she asked in an agonized whisper.

"I'm sure it gave you a nasty turn to see that handsome captain shot," Bridgit commiserated, "but the earl only meant to stop him from making off with you."

"He meant to *kill* him!"

"You don't know that, and you don't know that he's dead," Bridgit insisted stubbornly. "Though from what you've told me, I can't see how he wouldn't be. You may not have married the earl of your own free will, but married to him you are, and that young man had no business trying to run off with you. It was his own fault if he got shot. He wouldn't have if he'd acted like a Christian."

"And you think the earl acted like a Christian when he shot him in the back?" exclaimed Summer, shaken by spasms as she remembered those last horrible minutes on Biscay Island.

Bridgit side stepped the question. "I don't know what happened because I wasn't there, so I can't set myself up as a judge of other people's actions. But I stick to it that the earl had a right to protect you. A man can't just up and make off with another man's wife, and a good thing it is too. You've got to obey the laws, I always say, even when you don't like them."

"You'll never understand," Summer moaned. "You'll never understand at all."

"Many's the girl that has married a man she didn't know and lived to bless the day," persevered Bridgit. "We can't all go about taking husbands of our own choosing. Lordy, what a mess that would be. Leave it to the parents, I say.

They know something of the world and its ways."

"All they understand is money and power," Summer protested, but the laudanum was beginning to take hold and her words were slightly slurred. "No one cares about me."

"You have a nice sleep, milady." Bridgit covered her with the blankets. "You'll feel much better when you've had your rest."

"You don't understand," Summer mumbled. "Nobody understands."

"You close your eyes. Things will look better in the morning." Bridgit repeated the words like a litany, and Summer's eyelids gradually drooped until at last she was asleep. Bridgit adjusted the pillows under her head and tried to make her more comfortable.

"Poor thing, you've had a right cruel time of it, and you so pretty I sometimes can't believe you're real." She stroked Summer's brow, drawing the matted chestnut hair back from her face. "You might have been happier if you'd been plain. At least these wicked men wouldn't be acting like heathens, killing and stealing like they never heard of the Ten Commandments. You mark my words, old man Satan is going to have new souls for his fiery brimstone before long."

Summer, ostensibly the one for whom these stern words were intended, had fallen into the uneasy sleep that had sustained her throughout the voyage. She had never been fat, but she was mere skin and bones now. It won't do any good to force her to eat, Bridgit thought to herself, it would just come back within the hour. Even the sailors had been looking a little green during this latest spell of heavy weather. It was Bridgit's opinion that if God had meant for men to be going about on water all the time, He would have given them fins. Surely this foul weather was a judgment.

Bridgit settled back into her chair, draped herself with several shawls, and covered her legs with a thick blanket. Barely ten minutes passed before a sharp knock sounded at the door. "Drat the man," she grumbled. "Why can't he learn to leave well enough alone?" The knock came again, more impatiently this time.

"I'm coming," she hissed. "Leave off that knocking." She unbolted the door and stepped out into the passageway.

"I'm coming in," said the earl. "I have no intention of conversing with you in the passageway like a servant."

"This is the first good sleep she's had in days," Bridgit objected.

"That may well be, but the only time I'm allowed to enjoy my wife's company is when I come unbidden to her cabin." He peered at the sleeping girl. "I begin to wonder if she will ever rise from that bed."

"The countess is a lot stronger than you think, but it's a miracle she hasn't died, what with being locked up in this cold, damp cabin and her used to nothing but hot breezes."

"She'll have to get used to the cold when she gets to Scotland."

"But she ought to do it gradually, and not while she's so sick. Please, sir, let me have a heater. It's getting colder every day and we still have some weeks to go yet." When Gowan looked mulishly at his sleeping wife, Bridgit added, "It may be the only way to get her to Scotland alive."

"She doesn't look very good," he agreed. "Are you sure she's all right?"

"The laudanum makes her breath heavy, but she can't sleep without it."

"Is she still carrying on about that outlaw?" he asked bitterly.

"Mostly she talks about you."

"You don't have to tell me what she says," Gowan

growled. "I heard quite enough that first night. She has some hard lessons ahead."

"I hope your lordship means to take pity on her."

"I'm not going to beat her, if that's what you mean. But she will have to learn that I'm her husband and that I insist upon being treated with respect."

"I've been trying to bring her around to that, sir. Over and over I've told her the young captain had no right to steal her away from her rightful husband. You have to respect God's laws, I tell her, and abide by your father's decision."

"And what does she say?"

"It's not so much what she says as what she does. She begins to cry and talk about your murdering that poor boy."

"Have the kindness to refrain from calling me a murderer," Gowan ordered with cold fury. "That *poor boy* was a condemned killer and an international outlaw. Had he been taken alive, his death would certainly have been prolonged and considerably more painful. You might even say that I did him a service, though an unintentional one, in giving him a quick end."

"I'm sure he would agree with you," said Bridgit persevering in spite of the hopelessness of her task. "But the countess doesn't see it that way, and while she so sick it's hard to make her see reason."

"She must be made to understand."

"She has to get well first, and she can't when she's wrapped up in a dozen quilts, her wits chattering in her head, and her body shaken by the sickness."

"You can have your infernal heater, but see that you don't set the ship on fire."

"I know how to use a heater," Bridgit replied stiffly. "Probably better than those wicked devils you have running this ship."

"If you did your work as well as those *wicked devils*, the

countess would be sitting up in her bed and inviting me to spend the evening at her side instead of looking like she's ready for a winding sheet."

"You can thank me that she hasn't been laid out already," said Bridgit, firing up. "And we're not home yet, not by a long shot."

Chapter 35

After long hours of silence, faint sounds of movement within the house brought Smith awake; he yawned silently, and with stiff, noiseless movements walked over to the window. Already the first orange and pink rays of sunlight were lightening the surface of the sea. Another day was beginning; another night-long vigil had come to an end.

Smith's gaze went to the huge bed on which Brent lay motionless, his life hanging by the fragile thread that had kept him alive these past weeks. They kept a constant watch over him, the doctor and Pedro by day and Smith by night. Every sound, every shuddering breath, brought one of them to his side.

"I don't know how he holds on," the doctor remarked in amazement several times a day.

"I told you the captain wouldn't die," Smith always replied.

"But he's just as near dead as he was when that bullet tore into his back," the doctor would argue.

"He'll live."

"Maybe."

Chapter 36

Unable to sit still for more than a minute, Summer wandered aimlessly about the cabin, fidgeting with anything within her reach and biting her lips until they were ready to bleed. She pulled at the tie of her best robe, a loose-fitting, frilly lace wrapper of bright yellow.

"If you don't calm yourself, milady, you'll be worn out before the earl gets here," warned Bridgit.

"I'm too nervous," Summer insisted, her drawn face and sunken eyes giving her the look of a tormented spirit.

"You don't have to be upset on account of the earl. He's been very tolerant of your illness, and I don't expect him to go changing now."

That wasn't why she was upset, but Summer didn't feel she could share the true cause of her agitation with Bridgit. From the moment she had been well enough to think of anything other than her nausea and her aching body, she had been preoccupied with worry over the future of her unborn child. Miraculously she was still small, but it was too late to think of passing the baby off as the earl's child even if she could have forced herself to let him touch her. She had to find another way, but what?

Maybe she could throw herself on his mercy. She was prepared to promise anything as long as she could keep her child, but did she really believe he would allow another man's child to be reared as his first born, especially after he learned that Brent was the father?

A voice inside her screamed that she was a fool to think the earl would allow her to keep the baby, but she refused to accept the evidence she had of his unforgiving, vindictive character. She told herself that she hardly knew him. Surely there was a way to persuade him if she just approached him at the right time and in the right way.

Maybe he would let her go. She didn't know what she would do, but she was prepared to face any peril for the sake of Brent's child. There was no possibility that she could pay Gowan back—Ashton wouldn't give up the money even if he still had it—but she was ready to work on her hands and knees for the rest of her life if it would save her son.

Bridgit had worked to get Summer to accept her husband for weeks, but now when it seemed that she was about to do just that, the older woman could not dispel the feeling that this was *not* what Summer intended to do.

"I don't know what she's planning," fretted Bridgit as she tidied up, "but it isn't natural for a woman fixing to eat dinner with her husband to act like every sound signifies the coming of Lucifer himself."

"That was a excellent dinner, my dear," Gowan said as Bridgit removed his plate and set out the brandy. "It confirms me in my opinion that I did well to come after you."

"You were undecided?" Summer asked.

"From the wild story Brinklow told me, I supposed you to have been carried off by no less than a thousand ferocious savages. I was sure you'd be dead long before I could reach you. And even if you were alive, I suspected it would be impossible to overcome such a force as he described. It wasn't until the next day that the quaking fool remembered to give me Brent's message, and then I knew he'd exaggerated. I also knew that I had to move with great speed if I was to reach you before the good captain had time to work his mischief."

"Mischief?"

"I doubted Captain Douglas could be depended upon to honor the bonds of decency. It seemed to me he would never be so foolish as to abuse you at sea and not share his good fortune with the crew, and I greatly feared for your safety once he had you on his island." Summer didn't trust herself to comment. Voicing any of the words that fought for utterance would render her task hopeless.

"I had acted as his guardian after his father died. The young hothead lacked the mettle to do more than strangle an old drunk." If Gowan had thought to look at Summer, rather than his brandy, he might never have finished his speech. Implacable hatred was reflected in her eyes.

"The captain was very protective of me," Summer stated, trembling from the effort to keep her voice steady. "He only took me to Biscay Island after a caballero tried to molest me."

"He was just protecting his investment," Gowan replied indifferently.

"The captain treated me like an honored guest, not a prisoner to be ransomed."

"It's the custom to treat captives of high rank as honored guests," Gowan declared, and his oily superiority made Summer long to claw at his scar. "Brent Douglas may be a spineless fool, but he was brought up a gentleman."

"What would you have done if he had abused me?"

Gowan's third brandy caused him to miss the tension in Summer's voice. "Sooner or later I would have hunted him down and killed him." His scar curled menacingly.

"And me?" she said softly. "What would you have done about me?"

"I would not have recognized you. It is unthinkable that I should acknowledge a wife who had been dishonored by Brent Douglas."

The sound of her beloved's name on Gowan's lips cut Summer to the quick. Her hand flew to her mouth to cover a tiny moan.

"Are you feeling all right?"

"Yes. I fear my digestion is not yet used to such rich foods."

"Allow me to turn your thoughts to something more pleasant." He rose from his chair. "This is a small gift I slipped into my pocket to bring along." Gowan took a large case from his coat as he came toward her. "It's not an heirloom, but it's a nice little set." Summer nearly stopped breathing when he opened the case. Lying on a piece of white satin was a great ruby necklace set in a heavy gold-and-diamond setting. "You might say it's a wedding gift." Try as she might Summer could not keep from recoiling.

"You needn't be reluctant to wear it." Gowan misread her reaction. "It's yours. And so are these." He produced a second case which contained a pair of earrings and a bracelet, also rubies, diamonds, and gold. "And this too." He reached for yet a third case which contained a huge brooch; Summer was speechless. "How do you like them?"

"They are stunning," she gasped, awed by the sheer extravagance of so many jewels. "They must have cost as much as you paid for me."

"They're worth a lot more than that, but they're not nearly as valuable as what I received in exchange."

But Summer didn't hear his extravagant compliment. To her, the jewels were a symbol of Brent's death, and as she stared at the prodigal display, it seemed to change into something grotesque and horrible. Had Brent lived, she would never have received these expensive items. Had his treatment of her been known, she wouldn't even be on this ship. The jewels were blood money, a kind of dowry of death; she shrank from them as from a coiled snake.

"Let me help you put them on," purred Gowan, his expression warming at Summer's nearness.

"Take them away!" she cried in alarm. "I don't want them." She half rose in the chair, backing away from the necklace dangling in the air before her.

"You don't want these jewels?" Gowan's disbelief was evident.

"Don't let them touch me. They're covered with blood, Brent's blood." Summer knocked her chair over in her haste to get away from the table. She ran to the door and wrenched it open. "Bridgit!" she cried.

"Sit down and stop acting like a lunatic," ordered the coldly furious Gowan. "There's nothing wrong with these jewels."

"Keep them away from me, damn you!" Summer cried. Bridgit hurried in, and she hurled herself at the poor woman.

"What's the matter, milady?" Brigit was completely bewildered. She wondered what Gowan could have done to have caused the composed countess she had left to turn into the pathetically crazed girl now clinging to her for protection.

"For some reason that I'm at a loss to understand, the sight of these jewels has completely deranged her," Gowan stated. "One minute she was perfectly normal, the next she was a raving maniac. She's mad, I tell you."

Bridgit looked sadly at the distraught girl.

"You promised me she was better," the earl said accusingly.

"I never knew her to act like this," Bridgit declared helplessly, "not unless she was having a nightmare. Are you sure you didn't say something to cause her to remember your shooting that young man?"

"I hardly even mentioned the captain." Gowan's scar curled.

"Maybe she's tried to do too much."

"She invited me here," the earl reminded her.

"I know, but she's weaker than she thinks. Why don't you step outside and I'll see if I can get her to tell me what's wrong."

"I think she's completely crazy, and I will not suffer the disgrace of being married to a half-wit." Gowan said this more to himself than to Bridgit. "If she's not sane when we land, I shall deny that I have ever set eyes on her and will leave her to the parish house."

"She's not crazy," Bridgit insisted. "I've been with her every minute since you brought her on this ship. I've seen her when she was sick and raving, when she wept hysterically, and when she was scared half out of her mind, but never once did I think her crazy. Sick, exhausted, and confused—yes. Just let me talk to her. I know there's a reason for all of this."

"Try if you want," Gowan snapped, "but you're wasting your time." He picked up the three cases and left the room.

Chapter 37

Brent tossed about in the bed, dashing the damp cloth from his forehead.

"Señor Douglas, you've got to stop wearing yourself out like this, or you'll never get out of this bed," Juanita said, dipping the cloth in cool water and then replacing it on his forehead.

"I've got to get up," Brent muttered through the clouds of fever that clogged his brain. "I've got to find Summer."

"You will, just as soon as you're able to get about a little," the heavyset woman said soothingly. "But now it's time to take your medicine."

Brent turned away from her.

"And there's no use putting your face to the wall. If you refuse, I'll get Mr. Smith to come hold you so I can pour it down you."

Brent's wound had begun to heal, but a series of debilitating fevers had attacked him, each one more devastating than the last, until he was unable to do more than roll about help-lessly in his bed. But his fevered brain had not forgotten Summer. He accepted the medicine from Juanita's hands, but he was still restive, his half-formed thoughts still dominated by the need to find his love.

"I've got to get up," Brent insisted, but he barely managed to lift his head from the pillow before it fell back again.

"You rest for a while," crooned Juanita. "We're going to go after that nasty earl, but it won't do any good if you're so weak you can't even sit up in your bed."

"I'm too weak to move," he said, almost as if he couldn't believe it.

"And you're going to be that way for some time." Juanita pulled up the sheet that had fallen off during his thrashing about. "The doctor says you ought to be dead, so you should be thankful that you can open your eyes, let alone run about cutting up an earl."

Brent's struggles grew sluggish; finally they stopped altogether.

"Sleep," Juanita said soothingly. "You'll soon be up again, and then that earl will wish he'd never set eyes on the *señora*. It just about breaks my heart to think the poor thing was carried off by that disciple of Satan, all the while thinking you're dead."

The door opened on silent hinges, and Smith entered to begin the evening watch.

"How is he today?"

"Still fretting himself into a fever. And the whole time he's crying for the *señora* fit to break your heart. It goes against my grain to keep him so drugged up, Mr. Smith."

"You know he'd never stay in bed long enough to get well if we didn't, and it would kill him if he were to go after the earl in his present condition."

"I know, but he's going to kill us when he does get well."

"I'm the one who gave the order, and I'm the one who has to bear the responsibility for it. Go get your dinner. Pedro is waiting for you."

"You think the *señora* is all right?" Juanita asked. "Every time I go to sleep, I see that man's face and I'm in mortal fear for her."

"The earl has no reason to harm Mrs. Douglas. He think she's his wife, so does she."

"But what about the baby? She can't hide that forever."

"I don't know," Smith confessed. "We'll just have to hope she can take care of herself until the captain is well enough to go after her."

"When will that be?"

"It won't be long now." Smith looked down at Brent. "If I know Captain Douglas, he'll make us carry him on board as soon as he can sit up. I've already sent Williams to Havana to gather the crew. We should be on the high seas before the end of the month."

Chapter 38

Summer was restless and irritable. She had sent Lucy to bed with strict orders not to disturb her, but she couldn't sleep. She sat down and picked up a book, but she soon flung it from her. "I don't know what's wrong with me," she declared in a peevish voice. "I feel like a caged animal tearing at the bars. If having Gowan around is going to have this effect on me, I'll go mad before the year's out."

Summer's first month at Glenstal had passed quickly. Gowan had been away most of the time and when he'd returned she'd kept to her room, complaining of sick headaches and weak spells. At first, Gowan had accepted her excuses without question, but recently his temper had become so terrible that even the servants tried to avoid him. Her apartment was no longer a haven from the menacing forces closing in on her in an ever-tightening circle, for as Gowan showed increasing impatience with her illness, it was becoming apparent that before many days passed he was going to demand, and probably attempt to take, his marriage rights. Thinking of his touch, of his lips on hers, sickened Summer, but fear of what he would do when he discovered she was pregnant made her blood run cold.

The outline of her swelling belly was so unmistakable that the servants already suspected her condition. Very soon she had to tell Gowan, face the fire storm of his fury, or run away. But where could she go? She was penniless, and no one would help her hide from her lawful husband. Furthermore she had no idea what to tell him; months of thinking hadn't provided her with an answer.

"There's no use giving yourself a headache trying to come up with something clever," Bridgit had informed her when she'd begged the censorious housekeeper to help her. "Nothing on earth is going to keep him from having a conniption fit. You'd be putting your time to better use if you was trying to figure out how to keep from getting a broken head, for I tell you, milady, I fear for you when you tell him. I really do."

Summer didn't hear the door open; she looked up and found the earl standing on the threshold. He rarely entered her apartments and she was unsure of what had brought him to them that night.

"I hope you don't consider my presence an intrusion."

"Not an intrusion exactly."

"But unwelcome nevertheless?" He was being extremely cool, even for him, thought Summer.

"If there's something you've forgotten to discuss with me, I wish you would save it until the morning. I'm really quite tired."

"I approve of the changes you made here," Gowan replied, ignoring her request and looking about the room.

"It was much too somber for me, and please don't sit on that chair."

"Am I not permitted to sit in my wife's bedchamber?" he asked sharply.

"I doubt it will bear your weight, and I would rather you didn't stay."

"Nevertheless, I intend to remain, and as this is the only chair you have provided, other than the one you are presently occupying, I am forced to hope that it will not break." Summer eyed him uneasily. He was carrying himself well, but she was sure he had been drinking and she didn't like the set of his jaw. It was so rigid, his words seemed to come from between clenched teeth. Instinctively she pulled the dressing gown more tightly about her.

"I presume you've come for a specific purpose," she said, finding the long silence uncomfortable.

"Yes, and no," Gowan replied. "I have been away so much I run the risk of being entirely out of touch with your accomplishments. From what I hear, you've become a great favorite with all the old tabbies and encrusted titles for miles about."

"You don't make that sound like much of an achievement."

"You must forgive me if I put it clumsily." Gowan looked at her with eyes that resembled those of a predatory animal. "I might not find myself in agreement with all you seek to do, but I'm in awe at the rapidity with which you have accomplished it."

"I can't take the credit. Mrs. Slampton-Sands has been very kind."

"I haven't noticed the gentlemen holding back."

"Gentlemen may admire a woman as much as they like," Summer said coldly, "but it's the ladies who decide whether she's accepted or not. You can rest assured they wouldn't accept me if I offered improper encouragement to their husbands."

"I would never accuse you of giving *encouragement* to any man, my dear, not when you can't even bring yourself to allow me to touch you."

"I don't take that as a compliment."

"It is merely a statement of fact. I find your highbred coolness quite admirable. There is a little too much of the snob about it for perfect comfort, but I feel sure in time you can be brought to clothe your disapproval in a less obvious guise."

"If you mean by that twisted phrase that you hope I will be pleased to invite the vulgar men you call your business friends into my house again, let me assure you that is not the case." Summer's color heightened as her temper rose, but Gowan's faded and Summer was made extremely uncomfortable by the pause that preceded his reply.

"Let me first point out that this is *my* house, and I intend to invite anyone here I wish."

"But you can't force me to be polite to them," she replied mulishly.

"You will find there are more unpleasant ways to spend an evening than making polite conversation with even the most underbred person. And don't bore me again with the litany of how hard you've worked for me and how little you've asked in return. First, it was that I might not touch you. Now you will not meet my friends. Next I imagine you will forbid me to enter your bedchamber, and after that you will probably agree to meet me only at dinner.

"No, my dear, you will not be allowed to dictate the terms of our relationship. Until now, I have accepted your restrictions and have put up with your perpetual illnesses. I don't know where I found the patience to endure this deception for so long, but the time has come to bring it to an end."

"What do you expect me to do? Meekly say *of course, your lordship?*"

"That course of action would be quite suitable, though I doubt you will be sensible enough to take it."

"You can be certain I won't. Not now, not ever."

"That's certainly direct, but we can discuss it at another time. I expect you will eventually find we have more to agree on than otherwise."

"But the exceptions will be too important to be ignored."

"As to that, we shall have to wait and see. But there is a more immediate issue I wish to settle." Tension gripped Summer as Gowan fixed her with one of his hypnotic stares.

"I think the time has come for us to begin to live as man and wife."

"No! You promised." The discordant protest was torn from Summer. Struck by fear and revulsion, she struggled to stand on unsteady legs that gave credence to her claim that she was unwell.

Piqued by her impassioned outburst, Gowan said "I never made you that or any other promise. You cannot suppose that I would agree to something so prejudicial to my own interest."

"But you don't like me," Summer objected. "You never *have* liked me."

"It is true that I have not yet developed an affection for you, but whose fault is it that I have seen more of your maid than of you? At times I almost forget I have a wife."

"You have been gone two weeks out of every three."

"I was under the impression that you were happier when I wasn't at home." His eaglelike stare never wavered, and Summer felt herself becoming more and more defensive. "But that is unimportant. I intend to be in residence much more often, and we will have plenty of opportunity to become better acquainted."

"I look forward to becoming more conversant with your habits and pleasures," Summer replied. "I do not deny that I am not yet comfortable with you—"

Gowan interrupted her. "Nor have you tried to be. You have used every possible excuse to avoid me." The scar slowly curved in upon itself as his anger grew, a living reflection of his inner turmoil. "I neither know nor care to learn the real reason. The time for locking your door is at an end. I intend to have free access to your apartments, and I expect your maid to retire to her proper quarters when she has finished preparing you for bed."

"You can't do this." Summer was terrified. He was inexorably closing in on her. "You can't command me like a concubine."

"But I can. Even your beloved Mrs. Slampton-Sands would find nothing improper in what I ask."

"I won't! I can't! Don't make me!" she entreated.

"There's no need for actions that may prove prejudicial to our future relationship." Gowan rose from the chair, extending a hand in Summer's direction. "Come to me willingly and I will do all I can not to hurt you." Summer could see the evidence of Gowan's passion as he stood before her, and she realized he meant to have her this night.

"Don't come near me, you detestable creature," Summer wailed as she fled behind the day bed. All patience and all pretense of sympathy deserted Gowan, and in their place was implacable fury.

"But I will, my dear," he said savagely. "I will take you until you scream for mercy—and I shall not be gentle. At times I *like* to be very rough."

"I'll die first."

"I can't allow you to do anything so wasteful, for I foresee even more pleasure in your arms than I had anticipated." His malicious smile sent spasms of terror through Summer. "I'm going to make up for my inattention these past months by acquainting myself with every part of you, *intimately*." His voice dropped to a harsh whisper on the last word.

Summer flung at him, desperate, "I won't make love to anyone who cheats his ward and murders old men."

Gowan paused in his pursuit. "It seems the good captain did more than keep you locked away. When did he whisper this slander in your ears, in the dark of the cabin or the solitude of the bedchamber?"

"Curb your vulgar imagination," Summer snapped, such

contempt in her voice that Gowan felt he had been struck across the face. "His first mate told me. The captain usually refused to discuss you."

"A coward is reluctant to face his enemy."

"Coward?" she exclaimed, driven to make an unwise retort. "You robbed and cheated a helpless boy, yet you dare to call Brent a coward? As a boy he faced you in your own lair, knowing that you were a liar, a thief, and an unscrupulous villain."

"Take care before you go too far," Gowan snarled, now nearly speechless with rage. "You are now in my *lair* and at my mercy."

"But I know you for the unprincipled scoundrel you are."

"That may be, but you are just as defenseless."

"If a young boy could beat you senseless, you can't be much of a man."

With a fierce roar, Gowan grabbed for Summer, but she escaped to the far side of the bed. "You're a bully and a tyrant," she taunted. "You enjoy inflicting pain, breaking people with your cruelty."

"Do you always believe pirates and outlaws rather than the lawful, loyal servants of the King?" Gowan inquired, glaring at Summer with steely eyes.

"I believe what I see."

"You didn't see me steal or murder—"

"I saw you murder Brent!" she shouted in his face. "I saw you shoot him in the back like the base coward you are." Gowan rushed around the bed after her, but she scrambled across it, throwing the curtains that ringed the bed in his face. Fury distorted his features, eradicating his urbane façade. ___

"You will pay for each and every word you have uttered, you stupid, ignorant bitch!" he bellowed. "I will tear the flesh from your bones. I'll scar the face that is a source of pride to you."

"No torture you can inflict will cleanse your soul of its corruption," she flung at him. "And nothing can erase the perpetual reminder of your treachery from your face. You're branded by your own deeds, Gowan, just as common criminals are branded for theirs."

With a speed Summer didn't expect in a man of his age, Gowan threw himself across the bed. She managed to evade his outstretched hands, but in her frantic attempt to escape a rug slid out from under her and she went skittering across the floor. She quickly regained her feet, but the few seconds she'd lost gave Gowan the extra time he needed. He caught hold of the hem of her dressing gown, ripped away a layer of lace as she tried to get the day bed between them. Before Summer could slip out of the robe, his fingers closed around her arms, and with a powerful jerk, he brought her around to face him. Summer dealt him such a resounding slap his head reeled.

"I have killed men for less than that," he blared. "I can break your neck just as easily."

"Do it if you dare. Death would be a blessing if it would spare me the misfortune of being your wife."

"You're going to be my wife in the truest sense of the word," he said, attempting to unfasten her gown.

"Never!" she shouted and twisted out of his grip. "You'll have to kill me before I'll submit."

But Gowan moved faster than she did. He grabbed the back of her gown and pulled with all his might. The heavy material ripped down the back and tore lose from his grasp. But the force of his attack caused Summer to lose her balance and fall heavily to the floor, and with a shout of triumph Gowan roughly tore the rest of the ruined gown from her body, leaving Summer nude before his gaze.

"I have you now, by God, and I shall take you right here on the floor. I'm going to skewer you like a trussed lamb, harrow and seed you until you've been planted with my heir."

"You're too late," Summer said, her lips curling insolently.

"I've already been harrowed and seeded, and I bear the fruit of that cultivation." She patted her clearly bulging stomach, and a grim smile of satisfaction spread across the face. "I bear the child of Brent Douglas."

Gowan's horrified gaze remained fixed on Summer's stomach. "You whore!" he roared. "Did you service the whole ship?"

"I might have known you'd jump to that conclusion," Summer said disdainfully as she tried to cover her nakedness.

"Don't preach morality to me, harlot. Not after you played the whore for Brent Douglas." He threw the shredded gown to the floor and roughly brought Summer to her feet.

"He forced himself upon me to get revenge on you," she wailed. "This whole horrible nightmare is your fault."

"It's a judgment on you, hussy."

"A judgment on me?" Summer cried, struggling to break free. "It's a blessing because it prevents me from having to bear a child of yours."

"You prefer to whelp the bastard of a common felon rather than bear an heir for your rightful husband?"

"I'd bear the child of the devil himself first. At least he doesn't clothe his villainy in pious posturing."

"You can be assured you will receive no more politeness from me." Gowan flung her from him. "I feel contaminated from having touched you."

"May you die of the infection." Summer sneered as she tried to cover herself with her robe. But Gowan tore it from her and flung it away.

"You can't hide your shame, hussy. I'm going to drag you from one end of the castle to the other so that everyone will know you for the gutter-crawling bitch that you are."

"You're insane!" Summer exclaimed, staring at him with widening eyes. "Didn't you hear what I said? I was seduced, forced to suffer this humiliation because of you."

"But first I'm going to rid you of that child. I swore to

wipe the Douglas family from the face of this earth, and I won't have his spawn in my home."

"Stay away from me!" Summer warned, disliking the look in Gowan's eyes as he came toward her. He seemed to have lost his reason, and she was certain he was capable of committing any atrocity.

"I'm going to tear that pirate's spawn from your body," he said, balling up his fists. "I'm going to beat you until you spill it on the floor." Summer let out a piercing, blood-curdling scream as he lunged for her. Freed of her clothing and spurred on by bone-chilling terror, she sped beyond his reach. Then the two of them fenced, Gowan lunging after her, Summer springing beyond his reach, until she reached the table next to her bed. In a flash she opened the drawer and whipped out a loaded pistol. She cocked it and aimed it straight at Gowan's head.

"I've kept this for just such an emergency," she said, drawing a shuddering breath. "Don't think I won't use it. The only thing my supposed father did for me was to make sure I knew how to shoot." Gowan's eyes did not waver and Summer doubted he could be reached by any rational argument, maybe not even by fear. "Back away from me," she said. "I won't hesitate to put a ball in you." Gowan did step back. "Still more," she ordered, and he retreated three more steps. "I want you to turn around and leave this apartment right now."

"You know you'll never be safe from me," he declared in an ominously quiet voice. "You know I will not rest—"

"Milady, are you all right?" Lucy burst into the room before Gowan could finish his sentence. Summer's attention was distracted for only an instant, but it was enough. With a crazed roar Gowan was up on her; the pistol fell to the floor with a clatter and harmlessly discharged its ball into the wall.

"Help! The earl is trying to kill the mistress!" Lucy screeched. Then, without a thought for her own safety, she pitched herself onto Gowan's back. The weight and force of her landing staggered him, and she wrapped her hands around his throat, cutting off his air so that he was forced to give up on punishing Summer in order to free himself of the virago on his back. All the while Lucy continued to scream for help and to encourage Summer to "scratch his bloody eyes out" and "land one where it will do the most good."

With a bellow of virulent curses, Gowan finally threw the hapless maid from him. She landed on the antique chair and it broke into a mass of splinters. Gowan grabbed the still-naked Summer and began to drag her from the corner. But the pistol shot and Lucy's screams had roused the household, and Bridgit, closely followed by the butler, Gowan's valet, and a footman, burst into the apartment.

"Merciful God!" Bridgit cried, starting forward. "He's gone mad. Stop him before he kills her." Wigmore, the butler, and the footman were too stunned by finding the countess completely nude to do more than stare. "Move, you fools, before it's too late!" Bridgit screamed as she picked up Summer's robe from the floor and rushed to cover her mistress, receiving some of the blows meant for Summer in the process. "Stop him before he causes her to lose the baby."

Wigmore suddenly recovered his wits, and launched himself at Gowan. The earl threw him off, but the valet and footman, spurred on by Wigmore's example, pinioned their master to the wall so that Bridgit was able to drag Summer from his grasp.

"Devil plague the man! Look at what he's done to the poor dear, and her carrying his heir. Take him to his room," Bridgit commanded. "Chain him to the bed if you have to, but make sure he can't come near the countess again."

Gowan stared at Summer with a look of naked fury, but he allowed himself to be led from the room.

"Send Betty and Annie to me," Bridgit called after the men. "I need to help with the countess and someone has got to tend to poor Lucy." The kind woman then turned her full attention to making Summer lie down and to covering her with warm blankets.

"What could have made him act like such a madman?" Wigmore was completely baffled. "And he'd just learned he was to have an heir?"

"Don't you repeat a word of it, but that's your precious Captain Douglas's baby milady is carrying. And unless I miss my guess, learning that caused the earl to go crazy and try to kill her ladyship."

"But that can't be." Wigmore's wits were not capable of coping with any more shocks that night.

"I know for certain that the mistress has never let his lordship near her, not from the first minute. It's my belief she fell in love with Douglas and that he planted his child in her, by force or I'm a nanny goat. The countess is not the kind of lady to let a man who's not her husband couple with her, no matter how much she might love him."

"Then her life's not worth a groat." Wigmore had grown up on the Douglas estate and he knew of the long-simmering hatred Gowan nursed for his former employers. "If she's carrying Master Brent's child, he'll kill her and the child."

"No man is insane enough to do something like that, not here in Scotland, not with King George on the throne."

"Gowan's capable of anything. He's already committed one murder in trying to destroy Master Brent. Bend your mind to thinking what to do *after* it is born, for I tell you the earl will never allow it to be brought up as his heir, not if he has to hang from the gallows for it."

Chapter 39

Summer sat staring at the dreary winter landscape. The snow-covered courtyard was as bleak as her thoughts, and she turned away from the window. This was the first time she had left her room since the earl's attack nearly two weeks ago. She had come down to her parlor in the afternoon, content to do some needlework on a lace cap.

"Thank goodness I'm not very big yet," she said to Bridgit, "or I'd be too large to move by spring."

"A fat mother means a healthy baby," Bridgit recited from her store of country sayings. "You can't expect to have a big baby when you're as skinny as a scarecrow."

"Skinny!" exclaimed Summer. "I'm as big as a milch cow now. I hope it's not twins."

"You're never having twins," Bridgit pronounced confidently. "There's hardly enough of for one."

Summer looked up from her work, a little startled to see Gowan enter her parlor. "I would like to speak to my wife in private, Bridgit," he said, holding the door open.

"I dare not leave the mistress," the older woman objected, preparing to keep her seat despite all persuasion. "She still has no business being out of her bed."

"I will call you if she shows signs of becoming faint," Gowan said coldly. "I'm sure you *and* Wigmore will be just outside the door." Summer studied Gowan carefully and was uneasy about what he meant say, but she was certain he didn't intend to harm her.

"It's all right, Bridgit. I'm sure the earl won't stay too long."

Bridgit opened her mouth to argue, but closed it again at a sign from Summer. She, too, had dismissed the threat of physical harm, but she knew the earl was never more deadly than when he was cornered. She gathered up her belongings. "Don't keep her long. She never was strong, and that baby is taking more of her strength every day."

"Then let us hope that she will soon be delivered of it."

Bridgit sullenly passed through the door, and Gowan advanced toward the middle of the room. "I will not take much of your time. I just wanted to tell you what I intend to do about this bastard of yours."

Summer wanted to heap curses on his head, but she remained silent. Vilifying him could only make matters worse.

"Because of your swollen belly, everyone in the county knows you are with child, and thanks to Bridgit's tongue they believe it to be my heir. Is there anyone who knows the falsity of that supposition?"

"No."

"Are you sure?"

"I've told no one, not even Bridgit, who the father is."

"That seems to be the only sensible thing you've done," he said, taking a deep breath. "I'm sure you realize it is impossible, quite out of the question really, that I should allow the offspring of Brent Douglas to be reared as my own. That his child should be my heir is an eventuality too monstrous to even contemplate."

"But where shall I go?" Summer asked. "I have no dowry, and I can't support the child alone."

"I don't propose that you go anywhere or that you support the child. You must remain here as my wife. No explanation would cover your departure from Glenstal without discrediting me."

Cold fear gripped her heart. "What are you going to do?"

"When you are nearing your time, I shall announce that I do not trust the local doctors with the safe delivery of anything so precious as my heir. I shall take you to Edinburgh to be attended by specially chosen physicians."

"And . . ."

"It will be announced that the child has been born dead. In reality, I will secretly place it in a foster home far from here."

"I won't let you!" Summer was too dazed to be able to move. She stared at Gowan, on her face a mixture of fear and doubt, but his calculating impassivity did not waver.

"You will have no choice. It will be arranged ahead of time and you will agree to it."

"Nothing will make me abandon my child!" she declared adamantly.

"Even though it's the spawn of a common criminal?"

"It is my child, too," she said miserably.

"Why don't you confess that you were in love with Brent Douglas," Gowan demanded, now in a black fury, "that you couldn't wait to fall into his arms every night?"

"I did fall in love with Brent," Summer said simply, "more deeply than I had ever dreamed possible, but I didn't fall in love willingly and I didn't fall into his arms every night. I supposed it's a judgement of sorts that he should love the medium of his revenge and I the man who seduced me, but it's too bitter an irony to find myself wife to his enemy and to know his child is subject to your mercy."

"I can find no sympathy for your moving tale. Even if things were as you say, a woman of character would have continued to revile the man and spurn his embraces."

"No woman could be indifferent to Brent." A sad smile of remembrance came to Summer's lips. "I don't think any woman ever tried."

"And you call yourself an honest woman?"

"Yes. I tried not to love him, but I couldn't help it. After a while it hardly seemed worthwhile to keep resisting. Then he took me to Biscay Island, and I knew he loved me as much as I loved him."

"This tale is as mawkish as it is wanton. You are a lusting wench, and once this child is out of the way, I shall take pleasure in seeing that you have all the amorous attention you could possibly desire."

"You will never be able to separate me from my child," Summer cried. "I will never give my baby up."

"Don't force me to take drastic measures."

"I shall run away."

"Speak of that again and I shall lock you in your apartments and post a guard at the door until time for your delivery."

Summer was beginning to think that she had truly lost. "Please let me keep my baby. I don't want anything else. You can tell people both of us died."

"That would be easy to arrange if it were the result I wanted," Gowan admitted, and his cold, viper's eyes told Summer that he would calmly murder them both if that suited his ends.

"You can be as grief stricken as you like, but I will spare your child only on the condition that you divulge the truth to no one. Should you do so, your offspring will not live to grow up."

"No!" The cry was a soaring wail of anguish torn from the very depths of Summer's soul. "Don't make my life more of a living hell than it already is!" She slid from the chair to the floor and rocked back and forth on her knees. "I beg of you, just let me go. I promise you'll never hear of me again."

"You must remain here as my wife."

"Why? What can you want with a woman for whom you feel nothing but scorn and contempt, a woman who hates you and loves another man, a woman who bears the child of the one man in the world you loathe?"

"I find you very beautiful," he said flatly.

"That's not it," Summer insisted. "My beauty hasn't tempted you in all these months, so why should it now?"

"You're wrong. It has tempted me quite often."

"I don't believe that's it at all. There's some other reason, and I demand to know what it is."

"You're in no position to demand anything."

"I will make your life miserable. I'll fight your every move. I'll run counter to your every wish."

"You can be dealt with," Gowan said calmly.

"You can't keep everything that happens in this castle a secret. Abuse me and it will cost you any remaining loyalty your people have. They already hate and despise you so much they might even be willing to strike a blow to help me."

"Are you seriously trying to threaten me?" He found it hard to believe that this lone, fragile girl could actually think she could intimidate him.

"I'm trying to get you to tell me the truth. Why do you insist that I be your wife when you'd rather be married to almost anyone else in Scotland?"

"I'll tell you, since you will have it, but it will do you no good." His expression was so ugly Summer began to wish she hadn't sent Bridgit from the room. "I inherited Glenstal from a distant cousin I remembered only from one short, disagreeable visit. All I knew of him was that he had eloped after a whirlwind romance and had then died quite mysteriously. Years later I saw a portrait of a young girl, done by a painter who had visited the Indies. The girl was the image of my cousin. I remembered that the girl my cousin had eloped with had been quickly married to someone else and sent off to the Caribbean."

"My mother." Summer was beginning to understand the tangled explanation.

"Exactly. My distant cousin was Frederick Boyleston. At the time, only a few people knew he had eloped with your mother; none knew that he had a child. Even I had no suspicion until I saw your portrait. You are Boyleston's legitimate daughter and a possible claimant to these estates. I've never been able to find the records of that marriage and destroy them, but that's unimportant now. As your husband I control your property. I had no choice but to go after you."

"So you are as much tied to a wife you dislike as I am to a husband I loathe. That's why you brought me back even though you never believed I was still a virgin."

"It does seem an unfortunate tangle."

"And I'm bearing the son of the man you tried to ruin, the grandson of the woman you wanted to marry and the man who was once your best friend."

"Your perception is remarkable," said Gowan. Summer suddenly smiled and then laughed. She tried to check herself, but her laughter began to erupt in uncontrollable bursts. Finally, she sank down upon the sofa, helpless.

"You're hysterical." Gowan feared the madness that had struck her during the voyage had reappeared. "I'll call Mrs. Barlow."

"No, don't," she managed to say. "She'd never understand."

"Should I?"

"Don't you see that the joke's on you?" she asked.

"I can't see any joke at all," he said icily.

"You must see it," Summer choked out through her laughter. "I'm the heir to the estates you inherited by mistake. You can't get rid of me without losing the whole basis of your power because you've buried the money you stole from Brent into *my* estate to hide it from the world. And right here in my body is the one person who can rob you of everything you've struggled for your whole life. My child can destroy you and all your evil just by being born."

"Take care you don't drive me too far," Gowan warned.

"I'm safe for now," Summer said, rising from the sofa. "You don't dare touch me after that foolish attack, and once everyone knows I'm the real heir to Glenstal you won't dare to lay a hand on me."

"You won't be safe forever." Gowan was chafing under the knowledge that he was cornered. "I still hold the power to give or deny life to your child."

"But I shall discover a way to defeat you before he's born," Summer stated coldly, turning on him with a look of such hatred that Gowan was silenced. "You have given me the one thing I lacked: confidence. I shall beat you, Gowan Mc-Connel, I swear it. I shall bring you to a ruin so shattering that you will never have the power to harm my child." She then turned and swept from the room, allowing him no chance to respond.

Chapter 40

Impatient at being confined, Brent rose from his chair and stared out the porthole. "The storm is just about over."

"I hope you're not thinking of going on deck." Smith looked worried. "The wet and cold will make you sick again."

"If you tell me one more time how the four of you toiled to make sure I didn't die, I'll throw *you* into the wet and cold," Brent threatened. Doing what good sense told him would speed his recovery had him completely out of temper. "I still haven't forgiven you for keeping me in that bed an extra month."

"It was just long enough for you to be able to get about on your own," Smith said. "I was certain you'd head for Scotland the moment you were conscious, even though you knew you'd never make it."

"And now you're quite pleased with yourself, aren't you?" Brent grumbled. "You actually *enjoyed* being able to make me do exactly as you said."

"It was an experience I never expected to have," admitted

Smith, a trace of a smile on his lips, "but on the whole I'm pleased that it's over. You were a very difficult patient."

"And you're an impudent dog." Brent roughly disguised his affection for the man to whom he owed his life. He had been enraged when his mind had cleared and he'd found out what had happened to him, so he had continually abused Smith even though he knew the man was acting in his best interest. The constant verbal persecution kept his mind off what was really worrying him: what had happened to Summer?

Reason told him that she was probably safe, but he could not be sure. And his anger over imagining the earl was forcing Summer to accept his caresses paled before his worry over what Gowan would do when he learned she was carrying his child; Gowan's hatred was virulent and longlasting. Brent stared out the window again, a feeling of helplessness stirring rage in his heart. He wouldn't let himself think about those fears now, but Gowan would pay with his blood if he harmed either Summer or the child. Brent swore that oath anew each day.

Chapter 41

"Don't forget to tell Wigmore to pack the medicine for the Claxton child. She's not getting any better."

"I wish you wouldn't keep jaunting all over looking after sick people," Bridgit said disapprovingly. "I'm worried to death you'll catch something in one of those dirty cottages."

"I've never felt better in my life. If I didn't fear running into the earl, I wouldn't spend a waking minute in this apartment."

Wigmore entered the room on silent feet.

"I beg your pardon, milady, but a man who claims to be your parent has arrived and wishes to see you."

"That can't be. My father's in the Indies."

"So I thought, but this gentleman claims to have just arrived from the Indies. He also seems to be in possession of a great quantity of information about you."

"What does he look like?"

"I would not like to be disrespectful to your father, milady, but unless I'm mistaken, he has been drinking too liberally for this hour of the day."

"If it's Charles Ashton, he drinks too heavily for *any* hour of the day." Summer rose. "I suppose I must go down."

Ashton was pouring himself a liberal drink when Summer entered the salon. He turned and surveyed her swollen belly through bleary eyes. "My God, you didn't wait long."

"What are you doing here?" Summer inquired coldly.

"That's not a very warm greeting for your father," he said. "How about a welcoming kiss?"

"You're not my father, as you were at pains to point out just before you sold me."

"I was angry then, worn down with worry." Summer's expression didn't change, so he went on. "You're not going to hold that against me, are you? I was just upset."

"You're always upset, and when you're upset you drink too much."

"I've reformed. I've decided to make a complete change in my life."

"You can start by putting down that glass. Or is that one of your exceptions?" Ashton looked hurt, but Summer's eyes didn't soften. "Have you given up gambling as well?"

"Absolutely. I have sworn never to pick up a card again, not even in a friendly game."

They stared at each other like two strangers.

"Aren't you going to ask me to sit down? Don't you even want to know why I'm here?"

Summer motioned him to take a seat. "Why *are* you here?"

"I've come to visit my daughter, to see how she's getting along with her new husband."

"Have you sold the plantation? Is that why you've come? You must have left before the planting season."

"No, I didn't," he said testily. "I can't sell the damned hellhole. I can't even raise a penny on it."

"What happened? Did you lose it in a card game?"

"Your grandfather cheated me, he and your mother."

"You got half. Isn't that enough for you?"

"I didn't get anything," he complained, aggrieved, and then drained off the rest of the glass. "The whole thing belongs to you, every stick of furniture and stalk of cane. I don't get a penny." He poured himself out another glass and swallowed half of it. "Do you know what those thieving bankers told me when I went to see them?"

"No," she said patiently.

"They told me I couldn't have any of the money unless I stayed on the plantation and worked it. They said if they had to pay an overseer, everything would go to you. I told them they could have the bloody plantation and everything on it. I was tired of the never-ending heat and the damned hurricanes that scare a man half out of his wits."

"You were never sober during a hurricane."

"Did you expect me to get through one of those howling, screeching monsters without a few drinks?" Ashton asked with injured air.

"As I recall, it usually took several bottles."

"Just like your mother, always counting everything. Now you made me forget what I was saying. Oh, I told those bloodsucking swine that I was going to see my daughter. Told them you'd take care of me."

"But you're *not* my father, and you can't stay here."

"Why not? You've got plenty of room."

"I'd have to double the amount of spirits we keep in the house."

"You can't let the little tyke you're carrying come into the world without a grandfather."

"You aren't his grandfather either."

"Well you can't tell him you're a bastard, can you? Your husband wouldn't like that very much."

"My husband knows who my father is."

"You weren't fool enough to tell him a thing like that?"

"No, he told me."

"You're lying! He couldn't have known. He never would have paid a pound for you."

"That's the only reason he paid anything at all. I'm Frederick Boyleston's *legitimate* daughter, and this little tyke will be his grandson. Mother was married when she eloped."

"I don't believe it," Ashton said, his drink suspended halfway to his mouth.

"Maybe you'll believe me when I tell you the earl only married me to keep control of these estates."

"Damn!" Ashton slammed his glass down onto the table. "I could have gotten at least twenty thousand instead of a measly ten."

"That *measly* ten ought to keep you for the rest of your life."

"It can't. It's gone."

"All of it? Not even you could have gambled away ten thousand pounds in less than a year."

"There wasn't ten thousand left by the time I paid Carter. I ended up with a little over two, and that doesn't last long when you're in the middle of the worst run of luck that ever cursed a man."

"So you're out of funds."

"I've got less than twenty pounds."

"And you expect to live at rack and manger here?"

"It's not much to ask, seeing as how I took care of you for all those years."

"But you're not worth much, are you? I certainly won't be able to sell you for ten thousand pounds after I've put up with you for nineteen years."

"You're more like your mother every day." Ashton suddenly dropped any pretense of fatherly feeling. "Hard as nails and not an ounce of forgiveness in you."

"After what you did to me, I don't ever want to see you again."

"I'll wait for the earl. You may be the mistress here, but I'll wait to hear what he has to say."

"And just what is it you would like to have me say?" The unexpected sound of Gowan's voice startled Ashton into spilling wine down the front of his coat.

"Now see what you've made me do?" he sputtered, quite put out. "You ought to cure yourself of the habit of sneaking up behind people. It gave me a nasty turn. I've quite ruined this coat."

"I'm sure it can be replaced." Gowan's cold eyes regarded him evenly.

"That's easy for you to say, rich as you are, but I don't have a pocketful of gold pieces."

"As I recall, I gave you enough to fill even the most commodious pocket."

"Nothing lasts forever, especially money," Ashton declared cynically. "In fact, it's the first thing to go."

"I take it from the complaining note in your voice that a want of gold is the reason for your visit."

Ashton was pleased by Gowan's quick understanding, but he would have preferred that the earl had phrased it differently.

"I came to see how my daughter was doing in her new home, and to make sure you were treating her right."

"As you can see, I've treated her in the manner that suits all new brides, and she's doing quite well."

"Slap me if I expected you to settle the business so soon, but you hot-blooded young bucks will have your way."

Gowan, who was older than Ashton, fixed him with a glare that even that thick-skinned hedonist couldn't ignore.

"That is a subject I do not propose to discuss with anyone, even my father-in-law."

"As you like." Ashton took a quick swallow of his drink.

"Wouldn't want to upset you for the world. Just thought I'd stay on and see that she comes through the thing right and tight. After twenty years I've developed quite an affection for the girl."

"But one that could be set aside for a suitable sum, such as ten thousand pounds."

"Every girl has to get married, and there's no sense in turning down money when it's offered. Which is not to say that I'd have her let go for a measly ten thousand if I'd known she was Boyleston's legitimate daughter," he declared, aggrieved.

"Such constancy deserves some reward. You must stay for dinner, but I think we should go in while you are still able to see what's on your plate."

Summer was too upset to do more than taste the meal set before her. She avoided Gowan's eyes, but she could feel his cold, critical gaze upon her, and knew he was including her in the contempt he felt for Ashton. She longed to protest that since he had invited Ashton to remain against her wishes, he deserved what he got. But the more Ashton drank the more incautious he became, and she began to seek any excuse to leave the table.

"I'm a little tired. I think I should lie down for a while."

"Shall we see you when the tea tray is sent in, my dear?" Gowan inquired, his words really a command.

"I didn't think anybody still drank tea," Ashton remarked.

"It's not a requirement," Gowan replied. "We have more brandy." His tone would have warned a sober man to proceed with caution, but Ashton was beyond prudence.

"You scared me there for a minute," he said.

Summer was too mortified to move.

"Have you left the islands for good?" Gowan asked.

"I'm never going back to that stinking hellhole," Ashton stated as vehemently as he could after drinking for the better part of the day.

"What plans *do* you have?" drawled Gowan. "Have you seen your brother?"

"Yes, I've seen the prig, and the harridan he married," Ashton said bitterly, "and they've seen the last of me."

"I take it your visit did not prosper."

"No one could get along with that pinch-penny, money-grubbing pair. They turned Presbyterian on me too. Just about every pleasure is a sin according to them. It gives a man a sour stomach to hear that kind of talk all the time."

"I take it you don't include Grantley Manor in your plans. Do you intend to purchase a property?"

"I thought I might pay you a visit, now that Summer's about to give you an heir. Wouldn't do to ignore my grandson."

"He's not your grandson, and I've already told you I don't want you here." Summer desperately wanted to leave the room, but she was afraid of what Ashton might say in her absence.

"You know you don't mean that," said Ashton with feigned fatherly concern. "You're just feeling out of sorts because of the baby."

"It has been my experience that your daughter means exactly what she says no matter how poorly she's feeling," Gowan observed dryly.

"I wish you'd stop calling me his daughter," Summer snapped. "If you let him settle here, you'll never get rid of him. Why don't you go back to the plantation?" she demanded, turning back to Ashton. "The trustees would see you didn't starve."

"This's a fine way to talk to one who's been your father in name and deed, if not in fact," said Ashton, simulating dejection. "And after I came all this way to see you."

Summer uttered an inarticulate snort.

"You may stay as long as you require to satisfy your mind that my wife is well and happy," said Gowan, "and I am quite willing to arrange your return passage." Ashton looked rather uncomfortable and glared moodily at Gowan.

"To tell you the truth, I don't dare go back. There are a few people who would be happy to deal roughly with me," he confessed.

"Gambling debts?" Summer asked in disgust.

"What did you expect me to do with my time, spend it slaving like a common laborer?" Ashton asked angrily.

"Some people *do* work."

"You're being a little hard on your father, my dear," Gowan put in. "It would be rude to turn him out after he came all this way to see you."

"He can stay at an inn."

"Probably, but I fear he would soon feel compelled to tell his story, or what he imagines to be his story, for the price of a drink, and that would be undesirable."

"You wouldn't." Summer turned to Ashton.

"I don't think you want everyone to know you're Boyleston's daughter," he replied, proving that the earl had gauged his character more correctly than she had.

"I'd rather be the hangman's daughter than yours," she declared outraged.

"The earl wouldn't like it either. It would start people to asking questions."

"It is true that it would be awkward at first, but since the ultimate result would be that things stand as they do now, I don't foresee anything to worry about."

"Either you're trying to pull the wool over Summer's eyes, or you haven't read that will." Ashton sounded remarkably sober now. "Most of this land was Boyleston's grandmother's, and any heir, male or female, can hold this property in her own right." Summer looked questioningly at Gowan, but he was staring at Ashton with a look that should have warned the man that his tongue might prove his undoing. Summer didn't like Ashton, but she felt a sudden urge to warn him.

"I've already admitted that things might be awkward at first, but my wife and I would settle things between us," Gowan said.

"Not if your trustees are like mine." Ashton refreshed himself from his glass. "It's nothing to me who has the money, but wouldn't it be better to let me stay for a while rather than stir up a hornet's nest?"

"In other words, you're offering to keep your mouth shut if we provide a bed and all the brandy you can drink?"

"That's blackmail!" Summer stood up.

"There's no call to use hard words," Ashton said reprovingly. "It's just an exchange of favors among friends."

"I think you ought to throw him out," Summer announced brusquely, and stalked from the room.

Chapter 42

The next few days did nothing to improve Gowan's temper or to encourage Summer to hope she could soon get rid of Ashton. The man spent the better part of his first morning at the castle wandering about and making a mental inventory of its contents, managing all the while to keep himself supplied with drink.

"This is a fine place you have," he informed Summer when he met her in one of the halls. "I'd warrant I could stay here a fortnight and not run into you except at dinner."

However, by that evening Ashton had changed his mind about staying at Glenstal Castle. He'd met one of Gowan's business partners and, over a friendly pint, had learned that Gowan's yearly income exceeded fifteen thousand pounds. That had started Ashton on a new train of thought.

At dinner he suddenly turned to Gowan. "There's not much going on here. Even Edinburgh has turned pious. I think I'll go to London."

"Whatever for?" Summer was astonished. "You don't know a soul there."

"A man of means can always find his way," Ashton said loftily.

"Do you plan to live there all year round, or do you intend to visit the watering places as well?" Gowan's voice was deadly quiet.

"He can't get to the next county without having to borrow money," Summer declared scornfully.

"But you think you know where to find the funds, don't you?" Gowan said to Ashton in silky tones.

"It would be only natural for a generous husband to make his father-in-law an allowance," Ashton stated glibly.

"One ample enough to permit the man to travel to London and to other spots frequented by convivial spirits," Gowan said coldly.

"I'd come back here to rest up, but London is the only place for a man of means."

"Drawing all the while on my unfailing generosity," Gowan continued. His words were like the hiss of a cobra, but Ashton was too enthralled with his vision of having enough money to do as he pleased to pay attention to such warning signs.

"Your partner assured me your income was so large you didn't need the half of it," Ashton responded, already able to feel the money in his hands.

"And so you have offered to spend some of it. Don't hesitate to tell me exactly how much you need. Do you want it in gold, or shall we set up banking arrangements?"

Ashton demurred. "I don't think such things need be mentioned before ladies. I know we understand one another."

"I understand you perfectly," Gowan said smoothly, then he turned the conversation to another subject.

Summer was unable to believe that Ashton could be so stupid as to believe that Gowan would hand over a major part of his income, but a few days later, when Ashton came down to dinner in a new coat, she made some casual remark about its cost and was stunned by his reply.

"I told them I was the earl's father-in-law and to send him the bills."

"*You did what!*" she ejaculated, unable to keep the shrillness from her voice.

"I don't know why you're getting so worked up over a few clothes," Ashton said peevishly. "You can't expect me to go about dressed like a hayseed."

"You've got to get away from here now," Summer pleaded, near desperation now.

"It's too early to go to London yet. Besides, Gowan and I haven't talked about the money I'm to have."

"You really expect Gowan to hand over the money to you, just like that, don't you?" Summer asked, incredulous.

"He doesn't have any choice if he wants me to keep my mouth shut," Ashton said bluntly.

"Not even Gowan's *whole* income could keep up with your spending."

"I know I overdid things before, but I won't do that again."

Summer stared at Ashton, unable to believe that he could be so blind. "Are you fool enough to think you can scare Gowan with your pitiful threats? Do you think people would even listen to the accusations of a drunk?"

"You watch what you say—"

"No one will believe you if both of us deny every word you say."

"But that would make you a bastard." Ashton was a bit shaken.

"Not when they already believe I'm your daughter. It'll just convince people that you're trying to squeeze money out of Gowan. He already has some of his men looking for the record of Mother's marriage. He'll destroy it if he finds it, and you'll never be able to prove a word of what you say. Please leave this house, and don't come back. There's nothing but danger here for you."

In his own hazy way Ashton didn't trust Gowan, but neither did he believe the earl would do him any harm. And he couldn't turn his back on the possibility of a perpetual supply of money. He'd already been cheated out of one fortune after waiting for twenty years; he wasn't going to miss his chance for another because of cowardice.

Dinner was a depressing affair, and the atmosphere grew even more leaden when Gowan brought up Ashton's bills.

"You seem to have been remarkably busy these last few days. I must be quite obtuse not to have noticed such prodigious needs."

"I may have ordered a few more clothes than I really needed," Ashton mumbled, disliking the look in Gowan's eyes. "I can send some of them back."

"I wouldn't think of asking you to do that," Gowan said with sinister calm. "I couldn't have it said that I allowed my father-in-law to be unsuitably dressed . . . or short of funds."

Ashton's faith in the gullibility of others was restored, and he took another swallow of brandy. "I told Summer you wouldn't cut up stiff over a few little bills."

"My dear, how could you think that I would deny your father a mere five hundred pounds? One must provide the necessities."

Summer blanched at the figure.

"As much as that?" Ashton said. "Bleeding bunch of thieves, that's what those tradesmen are."

"They aren't all tradesmen's bills, but don't let that worry you. I shall see that they are settled."

Summer was relieved next morning when she learned that Ashton had gone for an early ride, but when he didn't return for lunch she began to worry. By the middle of the afternoon she sent her grooms out to search for him. It wasn't until she came down for dinner that she learned Ashton had been found at the bottom of a gorge, he had broken his neck in the fall.

Summer bit her lip and clenched her hands so they wouldn't shake. "Where was his horse?" she managed to ask. "Why didn't it come home?"

"It was grazing a short distance away. Nobody can understand how he could have fallen off such a lazy slug."

"Had he been drinking?" Gowan asked, coming into the parlor in time to hear the last portion of the story.

"He left with two quarts and both of them were gone."

"What has been done with the body?"

"It's in the stables awaiting your orders."

"I think we should consult the countess," he said, but Summer was unable to control herself any longer. With a despairing cry she jumped to her feet and fled the room. She knew Gowan had murdered Ashton, she could feel it, and she couldn't stand to be in the same room with him. Gowan had talked civilly to Ashton over dinner and had calmly murdered him the next day. That proved he could kill her baby just as easily; she had no choice but to run away.

Chapter 43

The camp lay nestled in a small clearing under a cloud-filled sky. Restless horses breathed clouds of steam into the cold night air, but spring was on its way and the gypsies were preparing to leave their winter quarters. Every now and then someone walked across the clearing or called out to a companion, but most busied themselves getting ready for the road.

A lone figure emerged from the darkness beyond the wagons. Staying within the shadows of the trees, he circled the camp, then sprinted across an open courtyard into the lee of a distinctive wagon. After pausing for a moment to be sure no one was watching, he put his head inside. There was no one within. Drawing back against the brightly painted panels, he remained undecided until he heard a throaty contralto singing the lilting strains of a plaintive Gypsy ballad. He then smiled to himself and carefully made his way toward an open barn door.

In the soft light of a single lantern, a handsome woman of

about forty years, with fine features, high cheekbones, and perfect mahogany skin, was busy packing the last of her household belongings. She hummed a mournful tune to herself, occasionally breaking into the words.

"Madelena, why so sad?" the stranger asked, stepping into the light. "You always used to be so full of laughter." The woman turned, on her face an expectant smile, but when she realized that the huge man was unknown to her, her friendly greeting was cut off in her throat.

"Who are you?" she asked.

"Don't you recognize me?" the man sounded hurt.

"I never saw you before, and if you don't get out of here I'm going to call my husband."

"How unkind of you to threaten me with Roberto, you beautiful old witch. I'm your own Brent Douglas."

"You can't be," she stammered, staring at him suspiciously. "He must be dead by now."

"You always said I was too lucky to die."

"But you were only a boy."

"A boy grows into a man in ten years." Madelena came closer, hardly daring to believe this stranger was the wild, tempestuous youth who'd so delighted her a decade earlier.

"You do look like your mother, but you're much taller than Lord Robert." Her eyes suddenly narrowed as she surveyed the muscular magnificence of his body. "Did you come back to escape the women?"

"I came back because of you and that jealous ogre you married." Brent laughed and moved toward her with his hands held out. "Where is Roberto, burying the body of your latest admirer?"

"I'm an old woman. I do not attract admirers anymore." Brent brought both her hands to his lips.

"Then every man must have become blind. You're still beautiful, still a very desirable woman."

"How you talk," Madelena said, beaming. "Stop smiling

at me as if you were a cat looking at cream and give me a hug. Roberto won't mind. I'm old enough to be your mother."

"I'd hug you even if he did mind," Brent said, and he picked her up and swung her around effortlessly.

"Put me down, you foolish boy. You'll have me dizzy."

Brent laughingly set her on her feet, but she clung unsteadily to him.

"See what you've done?" she scolded good-humoredly, but her infectious chuckle died aborning. "Roberto, no!" she shouted, and without warning she pushed Brent away from her. Caught off balance, he stumbled, and at the same moment he heard a knife pass through the air close by him. Before he could regain his balance, he found himself staring into the hate-maddened eyes of Madelena's husband, a second dagger pointed menacingly at his throat.

"I'm going to cut him up into little pieces, and then I'm going to beat you, woman, for falling into his arms," Roberto raved, consumed by his jealousy.

"You fool, that's the young master come home," Madelena informed him. "Those big muscles could break a little man like you in half, but see how he laughs at your stupid temper?"

Roberto stared hard into Brent's twinkling eyes. "He doesn't look like Lord Robert," he said, not lowering his knife.

"He's the spit of his mother, you blind fox. Now put your knife away. Is that the way to treat a man who's let you camp on his land for I don't remember how long?"

"Must I remind you of the time I told my father's keepers I was the one who shot the rabbits hanging from your belt?" Brent demanded, his eyes brimming with laughter.

"Master Brent!" The dumbfounded Roberto went from murderous rage to joyful recognition in the twinkling of an eye. "I was sure you were at the bottom of the sea." He helped Brent to his feet.

"Or the bottom of some ditch," added Madelena, and the joy of their reunion vanished.

"What do you mean by that?" Brent asked, turning sober eyes on her.

"You needn't pretend with me. I know the earl strangled that old man. I saw it with my own eyes."

"You saw Gowan murder Ben?"

"Not the earl, stupid, Bailey and Ceddy. Strangled him with his own scarf and tossed him into the ditch. And don't go thinking I could have told the sheriff what I'd seen because he'd never believe a gypsy."

"And the earl would have sent his cutthroats after us," Roberto added. "I don't doubt we could have taken care of our own, but there was no sense in getting cut up when you were dead and gone for all we knew. Why have you come back? It will take an army to drive him out."

"Nonetheless I mean to do it, but I need your help."

"Master Brent, you know we'd do anything we could for you, but you can't even show your face without landing in jail."

"Gowan thinks I'm dead. He stole my wife and nearly killed me." When Madelena and Roberto gaped at him, he laughed out loud.

"What? Are you mad?" Madelena finally managed to say. "Why would he do a thing like that?"

"Because I stole her from him first."

"You *are* mad." Roberto was stunned.

"Where is she now?" Madelena demanded, instantly consumed by curiosity.

"At Glenstal."

"But that's the earl's wife up at the castle," Roberto said, confused by the tangled story. "Everybody knows that she's—Ow!" he howled as he received a well-aimed kick in the shins.

"She's absolutely beautiful," Madelena finished the sentence for her afflicted husband. "But what you're saying makes no sense. The only woman at the castle *is* the earl's wife."

As Brent proceeded to tell his story, Roberto heard him out in speechless silence, but Madelena became so excited by the tale of romantic love that she could barely contain herself. "The marriage documents were never properly signed, so Summer was never legally Gowan's wife," Brent concluded. "It was a simple matter for Smith to get hold of the documents, substitute new ones with my name, and bribe a priest to attest that the marriage had taken place. Legally, I am Summer's one and only husband."

"I've never heard anything more outrageous in my whole life." Roberto shook his head.

"What do you want us to do?" asked Madelena, ready to commit the whole caravan.

"I don't want you involved in the fighting. I've brought more than enough men to take on Gowan's hirelings. What I want you to do is smuggle them in from the coast."

"That'll be easy," Roberto promised. "He's afraid to go on your land alone, and even his own men are beginning to distrust him after the way he's treated his young wife."

Madelena trod on Roberto's toe, but he refused to be quieted. "He can't go risking his neck without knowing everything, Madelena."

"Has something happened to Summer?" Brent was suddenly fiercely alert.

"In a way it has," Roberto said quickly to get the jump on his wife. "One night, some while back, there was a lot of screaming in the countess's apartments, and when they broke down the door, the earl had stripped her mother-naked and was trying to beat her to death."

"I'll kill him," Brent raged, charging to his feet.

"Nobody knows why he did it, but some think he went crazy when she told him she was going to give him an heir."

Madelena put out her hand to stop Roberto, but to her surprise Brent began to grin.

"Tell me, how is the earl taking the news?"

"They say he's ready to cut the throat of anybody who even mentions that baby. The butler—"

"Wigmore."

"—has organized the staff so she's never alone with him."

"That's my child she's carrying." Brent jumped to his feet. "I've got to get her out of there tonight."

"You're crazy," said Madelena. "You can't burst in there and hope to get out alive."

"I know the castle almost as well as Gowan does."

"And how do you plan to get her away?"

"On horseback of course. You've got some of the best horseflesh in Scotland right here."

"You're not going to make a woman who's eight months gone ride a horse across the moors at night?" Madelena was aghast. "She would lose the baby for sure."

"Then I'll take a coach."

"And I'm sure you'll drive slowly and carefully with Gowan's men pursuing you," Madelena said derisively.

Brent was stymied.

"You can't even tell her you're here," Madelena added softly. "The shock might send her into early labor."

"Where do you plan to take her?" Roberto asked. "You can't stay in Scotland, not even for one night."

Brent slowly sank to the ground, suppressed fury causing a blood vessel to bulge at his temple. He couldn't rescue Summer until after she had the baby, and he couldn't remain in Scotland unless he crushed Gowan. The happiness went out of his eyes and cunning took its place; he had not come back to run away again.

"I don't trust Gowan enough to wait until after she has the baby," he decided.

"That baby can't be more than a month away."

"Then I'm going to have to get her out right away. Madelena, you'll have to find some way to let her know I'm here. She must make ready to leave; I'll steal inside the castle while Gowan's out and be miles away before he can muster his forces. Then I can face him without fearing what he might do to Summer. How soon can you begin moving my men in, Roberto?"

"Tomorrow. We're having a spring fair, and caravans will be coming from all over. Your men would never be noticed among so many wagons."

"Madelena, I want you to find out everything you can about what goes on at the castle. I can't give you more than two days."

"We need someone inside," Madelena decided.

"Wigmore." Brent's lips suddenly curved in a smile. "Can you contact him?"

"You leave that to me," Madelena declared confidently.

"Come, let me introduce you to the others," Roberto said. "You have a lot of explaining to do."

"And a lot of planning," Madelena added, squeezing Brent's hand. "It's good to have you home."

Chapter 44

Summer was greatly relieved when the day for her escape finally arrived. She had continued to visit the tenants in spite of Bridgit's and Lucy's pleas to stop. "It helps me keep my mind off my troubles," she always said. But that was only part of the reason; the long excursions into the countryside enabled her to map out her escape route.

She finished her breakfast without breaking into tears, and refused once again to allow either woman to accompany her. "What can happen to me when I'm never off our land?"

"You go wandering over to Windswept, too, and that's a far piece."

"Well, you won't have to worry about any more visits after this. The earl plans to take me to Edinburgh in two days. Is the food packed?"

"I don't know why you're set on giving them enough for a month," complained Bridgit.

"Don't be so stingy. No one in the castle will go hungry." Summer smiled to herself as she drove down the rough cart tracks, remembering Bridgit's loud assertion that she wasn't wanting the food for herself, and if the countess thought she ate too much, she was surprised she hadn't been told of it already. As long as Bridgit was in a huff, she wouldn't sit by the window; Summer didn't want anyone to start looking for her too soon.

In her purse was enough money to purchase her passage and to provide for her and the baby until she reached her old home. A chuckle escaped her as she imagined the uproar that would ensue when she didn't return that evening. She had chosen a hiding place in the opposite direction from the farmhouse she was supposed to be visiting and on the road toward the coast. She had already visited her hiding place and had left some old clothing there, garments originally intended for the almshouse. A farmer's wife in an old wagon would attract less notice than a countess in a carriage.

Long before the ten miles had been covered Summer was wondering if she shouldn't have chosen some place closer, but shortly before noon she pulled up in front of the decaying farmhouse and let her weary arms fall to her sides. Her hands were swollen from holding the reins and every part of her shoulders and back ached, but she felt exhilarated. She had escaped.

The house was situated well away from the lane and behind a belt of trees. It showed no signs of having been occupied for many years, but the roof was intact and the door could be closed and bolted. Her first task was to get the food inside. Then she must stable the horse and hide the wagon. Both were essential to her escape, but either one might betray her hiding place.

The barn door sagged open on loose hinges. She drove the wagon inside, unharnessed the horse, and put him in a stall. She decided to see about closing the door later.

By the time she had carried everything up to the sleeping

loft of the farmhouse, she was completely exhausted. She made one final check for any signs of her presence, then pulled herself up to the loft and fell into an exhausted sleep on a straw pallet.

Brent was glad he was alone when he first saw Windswept again. Memories of his parents rushed upon him, and tears that had remained unshed for ten long years fell when he saw his mother's sitting room exactly as it had been when he'd last seen her alive. It was almost as though he had reached out and touched the past. He sat in her chair and let his stored-up grief escape its long bondage.

"I am home," he said to the empty room when his eyes cleared, "and I am here to stay." He had a future to build, a life to make for his family. He would not forget the past, but never again would he be governed by memories.

The sound of an approaching wagon caused him to hurry out one of the doors at the back of the house. He hadn't gone twenty feet when he saw Madelena's wagon traveling dangerously fast over the debris-strewn drive.

"What do you mean driving like a madwoman?" he asked as she pulled up. "You're liable to break an axle."

"The countess has disappeared from the castle. Tie your horse behind, and I'll tell you about it on the way."

Brent wasted no time in useless questions. Within seconds he had the wagon turned around, and they headed back to the camp at a brisk trot.

"The whole castle was in an uproar when I arrived," Madelena said, holding on tightly as the wagon took a corner perilously fast. "The men had been out all night without finding the countess."

"What happened?"

"I'm getting to that. The countess planned to visit some tenants yesterday and she wasn't expected back until late afternoon. When she didn't return by dinnertime, the earl called for a fresh horse and every man he could mount. But the countess hadn't been to the farm, nor had anyone seen her. They searched the roads until after midnight and were out again this morning, but they haven't found a trace of her."

"What do you think happened to Summer?"

"I think she's run away."

"At such a time? Where could she possibly go?"

"I don't know. They say she's been very secretive ever since the earl announced that he intended to take her to Edinburgh for the delivery of his heir."

"Do you think that's significant?"

"I don't think the countess trusts Gowan."

"To drive a poor girl to have her child out in the open, alone and unprotected, is completely inhuman."

"I don't think she's in the open. I think she's planned this for a long time. All that riding around the countryside wasn't accidental."

"But where would she go?"

"Where they won't look for her, but in the direction in which she plans to escape. Louise said the countess's household money is missing. I think she means to reach the coast and go back to her home."

"How could she possibly hope to hide from the earl? His men are everywhere."

"Not on your land," said Madelena. "And your land is closer to the coast."

"Madelena, you're a genius." Brent gave her a kiss, then whipped the horse into such a gallop she was sure the wagon would rattle to pieces. "If the baby's a girl, I'm going to name it after you."

"It's going to be a boy." Madelena held on for dear life. "And he's going to look exactly like you."

"You're a witch." Buoyed by the knowledge that Summer was free of Gowan, Brent laughed. He fully intended to settle the score with Gowan, but that could wait until he'd found Summer.

Fifteen minutes after they reached the gypsy camp every man and boy, and half of the women and girls were scouring the countryside in search of Summer's hiding place.

"If you run across any of Gowan's men, discourage them from staying," Brent had prompted his cohorts, but he'd stayed in camp, ready to deploy his men if necessary. He chafed at the feeling of uselessness, but he had been a leader too long to give in to the temptation to join the searchers. If he or his men were recognized, it would ruin everything.

"Stay with me," he told Madelena. "I'm no good with babies."

"Even the children know more about having babies than you do," she teased. But as the afternoon wore on and the sun sank beyond the hillside, Brent's patience wore thin and he subjugated each returning searcher to angry recriminations, driving some back into the dusk with orders not to return until they found Summer. When all but Roberto had wandered in exhausted and hungry, Brent made up his mind to go out himself. He couldn't leave Summer alone and unprotected without trying to find her.

"What do you think you can do in the dark?" Madelena chided. "My people know these hills like their own hands, yet they cannot find anything on this moonless night. Why should you be able to do more?"

"I can't stay here and do nothing while she may be at the mercy of any wild animal that roams these hills."

"I know it's hard to wait," Madelena said kindly, "but she's safe where she is. You'll do that child no favor if you kill yourself out there in the dark."

Brent unwillingly bowed to the wisdom of her argument.

"She sounds like a remarkable girl, this wife of yours." Madelena patted his hand reassuringly. "And smart too. She's outmaneuvered Gowan for months. I think she can do it for one more night."

"You're a jewel," Brent said, his voice choked with emotion. "If I didn't already love Summer so much, I'd run away with you."

"You're through stealing other men's wives," Madelena scolded. "Hasn't it gotten you into enough trouble?"

Brent laughed, and some of the oppressive weight was lifted from his chest. He held Madelena a little tighter and stared into the empty blackness.

Moments later they were wrenched from their abstraction by the horseman that galloped up to the campfire, sending dirt clods into the coals. The light revealed the taut features of Roberto.

"Into the wagon," he shouted without dismounting. "She's at the old Smithurst farmhouse, and already in labor." Brent would have saddled a horse for himself, but Roberto unceremoniously cut him short. "Drive the wagon. She needs Madelena and Fiona more than she needs you."

They were out of the camp and swallowed up by the dark night in a trice. No one spoke. There was no moon to light the way so Brent had to concentrate on threading his way through the treacherous lanes. The women knew what Summer was suffering, and they hoped there would be no complications because it would be nearly two hours before they reached the farmhouse.

Chapter 45

It was nearly dark when Summer woke from her nap that first afternoon. She was so tired she went right back to bed as soon as she had taken care of her horse, but lying in the dark with nothing to do except listen for sounds outside the farmhouse caused her to become nervous and jumpy. She didn't know who or what might be lurking in the woods or planning to use the farmhouse for a refuge.

Telling herself not to worry before she had reason to do so, Summer took out bread and some slices of beef, but as soon as she attempted to swallow the first mouthful, she remembered she had gotten water from the well for the horse but not for herself. When she returned, she found the smell of food had attracted two field mice. Stifling an urge to back down the ladder, she stamped her foot to frighten the mice from the loft, and then sat down to finish her meal.

When she had finished eating, she wrapped the food in a piece of oil cloth and tied it with a rope. Then, feeling along the rafters until she found a large nail, she looped the rope over the spike so the food hung well beyond the reach of any rodent.

Satisfied with that arrangement, she decided to remake her bed. She piled up straw until it was two feet deep and then covered it with a thick sheepskin rug. One of the extra dresses she'd brought, folded up and doubled over, served as a headrest, and a heavy cloak pulled up to her chin provided warmth. The bed was surprisingly comfortable, but no matter what she did she couldn't fall asleep; she found herself straining to listen for every sound.

She was certain there was nothing to fear; nevertheless, she found herself trying to identify every noise. She had no idea who or what might attack her, but as the lonely hours crawled by, she wished her imagination were not quite so vivid.

Finally, just as she was about to fall asleep, she heard a scratching at the door and sat up, shivering with fright, the hair standing up on the back of her neck. It was a large animal, much larger than a rat. Why hadn't she thought to ask if wolves or bears still lived in the hills?

Now the scratching was accompanied by a whining sound that became increasingly insistent. At least it wasn't a bear. She was safe as long as she stayed in the attic. The scratching stopped, only to begin again and then stop once more. Summer crawled out of her bed and went to the ladder. She could still hear the whining, now from one window and soon from the other. Summer wondered if the animal was attracted by her food. Unable to stand the suspense any longer, she picked up her pistol and climbed down the ladder.

With great stealth she crept over to the window, placed her face to one of the dusty panes, and peered into the night. A sudden scurrying made her reel back and scream. Her heart beating wildly, she stared into the big brown eyes of a huge sheepdog which barked a friendly greeting and wagged its tail so energetically its whole body shook.

Weak from shock, Summer sank to the floor, laughing at herself and her imagined fears. "I'll bet you want a piece of meat," she said, beginning to recover her courage. "I can't give you any food, but I'd be grateful if you'd stay and guard my door." The dog barked again, entreating her to let him in; instead Summer climbed the ladder and went back to bed. No further sounds worried her, and she soon fell fast asleep.

The sun was high in the heavens before Summer woke the next morning. There was no sign of the dog; but she was not lonely. She looked forward to spending a day in idleness, but this turned out to be the most boring day of her life. Summer was used to being busy, and after an hour she began to look for things to do. She was finally reduced to sweeping the dirt floor to keep from going crazy.

Summer was dozing when she heard the horse whinny. She sat up, listening intently. There was no answering call from the barn, but the unseen horse whinnied again. Then the whining and scratching of the past night started up; Summer was sure it was the same dog. She held her breath and waited. Minutes later she heard hoof beats in the lane and she fled up the ladder. For a time the only sounds that came to her were made by the dog, and she began to hope that the rider was just passing by. But just as she was trying to decide whether to go back down, footsteps approached the house and someone tried the door. When it didn't open, the stranger knocked and then tried the door again, then the windows.

"Countess, are you in there?" The man spoke with an accent Summer had never heard before. "I'm not one of the earl's men. I've come from Captain Douglas." Summer's heart lurched so violently she nearly lost her grip on the ladder.

Fool, she told herself, that's exactly the kind of cruel trick Gowan would employ. He wouldn't care if the pain tore you apart. But the voice kept calling, kept using Brent's name, until it rang inside her head with the insistence of a tolling bell. She fought the weight of sadness, the birth of hope, the tears and the racking sobs that had not been exhausted by months of grieving.

At last, unable to stand the torture any longer, she called out, "You're lying. Go away and leave me alone."

The intruder pushed on the door harder than before. The wooden bar was stout, but dry rot had eaten into its cradle and one mighty heave sent it crashing to the floor. As the door swung inward and banged against the wall, Summer reached into the pocket of her cloak and took out a pistol. She had hoped she wouldn't have to use it, but if she let this man go, he would tell Gowan.

Roberto smiled when he saw the freshly swept floor. It reminded him of Madelena. "Countess, I'm coming up," he called, knowing instinctively that Summer was hiding in the loft. "I don't want to harm you. I only want to talk with you, to tell you about Master Brent."

Summer closed her eyes. The pain was almost too much to bear. If he didn't stop using Brent's name, she would have to shoot him. She couldn't stand to hear him talk as if Brent were still alive, as if all she had to do was climb down the ladder and he would lead her to him. She blocked Brent's image from her mind, and forced herself to think only of the danger below.

Roberto placed one foot on the ladder and began to climb slowly and deliberately. When he put his head into the loft the first thing he saw was the pistol less than six inches from his forehead.

"Don't move," Summer commanded. "I'll kill us both if I have to."

Roberto stared at her, his breath coming quickly. "You are beautiful," he said, in awe of her, "just as beautiful as Master Brent said you were."

"I'll shoot you if you speak Brent's name one more time,"

she cried out, fighting back tears. "I know he's dead. I saw him die with my own eyes."

"He almost died," Roberto told her, advancing very slowly, "but he's well now, and he's here in Scotland."

"I don't believe you." Summer's tears were almost blinding her; but against her will, the seed of hope took root. "I saw Gowan shoot him. I *saw* all the blood. *I saw him die!*" She broke down and sobbed uncontrollably.

"He's very much alive. We started searching for you the moment we heard you'd escaped. We thought you might be on Douglas land."

"How? . . ."

"My wife visits your egg woman every day."

"Please don't say this if it isn't true," Summer begged. "I will go mad if I lose him again."

Roberto was in the loft now, but he made no move to approach Summer.

"I wouldn't lie to you. I've know Master Brent since he was a boy. I would do anything for the woman he loved, especially when she's carrying his child."

Summer instinctively covered her belly. "Why do you say that?"

"Brent swore you wouldn't let the earl come near you." A heartrending sob broke from Summer, but it was cut short by a stabbing pain.

"My labor has started," she gasped.

"You've got to get below," Roberto decided.

"I can't move."

"I'm going for Brent, and a midwife. We may not be able to move you by the time I get back so I'll hide you under the straw. My dog will guard you."

"A large sheepdog?" she asked.

"How did you guess?"

"He was here last night. He nearly scared me to death."

"So that's why he led me this way. I would never have taken this lane in the dark, but when my horse neighed I knew there was someone about. I hoped it was you."

A spasm of pain swept over Summer as she descended the ladder; she froze and held on until it passed.

"Are you sure you'll be all right? I can try sending the dog back alone."

"I'll be fine," she promised. "Just bring Brent as quickly as you can. And if you've lied, I swear I'll kill you." Roberto prepared a deep straw pallet for Summer, and as soon as she was comfortable, he left his dog with her and vanished into the night.

The wait was the most terrible torture Summer had ever endured. Sometimes she expected Brent to walk through the door and sweep her into his arms. At others she feared that Gowan would appear and drag her off to Edinburgh and those doctors who were willing to do anything for money. Only the huge dog sitting next to the door convinced her she hadn't dreamed it all.

As time inched forward, doubts scourged her newborn hope and the pains grew sharper and more frequent. She was slipping into semiconsciousness when she heard horses's hooves and wagon wheels.

Brent's nerves were stretched nearly to the breaking point by the time he pulled into the farmhouse yard. "She's on a straw pallet in the corner," Roberto called as he leapt from the still-moving wagon, taking the lantern with him. He rushed through the door holding the light above his head, his eager eyes searching the dark corners.

"Brent?" The weak voice came from his left. "Is it really you?" Turning in the direction of the sound, Brent beheld Summer lying in a corner, almost entirely covered in straw. Her tear-stained face was contorted by a spasm of pain, but when she recognized him joy relaxed her features. Brent tenderly took her into his arms, but Summer, laughing, crying, and saying his name over and over, was momentarily oblivious to pain. She covered his face with kisses, and clung to him, unable to believe that he was really alive. Brent, too, forgot the baby and returned her embraces with crushing strength. The three onlookers, gathered at the door, were mute witnesses to a reunion that moved even the pragmatic Roberto.

"Shouldn't she lie down?" Roberto asked, fearful that the tight embrace would injure Summer or the baby.

"Let them be," whispered Madelena. "The baby can wait."

When a contraction turned Summer rigid in Brent's arms, the more practical Fiona announced, "You can finish this later," and bustled into action, adding, "right now we've got to get her comfortable."

"Don't leave me," Summer begged.

"I won't stir from your side," Brent promised.

"This is no time to have a man about," Fiona admonished. "You go stay in the wagon."

"I'm staying here," Brent declared.

Fiona was disgusted by the foolishly adoring way Brent stared at Summer, but she was never one to waste time on lost causes.

"Then make yourself useful. A wagonload of things have to be brought in. You and Roberto see to it while Madelena and I try to get her settled."

When Summer refused to let go of Brent's hand, he said, "I'm just going outside. I'll never leave you again."

"I'm going to need a lot more straw," Madelena declared. "If you will have your baby like a mare, at least we can make a decent bed for you." She scolded the two men sharply every time Summer made a sound, but Summer was finally settled on a fresh bed. "Now go start the fire and heat some water while we get her out of these clothes," Madelena said to the men.

"Roberto can make the fire by himself," Brent argued. "I'm not leaving her again."

"If you can look at her in the straw and still think she's beautiful, I guess you're as besotted as she is," Fiona said huffily. "But you'll have to turn your eyes away while we change her. I'll not have you staring at her naked."

"How do you think she got this way?" Brent smiled wickedly at Fiona.

"Young people have no manners anymore," lamented Madelena. "If Roberto had spoken to my mother like that, my father would have shot him."

"If your father had seen Summer, he would have understood."

"Are you saying I'm so ugly it's a relief to turn away?" Madelena's eyes glinted dangerously.

"Everyone knows that Roberto still has to drive your admirers away with a knife, but look at her. Even now she's the most beautiful woman in the world."

"You're hopeless," said Madelena. "If you must stay where you have no business to be, get out of my way so I can do my work." Brent continued to hold Summer's hand and to whisper lovingly in her ear even when Madelena poked him in the ribs to make him move. She grumbled while she changed Summer's clothes, then made some pungent remarks on the behavior of young people as she drew the sheet over Summer; but later, when she stepped outside to confer with Roberto, her attitude was quite different.

"You should see the two of them holding hands and staring at each other as if there were no one else in the world. You'd never know they were in a crumbling shack on a dirt floor."

"I thought you would send him out, or haven't you changed her yet?"

"He's so blinded by love he wouldn't know whether she was mother-naked or wearing a golden gown. Did you ever feel that way about me?" she asked coyly.

"With you rolling about and screaming like a wild woman?" Roberto asked, aghast. "I stuck my head in the wagon once, and you let out such a screech I thought they were cutting you open."

"You have no romance in your soul. You couldn't really love me," she pouted.

"Then your sister pushed me off the step. Your father had to protect me."

"Master Brent's not afraid."

"Why should he be? You and Fiona treat him like a prince. Your mother and sisters treated me like an archfiend for getting you pregnant." He pulled Madelena roughly to him. "But I'd do it again in a minute," he said, responding instantly to the warmth of her body against his.

"Behave yourself," his wife scolded, though she was enormously pleased. "I'm too old for that kind of stuff."

"That's not what you said last night," he teased, breathing hotly in her ear.

"I've got to go back." Madelena blushed and tried to break out of his hold. "Fiona can't manage without me."

"Neither can I. You know that, don't you?"

"Yes," she said shyly. She gave him a deep kiss and then ran back into the farmhouse, feeling younger and more lighthearted than she had in years.

Chapter 46

The women took turns watching Summer throughout the night. "She's not going to be quick with her time," said Fiona. "It may take another day."

"How can she stand another day of this agony?" Brent asked, fretting helplessly as Summer lay exhausted after a wave of pain.

"There's nothing wrong," Madelena insisted, trying to allay his fears. "She just started her labor too soon. The poor thing is worn out, but she's doing fine." Brent tried to be reassured, but he became more and more worried as the morning wore into midday and then afternoon. He wanted several times to throw caution to the winds and send for a doctor.

"Don't be an imbecile," Madelena admonished. "How can you expect Summer to remain calm if you act like a spooked yearling? You can't tell me you carried on like this when your ship was in trouble. She needs someone to lean on, not someone to add to her fears. It's going to take all of her strength to deliver this baby."

Brent felt like an apprentice seaman being dressed down.

At sunset the pains intensified and started coming closer together. One hardly receded before another swept around Summer's body like the coils of a large snake, causing her to moan distressfully and arch her body in protest. The two women then came out of their state of seeming unconcern and busied themselves with preparations for the birth; Brent's offer of help was firmly refused. "You'll have all you can do to keep yourself calm," Fiona told him tersely.

So Brent, completely shaken by the terrible agonies Summer was being forced to endure, stayed by his wife's side. He had never considered what it meant for a woman to bear a child; the ordeal of birth was completely foreign to his masculine experience. Despite the pain of his own wounds, and the deaths and maimings he had witnessed, it nearly drove him mad to see the woman he loved being battered by this seemingly perpetual torment. He wanted to fight something, to curse someone for her pain.

It was a new experience for him to sit by while others were busy, but he clenched his teeth and curbed his rage as best he could for Summer seemed to derive comfort from his presence. It was his own fault that she was having this baby. If sitting by her side, holding her hand, mopping her brow—woman's work he would have scornfully called it just hours earlier—could make her trial any easier, then that was what he would do. It was the only way he could relieve the guilt he felt for having forced this misery on her. He made a silent vow never to do it again.

As the light faded, her pains grew worse. Summer reached out to clasp Brent's hand as a particularly vicious convulsion wrenched at her abdomen, burying her in a haze of torment. She felt that she was drowning in pain, her head rolled from side to side, and she was unable to stop the low moans that slipped from her compressed lips. Faces became unclear and voices seemed to be coming from a distance, but Brent's hand was her lifeline, the link that kept her from being pilotless in this storm of suffering.

Then the most terrible pain of all gripped Summer, and pushed down with violent force. A muffled scream escaped her lips, but before she could recover, another contraction, even worse than the first, seized her like the embrace of a constrictor. She felt a terrible pressure, an overwhelming desire to push down, to rid herself of the burden that tortured her so. Brent cradled her in his arms as still another wave gripped her and she tried to throw herself from the bed.

"It's coming," cried Fiona. "I can see the wee creature's head." Without knowing quite why he did it, Brent yielded Summer to Madelena. It was his child and his arms must be the first to hold it.

"One more push ought to do it," prompted Fiona. Summer tried to respond, but before she could gather herself, another wave washed over her. It was so all-consuming she felt swallowed by it. Through a haze she felt the baby's head slip from her body; another push, and the baby lay in Brent's arms. The brutal pains rapidly lost their force, and Summer closed her eyes. She had done it, she had given birth.

Brent stared transfixed at the tiny, wrinkled face. The infant boy opened his eyes, took his first gulp of air, and cried out in protest. Brent had looked forward to becoming a father and had thought in an inchoate way of what it would be like. But now that his dream had turned into reality, he felt as much at a loss as any man could.

"You'd think the man had never held a baby." Fiona laughed.

"I haven't," said the bemused Brent. "We don't have babies at sea."

"Bless me, I never thought of that. He really *doesn't* know what to do."

"Then it's time he learned," said Madelena. Brent came out of his fog long enough to discover he was about to drop the baby. The women laughed heartily as he tried to balance the infant, rear end in one hand and head and shoulders in the other. His hands kept going up and down like the weighing pans of a meat scale.

"Bless the man if he's not trying to juggle with it." Fiona was enjoying Brent's confusion. The baby, dwarfed by Brent's enormous hands, looked up at his father with clear blue eyes.

"Don't stand there laughing at me, woman." Brent was truly flustered. "Show me what to do before I drop him."

"You put the arm next to you like this, you clumsy brute." Madelena placed Brent's left arm horizontally across his chest. "Then you lay the baby in the crook of it, and you still have your right hand free to make sure you don't drop him onto the floor." Both women were greatly amused as the hapless Brent held the child stiffly, certain that the slightest move would cause him to drop it. He could hardly believe that anything so tiny would grow into a man. The baby waved a tiny fist at his father and uttered a loud cry.

"He's protesting your rough handling," Madelena crowed. "You've got a lot to learn before you can be trusted with a baby."

"Brent," Summer called softly.

He started so violently at the sound of his beloved's voice that he nearly did drop his son.

"Merciful saints," Madelena exclaimed, and took the child from the now completely unstrung father. "The man is a menace."

"It is a son?" Summer asked dreamily.

"It's a boy," Brent said moving quickly to her side, "but he's awfully tiny."

"The man's a fool," Fiona declared. "It's a fine, big man-child and the spitting image of his oaf of a father."

"Brent is not an oaf," Summer protested. "He's the smartest and bravest man in the world."

"See what love can do, even to sensible women?" Madelena placed the child in the outstretched arms of its father. "See if you can give it to its mother without dropping it." She spoke sharply, but her eyes glowed as Brent gingerly took the baby and placed it next to Summer.

"He looks like you," Summer said fondly. "I hoped he would."

"He's the very image of his father," Fiona agreed.

"How can you say he looks like me? He's tiny, red, and wrinkled all over," Brent said with unfatherly frankness.

"He's beautiful." Summer ignored the outraged Gypsies who threatened to drive Brent from the farmhouse. "I'm glad. You deserve a perfect son."

"The woman's bewitched," scoffed Fiona.

"No I am not," Summer declared, showing a hint of her old energy. "Brent is the most marvelous man in the world and he deserves to have nothing but perfect children. Don't you say anything against him, or I'll chase *you* out of the farmhouse."

"Listen to her," crowed a delighted Madelena. "She's the warring mother already. If you've got so much energy, feed that baby. He's got a lot of growing to do before he catches up with his father."

Brent helped Summer prop herself up on quilts stuffed with straw, and holding her son in her arms sent chills of pleasure through her tired body. She could hardly believe that the tiny baby belonged to her, that this was what she had carried around for all that time. How could Gowan ever think she could give up anything so wonderful? She guided the tiny mouth to her breasts. The infant didn't understand at first, but he soon began to nuzzle. The first tug on her swollen nipple stung, but her heart was filled with joy as she looked down into the precious face of her child. It was worth the pain, the months of fear and worry, the physical strain of carrying him; this one inexplicably wonderful moment was worth it all. She looked up at Brent and smiled wanly. He was watching her with the bewildered look peculiar to most new fathers.

"Are you pleased with him?" she asked.

"I'm proud of both of you," he replied. "But I promise I won't put you through this again. One son will be enough for us."

"Don't be absurd." She smiled lovingly. "I want lots more babies, especially if they're all as beautiful as this."

"You can't mean you want to go through this again?"

"Many times," she said ecstatically. Brent couldn't believe she was serious, but the looks on Madelena's and Fiona's faces told him he had stumbled up against one of the mysteries of the female sex. As much as he might love his son, he would never be able to understand how Summer could want another child so soon after an agonizing birth that had taken the better part of two days.

"We can have as many as you want." He smiled. "But how about a little time out in between. I'd like to enjoy you with a flat stomach."

"You're a wretched beast, Brent Douglas, and I'll never understand why I love you." Summer giggled.

"It's the curse of all women," said Madelena, a merry twinkle in her eyes. "I could tell you tales about Roberto that would make your heart cry." Their tension released, the adults gave way to unrestrained merriment.

They were so taken up in their hilarity that they didn't hear the distinctive call of a night bird, but a second and louder call prompted Madelena to pause and listen. "Something is wrong," she said, suddenly serious. "That's Roberto's danger signal. You'll have to go."

"I can't leave now." Brent was unwilling to abandon his wife and son. But the call came yet again.

"Move!" Madelena commanded, and her alarm communicated itself to the others. "Roberto would not call three times unless he feared you were in mortal danger." When Brent still hesitated, she hissed, "Hurry or we may yet lose everything."

Brent went to the window; he was surprised to find it completely dark outside. Roberto was kneeling before a small fire in front of the wagon. When Brent opened the door and listened intently, the sounds of shod hooves on stone were carried to him.

"Someone's coming, several riders from the sound of it," he whispered to Madelena. "Turn down the lantern and keep quiet." He darted out the door and around behind the farmhouse. Then he crouched low and sprinted to the narrow hedge that separated it from the fields. Moving along that until he came to a point just beyond the wagon, he halted a few yards from the fire and the crouching figures of Roberto and his dog. Stacks of rifles stood near the gypsy, and Brent cursed under his breath for forgetting to arm himself. He could not get to the rifles without revealing his presence.

The horses, still enveloped in the inky blackness of the night, came closer and closer until they halted just outside the range of the firelight.

"What are you doing on this land?" The resonant voice attracted Brent's attention as Gowan drew his horse close enough for the fire to illuminate his features.

"Camping for the night," Roberto answered without raising his eyes.

"I don't allow Gypsies on my land. Camp somewhere else."

Brent strained to see how many men accompanied Gowan.

"I can't," said the still motionless Roberto. "I was heading to the fair when one of my women took sick. She's lying in that farmhouse now."

"Go see if what he says is true," Gowan directed, and two men dismounted and headed toward the farmhouse.

"I wouldn't go in," Roberto cautioned. "She's infectious."

"What's wrong with her?" Gowan asked skeptically.

"Smallpox." The men fell back at those words.

"Don't stop," Gowan bellowed.

"I can hear some female groaning from out here, your lordship."

"You can't keep her here," the earl said irritably to Roberto.

"I can't take her away until she's better, or until she dies," Roberto responded phlegmatically. "I stopped here because it's far from the other farms."

"Where are the rest of your people?" Gowan was aware of the danger of smallpox, but he was suspicious. "I never knew Gypsies to travel alone."

"They've gone on without me. They don't want the pox either. Some may come back tonight." Brent moved noiselessly along the hedge until the mounted men were between him and the fire. Gowan had brought six men, all armed. He and Roberto would be hard pressed to hold off seven men alone, even with two dozen rifles.

"Have you passed any travelers these last two days?" Gowan inquired.

"What kind of traveler might you be looking for?" Roberto asked.

"One of our women is missing. She's expecting a child soon, and we think she's wandering in her mind. She may be lost and unable to find her way home."

"We didn't meet any woman on foot."

"She wasn't on foot. She was driving a wagon."

"We didn't meet any wagons." Gowan looked at the barn. "What's in there?" he said nodding in that direction.

"My horses," replied Roberto.

"But your wagon has only a single trace."

"I ride the other, or tie it behind," said the ever-inventive Gypsy. Gowan gestured impatiently and two men moved toward the barn. They had almost reached the door when a terrible scream came from the farmhouse and Fiona came running out. The other men stumbled all over themselves trying to get out of her way.

"I need water," she squawked, grabbing up a half-filled pail by the door and brandishing her fist in the air before rushing back in. The men drew back. They had seen Madelena bend over a writhing female in the dim light of the lantern and that was enough for them. They needed no encouragement to retreat to the fire. The one nearing the barn stopped outside the door, and the other only stuck his head inside long enough to catch the sound of horses moving about in their stalls.

"Just two old nags," he said as he returned to the fire. During the distraction created by the women, a Gypsy had materialized out of the night and taken up a position to one side of Roberto. He was watching Gowan with steely eyes. Behind the hedge, Brent smiled to himself; Roberto would have made a fine ship's captain.

Gowan peered intently into the blank face of Roberto, trying to see behind the mask. He had no reason to doubt his story, but he distrusted all Gypsies. He was still undecided as to whether to leave when the night air was punctured by a piercing wail. "I want you off this land first thing tomorrow, and don't bury her carcass here if she dies." Another Gypsy arrived and squatted by the fire, his head cocked. His keen ears had caught the sound of many feet approaching along the route he had just traveled.

"The old lord let us camp on his land," Roberto said sullenly.

"The old lord is dead, and this is my land now." Gowan had not failed to notice Roberto's reinforcements.

"What about the young lord?"

"The young lord's dead, too. There are no more Douglases." Gowan's last words were nearly cut off by the unmistakable cry of a baby.

"What was that?" he demanded, whipping around in the direction of the sound.

"That was the sound of a new generation of Douglases," Brent announced as he stepped from behind the hedge into the light.

Chapter 47

"*You!*" The monosyllable was torn from Gowan's unwilling throat.

"I'm not very easy to kill."

"I'll make sure you die this time." Burning with rage, Gowan shouted to his men, "Take him! Take him, you cowardly fools!" But while Gowan was gaping at Brent, the Gypsies had taken up their arms, and Gowan's men found themselves looking into the barrels of three very businesslike pistols.

"Your men can't help you now, Gowan. You're going to have to take me yourself, if you think you can."

Gowan's fury didn't blind him to Brent's formidable bulk, nor to the fact that it wasn't likely that one man would be able to overpower him. "You'll never get out of Scotland alive," he snarled. "I'll see that a dozen officers are waiting for you at every port."

"I'm not running away this time. We're going to settle this right now."

"You wouldn't dare try to kill me," Gowan scoffed.

"Why not?"

"They'd hang you."

"They can only hang me once—for two murders or for one."

Gowan's expression lost some of its arrogance. Instinctively he looked to his men and was shaken to see that a third Gypsy had materialized out of the night; the numbers were almost equal now. "Is this a pirate's idea of fairness?" he demanded, pointing to Roberto's armed men with feigned contempt.

"I've been shot in the back once already," Brent snapped. He was beginning to lose patience. "I don't want it to happen again."

Gowan's face became rigid with fury, and he gripped the reins so hard his knuckles turned white.

The protagonists were so completely involved in the confrontation, they were oblivious to approaching hoofbeats until Wigmore burst into the light astride a winded old gray. He was followed by Smith, a half-dozen of Brent's crew, and a score of his tenants. It was a small, ragtag army, but it bowled Gowan over.

"What are you doing here?" asked an astonished Brent.

Wigmore was too saddlesore to dismount. "Thank goodness I reached you in time," he said. "I was afraid I would be too late."

"Too late for what? And where did all these people come from?"

"I heard the earl say he was going to search your land. I ran into your first mate on the way, he insisted upon coming with me, and people joined us as we went along. I didn't know you already had help." He smiled at the Gypsies.

"You will pay for this," Gowan thundered. "You will all regret hindering justice."

"Justice is about to be served for the first time since Lord

Robert was foolish enough to entrust his family to you," Wigmore intoned dramatically, waving a handful of papers above his head. "At last, I have proof of your infamy."

"Do you mean we can prove he stole Father's money?" Brent asked, jolted into forgetting the danger Gowan still posed.

"That and a lot more," Wigmore announced proudly. "The sheriff is already at the castle with orders to arrest the earl."

"You doddering old fool. Nobody would take your word over mine," Gowan said disdainfully.

"They don't have to. I found the box you hid in the crypt below the chapel. When the countess mentioned her mother's marriage, I remembered where you and Mr. Robert used to hide things when you were boys. I don't know why I never thought of it before. Where else could it have been when I'd already searched the castle twice over without finding a thing?"

"You *dared* to search my home?" Gowan roared.

"Why else do you think I agreed to work for you?" Wigmore regarded his master with devastating contempt. "I even found the letters Lord Robert wrote to his wife."

"You have no proof that I've done anything wrong. The money was all lost in speculation."

"That's not what your clerk said."

The confident smirk disappeared from Gowan's face.

"He was *most* helpful after the sheriff explained that he could be held equally accountable. Furthermore the Gypsy woman saw Ben murdered, and Ceddy and Bailey can hardly wait to swear they were only following your orders."

"And Summer is *my* wife," Brent announced before the gathered crowd could completely absorb these last revelations. "Your marriage contract was never properly drawn up. A new one has been made, witnessed, and safely recorded in Havana."

Gowan could see the circle closing around him. The fruits of a lifetime were slipping from his hands into the hands of his hated enemy. His mounting rage was communicated to his horse and the animal became restive.

"You're dispossessed of lands, money, wife, and power at a single blow, Gowan. Not even your powerful friends can save you now," Brent declared.

Suddenly, the last of Gowan's control left him. "If I must rot in hell, I'll take you with me," he roared, and before the astounded onlookers he pulled a small pistol from inside his coat and fired point-blank at Brent. Anticipating some kind of treachery, Brent threw himself to the ground so quickly that the bullet only grazed his shoulder, and bellowing with black rage, Gowan dug his spurs savagely into the sides of his mount. As the pain-crazed animal reared and struck out with lethal hooves, the men that had surged forward drew back, permitting Gowan to wheel his horse and gallop the frantic animal through the heart of Roberto's small fire, killing the flame and scattering the coals in the grass. The Gypsies fired into the night, but darkness had closed about Gowan and they had no hope of bringing him down. Two of Roberto's men hurried to where they had hidden their horses, though they knew it would be almost impossible to follow Gowan on such a moonless night.

The women had followed the events from inside the farmhouse, but when the fire went out, they could no longer see what was happening. The sound of gunfire brought Summer up from her bed.

"Lie back down," Fiona ordered, picking up the baby from the bed. "You'll hurt yourself."

"I've got to find Brent," Summer rasped, staggering to her feet. "I've got to go to him." Ignoring Fiona's protests, she pulled herself across the room. No one noticed the bedraggled woman who appeared in the doorway, wrapped in a sheet. Haggard, she stared at the men around Brent.

"Brent." The piteous wail came from her when she saw him emerge from the group huddled outside, and then she sagged against the doorway. Brent was at her side and scooping her into his arms before she could slide to the ground.

"You shouldn't be out here," he said, forgetting Gowan in his concern for Summer. "Where is the baby?"

"I have him." Fiona emerged from the farmhouse. "She would get up no matter what I said."

"I couldn't just lie there while you were in danger. What kind of wife would I be?"

"The only one I'll ever want," said Brent, seating her gently in the chair Madelena was quick to provide. Fiona held out the baby to Summer, but she nodded toward Brent. He pulled back the edge of the blanket and gazed at the tiny face that stared back at him curiously. Clear blue eyes and fair hair, what there was of it, stamped the infant as Brent's son.

"Do you really like him?" Summer asked timidly.

"I like him very much, but not nearly as much as his mother."

"We come together."

"Then I guess I'll have to keep him," Brent said tenderly.

Summer rose from her chair and walked into his outstretched arms. Their long kiss was finally interrupted by their son's loud protest.

"He doesn't want you to forget about him," said Madelena. "He's part of the family, too." With a burst of laughter, Brent swept Summer up into his arms and carried her over to the rebuilt campfire. He motioned for everyone to gather around.

"I want to show you my wife and my son. Stoke that fire, Roberto. How can anybody see her in the dark?"

"No," he said suddenly. "We're not going to hide any longer." He swung Summer up onto the wagon. "Everyone is invited to Glenstal. We're going to light the courtyard and break out the beer and ale. This is a night of celebration. I'll not have a dry throat or a cheerless spirit around."

"I have a horse and wagon in the barn," Summer said to Wigmore. "You're welcome to hitch it up and ride."

"Bless you, milady, but I don't think I can get down from this beast." Brent helped Wigmore dismount, but the poor butler's legs buckled underneath him when he attempted to stand unassisted. The crowd roared with laughter, but Wigmore, dignified as ever, did not deign to notice.

"You can ride with us," Brent invited. "After what you've done, you deserve to be mounted on a royal steed."

"Thank you, but I'm quite content with a wagon," Wigmore said, shivering with horror at the thought of being astride a horse once again.

"Smith, round up your men and see that Roberto brings everybody from his camp. The rest of you, bring your families. I want every man, woman, and child from Glenstal and Windswept to share in the celebration."

When the flambeaux had been lighted and the beer was flowing freely, Brent took Summer and the baby and climbed up onto the back of the wagon; he motioned for the roistering crowd to be silent. "A new day has dawned for Windswept and Glenstal, and for everyone who has given loyal service during these difficult years. There is enough wealth to rebuild every farmhouse and to repair every building on both estates. It's not our intention to keep everything for ourselves because we believe that we will prosper as you prosper." He took the child from Summer and held him up so everyone could see.

"This is my heir," he announced proudly, and received a rousing cheer. "He is also my pledge that the greed and hatred that have divided these lands and oppressed you for so long are gone forever. In this child you see the future of these estates. Let us work to increase our strength until ours is the most powerful house in Scotland." A louder cheer rose from the crowd.

"We owe a great debt to Roberto and his people. They were my eyes, my ears, my hands, and my feet—my soldiers and my midwife. This is their success as much as it is mine. You must tell your children of what the Gypsies have done for us so that they may remember to be grateful and to treat them with kindness and trust. Your people are free to use these lands for as long as you like, Roberto. If you are in need or in danger, you may be certain of refuge among us, for truly we are your brethren." Brent clasped Roberto's hands in a symbolic gesture of brotherhood.

"And now I want to propose a toast to my wife," he announced, pulling a reluctant Summer to her feet so that she faced him. "If it had not been for her, I might never have found the courage to return."

Brent gazed lovingly into Summer's eyes, then slowly raised the cup to his lips and drained it.

The crowd drained their draughts more quickly and responded with yet another cheer. Summer heard their acclaim, but she was blinded by tears of happiness.

Chapter 48

I'm glad this week is almost over, Summer thought to herself on the afternoon when Bridgit had at last allowed her to get up and dress. It had been a week of dizzying changes tempered by lingering fears. It was hard to believe that she was Brent's wife and the mother of his child. When Brent smiled at her from across the room or when she felt his strong arms around her at night, she gave thanks all over again. And she often pinched herself to make sure she wasn't dreaming, that she was actually the contented wife of a wealthy landowner, not a frightened runaway.

All week long wagons had traveled between the two estates, transferring from Glenstal items that Summer and Brent needed to set up housekeeping at Windswept. Even though they were currently staying at Glenstal, they had decided to begin their married life in Brent's home. "There's so much that needs to be forgotten before I could be comfortable in this house," Summer had explained.

During this transition period she was confined to bed, and

her activities were limited to the care and feeding of her lusty son, Robert Frederick, named for both his grandfathers. She was content to leave the ordering of things in the capable hands of Wigmore and Bridgit.

"I'm proud to be serving another generation of the Douglas family," said the old butler when he brought in her tray. "It'll soon be like old times." Bridgit grumbled about leaving a perfectly good house for a moldy old barn, but she worked just as hard as Wigmore so that Summer could devote all her time to Brent and the baby.

"You can be sure that as soon as I sit down she will rise up from her bed, no matter how much harm it will do her, for make her do what is best for her I cannot. I can barely manage to keep her from sweeping the rooms herself. As it is, she's worn out from chasing after the young lord and nursing that baby."

None of the servants had any difficulty in switching their allegiance from Gowan to Brent. Everyone liked him right away, and, unlike Gowan, their new master appreciated their efforts. Within a few days Gowan was as forgotten as last night's bad dream.

Brent's wound was healing nicely, but his arm was still a little stiff. "I'm leaving him in your care this time," Smith had told Summer. Giving her one of his rare smiles, he'd added, "He's a very bad-tempered, ungrateful patient. He threatened to kill me if I ever again kept him knocked out, so I've decided to let you put your head in the noose."

Summer had thanked Smith so often that the poor man almost cringed when he saw her coming, but she couldn't keep her eyes from filling with tears and her heart from overflowing with gratitude every time she thought of the unselfish care he had lavished on Brent during his long illness.

Only one patch of fear now dimmed the brightness of her days; the sheriff had not been able to apprehend Gowan. He had been seen in Edinburgh several days earlier, but he'd disappeared when he'd learned that his property had been seized on behalf of Brent and Summer.

"I say good riddance," Bridgit confided to Wigmore. "He was a hateful, trouble-causing man, never happy unless he made your skin crawl or had you shaking in your boots. But it's so nice to work for Lord Douglas, and seeing the pair of them together is like something from a story book."

"I won't believe we've seen the last of the earl until I know he's in a coffin and under six feet of earth," stated Wigmore. "I know him, and he won't give up."

"You and your goblins," Bridgit scoffed. "You've lived in this moldy pile so long you can't think straight. Why should he show his face here when the sheriff is just waiting to clap him in jail and every tenant between here and Edinburgh would love to stick a pitchfork in his hide. Besides, every blessed thing he owned now belongs to the master and the mistress."

"To my way of thinking, that makes him all the more dangerous. A man that has nothing to lose has nothing to fear. You heed my words. You had best have a care. Milady and the baby are not safe yet."

"Piffle," Bridgit replied, but she couldn't rid herself of the nagging suspicion that Wigmore might know the earl better than she did.

The dingy, ill-lighted room was different from the surroundings Gowan was accustomed to, but in the past few days he had often had to make do with much less. Remembering days spent hiding in barns or woods and long nights in the saddle, a fugitive from justice and the legal prey of any lowly peasant's gun, he cursed Summer and Brent with awe-inspiring ferocity.

"I shall be even with you yet, Brent Douglas," he swore savagely. "You need not think yourself done with me so easily."

But it was at Summer and the son she had borne in defiance of him that he directed his most virulent hatred. He cursed them upon going to sleep and upon waking.

A tiny woman rose to meet Summer as she entered the salon. Her ample figure was tightly corseted, and her bosom was raised and accented in the style that had been popular thirty years earlier. An enormous hat was perched precariously on the side of her head, and abundant iron-gray hair framed her plain face, almost mulelike in its ugliness. She stared out at Summer from under her hat's broad brim, her shrewd eyes, not without a hint of humor, scanning the younger woman.

"I beg your pardon for taking so long. Did Wigmore look after you?"

"Someone brought me wine and cakes, but I didn't eat any. I don't approve of eating between meals." She nodded, indicating Summer's wraithlike form. "From the looks of you though, you could use some extra food."

"The baby takes a lot out of me," Summer said happily. "He's growing fast, and he's hungry all the time."

"You should get yourself a good wet nurse," Mrs. Slampton-Sands said disapprovingly. "It's not proper for a woman of your standing to nurse your own child."

"I may do that for the next one," Summer admitted, remembering sleepless nights and continual exhaustion, "but after the worry I had over him, I can hardly bear to let him out of my sight." She laughed suddenly. "Brent still hasn't talked me into letting him spend the night in the nursery."

Mrs. Slampton-Sands's face suddenly clouded over. "Have they found Gowan yet?"

"No. The sheriff thinks he's left Scotland."

Mrs. Slampton-Sands pressed her lips together and for a moment Summer thought she was going to say something about Gowan, but she seemed to change her mind.

"I've come here today to repair an oversight. I have refused to have anything to do with Gowan for so long—I haven't even set foot in this house in more than seventeen years—that I have been blinded to simple Christian charity."

"But you were kind enough to accept me and introduce me to your friends."

"No I wasn't," Mrs. Slampton-Sands insisted, and the rigid control no one had ever seen slip, not even her husband of more than twenty years, deserted her. "I accepted you because I harbored a guilty secret. I tried to erase it by easing your way, but that was not enough."

"Surely, you didn't—"

"Let me finish. It's a silly story, not very significant really, but it's important to me, and not very easy for me to confess to you.

"Many years ago your mother and I were good friends. I couldn't help but be jealous of her beauty, but I felt true affection for Constance. I was not as ugly as I am now. I was never pretty, still I was happy enough to accept Carleton's offer, even though I didn't love him, because I was unlikely to receive another. You see, both Constance and I had fallen in love with Frederick, but it was clear from the first that he never saw anyone but her. When her father stubbornly refused to even consider permitting them to marry, I helped them elope. I won't distress you with a recital of that needless tragedy, but at one point I was given the marriage documents to keep safe." She reached inside her large reticule and withdrew some papers tied with a faded ribbon. "I have them still."

"You have the proof that my parents were married!" Summer exclaimed, starting up from her chair.

"And there's more." Mrs. Slampton-Sands motioned for Summer to be seated. "I only heard from your mother twice in twenty years. The first letter was written just before she sailed. She said that she never meant to return, that she intended to cut herself off from her family and Scotland forever.

"Then about two years ago I received a second letter informing me that she had a nearly grown daughter. She said the child was Frederick's and that she meant to return to Scotland to see that her daughter was suitably married. She asked me to send her the marriage documents.

"I didn't do it. Oh, I meant to and I would never have withheld them from Constance had she returned, but I was jealous and afraid. I envied her for having Frederick's child—I'm childless, you see—and I feared for my position. I was never well liked; Constance was the one who was always popular, but over the years I had become the most influential woman in the district. I knew that if Constance returned, and if she claimed Gowan's wealth for you, I would once again be relegated to her shadow. I had struggled too long for what I had to give it up."

"Surely you aren't blaming yourself for all this?" Summer asked.

"Yes, I am. When I saw you, I knew what I had done was unforgivable, but I didn't know how to make it right. My coming forth with the documents wouldn't have changed your position, you might even have hurt by it, and my position would have been destroyed. I can only ask you now to forgive me for what I have done. I am perfectly ready to accept the consequences for my selfish actions."

Summer crossed the space between them, and kneeling before Mrs. Slampton-Sands, she took her hand.

"I can never express to you the importance of your unquestioning acceptance when I first came here. I was a young bride in a strange country, frightened, hiding a guilty secret. It would have been quite understandable if you had refused to see me. But that cannot compare with what you have just given me. To have these documents, Mother's letters—well, it makes everything all right."

"But the suffering you've endured . . ."

"In my possession, these documents would once have been my death warrant; I could never have kept them secret from Gowan. But now I'm free to claim my heritage, and I can face my husband and children with pride." Her eyes filled as she remembered how agonizing it had been to think that she was illegitimate. "If my mother had lived it would have been best to have sent them to her, but as things turned out it's better that you've kept them until now."

Mrs. Slampton-Sands didn't agree and probably would have attempted to convince Summer of her guilt, but Brent entered the salon and cut off her protests. Summer jumped up, ran to him, and placed the miraculous documents in his hands.

"Now you can stop worrying about being a proper wife for me," he said fondly. "Did you know that she once almost refused to marry me because she didn't have a dowry or a family?" he informed Mrs. Slampton-Sands. "Now she can claim an older name than mine and *two* estates. The next thing you know everybody will be accusing me of marrying her for her position."

"Not when you've got two estates of your own," Summer countered, "and one of them is a whole island."

"But Glenstal is worth more than Windswept, and that doesn't take into consideration Gowan's business."

"Biscay is worth twenty times what you could get for my little farm, without even considering Windswept."

"I'm delighted you two have nothing more important to do than argue over who owns the most valuable property," Mrs. Slampton-Sands observed, rising to her feet, "but since Carleton's illness I have to see to everything myself or our modest estate will grind to a halt."

"Please don't leave yet," Summer begged. "I want you to see Robert Frederick. He will be christened soon and I want you to be one of his godmothers."

"If you don't mind sharing the distinction with Madelena and Fiona," Brent added.

"I shall be honored," said Mrs. Slampton-Sands, the merest suggestion of tears in her eyes, "but I must go. I'm sorry to see you leave Glenstal. It's such a nice place and much closer to me. With so many houses to choose from, I doubt you will ever return, but I shall look forward to the day my godson brings his wife here."

"Not for many years, I hope," Summer cried. "I haven't had him long enough to be willing to give him up to another woman just yet."

"What you need is more children to take up your time. Then you wouldn't be so preoccupied with this one," Mrs. Slampton-Sands declared.

"I'm willing, but Brent hasn't quite worked up the courage for that yet." Summer grinned devilishly.

"You'll pay for that bit of sarcasm, wife. I'll see that you have twins."

"Only if you agree to feed one of them," Summer retorted, and Mrs. Slampton-Sands wondered if even Constance and her adored Frederick had been as completely happy as these two young people. She left unobtrusively, certain they were scarcely aware of her departure.

Gowan had traveled the seventy-five miles that separated him from Glenstal in one night, and now in the still hours just before dawn he crept toward the castle through the woods, far away from the stables and the cottages of the servants. The half-moon was periodically hidden by swift-passing clouds, and during these brief moments of near darkness he moved through the grounds, finally crossing the piece of open lawn that stretched before the south front. Gowan didn't fear the dogs, they knew him well, but he couldn't afford to alert any-one to his presence. Even a suspicion of it would send Brent's family hastening to Windswept and destroy all his plans.

Reaching the great house without being detected, Gowan could hardly keep from breaking into a cackle of pleasure as he slipped inside the cellars. No one would be moving about in these dank bowels for at least another hour, and he would have plenty of time to make his way to the upper floors. The castle had been rebuilt about fifty years earlier to make it more comfortable and easier to heat. To do this, it had been necessary to reduce the sizes of the rooms and to lower the ceilings. Consequently rooms had been placed within rooms, and there were double walls in much of the castle, walls that would protect Gowan as he searched out the whereabouts of his victims, walls that would hide him while he waited for the right moment to carry out his revenge. He would have to ex-ercise great care because these secret spaces were not all con-nected, but Gowan was certain that within a few days he would find the perfect opportunity to strike.

Chapter 49

Summer readjusted her pillow and turned onto her other side, but she still couldn't fall asleep. She had allowed Brent to talk her into letting the baby stay in the nursery for the first time, and she couldn't stop worrying. Her son had a perfectly good nurse and she had no doubt that he was sleeping soundly, but it was the first night he had been away from her and she couldn't settle down.

Next to her, Brent slept soundly, breathing steadily and softly, and she didn't have the heart to wake him. He had worked hard to see that everything at Windswept was in readiness for their move on the morrow; she felt very guilty knowing that all she had to do was step into the carriage, ride five miles, and step out again.

Besides, how could Brent understand what a mother feels when she's separated from her child for the first time? Not that Brent didn't love the baby—indeed, he seemed foolishly fond of his young son—but he didn't have the same attachment to him, the feeling of being connected to the infant twenty-four hours a day and of being aware of everything that was happening to him. Brent would undoubtedly say she was foolish and would probably order her to get back into bed, but she just had to check on her son one more time.

She hoped Bridgit didn't wake up because that tyrant would never let her forget this visit to the nursery. Summer felt surrounded by maddeningly practical, thoroughly prosaic Scots. It seemed to her that the dour, solemn Smith—she used to think he had no emotions—was the only one of them who had the least bit of romantic spirit. The rest of them were just as disgustingly stolid as the everlasting sheep that overran the countryside.

Summer eased out of bed, slipped into her robe, and tiptoed to the door, but just as she opened it far enough to slip through, Brent rolled over.

"Give the little fella a kiss for me," he mumbled, and she could just imagine the cheeky grin on his face. Summer smiled to herself as she quietly slipped out, happy in the knowledge that no matter how oblivious Brent might be to anybody else, he was never unaware of even the most trivial thing she did.

The door swung open on silent hinges to reveal a dark hole beyond. For a moment nothing happened, then a head was thrust into the room, next an entire body. Finally a tall man in badly rumpled attire stood up and looked about him. Very little light penetrated the heavy curtains at the windows, but it was enough for Gowan to make out the crib where the baby slept and the open door that led to the small room off the nursery where his nurse snored softly.

Gowan crossed the room noiselessly. A smile of cruel satisfaction masked his face as he gazed on the sleeping infant. It seemed odd that this helpless child should represent the ruin of everything he had worked for, yet it had been so amazingly simple to reach his room undetected. It would be even easier to smother him without leaving a single sign that he'd been there; but Gowan *wanted* Brent and Summer to know what had happened to their child, he *wanted* them to live in fear of the moment he would come upon them unheard in the night. Death was not a sufficient punishment for those who had robbed and humiliated him, changed him in a few minutes from a powerful and feared aristocrat to a fugitive afraid to be recognized by even the meanest peasant.

He turned to look for something he might use to accomplish his black deed, and found that the room offered him a wide choice. He made his selection deliberately, deriving sadistic pleasure from imagining Summer's reaction when she found her child lying dead. The babe was too young to struggle, too weak to offer any resistance; all he had to do was hold the folded blanket over its mouth until it breathed no more. Gowan bent over the crib and slowly lowered the deadly mask over the face of the sleeping infant; it was all so easy.

Summer opened the door slowly, taking great care not to wake the baby. She thrust her small oil lamp into the room before her, and the sight that met her eyes caused a blood-curdling scream to erupt from her throat. The entire complement of the castle was on its feet in seconds.

Gowan, leaning over the crib, looked up just in time to see Summer fling the lamp at him and an instant later he felt the impact of her body as she threw herself at him in a desperate attempt to drive him away from her child. Gowan dropped the blanket and half turned to face her, but she was on him before he could do any more than raise his arms to fend her off. The force of Summer's attack knocked him to the floor, and she tore into him with ferocious energy. Her teeth sank into the hand that tried to push her away, while her fingers clawed frantically at the face that would haunt her for the rest of her days. One of Gowan's arms was momentarily caught in the voluminous folds of Summer's robe and he was unable to throw her off or to effectively stem her assault.

Meanwhile, the lamp that had bounced harmlessly off Gowan had broken, splattering its warm oil all over the rush matting on the floor, and within seconds the nursery was engulfed in flame.

Suddenly becoming aware of the fire, Summer forgot Gowan and scrambled to her feet intent upon rescuing her child from the blaze. The nurse, awake now and running about screaming fit to wake the dead, reached the door just as Brent burst through it; she was knocked out cold. Smoke rapidly filled the room so that all Brent could see was Summer snatching her child from the flames.

"Get him out into the hall," he shouted. Brent hustled Summer into the corridor, and leaving the footmen to drag the nurse to safety, he began to beat the flames with the blanket that Gowan had dropped. There had been only a small amount of oil in the lamp so, with the help of the servants who arrived quickly, the flames were soon out.

When it was all over, Brent found Summer still in the hall only a few steps away, clutching the crying infant to her bosom and shaking convulsively.

"There's nothing to worry about now," he said, taking her into his arms and holding her close. "It was only a small fire."

"Gowan," Summer managed to say despite chattering teeth.

"What?" exclaimed Brent.

"Gowan . . . in there . . . trying to smother the baby."

"Merciful God," exclaimed Bridgit who had thrown a blanket around the pair of them. "You don't mean he started that fire to burn up the poor little tyke?"

"He was trying to suffocate him," Summer managed to say at last. "The lamp broke when I threw it at him."

"How did he get in here?" Brent demanded in a voice that captured the instant attention of everyone present.

"There is a door on the far side of the room that opens into an empty space," Smith said, emerging from the smoke-filled room.

"But that's just a closet in which we store things," Bridgit said.

"Glenstal was rebuilt some time ago, and there are many such empty spaces throughout the castle," Wigmore informed them.

"Then Gowan is still in the castle," Brent surmised.

"He's probably been here for some time, just waiting," Smith added.

"Judas priest!" Bridgit sat down with a plop.

"I can't stay in this awful place another minute," Summer cried. She was terrified. "He could be any place."

"I'll find him," Brent swore. The determined look Smith knew so well settled over his face.

"But you can't go after him by yourself," Summer protested. "He could be hiding anywhere, and you don't know this house."

"I will find him," Brent insisted. "Smith will take you back to your room. Bridgit will stay with you, but arm yourself and be on the lookout. I'll be back just as soon as I can."

"Would you like me to come with you?" Smith asked quietly.

"No. This is something I must do alone."

Summer started to protest again, but she knew it was futile. "Please be careful," was all she finally said. It didn't seem to be the time or the place to utter the other thoughts whirling about in her brain.

Brent waited until everyone had left the nursery wing, and then he entered the smoldering bedroom and made his way over to the still-open door. He held a lamp high above him until he could see the space that ran along the north side of all the rooms in the wing, probably giving access to every one of them. Gowan could move in and out of these rooms at will, and no one would ever know. He retraced his steps, and stood for several minutes, thinking, before he left the nursery and started down the hall.

The castle was silent, and Brent's footsteps echoed through the halls, but he didn't hesitate and he didn't take any notice of the shadows that leapt and dived as his lamp played upon the walls and furnishings, though they danced like a thousand ghouls as the boards creaked beneath his feet.

He stopped dead in his tracks when he reached the point where the corridor joined the larger hall leading to the main part of the castle. He could have sworn he'd heard bare feet moving swiftly along polished boards, but when no further sounds reached his straining ears and no flash of movement caught his eye, Brent moved forward, more cautiously this time. Someone was in the hall with him, someone who didn't want his presence detected. Brent was certain that the sounds had come from somewhere behind him, but he neither flinched nor looked back.

The light of the small lamp seemed to contract abruptly when Brent reached the stairway descending to the great hall. He could see only the tiny flame before him; the rest was in total darkness. He realized that he made a perfect target for a waiting assassin, but he continued to move forward, pausing only now and then to listen intently for the man he was now certain was following him.

Brent reached the ground level and paused long enough to blow out his lamp. He waited for his eyes to become accustomed to the deep gloom; he and his pursuer would make the last of their journey in the dark. Brent knelt down and removed his slippers, then he moved forward with great care in his stockinged feet. Suddenly he crouched and pitched a slipper into the inky shadows around him. The soft plop was followed by the sharp report of a pistol, running footsteps behind him, and the barely perceptible closing of a door.

Then all was silent once more.

Brent waited, but no sound came to his straining ears. At last he rose to his feet and proceeded across the hall toward a door that had been imperfectly closed. For several moments he stood before it, but he could hear nothing before or behind him. He wasn't sure of which way to turn, but after pausing to listen once more, he dropped to a crouch just as he reached for the handle.

Ever so slowly, Brent turned the handle, not making a sound, and began to open the door. He knelt, ready to spring into action, waiting only for a creak or any light noise that would betray the presence of his enemy, but the door continued to open soundlessly until Brent could see half of the room. He was in the library, the room where, ten years earlier, he had beaten Gowan into unconsciousness with a riding crop; he wondered if Gowan remembered that fateful night as vividly as he did.

Peering intently into the dark room, Brent was barely able to make out the small globe on the desk and he aimed his second slipper directly at it. The globe toppled, a second pistol shot shattered the dark, and Brent rolled behind a wing chair near a long heavy table.

"That's your last shot, Gowan," he said, addressing the dark shadows behind the door. "Now you'll have to face me with nothing more than your strength and cunning. Are you sure that will be enough? You don't have your men behind you now and the sheriff isn't combing the countryside for me."

Brent thought he could hear the sound of ragged breathing, but he couldn't tell where it was coming from.

"Come on out, Gowan, I'm not armed. I don't even have a riding crop this time." Gasping breaths again came to Brent's ears and he smiled. "There are no more secrets to hide, there is now no reason to play hide-and-seek in the dark. This is where it ends, right here, tonight." Brent could feel the tension in the room escalate. He felt about him, searching for anything to use as a projectile. He chose a book and slid it across the tabletop. The sudden whooshing sound, coming as it did in the dead silence, was quite startling and Brent saw a brief flash of metal across the room. Just as he'd thought: Gowan had a knife and was moving along the far wall in his direction.

Brent moved out from behind the table, headed toward the center of the room; he had to get Gowan between him and the sliver of light that came through the window. If he could just see the man's outline, he wouldn't need any cover, he would welcome Gowan's attack.

"Come on now, Gowan. Surely you're not going to let a coward—that was the word you used, wasn't it—keep you crouching in the shadows like an animal. But then I guess it doesn't take much to scare a man who preys on old men, boys, women, and now babies."

Brent thought he saw a shadow move.

"Just think of what your friends would say if they knew you couldn't even smother a helpless child without help. You could hear them laughing in London."

The shadow definitely moved.

"Of course if it ever got out that you were knocked down and mauled by a woman, you wouldn't be able to hold your head up, but I don't think anybody will be listening by the time—"

"Fiend! I'll kill you once and for all!" The words exploded from Gowan's throat as he launched himself in the direction of the maddeningly calm voice that had taunted and mocked him; the voice of the man who had eluded him for ten years and who threatened to do so once more.

Brent only sensed the shadow's movement, but he did see the glint of the knife as Gowan raised it above his head and he silently moved out of his path. Gowan stopped, confused when he found nothing solid in the darkness; he paused, panting from exertion, and waited, expecting the maddening voice to come at him from another part of the room.

"Your sense of direction is a little off. I'm over here." Brent was ten feet from where he'd been when Gowan had charged him. Gowan twisted sharply about and made painful contact with the leg of a heavy table.

"Maybe you can see me now," Brent called as he moved the curtain enough to allow a thin shaft of light to enter the room. Gowan immediately charged in his direction, but again he found only empty space, and the taunting voice, now coming from another part of the room, baited and mocked him until he was aflame with rage.

Twice more Gowan launched a murderous attack only to come up against ambient air and then to be driven to fury by soft, mocking laughter.

"It appears I will have to light a lamp for you," Brent jeered, "or you'll drop from fatigue before you find me."

"Come out and fight like a man, you slippery coward," Gowan roared. "You're the one who's afraid."

"No, only prudent." Brent had moved again, and Gowan whirled to face him.

"Stand still!" he shouted, half-mad.

Suddenly the library door opened, and Summer stood framed in the shadowy light.

"Brent, are you in here?" With a cry of triumph, Gowan rushed toward her, but a hand suddenly reached out and drew her into the safety of darkness.

Brent had been just as stunned as Gowan when she had appeared, but he had instinctively launched himself at Gowan's shadowy form, like a cat whirling to face danger from an unexpected quarter. Now reaching out in the darkness for a body he couldn't see, he brushed against Gowan's feet. He was unable to get a grip on him, but he struck out firmly enough to bring him down. Brent rolled into a ball and tumbled past Gowan just as a knife was driven into the floor where he'd been.

Gowan yanked his knife out of the wood and turned to face Brent; they grappled in the dark, the knife slicing into the warm flesh of Brent's arm and sending excruciating pain through it. But Brent barely noticed. He had located Gowan and the deadly knife at last. With terrifying strength, he twisted Gowan's arm until it threatened to break. Gowan dropped the knife and brought his knee up into Brent's stomach; then he drove his clasped hands down on Brent's neck in what should have been a stunning blow. He whirled to find the knife, but he had underestimated his foe. Brent was up and bringing him down from behind. With a powerful wrenching movement, Gowan turned over on his back and brought up both feet, intending to drive them into Brent's groin, but in a display of control and agility, Brent twisted away from the feet and threw himself upon Gowan, his hands seeking his foe's throat in a death grip. Gowan fought with the desperate strength of a man who sees death coming to meet him, but the hands did not relax their pressure until Gowan's body fell away, limp and unresisting.

Chapter 50

Summer poured the tea and then handed cups of it to Smith and her husband. The lawyers and representatives of the King's justice had taken up all of Brent's time this past week, but at last he was now free of the complications resulting from Gowan's death. Everything had turned out to be rather simple in the end, if not quick to settle, because of Gowan's passion for keeping records. It was easy to prove that his entire fortune had its beginnings in property and monies that belonged to either Brent or Summer. "It's all yours or your wife's," the lawyers had said, "so there's really nothing for us to do."

"It seems Gowan hoarded every cent he got his hands on," Brent said to Smith and Summer. "He only spent money on you, and then he let you slip right through his fingers into my arms."

"I can recall when neither of you was very happy about that," said Smith.

"We're happy now, and that's what's important." Summer was settled contentedly beside her husband.

"It seems that you have quite a considerable dowry after all," Smith remarked. "Young Lord Robert Frederick is going to be a very wealthy man someday."

"Young Robert will have lots of brothers and sisters with whom to share his good fortune," Summer promised. "I've discovered I like babies."

"Which brings us around to you," Brent said to Smith.

"To me?"

"To your help."

"All I did was wait comfortably in camp, only to find you didn't need me after all."

"I notice you don't mention following me down to the library and then pulling Summer out of Gowan's path when he tried to kill her."

"Did you know he was there all the time?" Summer asked.

"I never thought for a minute that I'd get one step past the end of the corridor without Smith dogging my footsteps."

"You couldn't have gotten that far. He didn't even take me back to my room. He made Bridgit and Wigmore go with me."

"Remind me to teach Bridgit to tie you down when you're supposed to remain in one place. I heard Smith follow me across the hall, but I wasn't sure he had gotten into the library and I nearly lost my head when I saw you in that doorway."

Smith tried to play down the value of his contribution, but Brent and Summer would hear none of that. "No more arguing. You and the men will be paid as I promised. And I'm going to give you the island as well. You can sell it and divide the money amongst you."

"We've already talked about it, and we refuse to accept the island or your money," Smith stated categorically. "But tell me this. Do you plan to go to sea anymore?" Brent looked at Summer and shook his head.

"I have too much to keep me here."

"Then make me captain of the *Windswept* and the men equal partners."

"I will, and I'll do the same with the plantation."

"The ship's plenty. We've done little enough for you compared to what you've done for us."

"Good Lord, what did I do besides help you risk your hides?"

"You gave us wealth, success, and work we can do with pride."

"But we don't need the plantations," Summer declared.

"Maybe not now, but someday you may want to return to them, if only for a little while. Remember, both of you have more roots there than in Scotland."

"Thank you, old friend. You have shown your selflessness once again," Brent said.

"I have done nothing of the kind." Smith smiled nervously. "I now have the best ship and crew on the Atlantic under my command. I intend to be as rich as you someday."

"And you will. Nothing has ever stood in your way."

"God bless you." Summer stood on tiptoe to kiss Smith as he prepared to leave. "I'll always remember your kindness and understanding. I hope you find someone who can make you as happy as you deserve to be. She'll be a lucky woman."

For once in his life Smith was left with nothing to say.

"You'd better go before she maps out the rest of your life," Brent warned. "Things she says have an uncanny way of coming true."

They said their goodbyes cheerfully, but Summer felt a sense of loss when the door closed behind Smith.

"He's the finest friend a man could have. I'm going to miss him," Brent stated.

"Then I'll have to see what I can do to distract you." Summer smiled and wiped her eyes. "When you get tired of thinking about improving farms and reducing rents, we might consider a sister for Robert."

"I don't intend to wait for that," Brent retorted, putting an arm around her waist and caressing her cheek.

Summer leaned her face against his hand, enjoying the contact that always made her pulse race. "I was wondering if you'd have enough energy for both," she said, giving him a challenging glance.

"You'll soon see how much energy I have," Brent declared as he swept her into his arms and headed toward the bedroom.

"Will you be as interested in me now that I'm a married woman who nurses her child and worries about whether the meat will be properly prepared for dinner?"

"Even as such a one." Brent kicked the bedroom door open with his booted foot. His voice had become husky and that peculiar greenish tint only Summer had the power to evoke was in his eyes.

"There is one more thing I want," he said, depositing her on the bed and settling down beside her.

"You always want that," Summer teased. Brent was responding as always to her nearness, but the soberness of his expression made her pause. "What is it?" she asked more solemnly.

"I would like us to be married."

"But we're already married," Summer pointed out, half sitting up in surprise. "We are, aren't we?"

"As far as everybody else is concerned, but we've never exchanged our vows. It was all done without your knowledge, even without your consent. I want to *hear* you say you want to be my wife."

"You just want a lot of people to hear me swear to obey you," Summer teased, but she was trying very hard not to cry with happiness. "I never could trust you when you started acting nice." Instead of matching her mood, Brent took Summer's face in his hands and looked directly into her eyes. There was no evasion, no teasing, only naked emotional hunger in his gaze.

"I don't care whether you disagree with everything I do or argue with me for the rest of our lives, I want to hear you swear that you love me, that you'll go on loving me forever, no matter what."

Summer's heart was so full she could hardly speak, but after a moment she responded. "I'll be proud to marry you, on any day you wish. I want every woman in the world to know you're mine, and that I don't ever intend to give you up."

Brent then kissed her with such passionate intensity that she felt dizzy.

"Now there's one thing I want," she said as soon as she recovered her breath.

"Anything."

"Don't tempt me like that." Summer smiled. "Promise that you'll always save a little corner of your life just for me, that we will never become so tied down with estates and children that we won't have time for each other. I'd die if I were to lose you, even if it wasn't to another woman."

"At least once every five years we'll run away, leave everything, children and estates, behind us. And we won't come back until we're so tired of each other we can't stand to spend another night together."

"We can't let our children grow up as orphans," Summer said her eyes twinkling. "As much as I admire Wigmore and Bridgit, I don't think they would make suitable parents."

Brent silenced her in the only way he knew.

LEIGH GREENWOOD

The Reluctant Bride

Colorado Territory, 1872: A rough-and-tumble place and time almost as dangerous as the men who left civilization behind, driven by a desire for a new life. In a false-fronted town where the only way to find a decent woman is to send away for her, Tanzy first catches sight of the man she came west to marry galloping after a gang of bandits. Russ Tibbolt is a far cry from the husband she expected when she agreed to become a mail-order bride. He is much too compelling for any woman's peace of mind. With his cobalt-blue eyes and his body's magic, how can she hope to win the battle of wills between them?

TEXAS VISCOUNT
SHIRL HENKE

Sabrina Edgewater, teacher of deportment, first encountered her nemesis in a London dockside brawl that earned him the nickname of "Texas Viscount." She never imagines that the lout will turn out to be the earl of Hambleton's heir.

Joshua Cantrell is brash and bold, a self-made millionaire who only agrees to become a viscount to ferret out an international conspiracy. The last thing he needs is to lock horns with a prissy little schoolmarm, even if she is cute.

The stakes are raised when Lord Hambleton offers Sabrina money enough to open the school she's always dreamed of if she'd only take the rough edges off his heir. Does she dare risk her reputation to achieve her heart's desire? Or is her heart's desire the Texas Viscount?

BRAZEN
BOBBI SMITH

Casey Turner can rope and ride like any man, but when she strides down the streets of Hard Luck, Texas, nobody takes her for anything but a beautiful woman. Working alongside her Pa to keep the bank from foreclosing on the Bar T, she has no time for romance. But all that is about to change....

Michael Donovan has had a burr under his saddle about Casey for years. The last thing he wants is to be forced into marrying the little hoyden, but it looks like he has no choice if he wants to safeguard the future of the Donovan ranch. He'll do his darndest, but he can never let on that underneath her pretty new dresses Casey is as wild as ever, and in his arms she is positively...*BRAZEN*.

A WILL
OF HER OWN
WINNIE GRIGGS

When Will Trevaron inherits the title Marquess, his grandfather demands he leave his beloved America and sail back to England. Not wanting to obey, Will hits on the perfect solution: a marriage of convenience to Maggie Carter. A union with a "nobody from the colonies" would shock and horrify his family and rescue from poverty the woman who once saved his life.

Will doesn't expect to fall for his wife. But as Maggie sets his household straight about what exactly an independent lady from a savage country would and would not accept, the new marquess sees that—her loving husband aside—his marchioness has . . . *A Will of Her Own.*
